P9-DCD-234

Fire Logic

Fire Logic

Laurie J. Marks

TOR®

A TOM DOHERTY ASSOCIATES BOOK
NEW YORK

FIRE LOGIC

Edited by Delia Sherman

Design by Heidi Eriksen

A Tor Book
Published by Tom Doherty Associates, LLC
175 Fifth Avenue
New York, NY 10010

www.tor.com

Tor® is a registered trademark of Tom Doherty Associates, LLC.

Library of Congress Cataloging-in-Publication Data

Marks, Laurie J.
    Fire Logic / Laurie Marks.—1st ed.
        p. cm.
    "A Tom Doherty Associates book."
    ISBN 0-312-87887-7 (alk. paper)
        I. Title.
PS3613.A369 F57 2002
813'.54—dc21

2001058352

First Edition: May 2002

Printed in the United States of America

0 9 8 7 6 5 4 3 2 1

For three enduring friends, who, with their elemental talents of fire, earth, water, and air, bound into this book their insights, truths, joys, and intelligence: Rosemary, Delia, and Didi

Acknowledgments

I am fortunate in my friends, a sustaining community of people who read this manuscript again and again, and whose thoughtful responses helped this book and its author to transcend her limitations. I am particularly indebted to the group known fondly as the Genrettes: Rosemary Kirstein, Delia Sherman, and Didi Stewart, whose cappucino-inspired insight saw to the heart of many an incoherent draft, and whose energized and entertaining companionship spirited me through a long labor. In addition, for commentary, advice, and support in every imaginable form, I am profoundly grateful to Deb Manning, Susanna Sturgis, Wendy Marks, Gretchen Marks, Diane Silver, Gillian Spraggs, Donna Simone, Amy Hanson, Ellen Kushner, and my beloved Deb Mensinger.

Fire Logic

Part 1

Foolhardy

What is worth doing is worth merely beginning.
——MACKAPEE'S *Principles for Community*

*Who breeches the wall breeches the trust of the
people, for without walls there can be no defense.*
——MABIN'S *Warfare*

Without a history, we cannot distinguish heroes from fools.
——MEDRIC'S *History of My Father's People*

Chapter One

In the border regions of northern Shaftal, the peaks of the mountains loom over hardscrabble farmholds. The farmers there build with stone and grow in stone, and they might even be made of stone themselves, they are so sturdy in the face of the long, bitter winter that comes howling down at them from the mountains.

The stone town of Kisha would have been as insignificant as all the northern towns, if not for the fact that Makapee, the first G'deon, had lived and died there. His successor, Lilter, had discovered the manuscript of the book in which were laid out the principles that were to shape Shaftal. During the next two hundred years, the library built to house the Makapee manuscript had transformed the humble town into an important place, a town of scholars and librarians who gathered there to study and care for the largest collection of books in the country. The library had in turn spawned a university, and the scholars, forced to live in the bitter northern climate, tried to make their months of shivering indoors by a smoky peat fire into an intellectual virtue.

Emil Paladin considered frostbite a small price to pay for the privilege of being a student in the university at Kisha. He was older than some of the masters, and his long-time teacher, Parel Truthken, had warned him that he might be more learned, as well. For ten years, since his first piercing, Emil had accompanied

Parel on the rounds of his territory, capturing fleeing wrongdoers and occasionally executing them when it was necessary. It was Parel who had finally arranged Emil's admission and who would be paying his fees. So now Emil had arrived for the spring term, with a letter of introduction that was about to bring him into the presence of the Makapee manuscript itself.

Despite expensive carpets, rooms crammed with books, and fires that burned year round to prevent the damp, the library was a chilly and echoing place where men and women in scholar's robes tiptoed about. Being admitted to the Makapee manuscript, which set forth the principles that now unified Shaftal, was like being admitted into a temple. As he put on the silken gloves that he was required to wear, it occurred to Emil that Makapee himself would have found this ritual tremendously peculiar. The first G'deon had been an obscure potato farmer, who sat by a peat fire all winter long, writing of mysteries in a crabbed, nearly unreadable handwriting. The paper, Emil had been told, still smelled of peat. He doubted that the frowning librarian would let his nose come close enough to the paper for him to sniff it, but still, Emil felt almost giddy with anticipation.

A door opened, and the sound of an urgently ringing bell intruded on the silence. The librarian turned her head, frowning. "What!" she breathed at the man who hurried towards her.

The man whispered in her ear. Paling, she turned aside and hurried away. Emil was left with the gloves on his hands and the door to the Makapee vault still bolted shut. He felt a tearing, a sense of loss so profound he could not believe it had anything at all to do with the manuscript. Something momentous had happened. Dazed, he went through the halls, following the sound of the bell out into the square that fronted on the library.

As the bell continued to ring, the square became crowded with scholars carrying pens with the ink still wet on the nibs, librarians carrying books, townsfolk wearing work aprons, with babies in their arms and tools in their hands, and farmers from the countryside in heavy, muddy boots, with satchels on their shoulders. The farmers must have spotted the messenger on the road, and followed him into town to hear the news. The messenger's dirty, ragged banner hung limp from the bell tower, and Emil could scarcely make out the single glyph imprinted on it. It was Death-and-Life, he realized finally, which was commonly depicted on glyph cards as a pyre into which a man stepped and became a skeleton, or, alternately, from which a skeleton stepped and became a man. It was the G'deon's glyph, carried through Shaftal only once in each G'deon's lifetime: when the previous G'deon died and the new one was vested with the power of Shaftal. It called the people to simultaneously mourn and rejoice. Soon, the messenger would announce the death of Harald G'deon, who had given the land protection and health for thirty-five years, and would name his successor.

Emil did not envy the young elemental selected to inherit that burden of power and decision. The government of Shaftal had been in discord for some years, and the coastal regions were occupied by foreigners who lacked the Paladin compunctions over the use of violence. This was a time that demanded wisdom, and the new G'deon would not have much leisure to learn it.

A townswoman with a child clinging to her leg turned to Emil and said anxiously, "Well, it's a pity about Harald. But what I most want to hear is the name of his successor. It would relieve my heart to know that the rumors we've heard are wrong."

"Rumors?" said Emil. "I'm sorry, I was isolated all winter, and have only just come into town."

"Well, they say that even though Harald has known since autumn that he was dying, he refused to name a successor. Surely he did it at the end, though. He'd change his mind when he felt the breath of death at his heels. And now all this Sainnite nonsense will come to an end, at last, for a young G'deon won't fear to act against them."

The bell stopped ringing. The messenger, whose road-grimy clothing had once been white, stood up on the bell platform to speak, but he could utter only a cracked whisper that those closest to him could scarcely hear. The people pushed a big man forward to stand beside him and listen to his broken voice, then shout his words in a voice that carried across half the town.

"Harald G'deon is dead!"

The gathered people nodded somberly.

"He vested no successor!" the big man boomed.

Some listeners groaned, and others cried out in dismay, but Emil stood silent in horror. It was unimaginable that a G'deon would allow the accumulated power of ten generations of earth witches to die with him.

"The House of Lilterwess has fallen in a Sainnite attack!" the big man shouted. His words were heard in stunned silence, followed by an outcry of shock and grief that swelled to fill the square. The big man's final words could scarcely be heard. "No one survived."

From every quarter, the townspeople shouted frightened, frenzied questions. The messenger sank down onto the bell platform and replied in his broken whisper, "I don't know. I don't know. I don't know."

Emil had already stripped off his silk gloves, and now handed them to a nearby librarian—the same one who had been about to admit him to the vault. "What will become of us?" she cried.

"Shaftal is at war," he said.

He pushed his way through the weeping crowd and headed for the nearest Paladin charterhouse, where he knew the members of his order would gather. He noticed that he himself was weeping, though, except for that first tearing sensation in the library, he felt nothing. It was a small thing, insignificant beyond notice, that the fall of the House of Lilterwess had severed Emil's soul, separating the scholar from the soldier, leaving his heart on the steps of the library while his duty called him away to war.

At the edge of the crowded square, an old man and a young woman observed the aftermath of the messenger's terrible news. Though they did not look like anyone else in the square, they were distinctly similar to each other: small-framed where the Shaftali were sturdily built, dark-skinned where the Shaftali were fair, with eyes and hair black as obsidian, where the townsfolk were generally tinted the color of earth. In dress also, they stood apart as strangers, wearing long tunics of finely woven goat's wool and jerkins and leggings of deerskin, while the working people wore breeches and longshirts. Both had long hair plaited and knotted at the backs of their heads. Let loose from its bindings, the young woman's hair would have brushed her thighs, and the man's hair would have reached his knees. Even their faces were shaped differently from those of the townsfolk: narrow and pointed, with hollows under the cheekbones and eyes deep set in shadow.

With their pack animals tethered nearby, the two strangers stood beside a pile of beautifully woven blankets and rugs. When the messenger first arrived, they had been negotiating a large sale to a trader of woolens. The old man turned from his consideration of the weeping crowd to speak quietly to his companion, in a subtle, singing language. "So we cross the boundary into a new world."

She said, "But I feel the world is dissolving away before us, like a crumbling ledge above a crashing cataract."

"Every boundary crossing feels like this," the old man said. "When we cross a boundary, it is a loss, a death, an ending. It always seems unendurable. It always seems like plunging over a cliff." He added kindly, "Zanja na'Tarwein, what has happened here portends a future that is more yours than mine. It is not too late to change your mind and refuse the gods."

Though she was young, her face did not seem much given to laughter. She smiled though, ironically. "How shall I do that? Shall I unlearn all I have learned, these last two years? Shall I tell Salos'a that now I have seen the world beyond the mountains I want nothing to do with it?"

"You could," he suggested. "The mountains protect our people like a fortress. You might retreat behind those walls and never come out again."

"No, Speaker," she said, seriously and respectfully, "I could not."

They stood silently for a long time, watching the crowd divide into arm-waving, wildly talking clusters. The youths sent from the farms left to bear their news to the waiting elders. Zanja imagined the people of the entire country standing about like this, bereft and bewildered. She said, "Now the Sainnites will overpower them like wolves overpower sheep." Her people got their wool from goats, who were brave and clever and sure-footed. She had no admiration for sheep.

The Speaker said, "No, I think not. Perhaps the Shaftali people are not wolves, but neither are they sheep."

The trader finally remembered his visitors and their pile of woolens, and came over wringing his hands. "I don't know what to say to you. Ashawala'i woolens are a luxury, and I don't know if I can sell luxuries to a country at war."

The Speaker said dryly, "Good sir, this land has been occupied by Sainnites for fifteen years, yet you never had any difficulty selling your wares before."

"But now the House of Lilterwess has fallen." The man could not continue. "Come back tomorrow," he finally said in a choked voice. "I need to consider my future."

"I am considering whether the Ashawala'i people would be better served if we sold their woolens to a more decisive trader. One who will not make us spend an entire afternoon unpacking and repacking with nothing to show for it." He gestured, and Zanja, who understood the value of drama, began painstakingly and with evident weariness to roll up the large, beautiful rug over which they had been dickering. The trader thought better of his caution, and money changed hands.

As they led their string of sturdy horses away, the old man commented, "We will travel more lightly now."

The Speaker had said he would bring her to the House of Lilterwess, to introduce her to its most important residents: Mabin, the council head, the other eleven councilors representing the Orders of Lilterwess and each of the regions of Shaftal, and Harald G'deon himself. Now, the House of Lilterwess was rubble, the twelve councilors were dead, and so was Harald G'deon. Now, Zanja asked, "But where will we travel to?" The Speaker did not answer.

They walked down one of the town's main streets until they reached a place where an inn stood on one side of the road, and on the other side stood a Lilterwess charterhouse. The yard was busy with horses being saddled and armament and supplies being distributed to a company of Paladins. Most of them seemed very young, not yet pierced with the first gold earring that would mark the day they took their vows to spend their life in service to Shaftal. Their senior officer, a woman whose two earrings glittered in the bright spring sun, came over to the fence. "That's a fine string of animals you've got there. The Paladins have need of them."

"I am the Speaker for the Ashawala'i before the Council of Lilterwess, and these are the only horses and donkeys owned by my people. Without them, the trade between my people and yours would come to an end."

"That seems a small matter when the world is coming to an end."

"It is not a small matter." The Speaker leaned his elbows unconcernedly on the fence. "And you will not take my people's stock, for we are protected under the law."

"What do we know anymore?" the commander muttered. "Isn't it against the law for children to ride to war? Isn't it against the law for the House of Lilterwess to be turned to rubble?" She turned rather agitatedly to shout something at someone.

"You may *borrow* our donkeys," said the Speaker, "If we accompany them."

"We ride out on Paladin business."

"It is the Speaker's duty to advise and protect our people. For that, we must know all we can about events in Shaftal. And we are *katrim*, warriors like yourself, with vows to fulfill. We will observe, and not interfere, and perhaps we might even be of some help."

The commander looked at them then. She saw two schooled faces and disciplined stances. The Speaker's hands had many small scars, of a kind a blade fighter might get in practice bouts. His young companion's hands were scarred also, though not so heavily. Both of them had a rather unnerving quality to their gazes, an intentness and seriousness that seemed almost unnaturally alert and intelligent. Perhaps these two had elemental talents. In any case, they almost certainly would be valuable companions.

The commander said, for she was desperate for beasts to carry the gear of war, "We ride to a gathering of Paladins, and after that we ride against the Sainnites. Come with us if you like, but I can't promise your safety, or the safety of your animals."

Seeming amused, the Speaker accepted her terms.

Zanja na'Tarwein closely watched these negotiations. Like her, the Speaker once had accompanied his predecessor when he was a young *katrim*. Like her, he belonged to a fire clan, and had been born with an elemental talent for languages and insight. And, like her, when he went on his vision journey he had dreamed of the god Salos'a. Now, by watching him she continued to learn what it meant to be chosen by the one who crosses between worlds, who sees in all directions. Though the hawk, the raven, and owl were all associated with death, Salos'a was not a killer like the hawk, or a trickster like the raven. The owl conducted souls to the Land of the Sun, and was a restless wanderer who acknowledged no boundaries.

Zanja had already learned that she who crosses between worlds is a stranger everywhere, even in the land of her birth. Having lived for six seasons with a Shaftali farm family, she had developed two minds and two ways of seeing, to go with her two languages. After that, her own family found her peculiar, and said that she stumbled between contradictory cultures and languages like a drunken fool. The Speaker had explained, "That is what it means to be a Speaker. Did you think it would be easy or graceful?" He had added, no more reassuringly, "What you see and know depends on which eyes you see with."

Today, she had come to understand more clearly why a crosser of boundaries must learn to see through the eyes of strangers. Twice today, the Speaker had settled a difference in his favor by constructing an argument from the materials of his opponent's self-interest and values. As they began the journey southward in the company of Paladins, she considered in silence the Speaker's methods, and what he had needed to know about the person he spoke to in order to properly advocate for his people's interests. Now, when he spoke to her about the towns they passed, and described the peculiar ways and customs of the people there, she listened attentively, thinking all the while about the potential usefulness of the information.

The Paladins with whom they journeyed seemed a random collection: some were well-equipped and travel-hardened, others had the pale skin and soft hands of scholars and their riding gear was creased from having been folded away in trunks. More than half of them seemed to have only recently left their family farmholds. Except for the fact that they all traveled armed, and they shared a propensity for lengthy, arcane discussions of philosophy, it might have been difficult to tell that they all were members of the same order.

One of the Paladins had been riding somewhat separate from the others. A man neither young nor old, he did not eat or drink or join in conversations, and walked away alone when they stopped to rest the horses. "What about him interests you?" the Speaker asked Zanja, when he noticed her watching the man.

"He is so solitary," she said.

"Is that all? You must listen more carefully to your intuition, or you will not survive for long."

She considered the lone man, who now stood a good distance away, gazing at something beyond the far horizon. "He is not merely sad," she said. "He is complex. He knows so much that it weighs him down. And yet I think he could be merry. The same knowledge that he finds so heavy might also give him joy."

The Speaker grunted approvingly. "You're guessing, of course. But you're learning to let your guesswork reveal the truth. Now tell me what kind of man you have described."

Zanja considered some more, and abruptly felt quite stupid. "Of course, he is a fire blood, like us."

"Next time," the Speaker said, "It will not take so long for you to realize it."

✣ ✣ ✣

They had neared their journey's end when the solitary man, with apparent effort, began making himself more convivial. Eventually, he dropped back and walked his horse beside the Speaker's and soon had convinced Zanja's teacher to give a lengthy, detailed exposition of the differences between the Ashawala'i and the Shaftali people.

The solitary man's name was Emil. He told them that after fifteen years as a Paladin, he recently had been pierced with the earring of Regard. He self-consciously fingered the two gold earrings in his right earlobe. "I suppose they'll make me a commander now," he said, without enthusiasm. "And what will become of you, now that we have no G'deon or Lilterwess Council for you to speak to? How will you advocate for your people?"

The Speaker said, "In just a few years, these problems will be Zanja's, so perhaps she should answer your question."

Zanja was unprepared, but she could not defer to her elders when the Speaker made it so clear she must think for herself. "As Shaftal changes, my duties must change as well," she said. "But how could I say how Shaftal is going to change? Perhaps Shaftal will form a new government, to which I might be an ambassador. Or perhaps the Sainnites will." Emil looked rather startled by this grim possibility, but refrained from objecting. "Perhaps Shaftal will become a land of violence and confusion," she continued, "And I will keep that turmoil from affecting my people."

The Speaker grunted with approval, which encouraged her to add, "Perhaps my duties will become impossible to fulfill."

"Perhaps they will," the Speaker said.

But Emil, who seemed much impressed by her answer, said, "Impossible! For a woman of less talent, perhaps."

The Ashawala'i did not compliment each other so directly. Zanja glanced confusedly at the Speaker, who said on her behalf, "You are too kind."

"We have arrived," said Emil, standing up in his stirrups to see better. For some time they had been traveling among wagons laden with food being transported from the farmholds of the region. Now, the woods had opened up into a vast clearing filled with Paladin encampments, wagons, animals, equipment, and food tents. A harried woman directed the wagons in one direction and the Paladins in another. At the top of the hill before them stood a complex of buildings, a Paladin charterhouse. "The generals will be there," said Emil, "and that's where I must go, to learn my future."

He took each of their hands in turn, as he bid them farewell. "Perhaps we'll meet again," he said, and rode up the hill.

Along with the hundreds of fretful Paladins, seething with rumors and tales of fresh disaster, the Speaker and his student camped upon the hillside. Before nightfall, a wagonload of travelers, accompanied by a handful of Paladin outriders, made its way up the dusty track from the highway. Word swept through the gathered Paladins like the turning of a tide: the new arrivals were refugees from the House of Lilterwess, and Councilor Mabin traveled among them, unharmed. "I believe this rumor," said the Speaker thoughtfully. "The House of Lilterwess was like a city within a building, with hundreds of residents and plenty of defenders. I found it difficult to believe that no one at all escaped the attack. And Councilor Mabin has always struck me as someone who would survive, whenever survival is possible."

Though the gathered Paladins crowded expectantly around the charterhouse, the hour grew late without any fresh news, and finally the companies began making ready for bed. Zanja and the Speaker also slept, but he awoke her before dawn, and they quietly made their way among sleeping Paladins and smoldering campfires. The blacksmith slept beside his anvil, the horses dozed in their field, the guard at the hostel door seemed asleep on his feet and blinked at them blearily when the Speaker addressed him. "Tell Councilor Mabin that the Speaker of the Ashawala'i wishes to discuss the future with her."

"You would disturb her rest?" slurred the sleepy guard.

"I know she rises early, before the sun, if she sleeps at all."

The guard sent for a Paladin officer, who inquired about the Speaker's business and informed him that Mabin was not to be disturbed. Eventually, though, the Speaker's courteous persistence was rewarded and they were brought into the silent, plain building, and shown to a disarranged room where a brisk fire burned and a woman sat busily writing at a desk scattered with candle stubs. "Speaker," she greeted him, without setting down her pen.

"Councilor. My apprentice, Zanja na'Tarwein."

Zanja, remembering that the Shaftali do not kneel to their elders, bowed instead.

"I think that's a fresh pot of tea," Mabin said distractedly.

Zanja served the tea in the Shaftali style, and the Councilor took no notice of her, even when Zanja handed her the cup and offered her the plate of bread. The Speaker politely expressed his delight at finding Mabin unharmed, and his sadness and concern at hearing of the G'deon's passing. Apparently finished writing, Mabin rose from the desk and said impatiently, "Harald G'deon was a fool, who brought this disaster upon his own people with his obstinacy and idiocy. Now I alone am left to rebuild this ruin. Do you think I even want to hear his name spoken again? I only wish he had died sooner."

She paced angrily to the fireplace, drained her teacup, and held it out for Zanja to refill. "Speaker, I will instruct my people to treat you as a Paladin commander, so that you may be as informed as anyone is about Harald's death and the Fall, and our plans for the future. Now, as I am the only governor left alive, I am being taken into hiding until we can rebuild our strength and organize the defense of Shaftal."

"I am certain you intend no insult," the Speaker said. "But I am as important to my people's survival as you are to yours. Surely you can spare a little time to advise me."

There was a silence. Mabin took a piece of bread from the plate Zanja offered her, and this time seemed, momentarily, to see her. "Are *all* the Speakers fire bloods?"

Though it was surprising to be assessed so accurately with a mere glance, Zanja replied, "Yes, Councilor. A fire blood's insight is useful when wandering a strange land."

Mabin looked away, seeming to dismiss, not just her but all fire talent. She said to the Speaker, "I suggest you tell your people to guard their passes. And you should make certain the Ashawala'i remain beneath the notice of the Sainnites. They kill those who threaten them, exploit those who can help them, and ignore everyone else. Make certain that your people are ignored."

The door opened, and a young woman, somewhat older than Zanja, entered. She wore black, bore arms, and her hair was cut short like a Paladin's. Her gaze paused briefly on Zanja, leaving her feeling like a pot that has been scoured. "Madam Councilor, we are ready to leave."

"Will you pack up those papers for me?" Mabin went out to speak to someone in the hall, and returned to tell the Speaker the name of the commander she had designated to deal with his concerns. She said to the young woman in black, "They are gathering the Paladins so I can address them before I leave. You travel ahead in the wagon, and I'll catch up with you on horseback."

"Yes, Madam Councilor."

The Speaker scarcely had time to thank Mabin. The councilor was swept out into a crush of commanders who had arrived to escort her to address what remained of her army. The door shut behind her, and now the room lay silent. The Speaker sighed as if with relief, and Zanja hurried over to pour him a fresh cup of tea as he sat down in an armchair by the fireplace. He sipped from his cup, gazing into the flames as his damp boots began to steam. Papers rustled as the young woman in black ordered them meticulously into a pile and then wrapped them and tied them in a leather cover. Zanja stood by the tea table and watched her covertly.

Zanja could not easily categorize this discomforting young woman. She seemed hard and tired, which might be expected in one who had recently survived and escaped a devastating attack. Though she looked like a Paladin, Zanja did not think she was one. She was old enough to have taken her vows, but her earlobe was unadorned. Plus, she had an unsettling quality that made Zanja suspect an elemental talent, though she did not recognize which element.

The young woman looked up and caught Zanja's eye. Her gaze was almost unendurable. Trying to back away, Zanja stumbled into the tea table. The young woman turned aside without a word, picked up the packet of papers, and left the room.

The Speaker said, without removing his gaze from the fire, "We have none like her among the Ashawala'i."

"She is an air blood?" Zanja guessed, for the Ashawala'i had only earth and fire clans, and water bloods were rare everywhere.

"She is an air elemental, and a Truthken. Now you know why the Truthkens are so feared."

Zanja still felt the effects of that young woman's regard, even though she was no longer in the room. "Yes, I felt as though her look invaded me."

"In time she'll learn more subtlety, I assume. Do you want to hear the Councilor's speech? I myself have no interest in it."

"I suppose she'll be inspiring," Zanja said.

The Speaker glanced up at her, amused. "I have never learned to love Mabin either, though she has many admirers. Have a cup of tea, at least. You may never again taste green tea as fine as this, and if we don't drink it, it will go to waste."

She poured herself a cup, and went over to the room's one small window to look out at the dawning day. The window viewed the back of the charterhouse, an unkempt garden of herbs and flowers that were just starting to bloom, and the track that led to the stables. As she watched, a wagon was brought out and loaded with baggage and people. The last to arrive was the young Truthken, still carrying the packet of papers, but now escorting another person. Zanja pressed her face to the windowpane, intrigued by the strange appearance of the Truthken's companion. She was very tall—taller than a grown man—but thin and gangly as an adolescent in a growth spurt, with big hands and feet, wearing clothing she seemed to have outgrown. Her hair was a tangled bird's nest. The Truthken walked her to the wagon as if she were a prisoner or a puppet. On the tall woman's face was an expression of blank, stunned despair.

Zanja watched the wagon roll away. She did not know what she had seen, but she knew that it was terrible. She remained at the window long after the wagon had passed out of sight.

Chapter Two

One fine day in early autumn, nine years after the fall of the House of Lilterwess, two Sainnite soldiers impatiently waited for the stablehand to bring them their horses. The cool air was freshened by winter's distant breath, but no hint of the mud season's first rainclouds had yet appeared in the sky. The soldiers complained about the cold, as though they had never lived through a Shaftali winter, and did not know they would soon be longing for a day this warm.

"A thankless day's work it will be," grumbled one, tightening the buckles on her cuirass of boiled leather.

"Is this a soldier's work?" Her companion was younger and bulkier than she, and carried a number of weapons: swords, daggers, even a small battle-ax, as though he intended to spend the day in grueling, hand-to-hand fighting. "Breaking heads to force reluctant peasants to hand over a few coins . . ."

"We'll take supplies instead of money. Gladly." She checked her three pistols to see that they were properly loaded.

"What, are we filthy tradesmen?"

"We are soldiers," she said, "who need to eat. And the peasants—"

"—don't know their frigging place—"

"—literally!" she concluded. "If they would just lie down and do what they're supposed to do . . ."

Their conversation deteriorated. The stablehand,

who had become all too familiar with the Sainnites' assumptions about what non-Sainnites were good for, deliberately knelt in horse dung as she checked the horse's hooves. She was grimy already, but wanted to make certain the soldiers found her unappealing.

"How long does it take to saddle two horses?" said the man, banging his booted foot against the floor as though he were a horse himself.

"That stablehand is always slow. A simpleton."

"All barbarians are. And they live like animals." The soldier's lip curled as the stable hand brought out the horses. "Look at her. She's been rolling in horse dung. She may even eat it, for all we know."

The woman companionably made a retching sound, and set to work checking over her mount with insulting care, testing every strap and buckle. The stablehand stood back, gaze humbly lowered. Though the soldier had found nothing wrong with the horse's gear, she cuffed her casually on the way out the door.

As the two soldiers rode off to harass the people they called peasants, the stablehand raised her dark eyes to gaze after them. She said softly in her own language, "You two will die today." It was no idle threat. She sensed the death awaiting them, hidden in the woods not too far out of town.

Zanja na'Tarwein's prescience had been particularly heightened this year, for to live safely among the Sainnites required a degree of caution and conscientiousness that verged on the supernatural. For months now, she had been dodging attention as meticulously and instinctively as the rat that lives underfoot, unnoticed. The gift of prescience was a troubling talent: useful when it came to guarding her own safety, distracting and unnerving when she became conscious of pending events in which she did not care to intervene. Perhaps a dull winter at home among her people would suppress her foresight to a more tolerable level.

She had returned to the dreary work of mucking out the stalls, but paused at the thought of home. Suddenly, between one breath and the next, she decided it was time to leave the Sainnite garrison. She had covertly learned their language, and she had learned much else that left her worried and distressed. The Sainnites were skilled fighters, accomplished tacticians, and ruthless oppressors. She did not want to know any more. She had done her duty; she had crossed into the Sainnites' world. Thankfully, the same god that required her to travel between worlds did not forbid her to travel home again.

Zanja na'Tarwein leaned her pitchfork on the wall, fetched her money pouch from its hiding place, dropped it down the front of her filthy shirt, and left the stable. At this time of day, the garrison was lively with the orderly and energetic activity that she had re-luctantly come to admire. A company of soldiers was delicately weeding a flower bed—the Sainnites loved flowers, and cultivated them in every inch of bare ground. Disabled soldiers were busy with the housekeeping: sweeping and scrubbing one or another item that Zanja would have sworn had just been cleaned the day before. Pigs were being slaughtered in the kitchen yard, and the practice field was crowded with soldiers who sweated and grunted and shouted with triumph or dismay.

That spring, when she had first presented herself at the garrison gate, a good portion of the day had passed before she was able to communicate that she had learned there might be work in the gar-rison for border people like herself—barbarians, according to the Sainnites, who stupidly assumed that the border people could not be spies because they had no ties to the land of Shaftal. Now, leaving the garrison in early autumn, Zanja had to wait no longer than it took the bored soldier to unlock the gate. She didn't even have to display the empty bottle of horse liniment she had brought with her as an excuse for going out.

By contrast to the garrison, the streets of the city were practi-cally deserted. As the work of harvest drew to a close, the city would fill with farmers. But now, Zanja walked down an empty street hung with tradesmen's shingles, marked with glyphs that Zanja had never learned to interpret. One had an Ashawala'i rug on display that Zanja remembered selling to a northern trader the year before. She proceeded cautiously, for even though someone as ragged as she seemed an unlikely target for thieves, smoke addicts were known to steal anything from anyone, often in broad daylight. She had been forced to go unarmed all summer, and though this was not the first time she had wished earnestly for a weapon, she hoped that it would be the last.

She turned down a side street and stepped into the narrow doorway of a public bath, startling the proprietor from her doze over the account books. Surely the woman had seen plenty of dirty people come through her door, but still she wrinkled her nose. "I hope you have something clean to wear."

Zanja said, "Yes, I stored my belongings with you in the spring. You'll remember me when the dirt is washed off."

"Oh, yes," she said. "Shaftal's Name, you certainly are changed. I'd better get the water heating. A lot of water."

Alone in a private room, Zanja sat naked on the bench and painstakingly undid the tight plaits of her hair. When the woman and her assistant arrived bearing between them a vat of hot water, Zanja knelt over the drain and allowed herself to be doused with water, briskly scrubbed with brushes and foaming soap, and doused again. Her skin was raw before the last of the dirt had been scrubbed away. The two bath attendants chattered about people she had never met and would never meet as they washed her hair, treated it with various mysterious unguents, and combed it for her. In an ecstasy of cleanliness, Zanja gladly paid what they charged, and when she left was dressed in her accustomed goat's wool and deerskin clothing, with a dagger at the small of her back and her stablehand's rags left behind on the ash heap. She doubted that the Sainnites would even notice that she was gone.

The city was built on a hilltop. As she left the last of its crowded buildings behind, the land opened up below her: fields and forest bright in the vivid light of autumn. Some fields lay barren, their bounty already picked and plowed under. Some were striped with hay rows. Others were alive with industry, as wheat fell before the scythe and potato forks turned up the soil. Zanja, though her back and shoulders ached from the summer's dreary labor, felt a moment's guilt at her laziness in such a busy time. She decided to avoid the farmlands and sleep in the woods, lest she find herself recruited, willy-nilly, into the frenzy of harvest. The weather would hold, she thought, examining the sky. She settled her burdens on her shoulders and started briskly northward, toward the mountains that at the moment lay far below the horizon.

A few hours later, she found the dead soldiers. The ravens had arrived before her, and hopped reluctantly away as she approached, uttering insults in their harsh, secret language. The Paladins had done their work as briskly as any butcher, and deliberately left the bodies to be found. The man who had banged his foot on the floor like a horse had been shot with a pistol and then finished with a dagger. The woman whose fist had left an aching bruise on Zanja's cheekbone had been shot three times. The horses had been re-cruited to serve the resistance, Zanja assumed. The two Sainnites must have been ambushed here by a number of concealed marks-men, now long gone, perhaps hunting the other Sainnites who had foolishly assumed the members of the resistance would be at home helping with the harvest.

In the near distance, Zanja could hear the voices of the farmers, breathlessly singing a working song to keep their energy from flag-ging as the afternoon grew old. The smell of violence suffused the bright air. The ravens jostled each other impatiently, edging their way back to the feast. This was still Shaftal, Zanja told herself, but it seemed like an alien land.

A year after the fall of the House of Lilterwess, Councilor Mabin's book, *Warfare*, had become the manual for insurgency throughout Shaftal. People whose lives had until then been the very model of peacefulness joined the Paladins—the new Paladins, Mabin called them, for they did not give up their families or take complicated vows. Soon, every region of Shaftal that the Sainnites occupied also supported a company of irregular fighters who made it their business to cause the Sainnites no end of misery. The retaliating Sainnites, perhaps thinking to prevent any book from having such an impact again, destroyed all the printing presses, the paper mills, the schools, and the libraries. They executed everyone whose ear was pierced, everyone who appeared to be learned, everyone who had or was ru-mored to have an elemental gift. They hunted and killed any mem-ber of an old order, even the Healers, though their vows forbade them to fight. To escape the harassment of the Paladins, the Sain-nites built garrisons in which they could secure themselves, from which they exercised an iron control over the commerce of the cities upon which they depended for the taxes that ensured their survival. The countryside, however, remained firmly in the control of the Paladins and of the farmers who fed and sheltered them.

Zanja's teacher developed a shortness of breath that left him unable to endure the rigors of travel, and she became Speaker at age twenty-two. Traveling beyond the borders, she became adept at avoiding the frequent, brief armed confrontations between Sainnites and Paladins. She learned the side roads and byways, since the main roads were frequently patrolled by foul-tempered Sainnites. She could not avoid the cities, though, where to sell her woolens she first had to bribe the guards, and afterwards hand over a substantial portion of her profits. In the countryside, the Paladins sometimes were not much easier to deal with, for, like the Sainnites, they had become violently suspicious of any stranger, and especially a stranger like Zanja, whose dark coloring made her uncomfortably visible, and whose presence and purpose could not be easily explained.

She continued to serve her people and her god, however precariously. But every year, she wondered how long she could continue. That she would eventually be caught up and killed in the random violence of the unending war seemed inevitable. But this year, as she reclaimed her horses from the farmers who had looked after them that summer, and continued homeward on northerly roads, she carried a new fear with her. The fear haunted her as the roads became narrow tracks and finally disappeared entirely, leaving her to navigate her way by the stars, the shape of the land, and sheer common sense. The fear followed her as she entered and scaled the mountains, following ways so rarely traversed that scarcely the trace of a path could be seen. She returned home to her people, as she did every autumn, but this year, living among the Sainnites had left her wondering whether her people's future was any more certain than her own.

The flashing mirrors of the sentinels alerted the village of her coming, and her clan brother, Ransel, met her on the path as he usually did. "Zanja! Home so soon? Did you grow tired of breaking the hearts of the Shaftali women and decide to break the hearts of *katrim* instead?"

She gave a snort of amusement, for Ransel knew perfectly well that she had no great accumulation of discarded lovers on either side of the border. "I grew tired, anyway," she said.

"And you missed me?"

She eyed him with mocking doubt. "Well . . ."

He laughed. Ransel was always laughing, always mocking, always telling jokes or making up crazy riddles. The raven god, a trickster himself and a great practical joker, had chosen Ransel to serve him, and Ransel did so with unremitting enthusiasm. "Say you were lonely!" he teased. "Admit that the inconquerably self-sufficient Zanja na'Tarwein was about to expire from the poison of solitude! Say that—"

He could go on like this forever if not interrupted. "I was," she said. "Terribly lonely. As I always am."

He fell silent. She put her arm around his waist, and he gripped her affectionately across the shoulders. "Well," he finally said, "You're lonely no longer. Let's go climbing tomorrow."

"Climbing! And what exactly do you think I've been doing for eight days now?"

"You've been climbing alone. Climbing with your brother, that is completely different."

"No doubt. Anything done with you is completely different. But the elders will want me tomorrow."

"Oh," he sneered. "The elders!"

"Has the weather been fine?"

"Other than the occasional touch of frost and flurry of snow."

"Will it hold until the day after tomorrow?"

"It might. But whether I will be offended at being put off to accommodate a bunch of creaking, self-important—"

"—Leaders of the people," she said pointedly.

"You're no fun," he grumbled. "Did you bring me something?" He glanced hopefully at the heavily laden horses.

"I'll answer that question when we go climbing."

"Aha! A bribe! Well then, since you know my price, I shall agree."

They walked companionably together, behind the horses, who kept up an eager pace because they could smell the nearness of home. "So tell me the news," Zanja said. She did not usually have to prompt him.

He said, soberly for once, "Well, I don't know a good way to tell you this, my sister. The Speaker is dead."

She stopped in her tracks. Ransel's momentum carried him a couple of steps beyond her, and he turned around. "Here," he said. "Sit for a moment. The horses know the way."

He squatted on his heels beside her in the middle of the path. "It was a quiet thing. One morning, he simply did not wake up. Salos'a had come during the night to carry him across his last boundary."

"Without anyone there to remind him of the stories of his life."

"I am sure there was no need. Salos'a knows his life already."

"I wanted to be there at his death. And I needed to ask him . . ." To the astonishment and embarrassment of them both, she abruptly began to weep, and could not get herself under control for some time. As much as she looked forward to Ransel's staunch affection, she had looked forward to her long conversations with her old teacher, the only one she could confide in. Though she had taken over his duties and position, she still relied heavily on his advice. Now, when she needed most to ask him what to do, Salos'a had taken him off to a far land where he could not possibly be so badly needed.

She raised her head at last. Ransel, uncertain what to do in this unprecedented situation, had simply looked away and was courteously pretending not to have noticed her tears. She stood up, wiping her face, and they continued down the path. After a while, Ransel, somewhat muted at first, began to tell her all the other events of the summer, as he always did. By the time they reached the Asha Valley, where Zanja's people thrived in peaceful comfort, she had gotten more surefooted as she tread the precarious edge of sorrow, and was able to keep from falling into it again.

The next day, she spoke to the elders, who gathered in the elderhouse to hear her. She told them of her summer with the Sainnites, and she told them of the fear she now carried with her. While living with the Sainnites, she had learned the extent of their arrogance and their ignorance. She had learned that the Sainnites feared Shaftal: they feared its supposedly conquered people for their tenacious refusal to give up the fight; they feared the rage and bitterness that they themselves had caused; they even feared the long, harsh winter that to them seemed arbitrary and undeserved as a curse from a vengeful god. And she had learned to fear the Sainnites in return, after she learned that, because they were exiles in a land they detested, they could be destructive and vindictive in a way no sane people could tolerate. She reminded the elders of the weapons that kill at a distance, and of the smoke drug that insidiously killed the will and spirit of Shaftali city dwellers.

All morning and well into the afternoon, she tried to convince the elders of their danger. When she was finished, they placidly replied that the Sainnites were indeed dangerous, and so it was fortunate that they had no reason to even notice a remote tribal people like theirs.

They agreed to post additional sentinels in a wide circle a day's journey outside the valley, so that if a danger were to approach them, they would at least know of it in advance. But they refused to develop a plan for how to defend the village against attack, since it would have required them to explain the danger to the Ashawala'i people. "When you are old," they said to Zanja, "you will understand. Now, it is difficult for you to see how easily that which is right and good can be changed, and how difficult it is to change it back again. You say that our people are endangered by these Sainnites. But you do not see that fearing the Sainnites would endanger them even more certainly."

On a day as warm as summer, Zanja and Ransel went climbing to a place they knew, a high meadow not too far from the groaning edge of a glacier. From there, it seemed they could see to the end of the world. Ransel entertained her with accounts of his many love affairs, and then advised her at length about which of the women *katrim* might be amenable to her advances this winter. She listened carefully, for he was a good matchmaker. Eventually, their conversation trailed off, and they lay a long time in silence, half-asleep in the warm sunshine.

"You are like an umbilical cord," she said to him after a while.

Ransel had a sweet tooth, and she had surreptitiously brought him a tin of sweetmeats from Shaftal. "An umbilical cord!" he exclaimed stickily. "What kind of compliment is that for a *katrim?*"

"I didn't mean to compliment you. You're conceited enough already. I meant to say that the Speaker had no friend like you, and I'm thinking that he must have dreaded coming home much more than I do. Even with your help, it's a painful passage."

Ransel unwrapped the stiff waxed paper from another sweetmeat. "He never was contented," he said. "But then, neither are you."

"I'll always think I am his student." Zanja rolled over in the warm grass, startling a couple of tiny rabbits back into their holes. "An umbilical cord," she repeated. "You connect and nourish me, and I do nothing but kick you in the stomach."

Ransel gestured with the sweetmeat tin, his mouth too busy for talking.

"I corrupt you," she interpreted, "with forbidden luxuries. That is no gift."

"Mmm," he said. "Good thing your grim moods always pass, for they are very tiresome. I love you out of self-interest, as you know full well. Even though you whisper not a word to me of all you see and know, people still think that I am privy to your secrets, which gives me an excuse to act self-important. Not only that," he continued, while she uttered a snort of laughter, "but since you are a presciant, you can save me from my own idiocy, if you care enough to do it."

"So long as I'm beside you."

"Well, your lengthy absences are a drawback. But when matters go badly, you surely are the one I want guarding my back. Whoever's with you will survive just as you will. Won't your prescience send you running home when I most need you here? If it does, I swear I'll do whatever you command, for I'd rather be alive and humble than dead and proud."

Zanja closed her eyes and pretended to doze in the sunshine. She felt so tired after her summer with the Sainnites that she wondered whether an entire winter's rest would revive her. But she had not slept well since her homecoming, which was one of many things she could not tell Ransel, lest she do him a worse disservice than she did by smuggling in comfits for him. Only the elders of the people were judged mature and experienced enough that they could safely know of the world beyond the mountains without being changed or corrupted by the knowledge.

"Why do you sigh?" Ransel asked.

"I suppose I do have talent," Zanja said. "But it never seems talent enough."

Ransel nodded, and said sententiously, "The na'Tarweins are never satisfied."

Chapter Three

Much that Zanja admired about the Shaftali people began to disappear. She saw hospitality replaced by suspicion, and open-handedness replaced by closed fists. When once strangers had been happy to sit down with her and talk about their lives, she now could not enter a tavern unless she was willing to sit in solitude with a circle of silence surrounding her. Meanwhile, in the Asha Valley, her people looked after their croplands and hunted in the forest, herded their goats and spun the goat's wool. Children respected and learned from their elders. *Katrim* visited other scattered peoples that inhabited the mountains, and returned with gifts of beautiful pottery, beaverskin robes, and delicate shells. The *katrim* patrolled and watched over their territory, and no danger appeared. Zanja, who year after year was reminded anew of the Sainnites' brutality, did not become complacent. But in the Asha Valley, the peaceful, timeless effort of her people's lives remained undisturbed and unchanged. Perhaps it was true that ignorance would protect the Ashawala'i against corruption.

Fifteen years had passed since the fall of the House of Lilterwess, when one summer Zanja began to hear of trouble in the Midlands, where in the region of Rees a particularly brutal Sainnite commander was devastating the countryside in a largely successful effort to decimate the Paladins who opposed him. Working her way southward to find out as much as she could, Zanja was accosted in nearly every region by wrought-up Paladins. Finally, four days' journey from the border of Rees, she found herself surrounded by one-time farmers, whose hardening to Sainnite violence had left them incapable of recognizing the subtle fact that not all strangers are enemies.

They confiscated her dagger, her horses and pack animals, her money, and all her gear and trade goods, and told her she should be grateful to be escaping with her life. It was useless and dangerous to argue with them, so she did as she was told, walking away down the road in the opposite direction from the one she wished to go. But as soon as she knew she was no longer observed, she returned back through the woods. She was able to travel quickly across country, running most of the time, keeping the road in sight until she had caught up with her stolen horses and their gleeful escort. She followed, careful to keep anger from overriding common sense, and watched from a distance as the Paladins finally divided her belongings and separated, each going in a separate direction.

It seemed clear that they were not bringing her horses and belongings to their company commander. Zanja returned to the original watchpost by the side of the road, and spent an uncomfortable night in the undergrowth, within hearing of the garrulous farmers, who kept themselves awake with storytelling. At dawn, a lone foot traveler approached through the woods to take their report and bring them fresh bread to eat. When the lone traveler left, she led Zanja to a remote, apparently abandoned farmhouse. Zanja had only to walk up to the door and knock.

"I seek the commander of Damar Company," she said politely to the startled Paladin who opened the door. "I am Zanja na'Tarwein, the Speaker for the Ashawala'i."

She heard the distinct voice of the woman she had followed these two days, exclaiming, "Name of Shaftal! I kept thinking someone was following me, but I thought it would be impossible . . ."

So many of the Paladin commanders had been killed during and shortly after the Fall that a great number of people had been promoted beyond their abilities or talent. Fortunately, when she was allowed to enter, the commander of Damar Company eyed her with a certain intelligence, at least. "You are a long way from the Ashawala'i," he said.

"I try to learn what I can about the dangers that might threaten my people. When I heard about the troubles in Rees, I came down to see what was happening."

The commander said skeptically, "Rees is no place for dilettantes this year."

"I am a soldier like you." Zanja folded her scarred hands before her, though she doubted he could see them in the dim light. "But the people of your command took my weapon—not here, but on the road to Rees. And they took my horses, my money, and my trade goods."

The woman exclaimed, "They never mentioned—"

The commander hushed her. "Fighting the Sainnites is expensive, I regret to say, and Damar is a poor region."

"So the Paladins of Damar have become thieves?"

The commander gestured impatiently. "We are at war," he said, as though that excused every immoral act. "But I will see to it that your horses and belongings are recovered."

He did not say that he would punish the wrongdoers, but Zanja had no choice but to be satisfied for now. So, because there was no help for it, she became the guest of Damar Company while waiting for her belongings to be recovered. At least she was able to use the time to her advantage, for the commander sent her with an escort into Rees.

In Rees, she saw a village that had been burned to the ground because one of the households had sheltered a Paladin. She heard about entire families slaughtered because one member served in Rees Company. She saw pale, hopeless veterans with legs and arms amputated. She finally met some of the survivors of Rees Company: harried, half-mad fighters who hurried her out of their camp because they feared that the Sainnite commander would exercise her near-supernatural ability to find them wherever they sheltered. Zanja and her companion gave the poor souls all the food they had, for the Rees farmers were so terrorized that they dared not feed their own soldiers any more, and the few surviving Paladins were starving.

Zanja returned to Damar much sobered, to find that most of her goods and horses had been recovered, and that the rest, the commander assured her, would arrive soon. Soon after her return, a messenger arrived, and the commander summoned Zanja. "Can you read?"

"I can read the alphabet, but not glyphs."

He showed her a note, much begrimed with long travel, that included a description of her and her gear, and requested that if she were spotted anywhere, she be directed to return home at once.

Never before had Zanja, or the Speaker before her, been summoned home like this. She left her goods and pack animals in the care of some honest farmers and hurried homeward by the most flexible and least noticeable means of travel, her own two feet. She was a hardened traveler, but even though she ran whenever the way was reasonably flat, the journey seemed interminable. It was nearly mid-summer when she saw before her the sky-piercing peaks of stark gray stone where Winter set by next year's supply of snow.

Katrim watched all the passes from the high vantage of nearly invisible shelters of stone and mud, and for many years now the easy paths had been left choked with stone as barriers against invasion. She followed a narrow, precarious way that paralleled the river down the mountainside, gradually losing altitude, until trees came crowding up the canyons once again. At a bend of the river, the valley opened up and the village of Zanja's people came into sight. Ransel was hurrying up the path to meet her.

"How long has it been since you saw the Asha Valley in summer?" he asked. "More than half your life, I think."

It was indeed quite odd to see the trees in leaf, the fields of corn and squash being hoed, the goats grazing in the flood plain, and the children swimming in the river. She had almost forgotten what a fine place this valley was in summertime.

"Well, Alastad na'Parsa is dead," Ransel added.

She gazed at him, baffled. For seventy years, Alastad had guaranteed the success of the Ashawala'i crops, given health to the newborns, advised the elders, predicted the weather, suggested the best times to gather nuts or hunt deer, and eased the dying into death. The Ashawala'i had been fortunate to have an earth witch of such talent for so many years, and it was certainly a matter of concern that he was dead, and that no earth clan had yet produced another so gifted. "But that is no reason to fetch me—"

Ransel had become one of the finest *katra* dancers in the village, and had the scars to show for it. He had a fresh cut on his arm, sloppily bandaged and leaking blood. "I know that something untoward has happened," he said. "Some *katrim* and hunters are in disgrace. The elders need your advice. That's all anyone will say."

They walked together across the valley and into the village. Busy, preoccupied people shouldered their way down narrow pathways between the close-built clan lodges. Summer's warmth had brought forth the village's miasma. Outside its limits, the most noticeable smell had been that of the latrines. Now, the changing scents marked the delineations of the village's many industries: from the stink of the dye vats to the piercing smells of the tanner's yard. The smell of burnt fat and roasted corn distinguished the na'Parsa lodge, where a funeral feast must have recently been served.

They reached the lodge of the na'Tarweins, upon whose walls each of the nine bird gods were painted with equal skill and prominence, so that none would feel slighted. Painted elemental flames writhed around the doorway, where a loosely-woven summer rug kept out the flies. Ransel told her that the na'Tarwein elders wished to see her alone, so she bid him farewell and promised to find him in the summer camp, after sunset.

Zanja stepped into the lodge and dropped to one knee. The mother of the na'Tarwein clan, a hazy shape in the dim light of the lodge, rose up from her stool and stepped forward to accept her greeting. As Zanja's eyes adjusted to the shadows, she identified three other clan elders, each seated upon a low stool, with an attendant child cross-legged at their feet. Still kneeling, she greeted each of the elders in turn, and only then stood up to be clasped in the clan mother's arms and accept her offer of tea.

One of the children hastened to pour a cup of tea from the pot upon the hearth. The precious porcelain cup fit perfectly into the palm of Zanja's hand, and felt light and smooth as a leaf from a tree. She sat down upon the floor at a gesture from the clan mother, and slurped politely from her cup.

The clan mother said, "With the death of Alastad, I fear we may lose the prosperity of the people."

Zanja replied, "Surely an earth child will soon take Alastad na'Parsa's place."

The elders shook her heads and murmured with regret, as the clan mother said, "Earth witches are rare. Hard times lie ahead, I fear."

"When last I saw Alastad, he seemed in good health."

Zanja drank her tea while one of the elders recounted the tale of how the aged earth witch had been suddenly stricken with a strange paralysis, and how the herbalists' frantic efforts to revive him had failed. Zanja became impatient for the end of this overly complicated tale, but restrained herself from rudely interrupting her elders. She was finally able to say, "I am glad you sent for me, Mother."

"I would never have called you home for one person's death, even one so important as this. It is not as if your presence could bring Alastad back to life."

Zanja set her empty cup upon the floor before her. A child hurried forward to collect it and carry it carefully to safety. "What else has happened?"

The clan mother rose to her feet once again. "Come with me."

She led the way between the hanging rugs that divided the public space of the lodge from its cavernous living and work space, currently occupied only by a young woman with a belly like an empty bag, whose newborn infant slept in a basket beside her. In summer, the people stayed out of doors as much as possible. They would see enough of these walls during the long and bitter winter.

At the far end of the lodge, another curtained doorway gave entry to the sickroom. There two na'Tarwein *katrim* stood rigid guard over a man sprawled upon the floor. The guards, their gazes evading hers, gestured welcome to a fellow *katrim*, but clearly were to discomforted to speak. Their attitudes, as much as anything, alerted Zanja to the shamefulness of the situation, though what she saw was deeply puzzling: her clan brother, Tarin, a hunter of some renown, apparently ill, but wearing a goat harness by which he was tethered to the wall. She squatted down to shake him gently by the shoulder. His drooping eyelids opened, but he looked at her blankly, idiotically, his black irises hazed with a dull film.

Zanja felt a sickness descend on her. She said, "Tarin, stand up."

He did as she said, clumsily but promptly. He obediently complied with her demands that he make a variety of moves and gestures, and then he remained standing until she told him to lie down again.

Now she noticed the sour, moldy scent that sometimes lingered in the alleyways and dark doorways of Shaftal. She said, more to convince herself than to confirm what the clan mother already knew, "This man is addicted to smoke."

The clan mother did not reply. Zanja stood up, feeling the sickness not just in her belly, but throughout her body, even to her fingertips. "How did this happen?" she cried.

"Tarin met a Shaftali wanderer out in the forest, some three or four days' journey to the south," said the clan mother in a voice like rawhide. "Though he and the stranger could not speak each others' language, they became friends, he says. They smoked many pipes together. Tarin began bringing gifts for the man, and when that did not seem to be enough, he introduced others to the smoke."

"How many in all?"

"Seven people, from three clans. But he is the only one who used the drug so much that now he cannot live without it."

"And the man in the woods?"

"We cannot find him. Is it true that Tarin will die without the drug?"

"So I have heard."

"Then he will soon pay a high price for his foolishness, for his supply has almost been depleted. I have daily looked for your arrival, hoping you would return before he died."

Zanja followed the clan mother out of the closed room, back to the common space where fifty or more people could comfortably take shelter. They stood together in the hot room. Flies buzzed in the corners, and the infant made sucking sounds in his sleep.

The clan mother said, "In all these years that you have warned the elders about the dangers that threatened us, no one heeded you. Now we have sent for you. Think hard on what you wish us to hear."

"I will consider," Zanja said, but her thoughts were in turmoil.

The na'Tarwein sighed. "These are uneasy times. Would that we had a single seer! But our only seer is you, and what you see is not the future, but the present."

In the old days, the Speaker would have gone directly to the G'deon to complain of this intolerable encroachment on the Asha-wala'i, and the problem would have been dealt with. Now Zanja said in frustration, "Smoke is a Sainnite drug. Was the man in the woods a Sainnite? Or was he just a trader trying to lay his hands on Ashawala'i woolens?"

"We do not know."

"Then I must talk to all of those who smoked this visitor's pipe. Their description of him will let me know if he was a Sainnite."

"But you have had a hard journey, and now you are angry and worried. Tonight you must think and rest, so that tomorrow you can address the problem with serenity and clarity."

"Yes, Mother." Though Zanja's body was rigid with rage, she was pleased to see that not a trace of anger found its way into her voice. She took her leave, and went out in search of her friends.

The summer village, which by day looked like nothing more than a collection of pots and fire pits, at night scattered the flood plain with cook fires and cranky children. Zanja sat late beside the *katrim*'s fire, while they regaled her with warrior's tales of the past season. To listen patiently eventually strained her courtesy. The concerns of these, her fellow *katrim*, seemed trivial to her, just as hers would seem fanciful to them. Surely, she thought ungraciously, she was like a captured hawk, forced to listen to the tales of mice until it drove her mad. At last she lay down where she had been seated upon the much trampled grass, and shared Ransel's blanket, as they had done since childhood. She slept badly.

In dead of night, Zanja awakened to a silence so profound that she could hear a night breeze hunting through the cornfields in the flood plain. What would it take, she wondered, to silence the normal din of the river banks: the shouting frogs, the screams of the accuser bugs, who carried on all night long until dawn light finally stilled their glee? A cold terror took her, and she shook Ransel violently until he sat up, protesting. "Gods' names, Zanja, a fine dream I was having."

"Shut up and listen."

In a moment, Ransel muttered, "Who tramples through the frog lands, eh? And at an hour when ghosts go wandering? This is a mighty strange silence."

Zanja had already put on her boots, and went around the *katrim's* circle, awakening all she could while Ransel tied his boot straps. The *katrim* were less than pleased with her for disturbing their sleep, but ceased their grumbling when she said sharply, "The people may be in danger." A precious fool she'd look like later, if her panic was caused by nothing but a froggish whimsy.

"Let's go see what's on the frogs' minds," said Ransel.

The two of them ran full tilt across the crowded plain. They tread on embers, trampled fragile pottery, and tripped over peaceful sleepers, who uttered cries of fear that turned to shouts of outrage in their wake. Babies marked their passage with startled wails. Zanja could see Ransel's teeth in the darkness. Perhaps he was amused, or perhaps this was no grin, but a grimace, as he considered his lifetime of experience with Zanja's whims—which rarely, if ever, turned out to be mistakes.

Let me be mistaken now, she thought, or prayed, to whatever god might be paying attention. Let this disturbance we've created be on my head. Let me be a laughingstock. Just let me be wrong.

They left the summer village and ran through cultivated fields, along a track of pounded dirt with ditches on both sides to channel the rainwater. Corn tasseled to the left, and to the right lay mounded squash plants, their buds ready to twist open with the dawn. Crickets sang in the cropland, but ahead lay silence. Zanja and Ransel slowed to a walk and cautiously approached the edge of the long downslope, at the bottom of which journeyed the river.

It was called the Asha River both within and without the borders. Its cobbled banks kept trees from thriving at its edges, and so Zanja could see its glimmering water, which was cold with melting snow even at mid-summer, and the horde of soldiers that waded through it. They dragged their equipment and armor behind them on little rafts, and those that had completed the crossing drew on their boots and buckled their cuirasses in haste and silence. Even the war horses, which must have crossed first, as their riders were already mounted and standing guard, uttered no sound, and stood still except for the nervous twitching of their bobbed tails.

"Oh, my brother," Zanja breathed, and groped for Ransel's hand.

His fingers clenched hers. "Is it Sainnites?"

"Yes, it is." She pulled him back from the edge of the slope. They stood for just a moment, staring at each other in the darkness. Zanja thought there might be as many as fifty war horses, which meant a full battalion, with twenty heavily armed foot soldiers for every horse. They outnumbered the *katrim* by ten to one, and the katrim's daggers would be no match for the Sainnites' armor and weaponry.

Zanja said, "The people must flee for their lives."

"Then we'll need to defend the northern trail, so they can climb the cliffs into the forest."

"You go back and shout the alarm. You have the voice for it. Take half the *katrim* to defend the trail, and send half to me, so we can delay the Sainnites to give our people time to escape."

For a moment, Zanja thought Ransel would actually waste precious time in argument. But then he bared his teeth in a bitter, mocking grin. "My commander speaks and I obey."

"Honor to you, Ransel na'Tarwein." She forced herself to release his hand.

"Honor to you, Zanja na'Tarwein." He gestured a brisk, graceful salute, and dashed into the darkness. She watched until she could not distinguish him from the shadows. *I will never see him again,* she thought. For a dreadful moment, she could not bear it. She almost called after him. The two of them would flee . . . and live in shame forever after. She took a breath and turned to face the enemy.

The soldiers below efficiently and silently crossed the river. Fifty war horses she counted, and three hundred or more foot soldiers. The Ashawala'i numbered some 1,500 souls, but only a hundred of them carried weapons. The *katrim* were fine fighters, and fought with each other incessantly: neat, graceful, courteous encounters that rarely drew blood. To the Sainnites they would seem like children who merely played at war.

Trembling now, Zanja heard Ransel's voice, clear despite the distance. "Rise up, Ashawala'i, and flee for your lives! The enemy is upon us!" Three times Zanja heard this cry, until Ransel's voice was swallowed in the rising uproar.

The Sainnite commanders, certainly hearing the noise, shouted sharp orders. The soldiers, working with terrible speed, began to form a battle line. Zanja stood alone between her people and disaster, trying to hold it back by will alone. She imagined Ransel and the *katrim*, running ahead of the fleeing people to secure the northern trail, the only route up the cliffs that could safely be climbed in the darkness. She imagined the Ashawala'i, confused and disorganized, with panicked children and crippled elders in tow, running across the grassland. And how many of the *katrim* would have the courage to run the other way, towards the river and the enemy?

Oh, but the *katrim* were arrogant. Zanja had scarcely begun to doubt them when they began to arrive, breathless and excited, with their boots on their feet and their blades in their hands. Some hunters arrived as well, with their deer bows and longest arrows. They could see well enough to shoot the horses, they assured her, and she chose not to tell them that the horses were wearing armor. Their courage came from ignorance, and she wished that she had more of both.

She locked her terror into a distant dungeon where it could do whatever it liked, unnoticed, and hastily sorted the *katrim* into a battle line. A few of them had lances, and she put them first, to try to stop the horses. The hunters she poised behind them, and the *katrim*, with their daggers, standing to the rear to await the foot soldiers who would follow behind the cavalry. She took a lance herself and stood in front, not from courage but from eagerness for the excruciating wait to end. She noticed, with relief and horror, that the cavalry had begun its charge.

How much time had passed? How quickly could the tribe climb up that single, narrow path and flee into the safety of the forest?

Even though they had to run up slope, the horses picked up speed, and she saw ephemeral sparks flash from their iron hooves.

The *katrim* began to shout: an eerie, shrill, challenging cry. Zanja felt a jolt of pride. *Perhaps*, she thought, *we will survive.*

She screamed defiance at the monstrous shadows that reached the top of the slope and blotted out the stars. Arrows clattered uselessly on the horses' iron plates, but the *katrim* shouted with satisfaction as one rider fell. And then the dust washed over them like smoke. Choking, Zanja felt a wave of riders veer past as her lance point jarred off a horse's armored side.

Like a fist through parchment, the cavalry punched through the line of *katrim*, and wheeled around, sparks showering where iron struck stone. The clenched groups of horses opened up like hands and formed a line, and part of Zanja remembered how she had once watched Sainnite horsemen practice this very drill. At her back now, the foot soldiers were running up the slope. The *katrim* were trapped, like a fly between two clapping hands.

Zanja cried, "Ashawala'i!" She charged a horseman with her lance and dove between the horse's hooves to drive its point into the underbelly. The rider's ax shrilled past her ear. The horse screamed. She rolled away as the monster fell, hooves thrashing, the rider tangled in the stirrups. She jerked her dagger from its sheath and turned to face a foot soldier, whose blade clashed upon hers once, twice, three times. She never even gained her balance, but simply moved her weapon to block his, with the rest of her body tumbling after it, whichever way it happened to go. There was no grace in it, she thought sorrowfully. She pierced him with a blow that was more luck than talent, and saw him fall to his knees, with her dagger still caught in his ribs.

She leapt forward to snatch her dagger back, but a horse bore down on her. Empty-handed, she dodged spiked hooves and gnashing teeth. The horse reared, and wheeled. Choking in dust, Zanja found the fallen soldier and jerked her gory dagger from his chest. The horse was on her once again. Horse and rider both bared their teeth at her, laughing, no doubt, for she was no more than a bee trying to sting them with her little blade. The rider's ax came whistling down at her. She fell to the ground and felt its edge slash across her tunic. His lance, held in his other hand, glimmered faintly. She rolled, jumped back to her feet, and ran under the horse.

The horse reared. She tripped, and saw the big, iron-wrapped hooves come down at her. She felt a moment of stunning pain, like a blacksmith's hammer striking her head over an anvil. The dust-masked stars went out like candles.

The war horse trampled her into the stones and dust. The *katrim* died all around her. The peaceful history of the Ashawala'i reached a bitter, bloody conclusion. Zanja lay with the others, her blood soaking the dry soil, and the dust slowly settled around her.

She opened her eyes to the heavy mist of dawn. Far away, muffled voices called in Sainnese. She struggled to her knees, vomited from pain, and fainted. She regained consciousness with her head resting on the cold flank of a dead horse. Without moving, she raised a hand to feel her bloody head. The morning breeze blew the smoke of the burning village across the valley. In the rising light of day, she saw Sainnites working their way methodically across the battlefield, claiming their dead, finding their injured, killing any enemies found alive. She could not stand, but crawled across the bloody bodies of her kinsmen, into the smoke.

When she opened her eyes again, she lay wrapped in a fine woolen blanket, in a neat hollow guarded by giant stones. Overhead, the sky was a deep blue, with the stars starting to come out. "My sister," Ransel said, "a dozen times today I have thought you were dead."

"I *am* dead," she rasped, in a voice harsh with smoke and blood.

"So are we all. Here." He tilted a gourd cup to her mouth. She drank. He said, "You breathed too much smoke, and you have some burns and bruises, but your head is your worst injury. A horse trampled you, I think."

"How did you find me?"

"You found me," he said. "I was looking for you, and you came out of the burning village."

"What happened to our people?"

"When they heard my warning, they left their belongings and followed me and the other *katrim* to the cliff path. Sainnites lay in wait at the top of the path. We fought them. But they were many, and they have strange weapons that explode with fire."

"Names of the gods!" Zanja groaned.

"We fought them a long time," Ransel continued quietly. "What was accomplished I do not know. Did even one of our people escape? I wish I knew the answer, but I do not know. I and some other *katrim* fled when the Sainnites came up the path behind us. The cliff path is now choked with bodies. The village is a smoking ruin. I walked through the valley hunting for you, and everywhere

I went, I saw our people slain: elders and children, warriors and farmers. The only people alive are those you see here."

Zanja saw that other *katrim* were gathered in this hollow, and that many had drawn close to hear the conversation. Her vision was blurred and she could not count them, but it seemed there were fewer than twenty.

"I was pinned under a fallen horse," one of them said. "I lay there all night, watching the butchery. The Sainnites did not rest until no one was left alive. Finally, I pulled myself free and escaped in the smoke, as you did, Speaker."

Others also told their stories, in voices as harsh and lifeless as the voices of ghosts are said to be. Zanja listened, thinking that surely she also had witnessed the horrors they described, but she only remembered a sensation of chaos and then of stillness. To have forgotten so much surely was a mercy, but it also was dreadful to gaze at these shattered tribesmen and feel confusion rather than sharing their horror.

"The Sainnites must have taken the long path through the mountains," one of them said. "For they have wagons and horses that could not have surmounted the steep passes."

"They must have killed the watchers before they could spread the alarm," said another. "Though the watchers were hidden and it should have been impossible . . ."

"No, they knew exactly where the watchers were," said Zanja. "Tarin must have told them—told his friend in the woods, in payment for smoke. He betrayed his entire people."

They were silent then, for this was something they had not known, and could scarcely begin to understand. But Zanja understood that if she had only taken action immediately to find out what exactly had happened to Tarin, rather than delaying to let her anger cool, she might have discovered his betrayal immediately and been able to forewarn her people of their danger. Not for the last time, Zanja wished that the war horse's kick to her head had been harder.

Ransel did not know of how she had failed the Ashawala'i, and she was too stunned by shame to tell him. He gently tended her wound and gave her more water to drink. She could not resist sleeping again, and in her sleep she dreamed of Sainnites. She dreamed that they sat around a fire where they roasted a slaughtered goat. In their own language, they talked about the hard work they had done and about the dreary journey home that lay before them.

When she opened her eyes, she saw stars burning. The *katrim* roasted river trout over a small fire, and talked about revenge. Ransel hovered nearby, and drew close when she stirred.

"The Sainnites will march out at first light," said Zanja.

The other *katrim* abandoned their meal to come over and hear what she had said. "Speaker, how do you know?"

"They told me in my dreams."

"Then we will follow them, to haunt them like ghosts, to kill as many as we can."

"If we do this, we all will die." She could see them more clearly now: some fine warriors and some she had long considered fools, but with the foolishness burned out of them now.

"What does it matter, so long as we can die in honor?" said Ransel.

They all murmured agreement, their voices empty and bitter with loss.

"Then we shall follow them," Zanja said. She did not understand how she had become their leader, or why they listened to her, when her certainty might be nothing more than the delirium of a broken head.

She shut her eyes and slept the night through. At dawn, they began hunting Sainnites. Zanja went with them, leaning on one or another shoulder, carried sometimes, as they ran lightly across the mountaintops while the Sainnites, burdened by armor and horses and wagonloads of supplies, trudged below. The Sainnites did not realize what haunted their journey until that night, after the *katrim* slipped into their camp like the ghosts they were, and used the hay the Sainnites carried for the horses as tinder to set fire to all the supply wagons. Zanja could not make that raid with them, but despite her blinding headache, she told them where to find the hay wagons and how to avoid the pickets, and only two *katrim* were killed. Fifteen remained, including herself, but they bore the weapons of dozens more dead companions, and they knew how to survive in these ungenerous mountains. They waited a few days to let the Sainnites lower their guard, and they struck again, once or twice a night, night after night, and during the day made it impossible for the weary Sainnites to safely forage for food, or use the latrines, or even take off their armor. While the *katrim* ate roots and greens and berries and trout, the Sainnites began butchering and eating their starving horses.

Zanja and her companions lived ghost lives. They did not speak of the past, or of the dead, or of their own deaths. They watched the Sainnites, and slipped through the mountains like shadows, and from time to time let fly a precious arrow, or cut the throat of a straying soldier. One by one, Zanja's companions disappeared. Like the Sainnites, the *katrim* were leaving behind them a trail of abandoned bodies that they dared not try to find and had no time to burn. The mountain vultures and ravens followed them. Zanja could walk on her own feet now, but was often disabled by dizziness or blinding pain. The Sainnite soldiers continued to speak in her dreams, telling her all their secret plans and terrors and blood lusts.

The fifteen *katrim* became twelve, and then seven. The seven became five. With more warriors and more time, they might have eventually destroyed the entire Sainnite battalion. But now, with only five of them remaining, and only one more pass to climb before the Sainnites could safely exit the mountains, they knew their time for vengeance would soon come to an end. None of them wished to survive. They camped among stones, high above the miserable Sainnites and their disgusting horsemeat. They ate sweet trout flesh and sucked on the transparent bones. They ate tart berries and crunched the seeds with their teeth. They tallied the Sainnite dead and were satisfied.

Only Zanja had ever traveled so far east of the Asha Valley. She told about a treacherous canyon they soon would pass, and suggested that one of them might lure the Sainnites into the canyon, while the others dislodged stones to fall down on their heads. They drew lots, and Zanja chose the longest stick. That night, Ransel put his arms around her and said, "Wait for me in the Land of the Sun, my sister. I will not be far behind you." She fell asleep with her head in the hollow of his shoulder.

She would always remember the moment when the mountain fell on her. It was her second death, and far more satisfying than the first. She would remember the Sainnites gleefully chasing her up the canyon, the four *katrim* levering the rocks overhead, and the canyon wall collapsing onto the people below. Mercifully, she would not remember much else: She would not remember when the surviving Sainnites dragged her out from under a boulder with her back broken. She would not remember how they tortured her, when they realized she was still alive. She would not remember when they killed Ransel, who might have been trying to either rescue her or deliver her with a merciful blow of the dagger. She would not remember that she mistakenly thought she was already dead, and he was coming to join her. She would not realize for a long time that in fact he had left her behind among the living.

Chapter Four

In a stone cottage tucked into a hollow in the iron-rich hills that surround Meartown, Karis, a masters-mith of Mear, sat on the stoop in the morning sunshine, fumbling with her bootstraps. From where she sat, she could see a dark cloud rising as the furnaces of Meartown were lit. She smoothed her big, sooty, callused hands across the stoop's worn stone, testing to see if the smoke paralysis had lifted sufficiently for her to at least be able to sense the hammer as she gripped it. The light of the rising sun was blinding.

Lynton moved slowly through the lush garden, his white hair gleaming among the bean plants. Bald Dominy came out the open door of the cottage with a packet of food for Karis's dinner. "It's bread, dried fish, some cheese and a couple of apples," he said. "Be sure you eat it all, whether you want it or not. A person your size has to eat."

She nodded. Dominy or Lynton had said these words, or something like them, every morning, all the years she had lived with them. She did not reply, for if she tried to talk she would slur like a drunk, since her tongue was still half paralyzed. The old man patted her shoulder affectionately. Before she moved in, he and Lynton had added an oversized room to their house to accommodate her oversized frame. After she moved in, thanks to their incessant fretting, she had finally put on the bulk to match her height.

The sunshine chased the lingering poison from her paralyzed nerves. She said, without too much difficulty, "Something has changed."

Dominy shouted to Lynton to be sure to pick plenty of tomatoes. "What's that?" he asked absently.

"Something has changed," she said again. She felt it, a shifting of the earth's weight, as though the earth and stones were gathering up their strength for a great effort. "I feel an urgency." She pressed her palms again upon the stoop. "What has happened?" she asked the warm granite.

Most of the time, Dominy treated her like any other metalsmith. Sometimes, she did something that astounded him, and he would remember that she was a witch. As she looked up at him now, he asked diffidently, "What does the stone say?"

"It speaks of blood and death throughout the land. That is not new. But it speaks of something else, a life." She shook her head. "I don't understand. It pulls at me." She looked down, as though a child were tugging at her shirt.

"You're going to be late," Dominy said.

She stood up. His head tilted back, and back, until it seemed he was gazing up at a mountain. He squinted fiercely in the sun. "I'm not going to the forge," she said. "I need to think."

"You want me to carry a message to the forgemaster, I suppose." Grumpily, he took the food packet out of Karis's hand. "I'll get a satchel for this. Where will you go? Out onto the heath? Better bring a water bottle, too."

Far from the danger and stink of the furnaces and forges, Karis walked through lands too dry and poor to interest farmers. The sun rose up in a breathless rush, the rocks shifted in their foundations, and the seedpods of summer shattered open. When the sun was high, she supposed she must be hungry and thirsty, so she sat down and ate. Afterwards, she lay on her back and listened. A *life*, the deep soil said to her. *Pay attention!*

When she came home, Lynton told her she was tired, and fed her a great bowl of vegetables from the garden. Dominy told her the forgemaster had merely nodded when he heard Karis would not be there. The sun hung low in the sky, and the only hunger Karis ever felt was consuming most of her attention: she needed smoke. Yet beneath that hunger, she still sensed the vague, irritating nagging of the earth. *A life*, it said. *You must do something!* But it never told her what she needed to do.

Often, when Karis lay awake, but still under smoke, a strange thing would happen: her spirit would break free of her insensate flesh to take residence in a particular raven. This raven traveled with Norina Truthken, far to the southeast. Norina usually contrived to be alone for the sunrise, and on this morning, she sat on a split rail fence at the edge of a harvested cornfield, waiting to see if the raven would speak to her.

Karis said through the raven, "There is a new presence in the land."

Norina rubbed her eyes, which were still crusted with sleep. "I don't understand."

"A person has come into Shaftal, and the land seems to cry out to me, demanding that I pay heed."

Norina gazed into the cornfield. "Is it an earth elemental? The one we have been waiting for?"

This possibility had not even occurred to Karis, and she cried out in surprise, "And if it is, what then?"

Norina said, quite calmly, "All this will come to an end."

"And the end of our friendship, too."

Norina turned sharply to the raven, then. "Is that what you think?"

"You will have more important concerns."

"I will always be your friend," Norina said. And, because she was a Truthken, Karis almost believed her. "So is it the one we are waiting for?" Norina asked.

"I don't think it is an earth witch. If it were, then surely I would understand what is happening better than I do. I feel an urgency, a danger, an impulse to intervene. Perhaps this person has been broken."

"And you want to go find this person."

Karis didn't have to reply. Norina knew her well enough.

"Whatever calls you," Norina said, "You must not let it call you out of hiding, or you will find there the hand of the Sainnites, stretching out to grab you by the throat."

Karis could not speak. Norina said, "Do you hear me?"

"I hear you."

"This presence—it makes you restive." Norina got down off the rail. "Don't do anything foolish. I'll be there in a few days."

Karis's spirit broke loose of the raven. When she came to herself, she lay once again in her bed, with the light of sunrise in her face.

By the time Norina ended her visit, she had reluctantly agreed to try to find the person whose presence haunted Karis. Autumn harvest began and was finished. The rains soon commenced, the days rapidly grew short, autumn began to turn to winter, and still Karis was haunted by nagging, inarticulate worry.

One day, she stayed later than usual at the smithy, and shadows barred the roadway as she walked to the tavern. There, she ate her pigeon pie in haste, and still could have left before sunset if not for the baked apple that appeared before her. "Did I ask for this?" she resentfully inquired of no one.

Someone—she did not know who—said, "Karis, you are getting thin."

The apple was a gift then, and so she had to eat it, and even to pretend that she appreciated it. As she ate and smiled politely, she felt the sun go down like a shutter slamming shut. A woman wrapped in sheepskin came in, and everyone shouted at her to close the door. "It's going to snow," somebody muttered, in a voice that spoke of shoveling the paths and carrying the wood and sharpening the runners on the sleigh.

Karis's plate was empty. She left the tavern without saying goodbye or uttering a word of thanks, and realized it too late, halfway out of town. Would they all forgive her one more time? Could she still depend on them? The presence in the land, which before had lured her into untoward expectation, had now begun to constantly distract her: not by its demand for her notice, but by its steady retreat. Half her attention constantly sought after it, worrying. With her attention so divided, she was forgetting to eat, losing track of time, forgetting common courtesy, making mistakes that could well be the death of her.

"I can't continue," she said. No one answered. The cold had driven everyone indoors. The wind carried frost-rimed leaves into shadowed places, and in the west stars had appeared. Karis tried to sing to them, forgetting for a moment that the smoke drug had destroyed her voice years ago.

She left the cobblestones behind and wandered through the icy mud of the wagon ruts, weaving like a drunk on her trembling legs. *Will I even make it home?* she asked herself, for the hill seemed to go up forever. And then home stood before her, a thatched cottage with a lamp flame in the window. A black thing dropped down from the treetops and struck her shoulder like a blow. She uttered a cry, then caught her breath. "So you're home."

Crisp feathers rasped on her ear as the raven folded his wings. She fumbled in her pocket for something to feed him—a bread end or a bit of grain—but today her pockets were full of stones. She could not remember why she had picked them up, or where. "I have to smoke," she said.

The raven spoke in a voice no more harsh than hers. "Then smoke."

"Come inside. I think Lynton and Dominy are already in bed."

In her room, she opened the window so the raven could come and go. While she filled her pipe with shaking hands, he ate the bread and bacon ends she had snatched up in the pantry. Now came a quiet, for with the pipe in hand, her panic eased. She could wait a little longer. In the fireplace, the coals caught in new wood and flames began to flicker. The raven drank from a bowl. "What did Norina find out?" Karis asked.

"Norina found nothing. Nothing to find, nothing to be done. There is a place shut up like a strongbox, which stinks of death. The Sainnites imprison people there—unfortunates who might have secrets to trade for a merciful death. People avoid the place, or stop up their ears so they won't hear the screams or be cursed by the ghosts."

"Is that all?" Karis cried, when the raven fell silent. "That cannot be all there is to know!" Karis paced back and forth across the room until she banged into the settle and felt a far-away pain in her shin. She forced herself to stop, to breathe deeply, to listen to the silence. For months the person who had been broken had endured in that place of horror while she and Norina argued. But now that bright spirit was a candleflame guttering in its socket.

"This person's life has become important to me. Much more important than my own life."

"And what does that mean?" the raven said, as Norina would. "Your life is not your own. You will not be foolish with it."

Karis looked at the pipe in her trembling hand. If she didn't smoke, she would die, and if she did smoke, that flame in the darkness might go out while she dreamed and drooled, drug giddy. "You must fly to that place of imprisonment, and find that person."

The raven drank more water, and shook out his dry feathers. "Tonight?" he said.

"Now." Karis took up a small pouch and emptied it onto a tabletop. She put in a dry crust of bread and hung the pouch around the raven's neck. "Go quickly, good raven. Or we will be too late."

As Karis, having smoked her pipe at last, sprawled upon her bed and watched the shadows dance, the raven flew over his kingdom, with darkness above and below. The lamplights below had all been blown out, and an impending storm had blotted out the lights of the sky. The raven flew on until morning, when the snow began to fall. He waited out the storm in the rafters of a barn, which he shared with an owl and some bats and an anxious flock of chickens whose eggs he ate surreptitiously, hiding the broken shells so the farmers would not know. When the snowfall ceased, he flew on, with the sun setting behind him. Below, a company of Sainnite soldiers trampled a path through the snow. Then they were gone, and night fell again.

The ruins of the House of Lilterwess passed beneath him, a great stone cairn for the martyrs of the defeat.

Once again, Karis lay under smoke. Sometimes smoke made her able to see through the raven's eyes. So she now saw the cairn swoop past, and she tried to make the raven circle it again, to examine the ruin of the bell tower by the front gate, where on the night after Harald G'deon's death Dinal had stood bravely ringing the alarm bell as the Sainnites broke through the gates. Dinal had been an old woman, the mother of four grown sons, a lieutenant of the Paladins, the beloved friend and lover of Harald G'deon. Karis had only known her as a kind stranger who appeared suddenly in the mad carnival of Lalali and offered Karis a way out the gates.

Harald, the last G'deon of Shaftal, also lay beneath the fallen walls of the building. Sometimes his bones spoke to Karis, but not tonight. After fifteen years of delay, watching the encroachments of these invaders and refusing to do anything about it, he had died before the final carnage began. The Sainnites, still fearing his power though they knew that he was dying, waited for him to die, and then attacked.

At this turning point of history, Norina came to show Karis the way to safety, and found her lying vacantly in bed while cannonballs smashed into the building. Sometimes, the memory still made Karis desperate with self-loathing. She should have saved the House of Lilterwess, but smoke made her incapable of even saving herself. Sometimes, it seemed impossible that Norina had been able to forgive her.

The ruins had passed, and now there was only darkness to be seen. Karis slipped deeper into sleep.

When Zanja opened her eyes to the bitter darkness of the wintry night, she was surprised to find herself still entrapped in flesh. It scarcely seemed possible her spirit could hold on for so many months when she had seen so many die so easily. A blow or two of the blade usually was all it took to sever soul from body, a moment of agony and then the soul was translated.

She had been dreaming of all the people of her village, gathered beside their summer fires in the Land of the Sun, chasing children, strutting before their rivals, stirring pots of fragrant *kich*. But just as the path Zanja followed seemed about to deposit her in their midst, it turned her mysteriously away, back into the wilderness, and she was lost again, trapped once more in a stinking box of straw, where she had been laid some months earlier like a side of meat being cellared for the winter.

She heard a dry, rasping sound, and turned her head. The moon shone through the barred window, as it briefly did sometimes, and faint light shimmered on the ice-encased walls of her cell. The floor by the window was white with drifted snow. Silhouetted against the white, a raven stood on the edge of her box, near her head. He preened his wing feathers, just like any other bird after a long flight, but she knew him: the Messenger, He Who Decides. At last.

She tilted up her chin so that his blunt beak could better reach her throat. "I have been waiting for you a long time, Lord Death." Her voice whispered like dry wind.

"It is not yet time for you to die," said Death. His voice was harsh, and echoed of the deep canyons where he made his home.

"How could it not be time? I have no home, no kin, no clan, no companions. I am broken, paralyzed. That smell—do you smell it?—that is my flesh rotting from my bones as I lie in my own shit. What more can the gods expect me to accomplish? What is left for me except death?"

"You are still bound."

"Bound to what? The gods?"

"To earth," the raven said, implacably. In the silence, he paced the length of the box, perhaps inspecting her in the darkness. The blanket covered some parts of her ravaged frame, but to cover her feet required that she lever herself up with her arms to toss the blanket, and she had not been strong enough to do this in quite some time. Surely the sight of her feet, spastically curled and with half the toes hacked off, would convince even a god that her usefulness in this world was at an end. But Death paced back to her head again, unperturbed, and fed her a crust of bread, dry and stale and hard as stone, as if she were his fledgling. Her mouth was dry; she could not chew. He brought her a beakful of snow from the drift by the window, and she managed to swallow the dry crumbs. They burned within her like coals in a hearth, and warmed the parts of Zanja's body where she could still feel the warmth: her torso, her arms, the shattered places of her heart. But the physical agonies that had only recently been numbed at last by cold were not renewed. For a while, she dozed, and awakened to find that her strength had gathered and concentrated around the center of that warmth in her belly. No, she would not step across the threshold just yet.

"Are you still there?" she asked.

"Yes," said the god. The moon had crossed her small window. Pressed against the darkness, the god still perched at her head, not a handspan away, invisible.

She said, "You say I am still bound. Perhaps you mean that I am bound to die in honor, as I am a *katrim*."

Death said, "What do you think should be done so that you could die as a *katrim* should die?"

"It is the way of the *katrim* to die in joy." She had spoken the words of an old lesson, a child's lesson, easy to recite when Zanja first stood up in the presence of her clan elders and named herself a *katrim* and proudly said that the owl god Salos'a had chosen her to travel between the worlds. But to recite this lesson now seemed a bitter joke, though Lord Death did not laugh.

"How might you die in joy?" asked Death.

"You mock me with impossibilities."

"I do not mean to mock you." Lord Death is a teacher, but the best teacher is the one who waits in silence. She heard the crisp sound of him unhurriedly preening his flight feathers, as though he intended to wait a thousand nights if necessary for Zanja to offer an answer to her own question.

She did not want to wait so long. She tried to remember what once had brought joy to her life, but the massacre of her people lay between her present and her past like an uncrossable divide. So she said, "Perhaps a joyful death comes from being able to understand one's life as part of a purpose or pattern. But that is the one thing I cannot do."

"Why not?" asked Death, as though he did not know.

"Because my memory is broken to pieces, and some of the pieces are lost, and the rest don't fit together any more."

"Then you must recover what you have lost, and remember who you are."

"Who I was." Zanja's bitterness brought forth weak tears, but surely there was no shame in weeping before a god.

When it is time for someone to die, the people of the dying one's clan gather around and tell the stories of her life, so that when she crosses the threshold she will still remember, and be able to tell that history to the people on the other side. But Zanja was the last of her people and so she had to tell those stories of her life to herself. This must be what the god wanted of her.

"Where shall I start?" she asked.

"Start where it begins," said Death.

So she began with her earliest memories of the clattering looms and the light drifting in to make the patterns shine as they were slowly revealed on the weaver's loom. She explained that her mother had been a weaver, and had been sorely disappointed when her daughter left the weaver's house as soon as she could walk on her own two feet, to return only by force. She told about the first time she realized the elders were watching her, the first time she understood that she was not like other children, the first time she and Ransel became friends in the midst of a desperate fistfight. As the night cracked with cold and her heart failed in her chest and her flesh moldered in the straw, she told Death all she knew: all that once had mattered, all that shaped her and now left her, like trash tossed into a midden heap to be eaten by worms.

When Karis awoke in the winter woods, it was still dark, and the stars were falling. They briefly flared and then were quenched, their spectacular suicides watched, surely, by none but her, for even the poorest people of the earth would have found some kind of shelter from this bitter night. Stiff hair prickled against her face. For warmth, she had curled against the belly of a shaggy gray plow horse. When she lay down to sleep, she apparently had not concerned herself with the danger that she might be smothered by her gigantic bedfellow. Stupidity, or daring, or innocence, she never knew what to call the peculiar logic of herself under smoke.

She got clumsily to her knees in a loud crackling of frost. The horse lifted his huge head and yawned, ground his teeth, then snorted wetly. They had made their bed in the undergrowth at the edge of a wood, where the snow had largely collected overhead rather than on the ground. That had been sensible of them, though most of the sense had probably come from the horse.

Karis tried to stand up, but staggered to her knees again. The horse blundered to his feet, dislodging a sudden avalanche of snow from overhead. He nosed her encouragingly. "Smoke," Karis explained. "But never graceful. No more than you."

With the help of a slender tree trunk, she hauled herself upright. Despair was always worst in the morning; she fended it off with curses and eventually was able to drag her ungainly body onto the horse's back. Stung by her urgency, the horse jumped forward. She clung to him grimly, angry at her weakness, angry at the irresistible impulse that drove her out on this insane fool's errand, angry at the bitter poverty of spirit from which her anger came. This dark and frigid morning, where dawn seemed unlikely ever to break, did not bode well at all for the day that lay ahead.

Zanja's voice gave out. In the bitter cold, the god stood sentinel, silent long after she had ceased to weep. When she turned her head, the straw crackled where her tears had frozen. A hush had fallen, and she saw the faint shimmer of snowfall outside the window.

Zanja's story was nearly done, and soon Lord Death would let her go free. She continued, "I don't know why the Sainnites didn't kill me. When they reached their garrison, it seems they were disgraced. Perhaps, in the confusion, orders were bungled, papers were mislaid. Perhaps they simply wanted to get me out of their sight. I don't know how, but somehow I ended up here."

"Ha!" said the god.

"So I did not set out to cheat you. Haven't I spent my days in pleading with the gods to allow me to die? I am tortured even in my dreams. I walk the path to my village and I see it filled with my people. Ransel is there waiting for me. How will I explain my long delay?" The raven seemed to shrug, and Zanja was tempted to grab hold of him and twist his neck until the backbone popped, just to let him know what paralysis was like. She could no longer take deep breaths to calm herself. The god moved cautiously out of reach. Zanja spoke, her voice shaking. "You bid me die in joy rather than in despair, but the only joy I can imagine is to walk down that path, to enter the Land of the Sun and be free of this body, this prison. Is that too much to ask?"

The god said, "You ask not for too much, but for too little."

"What?" Zanja peered into the shadows at the black shape of the raven, who she suddenly remembered was a trickster. "I am too stupid for riddles."

"It is no riddle, but a choice. Do you *choose* to die?"

She stared at him. Her heartbeat sputtered like a candle about to go out. In the silence, she thought she could hear a quiet footstep in the hall outside her door. But it was too early for the guard to make his noisy rounds. Bewildered, she whispered, "Now you mock me, Lord Death."

"No," said the god gently. "I am giving you the choice."

No keys jingled in the frozen silence, but Zanja heard the lock of her cell door turn. The guard had not come in to feed her for days, but the door swung open without a creak from the rust-caked hinges. A presence filled the doorway. Lord Death spread his wings and lifted suddenly into the darkness.

Zanja spoke to the vacancy where the god had been. "Then I choose to live." Then, she lay stunned by her own stupidity, asking herself what she wanted to live for.

She heard Lord Death's voice in the darkness, but he was not speaking to her. "I am your witness."

"I heard, good raven," rasped a voice as harsh as Lord Death's laugh.

Zanja heard a sound like the snapping of two fingers. A red spark danced like a firefly in the darkness, then flared, and became a sputtering flame. The flame advanced until Zanja could feel its faint heat upon her frozen skin. Her heart managed another weary pulse.

An enormous, long-fingered hand held up the burning wand. Another reached down to turn aside the decayed blanket and uncover Zanja's ravaged remains: ulcerated skin, tightly stretched over thinly clad bones, a stick-fingered hand still curled into a fist. The stink rose up, muted but not conquered by the cold.

The hand touched Zanja's emaciated chest. Like a coal in a snowdrift, heat shocked into her flesh. Zanja's heart gave a mighty thud. She grunted, as if she had been struck, and gasped burning air into her lungs. Her heart thudded again. A river of heat rushed through the conduit of her flesh, up her neck, and into the vessel of her skull. Color exploded across her vision. Bedazzled and stunned, she uttered an animal cry.

The voice spoke again, in Shaftalese. "Do not be afraid. I have come to help you."

Zanja would not have been surprised to discover that those warm fingers had folded back skin and bone to lay bare her faltering heart. "I'm not afraid," she lied.

"Tell me your name."

"Zanja na'Tarwein," said the raven, who now rode upon the woman's broad shoulder.

"Zanja na'Tarwein, my name is Karis. My raven has traveled ahead of me, and kept you alive at my command."

"Your raven?" Zanja said. "He is not a god?"

"You thought he was a god?" The woman dropped down beside the box of straw, never lifting her hand from Zanja's breast. "No, he is just a raven. And I—take the light and look at me."

The slender, insubstantial rush light was placed between Zanja's fingers. The sputtering flame trembled in her weak grasp as she lifted it to illuminate clearwater eyes, a sun-bleached thicket of hair, deeply drawn lines of worry, weariness, and perhaps some laughter. The woman smelled of sweat and wood smoke, and there were pine needles trapped in her hair. Her ragged shirt sleeves were rolled to the elbow, revealing bulky, muscled forearms. The palms of her hands were gray with ground-in soot. She had strolled through the locked door of this prison like a phantom, yet she was substantial, physical, powerful. The vitality coursing through Zanja's veins gave her an eye-aching clarity, and as she looked at Karis she could not help but know what she was made of. She said, "You are neither god nor ghost, so you must be an elemental. I think you are an earth witch."

Karis said, "And you've gone from mystery to understanding without asking a single question, so you must be a fire blood." She turned her head as though she heard something, and said, "I think the prison guards are up and about. How long until they come this way?"

"Not until after dawn."

"It is well after dawn now. A storm rolled in before first light, which is why it seems so dark now. Good raven," she added, "your work here is done."

The raven lifted from her shoulder, flew to the window, and was gone.

Zanja said, "Perhaps your raven is no god, but he taught me something I did not know. *Serrain*, I am dying, but even crippled as I am, I'd rather live. I ask your mercy."

Karis gazed at her as though astonished by her good manners. But it seemed that Zanja's careful words had not struck Karis as ridiculous, for she said, "As it happens, I am a great mender of broken things. Let me see what I can do." Karis took the rush light and wedged it in a crack between stones. "I need to touch you," she said, as though Zanja's heart were not still beating eagerly against the palm of her hand, and as though her callused fingers did not scratch Zanja's bare breast every time she shifted her weight. The shock of heat again, and Karis lifted and turned Zanja as easily as if she were an infant, so that she faced the ice-clad wall. Karis stroked a hand firmly down the weeping sores of Zanja's back. Zanja expected pain, but she felt something else: the startling warmth of Karis' touch, and an eerie, crawling sensation as her ruined flesh hastily knit itself together.

Then, in the place where her back had been broken, below which she had felt only dead weight for months, pain blossomed. Her entire body began to spasm. "Hold fast," said Karis hoarsely, and pinned Zanja down with her weight.

When the fit had passed, Zanja tasted blood from her bitten tongue, and the sharp salt of sweat. The weight of Karis' body lifted. She was gasping for breath, as though she had run a long way at a desperate pace.

Zanja had been long enough removed from the lower half of her own body that her legs felt foreign to her: ungainly contraptions of sinew and bone; but at least she felt them, and even could make them move, however reluctantly, with the lever of her will.

She breathed something in her own language, stupefied.

"Hush," Karis said absently. She had moved the rush light, and so Zanja watched by its light as those big hands delicately kneaded her feet, straightening the clenched muscles and stretching and moving the flesh with her long fingers to form new, perfect toes, one by one. Karis frowned as she worked, like a potter at the wheel, with her eyes half closed, seeming to feel her way with her fingers. Her sweat shimmered in faint light as it fell, drop by drop, from her chin.

Half drowned in the tingling, burning, cramping sensations of her repaired flesh, Zanja felt the pressure of those fingers only remotely, but as new toes budded and grew upon her disfigured feet, the feeling of it was so bizarre that it was all she could do to keep from snatching her foot from the witch's grasp.

When Karis laid Zanja's foot down, she rested her head in her hand for a moment as though exhausted or overwhelmed by her labor.

"*Serrain*," Zanja said again. Even her voice trembled shamefully. Having given Karis this title of great respect, she could not think of what to say, or what to ask, or even what words might begin to be adequate.

Karis lumbered to her feet, a great, graceless woman who seemed suddenly weary to the bone. She did not speak, but dressed Zanja in gigantic clothing, and then tied her onto her back with rope, where she could neither aid nor impede her.

The fugitive journey felt like a fever dream. Karis strode rapidly down dark ways where dawn's faint light had not yet penetrated, bent over in a crouch to avoid the rough-hewn beams of the low ceiling. From behind the steel-clad doors where other prisoners stared or froze in terrible solitude, there was no sound. Karis turned, and turned again, unhesitating. And then they were mounting a narrow, twisting stairway that pressed in on both sides and clawed at Zanja's knees. They climbed into light that wormed its way through narrow slits of windows and dispersed like dust through the darkness. Karis stopped short, and her rapid, shallow breaths swelled and receded within Zanja's tightly bound embrace.

". . . this cursed country!" said a voice harshly in Sainnese. Boots rasped upon stone.

"Remember the grape arbors of Sainna. In winter they dropped their leaves, that was how we knew the season. And the wind came in from the north, bringing rain." The speaker paused, perhaps overcome by his own poetry.

"And we sat indoors drinking warm wine." The guard spat. "I'd rather almost have been killed than be exiled in this barbaric country."

"Our hearts are turned to stone in this land of stone," said the poet.

The angry man snorted. "A land of ice, more like."

"Have another swig."

Zanja smelled the harsh fumes of distilled liquor. The echoes of stone made the sound tricky, but by the smell she realized that the two men stood very close by. She took a deep breath and smelled the rancid tallow with which they had waterproofed their cuirasses. All Sainnite soldiers smell the same because of that tallow; she had sometimes been able to track them through the woods by smell alone.

"Well, it's not getting warmer," said the angry man. "I might as well go feed the beasts. They'll whine like dogs today."

The poet only grunted. His poetry he reserved for speaking of his native country. Like Zanja, it seemed he was a refugee. The two men separated, and for a moment, a shadow blocked the dim light at the top of the stairs, then passed. Zanja felt Karis begin to breathe again. "I wonder what they were talking about," she murmured.

"The weather," said Zanja.

"Do you speak their language, or are you just guessing?"

"I do speak it, though with a terrible accent."

"You speak this language with an accent too, though I'd not call it terrible." Karis stepped out into the wide corridor, into which opened double doors wide enough to admit a wagon such as the one that had carried Zanja to this place. Karis ignored these massive doors, and went out through a nearby postern door, around which mud and slush brought in by the guards' boots puddled.

At first, all Zanja could see was snow. Then the walls took shape, a solid gray against the white sky. The low stone buildings to the right looked like stables; those to the left the guards' quarters. One set of buildings looked no different from the other except that one had chimneys and smaller doors. The wind picked up and for a moment the entire scene disappeared behind blowing snow. Karis started boldly across the yard. The snow on Zanja's face felt like sparks from a fire.

They reached the wall. Karis lifted a hand to the rough stone, and for a giddy moment Zanja thought she would simply push her way through, like a mole through earth. But she was testing a gray, snow-speckled rope that lay nearly invisible against the stone.

Already shivering, Zanja felt as though she were drowning in snow. The prison building was nearly invisible. Karis took hold of the rope, dug her toes into the thin cracks between the stones, and began to climb. She did it gracelessly, hastily, almost carelessly. Zanja hung upon her back, helpless as a bundle of laundry. When she turned her head, she could see portions of the compound, made ghostly and distant by the gray light and the falling snow.

The snow cleared suddenly, and the central building appeared, squatting sullenly under its dusting of snow. On each corner of the square enclosure stood a guard tower, whose guards surely could see Zanja as clearly as she saw them. Then the snow began to fall again, but not soon enough. She heard the distinct, echoing report of a musket shot.

Karis muttered a curse, and hauled herself up to the top of the wall. There was a blare of alarm horns. Zanja imagined what she could not see: the doors of the guards' quarters bursting open, and soldiers in their uniforms rushing for the stables and for the gates.

The sky swirled as Karis swung down the other side of the wall and swarmed down the rope to where a huge horse waited with stolid patience. And then she stood in snow, breathing heavily, holding Zanja by the wrist as she cut the rope with a sharp knife, until Zanja dangled loose across her back, feet dragging in the snow. The rank sheepskin doublet that Karis wore kept Zanja from feeling the muscle of that back, but after these demonstrations of strength she was not at all surprised when Karis simply picked her up and set her upon the horse's back, then dragged herself up behind her.

The horse jumped as if she had flicked him with a whip, and lunged headlong into the woods and down the hill, spraying clots of snow around him. No horse could keep up such a pace for long in snow so deep, but by the time he slowed, Karis seemed satisfied. "They already are turning back," she said. "They have no stomach for this foul weather."

Zanja lay slumped against Karis's shoulder, too weak to sit up on her own, hardly able to even hold up her head or lift a hand to brush the snow from her face. "This has been a very strange day," she murmured. And then sleep overwhelmed her.

Chapter Five

Snow was still falling when Karis hid Zanja and the horse in the hills, and went on foot to let herself into the barn of a fine farmstead near the edge of the forest that hems in West Hart. Like everything in this part of Shaftal, the barn was built of stone and mortar within a sheltered hollow, with a roof so low the beasts sheltered there could scarcely lift their heads. Two cows this farmstead owned, and two horses, and a dozen or more sheep. This farmstead was far off the beaten track, far enough that perhaps it had never been raided by Sainnites, who had been known to butcher the milk cows and strip the cellars to the walls. The dark day and shuttered windows had fooled the chickens, who had gone to roost in the low rafters though the sun would not set for some time yet. No doubt the numbers of this substantial flock would be sadly diminished come spring.

These people were not wholly hostile to strangers, for a loaf of pauper's bread, wrapped in wax cloth, rested upon a shelf just inside the door. A wide-mouthed jar with a stopper hung there as well. Karis milked a cow into the jug. She found some hen's eggs in the hay and tied them up with the bread. She could find nothing to carry oats in, and finally took off one of her shirts and made a bag out of it by tying the sleeves together and pulling tight the neck string. She left some coins in compensation for having taken

68

more than was customary, and returned the way she had come, walking in her own footprints.

In a goat's burrow hidden in the nearby hills, Zanja lay as Karis had left her, wrapped in the horse blanket, watched over by the raven. She still slept like a child, her skin flushed as with fever, her hair a matted tangle, her hands limply open against the earth. Her fingers were thin as sticks, and every bone stood out harshly in her sharply angled face. Karis lay down the fistful of oats she had reserved for the raven, and sat in the opening of the burrow, just out of reach of the falling snow. She heard faintly the horse crunching dry oats with his big teeth. He needed to be stabled and fed properly, but a good bit of grueling travel still lay ahead of them this night.

Zanja had slept the entire day through, collapsed in Karis's arms like a jointed puppet with the strings cut loose. While she slept, Karis nourished her, and felt herself slowly emptied, and knew the giddiness that comes from too much generosity. When the raven rejoined them, he crept inside the shelter of the blanket that wrapped them both, and he muttered in Karis's ear all he knew, every word Zanja had spoken during that strange night. It had been genius to send the raven, Karis supposed, but now there seemed something diabolical in his masquerade. She had created him intelligent, but he was also without compunction.

Now sunset was approaching and Karis still could not decide what to do. When she turned her head, Zanja was looking at her.

Zanja awoke in a cramped cranny between two boulders, which was blocked at one end by brush and stone, and at the other end by Karis, whose extraordinary length folded impossibly into the narrow space. Her back bowed to match the curve of the stones; her legs fit tightly to her chest, and her arms tucked to her sides, bent at the elbows, with her hands atop her knees. Her shirt hung loose at the neck and wrist, and oat grains were stuck in the weave of the fabric. Slush and melted snow puddled at her feet and dripped from the curled tips of her hacked-off hair. She looked as worn as her stained and poorly patched clothing: a used-up woman on the verge of going to rags.

Why did her kith and kin let a woman of rare and valuable talent go hungry, cold, and poorly clothed like this?

Karis turned her head, and Zanja caught her breath. She sat up, tossed off the heavy horse blanket which covered her, and took off Karis' sheepskin doublet.

Karis said hoarsely, "No, you wear it."

"Not while you are cold."

"I'm not."

"But you're trembling."

Karis lifted one of the hands with which she clasped her knee, and examined its tremor without surprise. "It's nearly sunset."

"It is?" Puzzled, Zanja examined their droppings-strewn shelter: the raven, who ate oats greedily, the plain round loaf of bread and the jug and eggs that waited beside it on the ground, and Karis again, who gazed at her steadily, as though waiting for something. Zanja remembered how the day had begun, but she remembered nothing else. Now, a green and raw energy pulsed in her wasted body, like sap rising in winter's skeletal trees, and Karis, who that morning had seemed gigantic in spirit as well as body, now seemed diminished, exhausted, worn to the bone. It was as though she had poured herself into the wreck of Zanja's flesh until all her reserves were exhausted.

Zanja said, "*Serrain*, I don't understand you."

Karis slid into the cleft and crouched close to Zanja, so close that drops of melting snow from her hair stung the skin of Zanja's hand. "Why do you call me 'Serrain'? What does it mean?"

"I—honor you. I don't know how it's proper to address a Shaftali elemental . . ."

"So you're making me a stranger."

"No, my people value formality—"

Karis looked away, the line of her body a cipher of frustration. "But if you were being impetuous, even foolhardy?"

"Karis." It did seem foolhardy, even to call her by name like this. "You could have my servitude, for surely I owe you whatever you demand. So why demand a friendship, which requires an obligation in return?"

"How else could my behavior possibly be explained, except as fulfilling an obligation? Well, madness, I suppose."

"It does seem like madness," Zanja said.

"Do you think so?" In body and in spirit Karis filled a great deal of space, and Zanja was fighting with herself to keep from backing away. There was something of the raven in Karis's way of waiting for Zanja to speak: intent, expectant, almost apprehensive. Unlike the fire bloods, earth bloods normally were stable as stone, but it appeared that Karis doubted her own sanity.

Zanja said, "Perhaps it only seems like madness since you are a complete stranger and have no reason to be obligated to me. But—" The inexplicable certainty of insight rose up in her and she said in astonishment, "but in the future, I will serve you, and you will indeed be obligated—"

Karis let out her breath as though someone had suddenly slammed a fist into her back.

Zanja reached for Karis's hand. It was surprisingly warm, and had a fluttering tremor, like a palsy. Karis's other hand rested upon her thigh. When Zanja touched it to turn it over, it flexed involuntarily but did not pull away. Upon this wrist, as upon the other, was inscribed in faded scars an old despair. There had been a time, years ago, when Karis had tried to kill herself.

And then she remembered: the gangly, extraordinarily tall young woman, a refugee from the fall of the House of Lilterwess, being escorted like a prisoner to the waiting wagon. She remembered how she had watched her being carried away, and how the sight had laid a horror upon her heart.

She looked up into Karis's shadowed face. That despairing prisoner certainly had been she, though she hardly seemed helpless any longer. Karis broke the silence with a voice that strained to seem indifferent, "If I simply sat here in silence long enough, would you discover all my secrets?"

"I'm beginning to think I might."

She still held Karis's trembling hand. In the silence, she could hear how unsteadily Karis breathed. Zanja didn't say anything, fearing that she had already been too presumptuous. Then Karis said, "There was a time that I could not endure my life. I wish it were my worst dishonor or my greatest shame. But the truth is that I dishonor myself every day, and will do so again today."

She had spoken these terrible words with a bleak hopelessness that defied response. Zanja groped her way out of that silence with uncertain words. "Surely . . . if it were true that you have no honor, then there would be no reason for you to be so tortured."

"I have no honor," Karis said heavily. "I would—and can—do anything for smoke."

Three months ago, Zanja would have dropped Karis's drug-palsied hand and pulled away in involuntary disgust. But she had seen repugnance in the eyes of her Sainnite guards every day since then, as they recoiled from her crippled body. Karis, though, had touched her without hesitation or disgust. So now Zanja held onto Karis's hand. "You consider yourself responsible," she said. "Call it what you will, it seems honorable to me."

A long time Karis gazed at her, until the raven said harshly, "You are in dire danger!"

"Oh, shut up." But Karis gently eased her hand from Zanja's grasp.

Zanja said, "What kind of danger?"

"More kinds of danger than I can begin to name," Karis said briskly, and served without ceremony the scavenged meal of bread as hard as stone, milk fresh from the cow, eggs raw in the shell. Zanja ate like the starved soul she was; Karis ate as though she were doing the food a favor. While Zanja ate, she considered whether she might demand to be told what Karis had to fear. If she had been caught up in this strange woman's destiny and was somehow to do her a great service, then surely she might be in a position to insist upon the truth.

When the last dry crumb was gone and the raven had pecked apart the emptied eggshells, Karis said suddenly, "Well, there's a farmstead not far from here, where I imagine they would take you in, and even marry you into the family. Isolated places like this get hungry for new blood, and it's a prosperous little farm. I could give you a bit of a dowry, to ease your way."

Zanja said, bewildered, "Wherever you go, I am going with you."

"No, you are not." Karis busied herself with getting ready to go.

The day had succumbed to a cold twilight. Zanja looked down at her wasted limbs. "But I am no threat to you. Even in my full strength—"

Karis looked up sharply, and Zanja saw how distressed she was. "Under smoke I am utterly defenseless."

"After you saved my life and took such risks, I couldn't even think of harming you."

Karis slung the horse blanket over her shoulder.

"But still, you dare not trust me? I'll swear you an oath. My word is my honor—your raven, who knows my entire life, can tell you as much."

Trembling, glassy-eyed, Karis said, "An oath would make no difference. I can't take you with me."

Zanja said, "Then leave me where I am."

"You'll freeze to death this very night!"

"I do not want a life that has no purpose."

Karis said angrily, "I'll carry you to the farm against your will, if I must."

Zanja waited. Ransel always said there was something uncanny about her ability to distinguish a true threat from a bluff. Karis sat back on her heels. "What oath?"

"Before my god Salos'a, She Who Travels Between the Worlds, I swear I will value your life as my own, protect you from harm when you are injured, serve your interests when you are absent, guard your back in every battle, love your friends and hate your enemies, and honor your name in life and in death." It was the oath Zanja and Ransel had sworn to each other when they were scarcely more than children.

Karis said, "Now you are being foolhardy."

"You think I would choose to sit warm and dry in some farmer's cottage, while you go forth alone into the bitter night? That I would be content to live out my days bearing children and hoeing corn when I could have embraced a perilous destiny instead? You do not know me, Karis."

"I know Norina, to whose house we are going. She will blame you that I put myself at your mercy. And you will indeed be in peril." Karis crawled out of the burrow and whistled shrilly for the horse.

The snow lay deep upon the barren hills, which swelled like a lovely woman's breasts under a gray silk sky. In the cleft between them clustered groves of leafless trees, and far away in the lower country Zanja thought she spotted a speck of light, perhaps a window of that farm where a warm fire burned behind thick windowpanes.

It was cold, bitter cold, and would be colder still if the wind picked up. Karis waded in knee-deep snow as she carried Zanja down the hillside to the waiting horse. Trembling had taken over her entire frame, and she stumbled in the snow like a dying animal struggling to remain afoot. Her skin, where Zanja touched it, was clammy, and the color had drained out of her face. Zanja had seen many a warrior stricken to the heart who looked no better than this: dazed and shiny-eyed as her soul already started down the last path. Karis managed to lift Zanja to the horse's back, and stood leaning against the beast's broad shoulder, breathing shallowly as though she might faint, fumbling one-handed at the buttons of her woolen shirt.

Zanja worked one hand under the cinch to hold herself steady on the horse's unsaddled back. "Can I help?"

The raven, now perched upon the horse's rump, said, "Leave her be."

Zanja looked hastily away as Karis drew a smoke purse out from within her shirt. Zanja once had curiously examined such a purse in the marketplace, not realizing until later what it was for. It would contain a tin matchbox filled with expensive sulfur matches, a charred pipe of carved wood, and a supply of the drug, each small piece wrapped in a twist of waxed paper.

The raven said, "The horse will be unable to carry the two of you in such deep snow. You'll have to ride alone, while she walks."

"I will stay on the horse somehow," Zanja said. She would tie herself to the cinch if she had to.

She heard the crack and sputter of a match being lit, and smelled the stink of sulfur, and then a second smell, like burning mold, the scent of dark alleyways and dilapidated doorways. Karis sighed out her breath and said, suddenly and clearly, "Zanja, the raven is only clever in certain ways. You will have to use your judgment."

"I understand," Zanja said, continuing to gaze out at the landscape.

"And you must instruct me—much as we both . . . dislike the idea. I will obey you. I will—have to."

The raven said, "You didn't take a second breath of smoke. Do it now." Karis said nothing, but Zanja heard another heavy sigh. "Now pack the purse—shake the ashes out of the pipe first—and button your shirt."

Zanja took off the sheepskin doublet and leaned down to put it on Karis. Karis allowed herself to be clothed and fastened against the cold, all the while gazing into Zanja's face with the eyes of an infant: startlingly blue and terribly, invitingly helpless. Zanja said to her, her voice strange and rough in her ears, "Good raven, does she have no cap to wear?"

The answer, it seemed, was no, and neither could the raven reassure Zanja that Karis's boots were well greased or her stockings warm enough to keep her feet from freezing. Karis had embarked on her cold journey no better equipped than a pauper.

Zanja would have to keep Karis moving so that she would not freeze, and perhaps in the end the horse would still have to carry them both. For now, though, Zanja wrapped herself in the heavy blanket, and hoped that their journey would not take so very long.

"It will take half the night at least," the raven said, when they had started in the direction he told her.

Zanja sighed, dismayed anew. "Is Norina her commander? Her lover?"

The raven cawed a harsh and even bitter laugh. "Lover? Smoke deprives its users of both agency and desire. And," he added gleeful at her shock, "Norina will happily kill you."

Some hours had passed when the clouds parted to reveal the light-edged blades of the stars, none of which seemed to be in quite the right place any more. Zanja gazed up at them, stunned by cold and by the beauty of the night sky, which she had never expected to see again. The relocated stars reminded her how far she was from home, and how much she was altered, and how much she had forgotten. The obedient giant trudged listlessly through the snow, breaking the way for the horse and perhaps being broken in the process. The snow cracked like ice beneath her weight. The iron chill invaded Zanja's flesh, cutting like knife to bone.

When Karis tripped over the road stones and fell into the road, Zanja dazedly thought that it must be her fault. And then she came out of her daze enough to realize what danger they were in. "How close are we?" she cried to the raven, who had flown to Karis and flapped around her as she floundered to her feet again. There was blood, Zanja saw, in the snow. Earth blood. The spilling of it would bless this spot, and the road workers would curse the weeds that would displace the stones here with grand abandon, come spring, and only Zanja would know why, if she lived until then.

The horse had followed Karis into the road, and nosed her gently, as though she were a foundering foal. "Karis, come here," Zanja slurred. Karis came, and stood quietly as Zanja brushed the snow from her shirt front and her hair, stopped her nosebleed with the help of some snow, and then felt her hands, which seemed even colder than her own. She slipped her fingers into the breast of Karis's shirt. Karis gazed up at her, seemingly relaxed, with her lips parted, but suddenly breathing too quickly, and with her heart pounding against Zanja's hand. What did Karis fear? That Zanja

would embrace the temptation of that terrible, malleable innocence? Or that she would take the smoke purse and so take control
of all Karis's choices?

Zanja hastily removed her hand and said, "Karis, your heart is
still warm—that sheepskin doublet will keep you alive, at least. But
you're too tired to continue, and I am too cold. Perhaps the smoke
keeps you from even knowing that you're tired. But you were tired
to start with, and perhaps you didn't know it then, either."

The raven had been watching Zanja as if considering whether
to peck her to pieces. But now, he said with great civility, "We've
gone more than half the distance."

"How much more than half?"

"Not much at all."

"Then this journey is going to end badly, good raven. There is
no shelter nearby?"

"No."

Zanja's emaciated frame had begun to shiver uncontrollably,
with cold or with weakness. "Karis—should have abandoned me—
she could have ridden. I should not have been so insistent. Now
we both are in danger."

The raven watched her, with inscrutable raven's eyes.

"We will die without help," Zanja said.

There was a weight and warmth against Zanja's knee where
Karis had leaned suddenly. Perhaps, in that long silence, she was
considering Zanja's words, in however slow or strange a way. The
raven said, "Follow the road south to the third set of milestones,
and then go east into the woods. Due east, until you reach a ridge,
then follow the ridge to the southeast. You understand?"

"Yes."

The raven still hesitated, as though he wanted to admonish her
further, or threaten her perhaps. Then, the raven spread his wings,
and flew into the darkness.

Following Zanja's instructions, Karis struggled to mount the
horse, and even using a large stone as a mounting block almost
could not succeed. But when at last she rode behind Zanja, with
the blanket wrapped around them both, they had a little warmth
for a while, which they shared between them like two starvelings
might share a piece of bread.

Only in winter did the sky seem at once so bright and so dark.
The sharp-edged lights of the night sky crowded down upon the
frozen earth, but their fires were cold. When it came time to leave

the road and go east among the trees, a steady shower of dislodged snow flung itself at them, like sparks falling from the stars' bitter fires. Zanja began to shiver again, and all her many disciplines could not keep her attention from wandering down unlikely and devious paths, which more often than not brought her up short at a shattered ravine where something had happened that she could not and did not wish to remember.

The horse also was wandering, indifferent to the stars that Zanja wanted him to follow, trying only to find the route of the shallowest snow and fewest trees. Zanja had not the strength to force him to do differently, and she wondered if they were lost, and how they might hope to be found on such a night. Then she ceased to be interested in such questions.

Some time later, she fell into a snowdrift, and lay there in a vast confusion of mind. The horse's big hooves stamped down not a handspan from her head, and for a moment she thought she lay once again in the Asha Valley, under the hooves of a Sainnite warhorse. There were yellow flames and an angry voice shouting, and then the horse blundered away. A lantern glared into her eyes, and beside it glared the scarred, narrow-lipped, hard-eyed face of a warrior, who seemed to be deciding the best way to make an end of her.

Lord Death flapped into the light. "She is under Karis's protection!"

"Karis is a fool!" The warrior tossed the raven roughly aside. She took Zanja by the arm, and jerked her out of the drift. Zanja landed in a tangle, but struggled to her knees. The warrior was going to strike her, and if Zanja ducked the blow the woman would draw the wicked dagger that, for now at least, remained sheathed. Zanja drew herself up to accept the fist instead. The blow never landed, and so she had leisure to remember what it was like to strike someone who neither flinched nor fought back. She had only ever hit someone like that once, and never forgot the shame of it. So now this warrior restrained herself, perhaps also remembering other blows struck in rage that she later had cause to regret.

The warrior said, after a moment, "You're a smart woman, whoever you are."

Zanja would have gotten to her feet then, if she could have, and faced this worthy opponent eye to eye and blade to blade. Even were she at the peak of strength and skill she likely would be defeated, but it would be an education worth its price in spilled blood and injured pride. Scarcely had she thought this when the warrior's scarred face creased with a grim amusement, and she unceremoniously hauled Zanja up and dragged her to the lightweight sledge that stood nearby, and dumped her into it like a load of potatoes. "How is Karis?"

The man she spoke to knelt at Karis's feet with a lantern nearby, feeling her bare toes with ungloved hands. He seemed unsurprised by the warrior's abruptness and violence. "She's fine, Norina. A touch of frostbite, nothing serious. Why did you never tell me your friend is a smoke addict? It explains so much . . ." He glanced over at Zanja, and his eyes widened. "Shaftal's Name!"

He left Karis to the brisk attentions of the warrior, and beat the snow out of Zanja's clothing, then wrapped her in a bearskin robe. "What happened to you? You're naught but bone in skin."

"Captivity," Zanja said.

"Drink some of this, if you can." He uncorked a small jug and gave it to her to drink. "I am J'han, of the Order of Healers."

Zanja let him feel her hands and breast, but stopped him when he reached for the heavy socks that Karis had given her. "Don't touch my feet."

"What?"

She could hardly blame him for being so bewildered, but the warrior's hand appeared suddenly on the healer's shoulder, and the woman said, "J'han, I guess I need to talk privately to—"

"This is Zanja," he murmured automatically, as though introducing friends at a festival.

"Just a few words with her."

The healer climbed out of the sledge and walked out of earshot, shaking his head all the while. "What did Karis do to you?" Norina said.

Zanja said, "When Karis found me, I was paralyzed. My back was broken. My flesh was rotting. Half my toes had been hacked off."

Norina snatched off one of Zanja's socks and looked at what Zanja did not want the healer to see: the incongruous, soft pink toes that lay against the others like replacement boards in a weathered barn. She muttered, "Karis, I will eviscerate you."

"You'll have to kill me first."

"And how difficult would *that* be? Listen: You were wise to keep J'han from realizing what power is at work here. And you'd be unwise to irritate me further. The way to guarantee that I don't simply toss you back into that snowdrift would be for you to promise to do whatever I tell you to do."

"I give you my word that I will do as you say," Zanja said.

"Good. Start by continuing to keep your mouth shut." She put dry socks on Zanja's feet, and called the healer back to the sledge. He came leading the hang-headed plow horse, which barely seemed able to drag his feet through the snow, and tied the lead to the back of the sledge.

"We'll go now," Norina said.

The man seemed to know better than to demand an explanation from her. He simply got into the sledge, and drew up a lap robe over his legs.

They reached a small stone cottage tucked among the hills, which had a chimney wall dividing its two rooms, kitchen at one side and bedroom at the other. In the bedroom, Norina stripped Karis naked beside the fire, tossing her wet clothing onto the floor, carelessly revealing a magnificence of muscle and form that might make a sculptor weep. With Karis folded into the too-small bed, then it was Zanja's turn to be stripped and dumped into a scalding bath, where she could not avoid seeing what the Sainnites had done to her. Beneath the grime, which at least could be washed away, her loose skin bagged over wasted muscle. Her joints seemed too big, like swollen knobs on slender branches. Her breasts had fallen flat upon her rib cage; her face, which never had been soft, felt like a skull under her fingertips. Her teeth even were loose, though by some stroke of good fortune none had fallen out. This alien form was made only stranger by the restoration to which it had been subjected. All down her back and buttocks, sensitive pink skin patched the brown.

Norina had left her alone, and came back in to find Zanja worn out with washing, too tired to resist or even to object when the hostile stranger washed her back and took on the project of her hair. Neither of them spoke, and Norina offered no gestures of pity, no matter what the sight of Zanja's devastated body made her think. Brusque and efficient, she hauled Zanja out of the tub and sat her upon the hearth wrapped in a blanket, and called in the healer to help carry away the tub. She returned again in a while, with a bowl of broth. The smell of food brought Zanja out of her daze.

Norina sat down upon a battered, three-legged stool that might have been older than the sagging stone walls within which they sheltered. Zanja said after a while, "I envy you your vigor."

The preoccupied, battle-scarred face turned as if surprised to find her a living being and not just a problem to be solved. She said, "You'll recover faster than seems possible, and you'll feel the effects of Karis's immoderate generosity for years to come. What is your name again?"

"I am Zanja na'Tarwein. I was Speaker for the Ashawala'i, but now my people are all dead."

After a long silence Norina said, "We have heard of the massacre of the Ashawala'i. You're the only survivor that we know of."

"Perhaps there were others, but I expect they would have killed themselves. Pardon me—if I am to answer your questions, I want to know who is asking them and why."

Norina said, "The speaker for the Ashawala'i by tradition has the G'deon's ear. Where did you serve as a diplomat, with the House of Lilterwess fallen?"

"I looked out for my people's interests in the northern border towns. Why is it your business?"

Norina looked up from her hands. The sardonic expression that the scar gave her face seemed much more pronounced. "You certainly are as incessantly polite and courteously insistent as any diplomat. But if you had a weapon your hand would be on it, am I right?"

Zanja said softly, "No, Norina, I would never signal my intent so carelessly, and so sacrifice the advantage of surprise."

Norina looked amused, as a wolf is amused by the antics of the rabbit she chases. "Tell me how you came to be in the Sainnite prison."

Zanja could play the game no longer. Wearily, so that the angry woman would leave her alone and let her sleep, she answered her questions as well as she could, considering how little she could remember of the events that Norina seemed to find most interesting. With months of pain and solitude and near insanity lying between this present moment and the massacre of the Ashawala'i, it seemed a distant event in someone else's life. She had become a ghost, and now Karis's hand upon her heart had raised her from the dead and brought her forth into a new world, a new body, a new life. The past seemed irrelevant.

As she struggled to remember those horrible, distant events, she gradually became unnerved by the dissecting quality of Norina's gaze and the weird accuracy of her sharply honed questions. And then, looking up impatiently as Norina asked a third question about something Zanja had twice told her she did not remember, she realized that the unnerving quality of Norina's gaze was not wholly unfamiliar to her.

She interrupted herself, and said, "We have met before."

"Really. How long ago?"

"How long has it been since the fall? Fifteen years?"

Norina opened her mouth, then closed it again without asking a question. Zanja had actually managed to surprise her.

Zanja said, "It was my first year to travel with the Speaker, my teacher. Do you remember, in the charterhouse, early in the morning, he was talking with Councilor Mabin? You came in to tell her you were ready to leave. You gathered her papers for her. I stood over by the tea table, watching you, unable to determine what you were. But the Speaker told me later that you are a Truthken."

Norina said indifferently, "Mabin and the Speaker were arguing."

"No, it was a cold but courteous conversation."

"I had just taken my vows."

"But you had no earring."

"It was just a few pages of paper."

"I remember thirty sheets, at least. I have wondered since then if she was writing her famous book—*Warfare*, is that its title?" Zanja added, forestalling Norina's attempt to quiz her on further details, "You were dressed in black. There was a brisk fire in the fireplace. The sun was just rising."

Norina said coldly, "Well, there's nothing wrong with your memory."

Zanja had thought it might help her cause to remind Norina of their common history. Now, she realized that she only had done herself harm, though she was too stupid with exhaustion to understand how, or why.

Her bowl was empty, and she wished it full again, but with meat and potatoes this time, and some fruit and cheese besides. If not for raging hunger she would have fallen asleep where she sat.

Norina finally said, "Your history is not important. I am charged with Karis's protection, and you have come in like a snake under the walls I've built around her."

"Karis chose to walk out beyond those walls."

"It was no choice. Fire attracts earth, and like all earth elementals Karis is particularly drawn to broken things that only she can fix. Certainly, you were sorely broken."

Zanja looked up at the Truthken then. "If I had done this to myself just to trick her out of hiding, then you would be right to kill me, for I would be an abomination."

"And there the puzzle lies." Norina stood up and took the bowl, and returned in a little while with meat and roast potatoes, an apple and a piece of cheese. Little wonder some people become convinced that Truthkens can read their every thought as clearly as though they had been spoken out loud. "J'han thinks I am insane," Norina said, "and he asked me to warn you that rich food will give you the gripe. You should tell him tomorrow that it did, even though it won't." She gave Zanja her eating knife, a valuable Mearish blade with an edge of startling sharpness, and sat with her booted feet stretched out to the fire while Zanja wolfed down the food.

Zanja had swallowed the last of the cheese and was struggling to keep her eyes open when Norina said quietly, "I wish I could make you my ally in protecting Karis, but we are at cross-purposes. No—" she held up a hand to forestall a protest. "I know you are virtuous and honorable and ready to die in her defense. I know that you have given her your loyalty, and that there is no truer friend than a fire blood. But your visions and passions and moments of insight would be like poison to her. So I have no choice except to keep you away from her. I don't expect you to be willing."

Zanja said, "I don't understand."

Norina sighed, and for a moment she seemed almost troubled. "I don't know how to explain it in a way you could accept. Karis is vulnerable and irreplaceable. You are an unpredictable visionary. With vision comes risk. Therefore, you must be kept out of her life."

"Karis wants me."

"Karis wants much that she cannot have. And you would do well to remember that Truthkens are executioners."

Chapter Six

Zanja awakened to pale light filtering through window shutters, and to the hushed crackling sound of cinders cooling in the fireplace. She had fallen asleep where she sat the night before, upon the hearth, naked, with a second blanket that she did not remember being tossed over her. Karis still slept restlessly among twisted blankets, with her legs hanging out over the end of the bed, but Norina was gone. Zanja used the chamber pot and considered the clothing—Norina's clothing, she assumed—laid out nearby for her to wear. The linen shirt and drawers would be worn next to the skin. The underclothing tied with laces, but the woolen outer clothing, both tunic and breeches, fastened with horn buttons. She then discovered buttonholes at the tops of the hose, and had to undress again, so she could button the hose to the underdrawers. She tottered across the bedroom in this warm but peculiar attire, and opened the door to the kitchen. There, in the light spilling through an unshuttered window, J'han Healer sat yawning at the scarred kitchen table with a reed pen in his hand. Bowls of dried herbs, a mortar and pestle, and a beautiful brass scale lay within his reach.

"You can walk!" he exclaimed.

"Not well." Zanja stumbled to the hearth, where her knees gave out.

"There's porridge already made; will you have some?" J'han tucked the pen behind his ear, and got up to serve her, following the porridge with warm milk and honey, several slices of buttered bread, and an infusion of herbs to build up her strength. He brought over a bucket of small green apples, and set it within her reach. "Have you had enough to eat?"

He had put so much effort into feeding her that it would have been cruel to tell him she was still hungry. He returned to his seat at the table, where he weighed and measured herbs into folded paper packets, and sealed them with wax. Though the healers, once renowned hospitalers, had become hunted wanderers after the fall of the House of Lilterwess, this one, at least, seemed to have found more than a home for the winter, for he and Norina had briefly awakened Zanja in the middle of the night as they made love in the kitchen.

He did not speak to Zanja again until she began to half-heartedly tear apart the mats in her hair. "Let me help—I'll get a comb."

So she leaned her head weakly upon his knee, and he seemed happy enough with his task, employing every trick Zanja had ever heard of to keep from resorting to the scissors, even before she explained, in response to a question, that her hair was uncut because among her people shorn hair is the mark of the outcast. She liked him all the more when he did not seem troubled that she wept as he worked, and she would even have thought he had not noticed, except that he commented later, "Someone you loved must have once combed your hair."

"My brother Ransel," she said. "He was killed near summer's end."

"I'm sorry to hear it. My brother used to comb my hair too. It's been years since I saw him last."

The healer had gotten up once to tend the fire, when the bedroom door opened suddenly, and Karis crouched through into the kitchen, red-eyed as a crapulous drunk. She dazedly examined the room as she fumbled with shirt buttons. Her wandering gaze chanced across Zanja's face, and paused.

"Try a swallow of this," the healer said. He had leapt to his feet, and offered Karis an earthenware flask.

"J'han," Karis rasped in her smoke-ruined voice.

J'han looked startled, as though he had not expected her to know his name.

She sipped from the flask, and lifted a hand to her throat.

"Those with Juras blood have such beautiful voices," the healer said.

Zanja looked at Karis, startled, as if she had not seen her before. She had heard of the Juras, a tribe of giants that were said to dwell far to the south of Shaftal, at the edge of a great waterless wasteland. It was said that the sound of their singing could cause the stars to tremble in the sky. Perhaps Karis's voice could not be fully mended, but the ghost of its lost richness echoed now behind the hoarseness as she thanked him and then sat down heavily in a chair that was too small for her long frame. With a crease between her brows, she reached down to brush a thumb across Zanja's tear-stained cheekbone. The gesture left Zanja speechless.

"Can you eat yet?" J'han asked Karis.

"Chew tongue," she slurred.

J'han seemed scarcely able to restrain his curiosity, and the corner of Karis's mouth quirked a bit. "Angry Norina?"

"She is on one of her rampages," he admitted.

"My fault." Karis's big, work-hardened hands folded together, finger by finger, and she rested her forehead upon this support as though she had much to think about. "Where is she?" she asked after a while.

"She needed to go to Leston."

Karis raised her head. "Did she sleep last night?"

J'han opened his mouth, then closed it again.

"No," Karis said for him. "Shaftal protect us."

Apparently having decided that Karis's mouth had been released from its paralysis, J'han distractedly served her some breakfast. She ate carefully, dutifully, without apparent appetite. Watching her, Zanja remembered something she had heard once about smoke addicts, but had not heeded because it seemed absurd: that they lived in lack of pain, and die for lack of pleasure. Karis ate as though she had been trained to do it; smoke surely had destroyed her sense of taste, just as it had her sense of touch. And so, Zanja realized with a shock, Karis would indeed be deprived of both desire and agency, since the earth bloods understand through physical sensation. It must have taken an enormous talent indeed for Karis to have healed and rescued Zanja with so little apparent difficulty.

"Is there a place where I can sit in the sun?" Zanja asked.

J'han had returned to his labors at the table. He said with some surprise, "It's bitter cold out there."

"I've been in the dark for months."

"Well, there's a bench out by the barn. I'll let you use my shoes, but I doubt you can walk in snow, considering the trouble you had with walking on a solid floor."

"I'll go out with you." Karis fastened her bootstraps, and Zanja put on J'han's shoes and his doublet of quilted wool that he had worn the night before. On the way out the door, Karis asked for a slice of bread, which she held in the air as soon as the door was closed, and the raven swooped down to snatch it out of her hand.

Supported on Karis's arm, Zanja made it to the frost-encrusted bench without falling. The light reflected from the snow was bright enough to make her eyes tear up. She said, "I don't know how much you remember. But last night I frightened you, and I owe you an apology."

Karis frowned as if she were trying to remember a dream. "That's right, you did."

"I should have explained first what I was doing. It didn't occur to me."

Karis sat down beside her. "Smoke and rape go together," she said, "like bread and butter. It's a lesson hard to forget, once learned."

Zanja felt a searing shame, for she understood far better than she should have the attraction of that helplessness. "You never should have taken me with you, and I never should have forced you into it."

Karis said, "But your oath was good."

"Of course my oath was good. But how could you have known that? And still, we nearly died of cold."

Karis closed her eyes to the bright sun, and murmured, "You sound so like Norina, it's almost funny. And you're even wearing her clothes."

Zanja did not find it funny at all, for she might admire Norina's genius and yet have no desire to imitate it. "She and I know the truth in different ways," she said. "My way is much more messy: confused and hazardous. I'll never have Norina's certainty, but I'll never want it, either."

Karis began to laugh, and seemed to find it hard to stop. "Blessed day," she said at last, wiping her eyes upon her sleeve, "You dismay me. What did Norina do to you last night, to leave you so bitter in the morning? Not that I can't imagine it, mind you, since I've known her half my life." When Zanja did not—could not—

speak, Karis looked over at her and said more gently, "You must have put her in a panic. I wish I could have seen such a rarity."

"You flatter me."

"I dared hope that once she'd seen beneath your skin you might become friends somehow. A fond hope, I know; but still, Norina can be a fine friend. She does it in her own way, but she's appallingly reliable."

"Did you wonder if we might be adversaries instead?"

There was a silence. Karis said in a muted voice, "I confess, that is a novelty that hadn't even occurred to me. I want to ask, adversaries over what? But that makes me sound naive." She leaned her head back and shut her eyes again, wearing her sadness like an old and familiar shirt. "But if you had wanted to try to control a wild power—" her voice was heavy with irony "—you missed your opportunity when you had my smoke purse in your hand and didn't take it. So it's not power you and Norina are adversaries over, and what else is there?"

Sitting beside Karis, with the warmth from her powerful left arm soaking into the wasted flesh of Zanja's right shoulder, Zanja abruptly found herself unable to answer; unwilling, in fact, to continue down this path of conversation that she had embarked on so boldly. She said, knowing that she had intended to say something quite different, "I have sworn you an oath of friendship, and I have foreseen that I am destined to serve you. But Norina says that my visions and passions would be poison to you, and she threatened to kill me if I don't stay away from you."

She felt Karis's muscles twitch, but when Karis spoke, Zanja heard nothing in her voice to explain that spasm of shock or pain. Without emotion, she said, "Norina often takes it upon herself to teach people their duty."

So, Zanja thought, I am to lead an empty life.

But Karis continued after a moment, her voice straining, "When I was young, not twelve years old, my master thought that smoke would make me a better whore. He'd gone through great expense to raise me from infancy, because he knew that my mother's size and strength had made her popular with the Sainnites. But I was such a disappointment to him: willful, disobedient, tearful, rude to the clients. And perhaps, as he realized how large I would grow, he also began to fear my eventual strength. So he made me into a smoke addict, to ensure my compliance."

Zanja felt Karis's weight shift, and she turned to find her peering into her face. "What would it take to shock you?"

Zanja said steadily enough, "You found me paralyzed and mutilated and lying in my own shit, yet you never shamed me for it. Surely I owe you the same courtesy."

Karis looked away, and for a long time neither of them said anything. In her full strength and clarity of mind, Zanja might have been able to interpret this silence, turning its raw material into a thread of her own spinning. But now she could only wait, until Karis took a breath and continued, "That I have a purposeful life now, in spite of smoke, is largely thanks to Norina's overbearing, cold-hearted, unscrupulous meddling."

Zanja said, "You owe me no explanations, Karis."

"No, I am trying to explain to myself why I would follow her advice in opposition to my own—wisdom." She paused again, as though astonished to hear herself use such a word. When she continued, it seemed she was arguing with herself. "I know it was wisdom, to save your life. And I would have done it much sooner, if not for Norina's interference."

Zanja said bleakly, "But now you will accept her interference once again. And what am I to do with this life, now that you have given it to me? If I am not to serve you, then what am I to do?"

Karis said, "Serve Shaftal, if you must serve."

"I am just one warrior. . . ."

"Is it an Ashawala'i habit, to display a false humility? It makes me wonder if you take me for a fool."

Zanja sat silent, and then, as Karis began to apologize, interrupted her to say, "I am not often admonished for having too little self-importance. But I might admonish you for the same thing."

"Oh, I know that I am important," said Karis bitterly. "Not a day passes that I am allowed to forget it."

When Norina came into sight, skiing behind the raven that flapped ahead of her like a black rag blowing over the snow, Karis walked part of the way to greet her, and they stood for a long time, leaning in each other's arms, as though, without the other, neither could stand.

Almost as soon as they ended their embrace, they began to shout at each other. Zanja, able to hear the tone of their voices but not the words, turned again to look at them only when they both fell silent. The sun shone full on Karis' stark face. Norina, in shadow, seemed grimly resolute. She had taken off the skis, and carried them on her shoulder. Karis bent down and took the satchel Norina had dropped upon the ground. It seemed a gesture of capitulation.

They turned, and started down the snowy hillside. Norina's head came to Karis' shoulder, and she took two steps to Karis's one. She wore a leather doublet over her sweat-stained wool longshirt; from a distance, it looked like armor. Karis plodded beside her, head down.

"I'm taking Karis away tomorrow." Norina's voice was tight with controlled rage. "You'll stay here for the winter, with me and J'han."

"That's very kind of you." Zanja made no attempt to conceal her irony. She had half-expected the command, for, much as Norina might hate it, she had no choice except to shelter Zanja. But there was no point in pretending to be happy about such an uninviting prospect as a winter spent in Norina's company. Little wonder Norina was so ill-tempered, Zanja realized. Even politeness, which was sometimes the only thing that made human company tolerable, was completely transparent to her.

"She has asked me to help you find a place," Norina said.

Zanja glanced curiously, not at Norina, but at Karis, who had pressed her lips together as though she didn't trust what might come out of her mouth. "A place in what?"

"One of the Paladin companies, perhaps."

"South Hill Company," Karis said.

Norina took in her breath and released it. "Karis—"

"The commander has a good reputation."

"Have you put this matter into my hands or haven't you?"

Karis replied just as sharply. "Are you going to do as I ask, or aren't you?"

There was no capitulation here, and Zanja was hard put to sort out which of them was giving orders to whom. She did not know enough about the old Lilterwess rankings, but a Truthken, as far as she could understand, outranked everyone, for in contested matters the law must take precedence. But there was no place in that old system for earth or water elementals; their very rarity precluded the creation of an Order to restrain them. No rule or way existed for Karis to follow, no law that gave Norina dominance. Karis could do as she liked.

"You should think," Norina said, "of what you're doing."

"I have. It makes no sense."

There was no possible reasonable response to senselessness. Karis could not be physically restrained, either. Norina seemed non-plussed.

Reluctant to put herself in the middle of a dangerous disagreement that she did not even understand, Zanja spoke cautiously. "*Serrainim*, I beg you not to sacrifice your friendship over so unworthy a cause."

They both looked at her as though they had forgotten her. Then Norina seemed to come to her senses and said quite prettily, "I beg your pardon. Of course you may not wish to join the Paladins or to concern yourself in any way with Shaftali troubles. What is it you want to do?"

"The Sainnites themselves have made this my war. But my first concern is that Karis endanger herself no further on my behalf. Last night, I placed myself under your command, and so I must agree to whatever you say, regardless of what Karis demands. So the two of you have nothing left to argue over."

Norina said, with scarcely a hesitation. "Perhaps I might reward your acquiescence."

At this point in a negotiation, Ashawala'i protocol required endless protests of one's unworthiness. But such insincerity in the presence of a Truthken would have been absurd.

"Karis?" Norina prompted, with somewhat less exasperation.

"I'll behave myself so long as you take care of her," Karis said.

"For what your promises are worth—"

"It's you who have sworn to make my life possible—"

"And how was I to know—"

"You're the Truthken!"

Norina threw up her hands. "But you are beyond comprehension!"

It was, Zanja realized, a truly astonishing statement for a Truthken to make. Not until Karis collapsed onto the bench beside her and roared with laughter did Zanja realize it had been a joke.

"It wasn't that funny," Norina said after a while. She had leaned against the barn wall, and seemed almost despondent. "It was the truth."

"And whose fault is that?"

Karis took Zanja's hand again, not to hold it, but to measure it against her own. "You're being very patient with us," Karis said to her, "While we fight like—"

"—A couple of sisters," Norina said dryly.

Karis glanced over her shoulder. "Loan me your dagger, Nori."

Zanja had noticed the night before that Norina's knife could serve as a substantial dowry. Now she saw that her fighting blade would have become an heirloom among Zanja's people, a blade with a genealogy, passed among the generations of the *katrim* as lovingly and devotedly as any story of heroism and self-sacrifice. Norina gave the dagger to Karis, and Zanja would not even touch it until Norina impatiently nodded her permission. It was a subtle weapon of austere beauty, with a blade deceptively slender and of startling substance. The metal had been folded upon itself, over and over, leaving a wavering, overlapping pattern inlaid in its shining steel, like ripples on sand. An extraordinarily skilled and patient metalsmith had sweated over, meditated upon, and lived with that blade, day in and day out, until it welded into the smith's very dreams and became itself a vision.

"You're cutting yourself," Karis said.

Zanja had involuntarily closed her hand around the blade, and it had casually parted the fabric of her palm. It could have sliced all the way to bone by weight alone, and she might never have even felt it. It seemed amazing, impossible even, that the blade had no Mearish mastermark. Surely only in Mear did the smithery exist to produce such a blade. But even a Mearish mastersmith might well have been awestruck by such workmanship, unable to reproduce it or even to say exactly how it had been done.

Zanja said shakily, "It is—an artwork. I've never seen its like." She returned the magnificent blade to Norina, who sheathed it absently, seeming preoccupied with a Truthken's arcane calculation.

Karis said, "Perhaps you'll accept a blade like it, as a poor substitute for the friendship we'll never have."

Only then did Zanja realize whose vision the beautiful blade embodied, and whose hand had held the hammer that folded that bright molten blade into its final form. "I'll send it to you by midwinter," Karis said. "Have you had enough sunshine? I think I might be feeling cold."

Norina's bundle contained bread and ham and a pair of new boots that fit Zanja as though they were made for her, though in fact they had been made for Norina. Norina sent J'han away to attend a difficult birth she had heard about while in Leston, and the three of them had a surprisingly peaceable day. Zanja slept and ate for most of it, and once when she awakened upon the kitchen hearth she found herself covered by the sheepskin jerkin, which smelled, she realized now, of coal smoke and the forge. Karis and Norina were chopping vegetables for a ham stew and discussing a book of political philosophy. Norina said something that Zanja could not understand, and Karis burst out laughing and put her arm around her. They stood so for a while, leaning against each other, silent, mysteriously united by ideas, knowledge, and experiences that Zanja did not, and could not share.

The na'Tarweins were infamous for their jealousies, but Zanja had so far managed to avoid that well-worn path. It seemed intolerable that Karis would leave, that Zanja would spend the winter here with this admirable but unlikeable woman, that these few hours she'd spent with Karis were all she would ever have. Norina was the barrier that stood between them. Unfortunately, thanks to the oath that Zanja had sworn to Karis, that barrier was permanent.

Zanja would have to make a life for herself alone, on the other side of this barren winter. But now she might steal a few more moments with Karis before sunset and smoke took her away, and so she sat up and asked Karis to explain what philosophy was, and what it was good for. That question took the rest of the day for Karis to answer. The sun set too soon.

Thus ended their brief and strange two-day friendship, for the next morning's brief and inarticulate good-byes hardly counted as anything more than empty ritual.

Part 2

Fire Night

Without courage, there would be no will to know.
Without the will to know, there would be no knowledge.
Without knowledge, there would be no language.
Without language, there would be no community.
— MACKAPEE'S *Principles for Community*

Who is seen to speak to the enemy must be silenced. Who
sympathizes with the enemy must lose their heart. Who dreams of
peace must dream no more. Those who ravaged the land will be
eliminated: without compromise, without mercy.
— MABIN'S *Warfare*

When I first met my enemy, she was a glyph, and it was I who
chose to read her as my friend. When my enemy first met me, I was
a glyph, and it was she who chose to read me as her friend. So all
people are glyphs, and every understanding comes from choice.
— MEDRIC'S *History of My Father's People*

Chapter Seven

Emil habitually wintered in a shepherd's cottage in the highlands, a place so solitary and forbidding that he rarely saw another living being, animal or human, between first snow and spring thaw. The cold became tiring, but he never grew weary of the solitude or the silence. When weather permitted, he would walk on snowshoes from one end of the highland to the other, and the austere and terrible beauty of that wild land would take root, and create in him a serenity all the more precious because he knew from experience how ephemeral and fleeting it would prove, come spring. When the wind howled and the falling snow made of the vast expanses a small and restless blank, he stayed indoors and read yet again by candlelight the words of the great Shaftali philosophers until whole passages became as palpable to him as a single word, a single thought. Every moment, every breath of frigid air, every flicker of candle and crackle of ice became precious. For most of the year his life belonged to the law, but in winter, his life was his.

Inevitable spring allowed him one last walk across the frozen water of the Finger Lakes, where he cleared the snow to watch the fish through ice as clear as glass. But as he stood on a rise of land about to turn toward home, he heard the sharp report of cracking ice. So the muddy thaw began.

Some twenty days later, during a break in the rain, he was planting flowering peas along the fence when something, a faint sound or a tingling of the skin, made him turn sharply, to see a pair of riders coming down the narrow from the direction of Gariston. In nearly thirty years as a Paladin he had come to trust his small talent for prescience, which never told him very much, but told it dependably. Knowing he had no reason for concern, he turned back to his pea planting until the travelers had ridden close enough to talk to. The horses were tired and muddy to the belly, for the roads surely had scarcely been passable. One rider looked cross; the other's face was a closed door.

"Emil Paladin?" said the cross one. "I am Norina Truthken."

He bowed to her in the old fashion, though he was not happy that the solitude of his last precious days had been disturbed.

The riders dismounted, and it was the silent one that Emil watched. Plain farmer's clothing could not obscure her exotic appearance: the dark coloring and the sharp angles of her face. She moved with the fluidity and precision of a blade fighter, who had learned her skills in a place where pistols and gunpowder had not yet eliminated all the beauty and skill from combat. She looked up to meet his gaze with her own: eyes black as night, with a flame in their centers.

"By Shaftal!" Emil reached to clasp hand. "I think I remember your name. Zanja, am I right? When I heard about the Ashawala'i, I wondered what had become of you."

"I guess they did make you a commander," she said.

"I'm afraid they did. And all these years I have been making the best of it." He gazed at her, feeling the distance from which she observed him, remembering the reserved but talented young woman she had been. She would be over thirty now, and for fifteen years her intelligence had been sharpened by bitter experience. He said, "I hope you have come to join my company."

"Yes, sir," she said impassively. Her face held back everything. Emil invited them to settle their horses and come in for tea.

Once they were all seated in the kitchen, with the Truthken choosing a chair and the tribal woman sitting on her heels, he poured tea from his small porcelain teapot and sliced bread fresh from the oven, on which they melted slices of midlands cheese produced from Norina's saddlebag. Though the two women had certainly been traveling together for days, they exchanged not a word with each other. A silent journey it must have been.

Norina said, "Well, Commander, I see I need not explain who

Zanja is. I have been charged with finding a place for her among the Paladins, and your company was suggested."

"They say that a few survivors of the initial attack all but wiped out a battalion," Emil said to Zanja.

"No, but seventeen of us did kill some sixty Sainnites."

"It is more than my company has killed in six years."

Her somber expression cracked away a bit. "Paladin techniques work well in the mountains."

Emil sat back to think and sip his tea, and finally brought himself to say, reluctantly, "You will not have an easy time of it in South Hill, and perhaps you would be better off in one of the northern units, where they are more accustomed to the sight of northern tribesmen."

"I am accustomed to being a stranger."

Norina added, "She is too well known in the north."

"Well, then."

Norina took a money pouch from inside her doublet. "She has no family to support her." She handed the pouch to Emil, who had not felt such a weight of funds in many a year. "A sponsor," she explained, though it explained little. Where would a solitary tribal woman find herself a sponsor in such uncertain times?

"This has been a day of many surprises," he said. The cups of the traveling porcelain tea set were very small, so he refilled them with the rare and expensive green tea. Though no one conducted hospitality rituals anymore, Zanja courteously complimented the tea's fragrance and flavor, leaving him with the impression that she could have fulfilled her role in the entire ceremony, uncoached, without missing a step. She was not a warm woman, he thought, at least not on the surface. But oh, she was careful, and, like him, she belonged in another world. He fingered his right earlobe, where once had dangled two gold earrings that he had dropped into a well many years ago. The holes had since closed, but the scar tissue remained.

Zanja sat on the floor of the cramped attic, beside a small window that let in a gray, rain-smeared light onto the page of her book. What with the rain and the thaw, sometimes it seemed as though the whole world was melting. The letters on the page pushed and shoved against each other like people on market day. They gave up their secrets only with much coaxing and study. Then, they offended her first by ranting at her and then by cozening her.

She leafed through the pages of *Warfare*. In the kitchen directly beneath her, where Emil also read while waiting for the rain to end, she heard him add a log to the fire. On a day like this, the Ashawala'i would sit around the clanhouses, mending their clothes, sharpening their tools, and telling stories. She wished Emil had told her stories, rather than handing her this battered book, with its disembodied demands and disguised angers. Mabin's *Warfare*, Emil had said, was the one thing held in common by all the members of South Hill Company. It was a language, philosophy, and history all in one. She needed to know it.

Nevertheless, a rainy day called for a story. Zanja turned the pages until a particularly worn page of the book caught her eye. "The Fall of the House of Lilterwess," she read, sounding the letters out loud. Though she had learned her letters as a child, during the year she lived with a Shaftali farm family, she had not needed to read very much since then. The book also made occasional use of glyphs, which she could not interpret at all.

She moved the book closer to the cracked windowpane and read out loud:

"When Harald G'deon died, I had been sitting at the head of the Lilterwess Council for three years. It had been considered strange, and even unheard of for a Paladin to head the council, but the majority of the council members had decided a warrior should lead in times of war.

"Unfortunately, Harald G'deon disagreed with the majority. It is commonly known that the G'deon and I, though we accorded each other a great respect, never were at peace with each other. It is still true that when my thoughts are in argument with themselves it is his implacable voice I hear. He was too great-hearted a man, for he could not believe that the Sainnites meant to harm us. While I argued and he remained unconvinced, the council sat paralyzed and the Sainnites continued to invade our shores. While the G'deon lay dying over a period of many months, he refused to the last to name a successor. So the great succession of G'deons, who for ten generations have protected and made fertile the land of Shaftal, arbitrarily and inexplicably ended, and no one will ever understand why—least of all myself. Harald G'deon at the very least committed a dreadful error. Some even call it a betrayal."

As Zanja read, she realized that she was imagining Mabin, who she had only met the one time, speaking these words. On the page, they seemed neutral and harmless, but speaking them aloud revealed the concealed anger and sarcasm. Harald had betrayed Shaftal with his naive obstinacy, according to Mabin. Zanja, disinclined to be generous to a woman she had disliked on sight, suspected that Mabin might be in the habit of considering stupid the things that she merely did not understand.

She continued to read, listening closely to herself now, and hearing how skeptically and ungenerously she interpreted Mabin's revered text. "The very night of Harald G'deon's death, the Sainnites attacked the House of Lilterwess. Harald G'deon must have known of the Sainnites' secret encirclement of our sacred home, but he died without the least word of warning that might have spared us all the years of sorrow which have followed. That night, many of us lay wakeful, fearful for the future. The Lilterwess Council never did sleep at all, but sat with our advisors and scribes, free at last to chart a new future for Shaftal. At dawn we planned to gather the Paladins and ride forth against the invaders.

"But the night was not even half over when an alarm bell began to ring. Some wakeful soul—commonly believed to have been Harald G'deon's companion, Dinal Paladin—must have discovered the breached gate or the assassinated guards. She was certainly the first to die that night, but not before her courage made it possible for some of us, at least, to escape by a secret way. As I stood on a far hilltop that terrible dawn and watched the smoke of destruction blur the sun, I and my companions had much cause to wonder for what purpose we had been spared, while our friends, lovers, children, and whole history were destroyed before our eyes.

"Now our hearts, first stunned by the magnitude of our defeat, then ripped apart with grief and rage, have become cold and hard as stone. The law failed us, we realize now, because it made us gentle. It relied upon a decency at the heart of every community, the willingness of each person in Shaftal to treat the next with generosity and understanding. When strangers came who were estranged from that decency, our kindness became our weakness.

"Therefore there is no longer a place in this war for acts of mercy. Lest we balk at this grim truth, let us always remember that this is a new Shaftal, a Shaftal created by the Sainnites. This is the land they wanted. Why should we suffer our pains while they become rich and fat from our labors? It is they who have created this new Shaftal. Let them pay the price."

Zanja lay down the book, and noted distantly that it had stopped raining. Oddly, Mabin's last bitter statements had caused her to think not of the Sainnites who had killed her people and who she had and would continue to kill in return, but of Karis. Nowhere did Karis appear in Mabin's account, except, perhaps, in the reference to unnamed companions. Yet she had been there, she and Norina, two precious talents saved from the destruction.

Zanja looked out the small window at the darkening sky, but what she saw was Karis, apparently a prisoner, possibly out of her mind with smoke, being walked by Norina to the wagon. She thought of the old suicide scars on Karis's wrists. Was it simple dislike that made Zanja want to make Mabin the source of Karis's misery, or was it fire logic?

Throughout the cold winter and into the harsh early spring, Zanja had scarcely thought of Karis. Karis had sent the artful blades she had promised as a poor substitute for friendship, and Zanja had accepted them. Now, she was a Paladin, and soon would wage war against the destroyers of her people. Still, thinking of Karis now, Zanja felt a restlessness, and a haunting loss. *Why?* she asked herself, and could not think of an answer.

She stood up, remembering almost too late to duck the low ceiling, and climbed down the ladder. In the kitchen, a pot of salt-meat stew bubbled on the hearth, and Emil darned a sock by the dim light of the fire. His supply of lamp oil was exhausted, he had told her, and the last of his candles had been eaten by mice. It was when he sat working in the dark like this, refurbishing his gear for the hard season ahead, that he seemed most willing to talk.

He said to her now as she knelt upon the hearth, "What do you think of Mabin's *Warfare?*"

"I notice she does not dwell much on heroism."

"She always argued that we would win through intelligence rather than bravery."

"And are we winning?"

"We merely resist. We keep the Sainnites from becoming comfortable, and we keep the people of Shaftal from forgetting that they used to be free. We outnumber the Sainnites, of course, but their advantage over us is too great."

"I have studied the Sainnites," Zanja said, "And I cannot see their advantages."

"They can make their living by stealing food from farmers—taxing them, they call it—while the people of Shaftal must either work or starve. To fight, as you and I will fight, is a costly luxury to people who live on the edge of hunger. South Hill Company survives on charity: the leavings of the already depleted harvest. So we often go hungry, while the Sainnites eat the fat of the land. That is their advantage."

Emil stitched away at the heel of his sock for some time. "I have not discouraged you?"

"No," Zanja said, thinking rather distantly about how her loss had left her with nothing to be discouraged over.

Emil cut himself another length of yarn. The yarn was a sorry sight, gray and lumpy with weed seeds, and the famous weavers of Zanja's extinct people would have sneered at it. Emil had spun it himself, probably, out of wool gleaned from a thorn bush, with a spindle cobbled together from a rock and a stick. He was not, she had noticed, ashamed to do things badly, so long as they got done. He glanced down at her, where she sat upon the stone hearth. "You don't like furniture."

"It just seems unnecessary."

Emil looked amused. "I think the rain is done for now. What do you say, shall we spend one more day here, or shall we leave tomorrow and slog our way through the mud?"

"Truthfully, my aimlessness wearies me more than any walk in the mud will."

"And the mud can't be avoided anyway, this time of year. Well then. Let's grease our boots and pack our bags."

Outside of Meartown, no one knew whose invention had made the Meartown pistols more accurate and reliable than those of the Sainnites. Years ago, Karis had determined that the pistol ball rattled about in the barrel when the gunpowder exploded, making its trajectory unpredictable. It was she who told the metalsmiths how they could make the pistol ball spin instead, by cutting spiral grooves on the inside of the barrel. Yet Karis had refused to make a gun or any part of a gun. She refused to even make a fighting blade, though the single dagger she forged long ago for Norina had become famous over the years, and connoisseurs of weaponry frequently appeared at fairs or even in Meartown itself, insisting that someone there could make a blade of rustless, folded metal that never lost its edge.

It was not only this refusal to profit from her own genius that baffled Karis's fellow metalsmiths. Though her apprenticeship was long ended, she had never been able to choose a glyph to be her mastermark. Even though she had been relentlessly educated, the glyphic syntax of metaphor and implication had resisted her every attempt to comprehend it. She was always too honest to engage in a purely mechanical exercise, and so when faced with the mechanical exercise of choosing a glyph to act as her mark of certification, she could not do it.

Without a mastermark she could not be a mastersmith. So Karis never opened a smithy of her own, and never took apprentices, and never went to stand behind her work at major fairs, and never dressed in silk or soaked her hands to leach out the soot ground into her skin. She kept working where she was, and her old master paid her five times an apprentice's wage to keep her from going somewhere else.

When the word got out in early winter that she was making a blade, the work of Meartown practically came to a standstill, as the mastersmiths of Meartown sent all their best apprentices to learn Karis's secret.

Metalsmithing, a dramatic and dangerous profession, was never practiced in solitude, especially not in Meartown. But Karis would rather have made Zanja's blades in private, for she engaged in a private conversation as she shaped them. She could have made a model of Zanja's right hand, including the blood vessels and the nerve endings, but to fit the blade to the hand was the easy part; it was the less tangible matters that preoccupied Karis to the point that she forgot her rapt audience and lost all track of time. She had never seen Zanja in her strength. Forging a blade to match Zanja's fighting style when Karis's only information came from an intimate knowledge of Zanja's wasted muscles and compact skeletal structure was a matter of the purest kind of speculation.

People fight the way they talk, Norina had said once, and so Karis made a blade for a gracious and graceful fighter whose manners were the velvet that covered the steel. Zanja would win by talent and persistence, not by power, so Karis gave the blade an edge that would slip in and out on the moment of inspiration and be gone before the recipient of that moment could know that he was dead. It was indeed an artist's blade, and that worried Karis. She realized as she forged it that if Zanja fought the way she talked she didn't belong in a war at all.

Karis loved the work of making the dagger and its companion

knife, but hated the aftermath. A half dozen people were injured trying to imitate her methods, and many others demanded that she show them again how to do one thing or another, and explain it this time. She couldn't have explained what she was doing even if she had been willing to do the demonstration. For a while her relationships with nearly half the townsfolk were in disarray, and various people had to go around reminding other people that she wasn't like the rest of them.

Later, when the blades had been delivered, Norina admitted that when Zanja unwrapped them she had nearly been in tears. She admitted that Zanja fought as if she were dancing, and that it was a beautiful but not completely impractical performance.

Now, with the spring mud season not even half over, Norina had come to visit. Her face was familiar in Meartown, and the people there at least vaguely understood her role as Karis's protector. The rain prevented them from walking the barren heath as they usually did, so Karis left the forge to spend the day in a tavern instead, and the metalsmiths who constantly sought her advice soon began to find her there. After one of these interruptions during which Karis solved a problem with a new kind of door latch that the smith was inventing, Norina commented, "Meartown's reputation has become practically legendary in the last ten years. While the people of this town conspire to maintain you in obscurity, the entire town has become notorious instead."

Karis pushed away the remains of a meat pie Norina had made her eat. "For years you have been congratulating yourself for your cleverness at hiding me here, 'one talented artisan among many.' "

Norina made a face at hearing her own words quoted back at her. "Well, this year I am less pleased with myself. Perhaps the Sainnites will never come here looking for an earth witch to slaughter, but surely they must be desperate to eliminate the metalsmiths that supply the Paladins with their fine weaponry. With Meartown so famous, how could the Sainnites not know where those weapons are coming from? They will come, Karis, and when they do, I fear you will not flee."

"And leave Meartown to face its attackers without me? Of course I will not flee."

Norina sighed. "So I was not so clever as I thought. Now, Karis—"

"Don't waste your breath. I can already recite your arguments in my sleep. These people have been loyal to me."

"They admire and rely upon your skill, but would they die for you?"

"Why should they?" Karis asked.

"Exactly!"

Karis glared at Norina, exasperated. "Well then, Meartown will have to rely on the Paladins, as we always have, to keep the Sainnites away."

"Do you know what lies between Meartown and the Sainnites?"

Karis said, "A couple of rivers, a small mountain range . . ."

"And fifty farmers who think they can fight."

"And two fire bloods," Karis said, for Norina had told her earlier that Zanja's new commander was also a fire blood.

"And what's that worth? Zanja may be a fire blood, but she never won a single blade match against me." She added, grudgingly, "I suppose that Paladin commander might prove more difficult to defeat, despite his game leg."

"You're awfully surly," Karis said.

"I'm pregnant."

"I noticed."

"It's your fault! J'han and I have been lovers for years, but the one night you sleep under my roof . . ."

Karis began to laugh. She couldn't help herself. Norina glared at her. "I want neither a child nor a husband, and I intended to get an abortion."

"Yet here you sit with your belly swelling. It's too late for an abortion now."

"J'han wants the child."

Norina's blunt, strong fingers tapped the tabletop. It was rare for her to betray any sign of upset, and Karis looked into her face more closely than usual. This was her friend, reliable as steel but much less pliable. It must have been a stunning moment when Norina decided to bear the child for her lover's sake; Karis regretted that she had missed it.

"How can I make amends? Shall I give you a painless birth?"

"I don't know a better midwife than you. But J'han wants to be with me. I'll go to my sister's house when the time comes, so she can foster the child. Her youngest will be just about due for weaning, and I have already written asking her to raise my child as her own."

Norina would not ask for money—she never did. But surely she would need some, for her family were plain fishing folk whose ability to live comfortably was unreliable at best.

"More ale?" asked the tavernkeeper. Norina grumpily waved her away.

"Did he like her?" Karis asked.

"Did who like who?"

"Did Emil like Zanja?"

"Zanja has mystery, integrity, and wasted talent. Any fire blood would like her."

Karis wondered, not for the first time, if it would be possible to know what Truthkens know and not be cynical.

"Now stop worrying about her," Norina said. "She's her commander's concern, now."

"I don't know why," Karis said, "but I can't stop worrying about her. I have no control over it."

Norina studied Karis's face for a long time, in that way that Truthkens have, that leaves one feeling like skin and flesh have been dispassionately peeled back from the bone. "Sometimes I get a hint," Norina said finally, "of why Harald G'deon all but drove Mabin insane."

Chapter Eight

For two days, Zanja and Emil walked through unnamed lands, following a river of mud that Emil claimed was a wagontrack. Then, they turned east and traversed an uneven, rocky land until they started to pass a few desperately poor farmholds, and finally reached something resembling a cobbled road, though it was in poor repair. The road improved as they traveled, until they reached a flooded, fast-flowing river and a sturdy bridge with a bridgekeeper's cottage on the far side. Zanja paused to get her bearings. To her north lay rising land, possibly even mountains, obscured by the lowering sky. "That's Darton," Emil confirmed. So Zanja placed herself on the sprawling landscape of western Shaftal, with Darton to the north, and the region of Mear to the north of that. South Hill lay on the other side of the bridge they were about to cross. To its north lay Rees, which the Sainnites had devastated last summer. North of Rees lay Damar, where almost a year ago Zanja's horses and gear had been stolen by rogue Paladins. It seemed like a long time ago.

This southward-flowing river marked the limit of Sainnite control. Zanja said, "So the duty of South Hill Company is to prevent the Sainnites from crossing the bridge?"

"Essentially," Emil said. As they started across the bridge, cold rain again began to fall.

They sheltered that night in a farmstead where Emil was welcomed like a beloved uncle, and was handed a bundle of letters and documents that had been accumulating for him all winter. The next day, his face was creased along its squint lines like pleated cloth, but he did not reveal to Zanja the bad news that surely had awaited him in that bundle of letters. The rain that had become sleet during the night became a downpour again by dawn, and they slogged on through mud the consistency of undercooked porridge.

They walked past many tightly shuttered farmholds, and it was afternoon before they turned up a narrow, flooded wagontrack, passing the leafless orchards and sodden fields of a large and well kept farm. Five houses and two barns clustered in the center of a pinwheel of walled fields: a prosperous and ancient farmhold, with its doors and windows latched shut against the miserable weather. But suddenly a door slammed open and the dogs stood up in their shelters to bark, though even they were wise enough to stay out of the rain. A young woman came running barefoot through the muck and the downpour, only to restrain herself at the last moment as though she remembered how austere and learned was this gray-haired commander she seemed on the verge of embracing. Ankle-deep in the mud, she took his wet hand in hers. "I'm happy to see you, Emil."

"I gather it has been a dull winter."

"The winters are always dull!" she cried. Then, her gaze turned to Zanja's face, and there was a moment that seemed to last much too long before she turned back to Emil, hostile and questioning. As the rain poured down and the dogs fell silent, Emil made introductions, describing Zanja as a newcomer to South Hill Company, and Annis as a genius with explosives. Annis gave Zanja not even a nod of greeting. "Come out of the rain," she said to Emil, and Zanja followed.

Inside the commonhouse, a roar of greeting lapsed quickly into silence, as though the people thought their old friend Emil had acquired a demonic shadow. The children rushed forward to help him with his boots and cape, but Zanja unstrapped her own boots and hung her own cape on the hook. Emil already had been drawn into the room by eager elders who wanted to hear the news. Zanja made her own way to the hearth, uninvited, where a dotty old man ensconced in a rocking chair smiled at her seraphically. Three hanging cradles, two of them occupied, swung from the rafters, and a nursing mother with an infant at her breast watched Zanja with surreptitious anxiety. Zanja squatted on the hearthstones, though someone nearby offered her a chair, and after a while her wet shirt started to steam.

The room was as crowded as any Ashawala'i clan house. A family so big suggested prosperity in spite of hard times: a large and fertile farm, carefully managed and not destroyed yet by taxes. The room was filled with industry. On the big work table many projects progressed: socks being knitted, tools being repaired, writing and other necessary skills being taught, bread being kneaded and shirts being seamed. Only the youngest and oldest were not working, and they were being watched and cared for instead.

At last, Emil, having done his guest's duty of exchanging news, said to Zanja across the room, "Are you getting warm? Perhaps some tea . . . ?" At least the elders were gracious enough to exclaim at their own rudeness once it was pointed out to them, and Emil escorted Zanja around the room, introducing her not as Zanja na'Tarwein but as Zanja Paladin. He knew everyone's name. Zanja constructed frail conversations out of the flimsy materials at hand: she admired babies and handiwork and what she had been able to see of the farm itself, and assured one stranger after another that she was delighted and honored to have wound up in South Hill. Emil said to her afterwards, "That was an impressive exhibition of good manners. You must be exhausted now."

"How many of these households do you have to visit?"

"Only ten or so right now. By autumn's end, though, I'll have visited them all. It's a foolish man who forgets that every loyalty is personal."

Zanja vaguely remembered having read something like that in *Warfare*. Though Emil frequently quoted the guidebook, and always with apparent seriousness, she already knew that while he did what he had to, it was not always without cynicism. Now, his performance was not for her, but for Annis, who had just come into the small sitting room with a tea tray.

"My parents want to know if you'll bide the night," she said.

Emil shook his head. "I want to be at Willis's house tonight, but I'm thinking I might leave Zanja here with you. If you would fetch Daye and Linde and a keg of gunpowder, we'll meet at Midway Barn in three day's time."

"She can lie in my bed," Annis said sullenly, and poured the tea. "Unless there's someone else you'd rather bed with," she added to Zanja.

"I beg your pardon, but I'm a stranger in this land and there's much I don't understand." Zanja expected she'd be saying these words, or words like them, rather frequently this season.

Emil seemed amused, and said to Annis, "The members of your family are afraid to talk to Zanja, but they'd sleep with her?"

Annis shrugged. "That's what I hear. Like you said, it's been a dull winter."

Emil shook his head. "It's not just a matter of sleeping," he explained to Zanja.

Zanja said, "My good manners have a limit."

Annis broke into a laugh and nearly spilled the tea. "Sleep with me, then," she said. "And I do mean sleep."

Zanja's first sight of South Hill Company was in a giant rebuilt barn on an abandoned farmstead with buildings fallen in on themselves and the fields long since returned to forest. She and Annis had followed a meandering course across the countryside, gathering companions and gear as they went. Among those who joined them was Linde, a middle-aged man who Annis said was heart-bonded to a man also in the company and Daye, a gray-haired grandmother, one of Emil's three lieutenants. Annis had been distant, offering grudging information only when Zanja asked for it, but Daye promptly set to teaching Zanja the lay of the land, the riverbanks and foot trails and hidey-holes where a hunted person could simply disappear.

Midway Barn was brightly illuminated by lanterns hanging from the rafters. The fifty people gathered there were uniformly pale-skinned, brown-haired, and stockily built. They seemed as feature-less to Zanja as stones that lie stubbornly in a field. Her companions of the last two days having melted into the undistinguished brown, the only dye color their clothing makers seemed to know, Zanja felt herself painfully exposed and solitary. She started across the barn towards the cauldron bubbling upon a makeshift hearth, where Emil perched upon his camp stool with one leg stretched stiffly out before him. She cut a swath of silence with her passing, and had not taken ten steps before a stocky, muscular man confronted her, demanding to know her name and business.

"Sir, I am Zanja, newly come to this company."

He looked her up and down. "You are no Paladin."

"Among my people I was a *katrim*, which is like a Paladin."

"What you are among your people matters not," the man declared.

"That is true," Zanja said, "since my people are all dead." She waited, cautious, wondering if the entire company would greet her with such hostility. But the others had fallen quiet, seeming content to listen while this belligerent man conducted the challenge and satisfied their curiosity.

The man turned and cried bitterly, "Emil, we are all kin in this company!"

Zanja heard Emil's quiet voice reply with supernatural mildness, "I am flattered to be counted among your kin, Willis. No doubt Zanja looks forward to the day that you accord her the same courtesy."

Zanja brought herself to say with a sincerity she hoped no one would realize was false, "Yes, sir, very much." But the belligerent man turned his back on her, ignoring the hand she offered. He squatted down among his cronies, who clustered around him like wolves greeting their leader. So Zanja learned, all in one moment, who her enemies were to be.

By the time the stew was ready, Daye had taken Zanja on a circuit of the barn, and told her the names and families of everyone present. She left her with Annis, while she and the other lieutenants, the belligerent man among them, conferred in a cluster around Emil, with their steaming porringers in their hands. "Willis is one of Emil's lieutenants?" Zanja asked.

"Willis, Perry, and Daye. The three of them started the company in the year of the fall, and we didn't get Emil until a year later. Until he showed up, Willis thought he would be the company commander forever. He and Emil get along now, but they didn't always."

Zanja glanced at Annis, astonished because up until now Annis had scarcely spoken a complete sentence to her.

Annis said, "Willis doesn't like outsiders. But we aren't all like him."

"Of course you're not," Zanja replied, thinking that it was possible Willis's hostility might do her more good than harm, in the end.

Annis took her over to the stewpot to fill her porringer, and then they joined a circle that had formed to share a bread loaf and butter pot. Zanja exercised the good manners Emil had so ironically admired some days ago, and the people she ate with gradually began to gain some definition. They noticed and discussed her battle scars, and they told her how Paladins fought primarily by ambush, avoiding confrontations that put the more numerous and heavily armed Sainnites at an advantage. She admitted she would have to learn to use the distance weapons, the pistol and the crossbow.

The increasing sobriety of the lieutenants' conference muted the surrounding conversations after a while, and when Emil finally stood up from his camp stool, the company, already watchful, immediately fell silent to hear his words.

"It's spring again," Emil said. "And amazing though it seems even to me, this is my fifteenth year commanding South Hill Company. When I first arrived, I said to you that I was astounded and humbled to find myself in command, and fifteen years later, that at least has not changed. We've learned some hard lessons together in the meantime, and this year, I'm afraid, we have some even harder lessons to learn.

"Last summer," he continued, "While we succeeded in assassinating the commander of Wilton garrison, our neighbors in Rees were decimated by an assault the like of which no company in Shaftal has ever seen. By summer's end, forty Paladins had been killed, their families' farmholds razed, and at least a thousand people left with neither food nor shelter to see them through the winter. By summer's end, in fact, Damar Company and South Hill Company were fighting the battles in Rees, for no one in Rees could continue to fight.

"Now, I have learned that the commander of Rees garrison has been reassigned to South Hill, and moved to Wilton garrison at the first thaw, along with most of the soldiers from her command in Rees. The number of Sainnites in South Hill has nearly doubled to some two hundred soldiers. There seems little doubt that South Hill is to be their next target."

He paused. The jovial people crowded into the barn sat silent, stunned.

"I have had a few days to think about this," Emil said, "but I am sure that all of you have been thinking, all summer and winter, about what happened in Rees and about what you would do if it were your family against whom the Sainnites took retribution. It is our families that make us strong, by sheltering and feeding us, but they also make us vulnerable. My first thought is that we must find ways to prevent the Sainnites from knowing who we are, so that they cannot identify our families, either. My second is that, once the spring mud is over, you all must not visit your families again until autumn. We will find some other way to get food to eat and we'll take shelter in the woods."

He continued, "I have a little more to say, and then I'd like to hear what you are thinking. The mystery of Rees is this: the Paladins there followed the strategies that have worked for all of us for fifteen years, but in Rees they did not work. The company could not avoid the confrontations they knew they could not win. The company could not take the Sainnites by surprise. The company could not successfully hide from the enemy. So we need new strategies, and we need to use the old ones cautiously, without expecting that they will succeed. Above all, we need to be prepared, to expect that this year will not be like every other year."

As quietly as he had begun, Emil ended his address, and sat down to hear the debate that followed. He did not speak again, except when he was directly asked for more information, questions he often could not answer.

The discussion lasted late, and then broke up into smaller debates, some of which continued even after Zanja lay asleep with Annis curled companionably against her back. In dreams, she heard people argue about the logistics of food and shelter, about battle tactics, ambushes, and bolt-holes. In dreams she returned to Rees, but this time it was she who hid in the woods, demoralized and terrified. Towards dawn, she began to dream about the massacre of her own people, and in her dreams she thought it was possible to prevent it this time, if only she could find a spare moment to read the book someone had handed her: not Mabin's *Warfare*, but a different book, with different rules.

She awoke thinking that there had been a mistake, that this was not her life at all. But, unfortunately, it was.

Chapter Nine

Annis began Zanja's education in a covert lead mine, where Zanja learned to recognize and extract lead ore, and practiced smelting it, and eventually poured her own pistol balls. The gunpowder lesson proceeded in much the same way. Not until Zanja had filled her cartridge pouch with rounds of ammunition made by her own hands from ingredients she herself had found did she finally learn to load and shoot her pistols.

With the rains over, the company was to gather in the woods, in a place they felt confident no one could find for the first time without a guide. Even Annis could scarcely find it, for the place was undistinguished and what landmarks existed were practically as hard to find as the place itself. At last, with the sun setting, they arrived at a natural rocky clearing surrounded by thick forest, just in time to fill their porringers with pieces of roasted chicken and lumps of hard black bread. Living in the rough hills, Zanja and Annis had eaten little more than ground corn, so this meal looked like a feast.

She looked up from the feast to find Emil behind her, with a basket over his arm. She had been reciting people's names to herself while pretending to be interested in their eager discussion of the lives and loves of people she had never met.

"Can I help you with that basket?" she asked.

"It gets lighter all the time." He handed out pieces of apple cake to her companions, then sat beside her on a convenient stone. "I promised Daye I'd give you the bad news myself. The company will divide into three units, to give the enemy smaller and faster moving targets, and you're to be under Daye's command, at her request."

"That is not bad news," she said.

"You will be responsible for collecting bread from the farmholds, and distributing it to the company."

"I see. Well, sir, I'll do my best."

"The next time you call me 'sir,' I'll demote you."

"But how would it be possible to demote me further?"

"Zanja, it was a joke."

After he left, someone said kindly, "Bread is important."

"It is a child's job," she retorted. No one contradicted her.

"At least your face will become familiar across South Hill."

Zanja suspected that the commanders had another advantage in mind: They wished to obscure the links between the company and the farmholds, but without bread they could not survive long. So they gave the duty of collecting food from the farmholds to a stranger, who had no relatives to be executed in retaliation, and who could legitimately pretend to have never heard of South Hill Company. It was a sensible decision.

Still, Zanja went to bed angry, and woke up angry in the middle of the night, with a dull headache and a full bladder, and a vague sense of dread that seemed related to the dreams she could not remember. She crept past her sleeping companions and went a little way into the woods. She had re-buttoned her breeches and stood wondering why she wasn't going back to bed, when a voice spoke in the leafless branches overhead. "Zanja na'Tarwein."

A dark shape flapped against the stars, leading her further away from the clearing. She followed, with her heart in her throat. The night gave a sigh, as a brief breeze lifted and then fell still. The raven dropped out of the branches and stalked at her feet like a restless rag of night sky.

Zanja sank into a squat. "What are you doing here?"

The raven said, "You were more courteous when you thought I was a ghost."

"But now I know you are just a messenger, and that your messages are not supposed to be for me."

"Ha!" the raven cawed. "Norina thinks I serve at Karis's will, but you should know better."

"Should I? What do you serve, then, if not her will?"

"I serve her secret heart."

The raven god of the Ashawala'i was an amoral trickster, so Zanja found herself unable to believe entirely in this raven's honesty. She said, "Well, perhaps you can ignore Karis's promises, but I have to honor promises of my own. I am certain Norina would forbid me to talk with you." She rose to her feet to leave, though she was not certain she could walk away.

The raven said, "This evening, as the sun set, I saw a thing that might surprise you."

Zanja often had wished she could see from above, like a bird. She said politely, "What did you see, good raven?"

"I saw Sainnite soldiers creeping through the woods."

Zanja's vague dread sharpened. "Are they creeping towards this encampment?"

"Oh, yes. They approach you from the west, spread out, to catch you in a net of soldiers as you try to flee."

"Then should we flee due east?"

"Northeast," the raven said. "The forest is not so thick there, and the land grows steep and rocky. It seems a good place to defend yourselves."

"Do you know if they outnumber us?" Zanja wondered, then, if the raven could even count. She could scarcely believe she was discussing battle tactics with a bird, and had to keep reminding herself that the raven shared Karis's intelligence.

"They are greater than your company, but not by much." She heard the dry sound of the raven running a wing feather through his beak. "Zanja na'Tarwein," he added, and she could have sworn it was the god that spoke to her, "you can be drearily punctilious."

He spread his wings, and, only mildly offended, she said hastily, "Well, tonight I appreciate your lack of punctiliousness. I'll try to leave some food for you in the camp."

She found Emil with no little difficulty, finally locating him by his gear: the box that contained his tea set, and the camp stool that was never out of reach. He awakened at her touch. "Zanja?"

"I think we are in danger."

He sat up, and seemed to consider, or perhaps to consult his own talent for prescience. "Yes, we are indeed in danger." He reached for his boots. "It is the Sainnites, of course. I wonder how they found us."

"That I don't know. But I think they are to the west, spread out in the woods."

"Yes," he confirmed, in some surprise. "There's a place to the north and east where we might stage an ambush. What do you think?"

"Why not?"

She gave him a hand up, and he grunted as he put his weight on his bad leg. He held her hand for a moment longer than necessary. "Two fire bloods," he said thoughtfully. "This is an advantage I had not considered."

"I'll pack your gear for you," she said. "I know how you like it arranged."

What followed was the most swift, silent, and orderly retreat Zanja had ever seen. She had scarcely managed to buckle her belt and sling her knapsack on her shoulders when the company began moving into the woods. She delayed a moment to put a chicken carcass and a handful of cracked corn atop a flat rock for the raven. By then, Daye had sent someone back for her, a laconic veteran who moved through the woods as a snake glides through grass. The abandoned clearing lay empty behind them, with only the warm ashes of the campfires to tell the story of how recently it had been occupied.

An occasional mimicked bird call, far ahead, gave the scattered company members a direction to follow. Zanja and her companion sometimes encountered others, traveling through the dark woods, but they separated again. The trees began to thin, and boulders loomed. Zanja realized from the ache in her calves that the ground had begun to rise. The trees dropped away. The bird call sounded: closer, but above her. She looked up and saw a rocky hillside pressed against fading stars. A dozen dark shapes climbed the rocks; soon she was one of them, hauling herself and her gear from stone to stone, sometimes being given a hand from above, and sometimes offering one to the climber below. At the top, the entire company had gathered, some gasping for breath, some loading their pistols and winding their crossbows. Daye had used pebbles to lay out a map on the ground. She looked up as Zanja squatted nearby. "Annis says you're not much of a shot yet."

"This is an opportunity to practice."

Daye grinned. "Well, first rule of ambush: Don't be the first one to shoot, not even if you feel like the Sainnites are right on top of you. And until you hear that first shot, don't even look to see where the Sainnites are. If you can see them, they can see you."

A half dozen late-comers stood or squatted around the impromptu map as Daye reviewed the plans for what must have been the third or fourth time. Others gathered around Willis and Perry, being instructed in much the same way, while Emil climbed to a high point and took out his spyglass.

The dawning day revealed a lone black bird soaring overhead. The last of the company members scattered to find positions in the bulwark of stone, and Zanja settled behind a boulder to wait, with her loaded pistols at hand. The dull brown clothing of her fellow Paladins melted into stone; their shapeless hats disguised their heads and faces. She watched the raven, wondering if with the flaps of his wings he sent signals that she could not read.

The rising sun had begun to cast shadows when Zanja heard the distinct, harsh tones of a tin signal whistle, and some time later faintly heard a few words spoken in Sainnese. No doubt the Sainnites were arguing whether to continue on, for to anyone with any sense the hillside was an intimidating prospect. She heard a few more words, angry now: a hot-headed commander, frustrated at having nothing to show for the long night in the woods. They were going to give up the chase, she thought, with a deep sense of relief.

A long silence followed, then she heard quite distinctly a woman just below her, saying in Sainnese, "They came this way, that's for certain. But I say they're long gone—scattered through the forest, impossible to find by now. They used the rough ground to obscure their traces."

A man said angrily, "That *seguli* swore we would have a proud victory this night."

"Well, the night has ended," the woman said.

"He has never been wrong before!"

The woman offered no argument, but it seemed it was her ill luck to be the target for her commander's wrath. "Climb up and tell me what you see," he said.

It was Zanja's ill luck that the woman began to climb where she stood, perhaps two body lengths below Zanja's hiding place. She waited, hearing the casual conversations of the Sainnites below, the chirps of a few early season birds, the faint, hoarse cry of the raven. The woman climbed swiftly, impatiently, and yet when she reached the other side of the boulder behind which Zanja sheltered, she paused, and Zanja heard the hiss of a blade sliding out of its scabbard. The Sainnite soldier came around the boulder weapon first.

For a moment, she looked, startled, into Zanja's eyes, and then Zanja quietly embraced her neck with her dagger's edge, and almost fell with her as the woman dropped her blade and grabbed Zanja by the shirt. Zanja hung on the hillside by her fingernails, and scrambled back to shelter, briefly seeing a dozen or more surprised soldiers staring up at her, or down at the flailing, dying soldier who had fallen practically on top of them. In almost the same moment, she heard Emil fire the first shot, and in the immediate volley the Sainnites fled for the marginal shelter of the thin woods.

Zanja and her companions chased them down the hillside. She leapt over the dying soldier, whose heart continued to pump blood onto the stones. She chased down a wide-eyed young man whose pistol shot dodged crazily past her shoulder and into the sky. He dropped the pistol and jerked a short sword out of its scabbard, but by then Zanja's dagger had sliced through his leather cuirass and into his chest so easily it seemed the man's armor and flesh were constructed of lard. She missed his heart, though, and had to try again, and in the moment between her first blow and her second, the panicked young soldier took a stumbling swing at her. She caught the terrified blow on her dagger, and felt it jar her arm and shoulder like a blow from a stave, but she managed to strike him again, and this time the blow was true, and the boy died.

In the woods, the Sainnite commander's tin whistle shrilled, "Come to me!" She looked around: scattered Paladins fought and chased the fleeing Sainnites. She ran to help a Paladin who seemed overpowered by a towering brute of a man in metal armor. She shot him at close range with her pistol, which seemed to do no good, then switched her dagger back to her right hand as the monstrous soldier turned to confront her. She would sooner take on an angry bull, she thought as she dodged the battle-ax that could have taken her head off, and leapt forward to slip her uncanny dagger neatly into his armpit. He scarcely seemed to feel it, but it bled like a mortal wound, and she and her companion took turns baiting him while he bled to death. At last he fell slowly as a slaughtered cow, still swinging his deadly ax.

She had a moment, then, to recognize her battle companion. "Is that your blood?" she asked, gesturing at Linde's scarlet-stained shirt.

"I don't think so."

They stood together, gasping for breath, watching the great soldier's eyes glaze over. "It took him long enough," Linde commented.

"I must have just nicked his heart."

"That was a tricky blow." Admiringly, he shook her hand.

"I've got a good blade," she said, which was the truth, though he took it for modesty. "What shall we do now?"

As if in reply, a volley of gunshots sounded in the woods, and Linde said, "The Sainnites have regrouped, by the sound of it, and Emil will be calling a retreat, since we no longer have the advantage. Let's look around for wounded Paladins, and start hauling them up the hillside."

They soon found the company healer, Jerrell, engaged in the same project, and the three of them hastily scoured the battleground for fallen Paladins, finding one wounded and one dead. They finished off two injured Sainnites as well.

With the exhilaration of battle starting to lift, Zanja fought an overpowering nausea. Her limbs trembled as she helped carry the dead and wounded to high ground. Her various victims had doused her with their blood, and she wanted nothing more than to find a quiet stream and rinse out her shirt. But she had been through this horror before, and knew there was no remedy except to wait for it to pass. Meanwhile, with the Paladins reappearing in the woods and gathering again on the hilltop, Zanja helped Jerrell to amputate the wounded Paladin's mangled arm. When they were finished, she commented unsteadily that she'd rather be a warrior than a surgeon.

Jerrell said grimly, "Well, I've done both, and I'd say killing a stranger is much easier than chopping off the arms and legs of my friends."

The raven circling overhead tilted its wings and flew into the sunrise. Perched on the hilltop with his spyglass, Emil reported that the Sainnites continued to retreat. Annis found Zanja, and her excited monologue gave Zanja some relief from thinking. She had time to change her shirt and to settle her stomach with a mouthful of hardtack before the company began again to travel, carrying the dead and wounded, some somber, like Zanja, and some, like Annis, giddy with triumph.

At mid-day, they stopped to rest and eat. Annis was called away to give her opinion on a faulty pistol, and Zanja sat solitary in the cool shade of a tree, pretending peace for a little while.

Emil limped over with his camp stool under his arm. "Daye says you have something to tell me." He had taken off his doublet, which had been stained with a distinct arc of spattered blood. He sat heavily upon his stool, and offered Zanja a wedge of cheese to go with her half-eaten piece of bread. She said, "I speak Sainnese."

He gave her a startled look, but said half-humorously, "Of course you do. And what did the Sainnites say?"

"Just before the battle began, I overheard a conversation between the commander and a soldier, the one I killed."

"The first of three, I hear."

"The commander was angry, almost as though he had been so confident of his victory that night that he could not believe it had been stolen from him. He said, 'That *seguli* swore we would have victory this night.' Then, he added, 'He has never been wrong before.' Then, because he was in such a bad humor, he sent that woman to her death."

"Hmm."

Though the days had begun to warm, in the cool woods it remained chilly, and the trees had scarcely begun to leaf out. Emil wore his tattered coat, and Zanja could hear the faint sound of his watch ticking in a pocket.

Emil said, "What is a *seguli?*"

"Unfortunately, I have never heard that word before. But I think the *seguli* may be our true enemy—a talented strategist, the same one who gutted Rees Company last year."

"If he truly has never been wrong before, our little escapade today will surely leave him—and them—a bit unnerved." For a moment, Emil looked as gleeful as a boy, and then he sobered. "Still, if not for you, they would have found us, and it would have been a massacre."

"We were lucky," Zanja said. It would not do for Emil to start relying on her to predict their battles for him. The raven was gone, and Karis would certainly see to it that he never returned.

"We were lucky," Emil agreed. "It's the kind of luck we need to survive this summer. I hope that it continues."

Chapter Ten

The important work of collecting and distributing bread to the scattered company proved as dull and tedious as Zanja had feared. The greatest challenge it posed was that of finding her way—first to the various farmholds that had agreed to supply the bread, then to the various encampments that needed it. The farmholds most often provided great wheels of hard rye bread that kept well and did not crumble easily, but they also loaded her poor donkey with whatever else could be spared from their own or their neighbors' storerooms: carrots, cheese, sausage, turnips, apples, potatoes, onions, and ham. At least, when Zanja succeeded in finding a company encampment, no one was sorry to see her.

It had become known that Zanja's prescience had saved the company that night. Although most of the Paladins could not bring themselves to treat her as one of their own, they were courteous enough, though in Willis's unit the welcome remained particularly cool.

"There you are at last," Annis said, when Zanja arrived at Daye's unit with a fresh load of bread. "We're running low on saltpeter, and I have to go to Wilton. Emil says to bring you with me, and we'll meet him and Willis along the way."

The next morning, on the east-west road just outside the river valley, they found Emil and Willis waiting for them. The road was busy with market day traffic. Willis and Annis, their weapons hidden in their longshirts, became indistinguishable from any other farmer. Emil might have been a rather seedy accountant looking for work. Zanja wrapped her hair in a headcloth, obscured her face with a hat brim, and hoped no one looked at her too closely.

"I want you to learn to read glyphs," Emil said to her, and produced out of his knapsack a sheet of paper. "I've written some out for you." He pointed. "The four elements, the four directions, the four seasons, the twelve implements."

Next to each carefully drawn symbol, he had written its name, followed by a brief explanation of the symbol's implications. The symbols seemed stagnant, their implications arcane and irrelevant. "Why?" Zanja asked.

"Indulge me."

She felt Willis glowering at her back. "Of course."

To understand the glyphs seemed like knowledge of the most tedious sort. Each glyph had primary and secondary meanings, and sometimes meant two things simultaneously. Each glyph had a history or special use, and some of them were accompanied by lengthy expository tales that complicated rather than clarified their meaning. In addition, the meanings of the glyphs interacted with each other, so that two glyphs together meant something different from what they meant separately. To fully understand these glyphs might require lengthy study, and the entire system, Emil told her, included a thousand symbols, though he was not certain if anyone remaining alive was familiar with them all. He himself knew about half of them, and had despaired of ever learning the other half.

His passion for this strange, ambiguous method of recording and understanding ideas was as evident as Willis's and Annis's excruciating boredom with it. If only out of perversity, Zanja struggled to comprehend what Emil was telling her about the glyphs. The more she came to understand them, the more genuine her interest became.

Wilton was as big as the largest towns Zanja had traded in up in the border country. Located near the junction of two major rivers, it was a warren of narrow byways and sudden plazas, with balconies on opposite buildings a mere hop apart from each other, and a casual attitude toward garbage that left her always on the lookout for dung and debris underfoot or falling from overhead. The rivers brought travelers from far-flung communities who were riding the current to the seaport and paused here to replenish their supplies and sell some of their wares. Many of these travelers looked no more like a South Hiller than she did, and some of them even resembled her.

"I won't say you can get everything in Wilton," said Emil. "It's not like it used to be, and it's nothing like Hanishport, where you *can* get everything."

"Everything but what you can get in Hanishport's neighboring town, Lalali," said Willis. "Of course, in Lalali you'll be robbed and murdered in the bargain."

The taverns had set up their tables in the streets, the better to entice the farmers to drink what money they had rather than buy seed or tools or pay their taxes. It seemed a hopeless enterprise, however. This early in the season the farmers come into town for market day hadn't much to sell, and they all had a pale, winter-pinched look, and a way of keeping their hands up their sleeves.

Emil and Willis had come into town to talk to Willis's brothers, who worked at the garrison. Annis left to make some arrangements with one of her chemist friends.

A row of beggars sat against a wall with their empty hands lifted, moaning tales of being reduced to poverty through no fault of their own. Emil tapped Zanja's arm and pointed at the garish sign that hung over the door. As was common throughout the country, the business folk of Wilton used glyphs to identify their shops. Merchants used only one symbol, the tavern keepers two, which made the name of the taverns amusingly ambiguous. However, the symbols were always represented as pictures. in the case of this tavern a wheel and a hoe.

The tavern was empty. Willis shouted for ale.

"So what is this place named?" Emil asked Zanja, as they sat at a battered table.

"Progress Through Hard Work," she hazarded. "It seems rather an odd name for a tavern."

It was an elementary reading compared to what Emil could do, but he nodded approvingly. "There's a humor in it—most people would miss the joke entirely these days, and simply call this place the Wheel and Hoe." A big, light-footed woman entered from the arched doorway that led to a steep stone staircase. Down its length echoed the wail of a baby.

"So sorry," she said. "I didn't know my husband had gone out."

She served them heavy mugs of ale and went into the kitchen to warm up some pies for them.

"Husband," snorted Willis. When Zanja glanced at him curiously, he added, "City folk use it to mean something completely different from what it truly means, and then they call *us* backwards. These are the same people who let their kin live on the streets, like those beggars out there, rather than keeping them decently clothed and fed."

"Those beggars are smoke sick," Zanja said.

"All the more reason why they need their families," Willis snapped.

"So what would you call this woman's man?"

"Not her husband," Willis said obstinately. "Where is the household? Where are the other parents for the child? It's just the two of them. That's no family."

Zanja took a swallow of the bitter ale she'd never developed a taste for, and ate the greasy pork pie the alewife set in front of her. The woman's husband returned, and they had a brief, bitter argument behind the closed door of the kitchen. When Willis's brothers arrived, the ale husband came out smiling and rubbing his hands, and wouldn't leave them alone until Emil threatened to go to another ale house.

Willis's brothers smelled distinctly of the stable. They were identical twins who dressed alike and ate alike and finished each other's sentences. When both of them turned their attention upon Zanja, she realized that they probably made love together as well, and she had to struggle to keep from revealing how repellent she found the prospect.

There was a certain affliction that every member of Willis's family seemed to share, a single-mindedness that sorely tried her patience. "Tell me about this new commander," Emil said. "You have at least seen her, haven't you?"

"She's young," said one.

"And handsome," said the other.

"How young? Is she one of this new breed, Shaftali-born?"

"She's older than fifteen!"

Emil rather wearily reminded the brother that, though it had been fifteen years since the Fall of the House of Lilterwess, the Sainnites had been a presence in Shaftal for a good fifteen years before that.

"I suppose she could be thirty," said a brother. "Maybe a bit older."

"What does it matter?" asked the other.

"The young ones sometimes speak our language, and they understand us much better than their fathers did. I think they are the more dangerous enemies because they don't make as many stupid mistakes."

The brothers looked at him blankly. "Sainnites are Sainnites."

"Exactly," said Willis impatiently.

Emil looked as if the three of them together were enough to give him a headache.

The brothers told him that the soldiers reassigned from Rees had arrived all at once, before the thaw. There were too many of them for the brothers to notice any one in particular. They complained at length about the great quantities of baggage the two of them had carried that day. In particular, they remembered some large, remarkably heavy trunks that the two of them had been unfortunate enough to have to move into one soldier's quarters. "Trunks full of rocks," they said bitterly. "A lot of rocks."

"Weapons," suggested Willis.

"Oh, sure, it could have been ax heads or something made of iron, though what one soldier wanted with so many of them I don't know."

"It was books," said Zanja.

Willis and his brothers burst into raucous laughter. "Books! Even we don't have books anymore, and at least we know how to read!"

But Emil said somberly, "Books? What kind of Sainnite would have such a collection of books?

"Perhaps a Sainnite young enough to be fluent in both languages, so he can read Shaftali books."

"And educated at least a little—though how that might happen I don't know. Some of them must be able to read, but not in Shaftalese."

"And he's influential enough that his commander allows him to fill a wagon, when most soldiers have only one small trunk, and whatever they can carry on their backs."

Emil turned to the brothers. "Find a man like that," he said. "A young Sainnite, fluent in both languages, educated, and influential, who arrived with the others from Rees. Find out everything you can about him."

The brothers gaped at him as though he was a street corner magician pulling coins out of children's ears. Willis, predictably, protested, "You don't even know this man exists. It's just guesses."

Emil said quietly, "No, it's fire logic."

Willis banged his tankard on the table. "I need more ale."

Zanja gave him hers. The thick stone walls retained the day's chill too well, and the fire on the hearth was stingy at best. Dour Annis came in, and greeted the brothers with indifferent kisses. Probably the brothers were her cousins, like just about everyone in South Hill. Then she kissed Zanja, much less indifferently.

The four of them left the brothers drinking their ale, and followed a circuitous route to a road that ended at the garrison wall. There was no gate; the wall rose up out of the road's debris. The city buildings stood aloof, with the basements of the buildings that had once stood there filled with the rubble of their demolished walls. The garrison wall had been built of reused stone blocks. As they stood there, a soldier strolled past along the battlement, eating an apple. He carried a long gun by a sling over his shoulder. He did not even glance down at them.

"The main gate is to the west," said Emil, "and there's two postern gates, all guarded. We've dreamed up half a dozen ways to break in over the years, but we've never actually done it. Let them hide away inside their walled city . . . if they'll just leave the rest of Shaftal alone."

They walked to the main gate, and Emil went into a shop within sight of it to visit a friend who had made it his habit to watch the comings and goings of the garrison. When he reappeared, he reported that his friend had nothing useful to tell them. If a Shaftali spy were visiting the garrison, he or she had the sense to go in by the postern gate, and if the owner of the trunks of books were going in and out, he looked no different from any other soldier.

Willis's mood seemed to have only grown more foul as the day continued. Apparently, he did not like that Emil taught Zanja about glyphs, nor did he like that their intuitions had proven so compatible. But why he was so irritated by these things Zanja could not imagine.

As they walked through the rich farmlands of the river valley, Annis talked to Zanja about her experiments with gunpowder and other unstable compounds. It seemed incredible she had not even injured herself, when she clearly deserved to be blown to bits.

In this community of huge, fantastically intermarried families,

Zanja's loneliness was becoming intolerable. She experimented with touching Annis's arm, wondering if she herself would be blown to bits. Annis turned her head at Zanja's touch, and her glance was not unfriendly. "We should go away somewhere so you can practice shooting," she said.

"Sometime soon," Zanja suggested.

Annis smiled. Apparently, not all South Hillers were hopelessly unsubtle.

The land slowly put on the clothing of summer: first white and pink, then many shades of green. The Sainnites regularly hunted South Hill Company, commonly by daylight, less commonly by night. Lookouts within and without Wilton signaled troop movements with fire and flag, and, inevitably, when the Sainnites arrived at one or another encampment, their prey would have fled. South Hill Company set traps, lay in wait, and struck back, though their enemy rapidly grew cautious and canny and so did not fall for their tricks often. Thus, every fallen Sainnite was a cause for celebration.

Zanja occasionally led the Sainnites on a merry chase through the wild wood, but more often she and her food-laden donkey took refuge in a thicket as the soldiers marched past, and instead of fighting or fleeing she spent much of her time straining her prescience, trying to calculate where and when she might find the hungry Paladins, who, by making themselves difficult for the soldiers to find, also made it difficult for supplies to find them.

The second full moon that Zanja had seen in South Hill was starting to wane as she and her donkey climbed wearily into the highlands where Daye's company had retreated for a few days of rest. A startled, haggard picket challenged her, for even in a place so remote from the garrison they dared not relax their guard. Zanja gave the poor man some bread and dried fruit, and made her way into the camp, where her appearance was greeted with an exhausted chorus of huzzahs. Daye intervened to keep the donkey from being stampeded, and handed over the fresh supply of food to the cook, who in turn sent a phalanx of helpers to fetch buckets of water and start chopping vegetables for stew.

"Tonight will be our first night's sleep in three days," Daye explained. "And we've hardly eaten since yesterday."

"I could not find you," Zanja said apologetically. "By the time I was done dodging Sainnites . . ."

"Well, I don't blame you. It's just frustrating, not being able to send my people over to the nearest farm for food when we get hungry. The lack of beds and baths, well, that's not so pleasant either. You're looking pretty tired yourself." She examined Zanja critically. "How long since you haven't spent a day on your feet?"

Zanja shook her head; it was too much trouble to count.

"Too long, then. You rest with us tomorrow."

"People will go hungry."

"Let them shoot a deer or snare some rabbits, like we've been doing."

Daye told Zanja the way to a nearby hot spring, in a rocky meadow where the turf would satisfy the donkey. The spring was easy enough to find, for it was marked by flapping flags of drying laundry. Though the pool's edges were trampled and some suds lingered, Zanja had the steaming, stinking place to herself. She tossed her dirtiest clothes in to soak, then lay herself down in the scalding, sulfurous water and decided she would never get up again.

People came to collect their laundry, and Zanja managed to exchange a few groggy words of conversation with them. They left; Zanja dozed, and was awakened by more laundry being tossed in to join hers. Then Annis came into the water and waded to the deepest, hottest part of the pool, where Zanja lay stunned by heat, with her head propped up on stone. Zanja put her hands on bare skin that was heated by the earth's center and slippery with minerals. Annis's hands stroked from ribs to hips and then to Zanja's breasts, and Zanja let her kiss her, lazy and slow, and eventually her hands found their way to the insides of Annis's thighs. For a while Zanja was unmoored, half drowned, dazzled by sharp flashes of sunlight, of pleasure, of simple release. Annis was a laughing, easy, and uncomplicated lover.

When they had finished, Annis got up and began briskly pounding her sodden clothes with stones. Bewildered, Zanja watched Annis sink to her elbows in soapy foam. Had she just been entertaining Annis, helping stave off boredom while her clothes were soaking?

"I had so much gunpowder in my clothes I was a walking explosion," Annis said cheerfully.

"I know what you mean," Zanja said.

"Listen," Annis said, not seeming to have heard. "I've invented something, and I think it might be rather fine. It flies! Don't tell Emil—I want to show him, and see his face light up."

When Zanja lay with her fellow *katrim*, it had been both intimate and perilous, for the *katrim* were simultaneously fellows and rivals, who with no immediate enemy to fight, could only pick fights with each other. To lay down their weapons for a while and offer each other intimacy and comfort instead was never casual, though it was always assumed to be short-lived. But Annis's carelessness, Zanja thought, was insulting.

"That was fun," Annis said, as she hung her laundry on the bushes, and did not even seem to notice when Zanja failed to agree with her.

The wearying, hectic game of dodge, retreat, and regroup dulled Zanja's pain, but honed her intuition. She stockpiled food at Midway Barn so starving company members could get supplies there even when it was impossible for Zanja to catch up with them. One night, she spotted the signal fires that warned Willis's company of an enemy attack, and she was able to guess where Willis would make his new encampment, and left food for them to find when they arrived. No doubt Willis would call it luck, or common sense. A few days later, she arrived at Midway Barn with a fresh supply of food, and was astonished to find Emil there, alone, sipping a cup of tea and reading a dispatch.

He was haggard, but grinned like a boy at her surprise. "I hear you've started leaving food supplies—not where the unit is encamped, but where they will be encamped soon. That's quite a trick."

"I've only done it twice."

"It's a pity you can't tell us where the Sainnites will be, the way they seem to do with us."

"It's a pity you can't do it either," she said.

"Yes. But apparently I can predict where you will be. Come with me to Bowen's Farmhold, will you? Three survivors from Rees Company are guesting there, and sent a message asking to be admitted to South Hill Company. We'll be there in time for supper, and the Bowens always set a good table."

It was a fine day: bright and warm, and shot through with swooping birds that dove like flame from out of the sun and swooped over the treetops, ecstatic with passion. The two of them took a high trail that Zanja had not followed before, with a slender rivulet chuckling along beside them. For half the morning, Emil thought his own thoughts, and Zanja, long accustomed to solitude, felt no need to interrupt with an attempt at conversation. They reached a high, remote meadow, where occasional fat bees shot past like pistol balls. There, they sat in the sun to rest, and the donkey promptly set to grazing. Emil took a packet wrapped in paper out of his doublet pocket and handed it to her. "This is for you. You'd have gotten it much sooner, but it took my friend in Wilton over a month to find."

Zanja did not know what to do with a gift. "Untie the string," he urged. "You'll laugh when you see what it is."

She opened the packet, and then she did laugh, for Emil had given her a pack of fortune-telling cards. "Emil, you are a desperate man."

"Yes," he said, suddenly serious.

"Glyphs!" she exclaimed, looking more closely at the cards.

"These cards were traditionally used to teach glyphs to schoolchildren. I'm afraid it's a rather artless deck. I've seen some that were almost too beautiful to touch—but I suppose you wouldn't want to be carrying artwork while running through the woods and rolling around in the mud."

Zanja shuffled through the cards, looking at the woodcut illustrations, printed in brown, and the glyphs stamped on each corner in red. Most of the glyphs she had not seen before, but even those she was familiar with seemed much less ambiguous when paired with an illustration. She found a raven, who dove earthward with a message satchel round his neck. She found an owl, who flew across a chasm with a person dangling helplessly from one claw. She found a woman standing in an open doorway, and lay that card flat upon her knee.

Emil took up the card and examined it critically. "The Woman of the Doorway really should look less grim and more ambivalent."

"Is she going out, or coming in? Or is she simply unable to make up her mind?"

"They say she stands poised between the danger without and the danger within."

"Of course." Zanja took the card from him and traced the shape of the glyph with a fingertip. "Uncertainty and judgment, and the dangers of decision. Possibilities and dangers and the fact of our existence here—" she tapped the woman's head, to show which "here" she meant. "Always deciding."

"To some fire bloods, the cards explain themselves. I suspected they might explain themselves to you."

She surreptitiously wiped her face dry. What was wrong with her? She restlessly sought and found the owl card, and showed it to Emil. "Is the person being carried a passenger, or prey?"

"Ah, well. That is the heart of the question, isn't it? Do we seek wisdom, or are we kidnapped by it?"

Zanja said, half to herself, "It was the owl god that chose me to serve her."

"No wonder your way has been so hard. That glyph must be your name sign, then."

"Which is yours? No—I will guess." She sought through the deck, and pulled out a card: a man standing alone on a hilltop, with stars shaped like arrows falling down on him.

"Solitude," Emil said. "Also sometimes called Contemplation. The man on the hill sees forever, and might be destroyed by what he sees. Yes, it's my card," he added, as she glanced at him inquiringly, "Now tell me: What is the threat to South Hill Company? Just pick a card and let me do the thinking."

She chose a card that depicted a plain box, with the lock broken, the lid half open, and the interior hidden in shadow.

Emil said. "But what is in the box?"

She pulled out and tossed down a picture of a burning flame.

"Whose fire is it?"

She lay a third card down, and cried in disgust, "That can't be right!" It was the Man on the Hill.

But Emil spread out the three cards in the grass. "Am I the one who threatens South Hill? Well, obviously my judgment on this matter is questionable, but I don't see how it could be possible. Let's consider what else it might be. The flame, of course, is the elemental fire that enlightens and destroys: love, rage, desire, revolution, creation, and destruction. The box has to do with secrets that might be revealed, so paired with the flame it suggests elemental divination or revelation. When the flame is paired with Solitude, it usually means fire talent, fire logic, the solitude that comes with being a visionary. And all three cards together . . ." He looked at them, frowning.

"It might be a warning that for us to practice divination like this somehow makes you the danger that threatens South Hill. Or it might be a suggestion that divination will allow us to counter a danger that is not yet revealed."

"It might mean either or both of those things. But I see a third possibility—one that I want to reject because it seems like an impossibility." They sat a long time in silence, with Zanja gazing down at the cards and seeing how their meanings ceaselessly shifted and yet somehow began to stabilize. Emil had looked away from the cards, and gazed out at the vista that lay before them. He said at last, "When those falling stars pierce the heart, it feels like this."

"It feels like an owl's claw," Zanja said.

He turned to her with a warm, wry smile, his squint lines all furrowed against the sun. "Well, what do you now see in the cards?"

"I see that the Sainnites have a seer."

"If that's true, then he must be a madman. To nurture a seer takes great care and deliberation, and the Sainnites seem incapable of both."

"He may be a madman," Zanja said, "but what he's done to us so far, and to Rees before us, seems more like genius."

"Yet—however difficult and exhausting the process—we continue to evade his insight. That may be the best we can hope to do against such an enemy." Emil stretched out his stiff leg, preparatory to standing up. She stood and offered him a hand, which he clasped in his so gently that she found herself again bewildered. The Ashawala'i were never so demonstrative, except perhaps with their closet kin. "To hell with protocol," Emil said. "Between the two of us, we can see through the tricks of an inexperienced seer—but not if I have to chase you across half the region every time I want to talk to you. These volunteers from Rees don't know it yet, but one of them—" he grunted as she helped him up, "—is going to be our new bread runner. Maybe more than one of them, since I suspect you won't be easy to replace."

Chapter Eleven

The three units rotated positions again: Daye's unit occupied high ground within spyglass sight of Wilton; Perry's unit retreated into the highlands for a few days of rest, and Willis's unit camped in between, in the thick woods west of the rich farmlands that surrounded Wilton. Since being promoted to runner, Zanja had traveled several times between Emil and Daye. It was never too difficult to find Daye's unit: it did not take a seer to know that they would be on one or another hilltop near the edge of the flood plain that surrounded Wilton. But to find Willis's unit would be tricky, even though, as far as Zanja knew, they had not decamped recently. She had been walking through the woods since sunrise, merely hopeful that she was following the right path.

Sweating in the warm morning, Zanja slipped through a thicket and emerged onto clear ground again. She paused to listen, and heard only faint bird song. Then a shot rang out, and a pistol ball smacked into a tree not a hand's breadth from her shoulder. A second ball whizzed past, singing in a high, thin whine, but by then she had dived into the thicket again. She paused to load a pistol and then crawled further into the thick woods, then lay down in the dirt and waited with her heartbeat thrumming in her ears.

The woods lay dead silent. The birds began to sing again. Her heartbeat slowed; her instincts told her that whoever had shot at her was gone. Still, she did not continue her journey until midday filled the forest with dull sunlight. It was afternoon when a watchful picket outside the encampment noticed her cautious passage through the woods, and challenged her. "Why are you lurking?" he asked, when he recognized her. "Do you want to get yourself killed?"

Willis kept his camps in exacting order, with all the gear packed away, so it could be easily snatched up should it become necessary to flee or fight. Lately, through, the Sainnites no longer chased the Paladins into the woods, and seemed satisfied to simply disrupt their sleep, night after night. It was a policy of persecution that did not subject their own soldiers to much danger, while continuing to wear out the Paladins. Willis had sent Emil an impatient message that next time the Sainnites approached his camp, he intended to attack rather than retreat. Emil had dispatched Zanja to find out his plans in more detail.

Willis sat talking with a sharpshooter who was said to be his lover, several other opinionated and incautious people, and a couple of his brothers, who tended to repeat whatever he said as though they had thought of it themselves. Whatever Zanja's assessment of their characters, these were seasoned and courageous fighters, and she supposed she might learn something about the value of aggression from them.

Willis spotted her and said with extraordinary joviality, "Well, well! Unfortunately, you have missed the midday meal."

"I was delayed by being shot at in the woods."

"That's strange. Perhaps a lone Sainnite is out there today. Either that, or it was that spy we've been watching out for."

Zanja said, "Well, I never saw who it was, but it makes no sense that someone who wants to avoid notice would have shot unnecessarily. Are you certain that it wasn't a member of your company taking a shot at me?"

"Well, if you didn't answer the hail—"

"No one hailed me."

"Then it was no Paladin. We don't shoot at our own."

"Of course not," Zanja said, and perhaps she might have left it at that, but the memory of the wasted afternoon rankled. "But how can I be confident that everyone in South Hill Company recognizes me as one of their own?" she asked.

She had said it quietly enough, but Willis reacted as she might have expected, with a roar calculated to make her regret having even mentioned such a possibility. "No one questions the truthfulness and honor of my people! If my man says no one answered his hail, then that is what happened!"

"No one hailed me," she said again.

"So it wasn't one of my people!"

"Then you have a sniper lurking in the woods, and had better beware. A solitary person could easily slip past your pickets."

"My pickets are always watchful," Willis said dismissively.

Mechanically, bitterly, Zanja gave him Emil's message, and then tried to listen closely as Willis and the others explained their plan to her. She had intended to ask Willis to show her the site of his intended ambush, but now could not convince herself to remain any longer than strictly necessary. If she left now, she could reach Daye's unit before dark.

"I didn't expect to see you again so soon," said Daye, when Zanja had found the encampment, shortly before sunset. They were dousing the cookfires to make it harder for the Sainnites to find them in the darkness, but the stew was still hot. The evening watch was already in position; the night watch slept; the day watch played cards or dice by the fading light. Daye claimed she had nothing important to do, and sat and chatted with Zanja while she ate.

"Is Annis away?" Zanja asked.

"She's conducting experiments again, now that she's got more gunpowder. That child is rather excited about something, but won't tell me what."

Zanja ate a few mouthfuls. "I need some advice," she finally said.

She had come to trust Daye during the months that she served under her command. Daye had been the first to congratulate her on her promotion, and to point out that now Zanja's swift mind would prove even more important than her swift feet. Now, Daye paused in plaiting her gray hair, and looked at Zanja inquiringly.

"I think someone in Willis's unit tried to shoot me today," Zanja said. "And I think that Willis commanded it."

"That man," Daye said, apparently not much surprised, "is an ass. I've known him his whole life, and he has always been an ass. It's hopeless." In silence, she finished plaiting her hair, and Zanja cleaned out her porringer with a bit of bread.

"I'm just a stranger—" she finally began.

Daye cut her off. "You're a smart fighter and that prescience is an asset to the company. I'll talk to Emil."

"I can talk to him myself."

"No, Emil and I have a long history. I am the one who tells him the truths that are so bitter no one else dares tell them to him, and he has to listen because I'm his elder. The older I get, the blunter I get. You young people waste so much time on niceties."

Zanja said, "I don't want Emil to think I'll run to him every time I have a problem rather than solving it myself."

"Well, this is the kind of problem he needs to know about. He's always had one good reason or another to put up with Willis, but he truly can't endure the man. So he ties himself in knots trying to be fair, and ends up looking the other way when he shouldn't."

Zanja said, rather astonished, "Should you be telling me all this about my superiors?"

"What!" Daye laughed. "South Hill thrives on gossip. Fertilizer, we call it, to make the crops grow." She added, more seriously, "When Emil told me about his decision to promote you, I could see there was more to it than simple admiration for your good sense. You and him, you seem like kinfolk to me."

Zanja awoke from troubled sleep to the sound of a pistol shot. Her unreliable prescience had once again failed her. Shouting, she leapt out of her blankets and snatched up her dagger. Gunpowder flashed all around the encampment. She ran through a chaos of confused Paladins at the closest gunpowder flash, following the distinctive oily stink of a Sainnite cuirass. The soldier was still blinded by the flare of his own gunshot, and, before Zanja was even full awake, she had dispatched him. She did not know where she had cut him, but the smell told the tale of her sloppy work. If she survived the night, it would be in clothing as foul as a butcher's.

Barefoot, half blind, she attacked another opponent. The two of them had come too close to killing each other before they realized they were allies. The guns flashed around them, deafening. She and her fellow Paladin screamed at each other, asking each other what to do. Then he collapsed at her feet and she stared at him stupidly. Pistol balls buzzed through the clearing.

Move or die. She dodged through the darkness and the billowing gunsmoke. How could the Sainnites keep shooting so long? In their zealousness they would surely soon be shooting each other.

She heard a metallic whistle, and the guns fell silent. By some devil's luck—too little luck, too late—she had broken through the ring of soldiers, and now as they tightened their noose upon the trapped Paladins, she was outside of it, as helpless to save them as they were helpless to escape.

With only a dagger in her hand, she followed the tightening circle of soldiers inward. She heard a scream, and bit her own tongue. The clearing seemed filled with soldiers. She might kill one more before she herself was killed, then no one would survive to light the signal beacon, or carry a message to Emil.

She got herself under command and slipped back into the dark wood.

She had scarcely gotten her bearings when she heard a tentative bird call. The racket of battle was already falling silent and she dared not whistle back, but stumbled about until she had found a handful of others: some survivors of the evening watch, who were booted and armed and frantic with guilt; some barefoot like her, with or without weapons; several of them injured, one certain to die before the night ended.

Knowing that Zanja reported to Emil, the people who had been on watch gave her a garbled account of not having seen a bit of movement in the valley all night, until suddenly the firefight erupted. "They must have slipped out of Wilton last night. Somehow, our spies there didn't notice. And they worked their way towards us from the north, along the rim of the valley where we couldn't see them. That's what we think happened."

Zanja paid no heed, for how this horror had happened seemed irrelevant. "We need to light the beacon," she said.

"There's three people up there already, like always."

"They would have lit the signal fire by now if they were still alive."

"Shaftal's Name!" someone said, raw voiced. "These Sainnites are devils!"

But they were too experienced to waste precious time cursing the enemies. The five that were still in condition to fight set out for the beacon hill, which pressed itself like a blunt knucklebone against the stars. But, as Zanja more than half expected, the hill crawled with Sainnites, with more arriving even as Zanja and her companions watched. It had been a well-planned attack, the Paladins bitterly told each other. The Sainnites must have attacked the beacon, the watchposts, and the encampment simultaneously, and now two-thirds of Daye's unit was almost certainly dead.

But now the Sainnites appeared to have nothing better to do

than to keep the Paladins from lighting the beacon. Zanja and her companions returned to the site of the encampment, finding it now occupied only by the sprawling dead. Daye had died fighting—"As she intended to," said one of the survivors dully.

Zanja sorted through her trampled gear, blinded by tears, feeling as choked for breath as though she were drowning. But one part of her stood distant from her grief, coolly reminding her that she had survived worse horrors than this. Mechanically, she found and put on her boots, holstered her pistols in the belt that crossed her chest, slung a light haversack upon her back, and abandoned the rest of her gear where it lay.

"Listen," she said to the others, who stood in an aimless, stunned group. "The Sainnites have bigger plans than this tonight, or they wouldn't be troubling themselves to secure the beacon. We need to learn what they are doing, and then we need to run messages to Willis, Perry, and Emil. Some of us need to go to the nearest farmholds to get help for the wounded and to carry away the dead. Do any of you watchers have a spyglass?"

They all walked the short distance to the overlook, where more bodies lay. It was impossible to see much in the dark, but the column of soldiers marching briskly towards them across the valley along the east-west road would have been difficult to miss. Zanja handed back the spyglass to its owner. "I'll carry the news to Perry and Emil," she said, and began to run.

The pallid light of dawn was warming Zanja's shoulders when the road began to edge its way around an appealing meadow, where anyone with any sense would break their journey to rest and water their horses, if they had them. She herself paused to fill her canteen at the brook, and then stood for a while, wasteful though it seemed to stand so quietly while disaster unfolded around her. Her thigh muscles quivered with fatigue, but surely the Sainnites also would be weary after marching all night, and even on a forced march would have to take the time to rest and eat. This meadow seemed a likely place for it.

She took herself up a gentle hillside on the far side of the road, and settled down among the dappled shadows to eat her honeycakes and fight off desire for sleep. Soon, a few outriders arrived on worn-out horses, and while the horses were being watered, the riders searched their immediate surroundings for lurkers. The bulk of the army arrived soon after: 150 soldiers, Zanja counted, all heavily laden with the kind of gear that might support a long and rigorous journey.

Perry's encampment now lay a hour's journey to the south. Zanja got heavily to her feet, and as soon as she had found a deer path to follow she began to run again, which relieved her from the need for further thinking, until the path abruptly popped her into the channel of a chattering brook. On the other bank, Emil sat waiting for her. Stupid with exhaustion, she gaped at him. Two of his messengers lay under the trees nearby, apparently sleeping.

He said, "I sent a message to Perry some time ago, and I expect his entire company will arrive shortly. Have you alerted Willis and Daye?"

"Daye's dead," she gasped. "Attacked last night. Most of the company was killed. I was with them." She sat down where she was, rather too quickly as her legs gave out under her. For a little time they sat in silence, with the brook between them. Then, Emil breathed in, white-faced, and asked calmly for more information. She told him all she knew.

He sat silent. She groped for something more to say. "How did you know to send for Perry's unit?"

"I heard a voice in my sleep. But when I awoke, it kept talking to me for a while. A voice in the sky. It was very strange. Perhaps," he added, not much seeming to care, "I am losing my mind."

Zanja looked around for any sign of a big, black bird. "Well," she said, in a neutral tone. But in the midst of her exhaustion, she felt an extraordinary relief.

Chapter Twelve

Throughout the afternoon and into the evening, until they could no longer see the way, Zanja and her twenty companions made a swift, hectic journey through the woods, following a path cut through the wild lands that they jokingly named Bandit's Road. The older Paladins told how that path had first been cut—how in the interval between planting and harvesting, Emil had recruited farmers and dray horses from all across the region to help in the enterprise, which none of them had thought necessary. Every year since then, a grumbling expedition walked the length of the path with saws and axes to clear away the year's growth and deadfall. Now, more than one old timer patted Emil's shoulder and apologized for cursing him behind his back.

The Bandit's Road paralleled the east-west road, but rather than meandering around the hills and wild lands, it cut directly through whatever lay before it, straight as a compass could make it. Zanja and her companions could not know how far ahead of the Sainnites they traveled, but that they were in fact ahead of them seemed certain.

That first night, Zanja awoke from exhausted sleep, and tottered out to the edge of their haphazard encampment. There she found Emil sitting by himself, weeping for his dead where no one could see him. She sat with him, dry-eyed. In time, he wiped his face and in a rough voice admonished her for not resting when she had the chance.

"I'd say the same to you," she said, "if you were not my commander."

"My blasted knee keeps me awake. But I drank a potion for it and should be able to sleep soon." He tilted his face back so the starlight shone on his deeply creased skin, and added, in a voice still hoarse with sorrow, "I've heard no speeches from the sky tonight."

Zanja said seriously, "Surely the voice will speak again if it seems we need more guidance."

"You believe we are watched over?"

"I believe the gods take the shapes of birds when they choose to speak to us."

"I am not a religious man."

They sat in silence, until Zanja said, "I imagine the Sainnites have their seer with them, and he will have realized by now that we are running ahead of them. So if we cannot take them by surprise, how are we to stop them from crossing the bridge?"

"Have you ever tried to shoot a mouse with a pistol?"

"I should think," Zanja replied after a moment, "that any self-respecting mouse would no longer be where it was, by the time the pistol ball arrived."

"Exactly. And where would the mouse be instead? I doubt even the mouse knows."

"So our best strategy is no strategy?"

"When seers predict the future, they are simply telling themselves stories, as you and I tell stories to each other. And they have the gift for knowing which of many possibilities are the most likely. The better educated they are, the better the stories they can tell themselves. But if all the possibilities are equally likely, then how will our enemy know where to point his pistol, and when to pull his trigger?"

"He will not know."

"That's what I hope. I suppose it depends on just how smart he is."

After a moment, Zanja added, "No strategy? Willis won't like that."

"Don't tell him I've been hearing voices."

When Zanja last crossed this bridge, the river had been flooded. But even though spring thaw and mud were long past, it remained a most intimidating river that muscled its temperamental passage between the steep shoulders of the hills. It could not be safely forded, someone told Zanja. Before the bridge was built, the river was so much trouble to get across that few people bothered, which explained why Darton had so few inhabitants to this day.

A cottage stood by itself on the hillside above the sturdy bridge and the wild river, with a vegetable plot in the back and a fat, pampered cart horse running loose on the grassy hillside. As Zanja and her companions came down the road, having reached the end of Bandit's Road and arrived at the east-west road with no Sainnites in sight, a peculiar old man came trotting down the hill to meet them. "You pay a toll to cross this bridge," he said, and counted heads and began doing calculations. Perhaps haggard, heavily armed brigands were an everyday sight to him.

Emil stepped forward. "Sir—"

"Don't interrupt!"

"Sir, I am Emil, Commander of Paladins, South Hill Company. I regret to inform you that we have come to tear down the bridge."

The bridgekeeper gaped at him. "You've got no right!"

"I am a ranking commander, authorized by the Lilterwess Council to act on behalf of the Shaftali people. I do have the right."

Zanja had flopped down with the others by the side of the road, too stupefied with exhaustion to even consider the enormous labor that yet had to be accomplished that day. When the bridgekeeper submissively started his way back up the hill, Zanja somehow got her legs under her and tackled him, and almost immediately regretted it. The man uttered a harridan's screech and swung his fist wildly, narrowly missing her nose. Still screaming, he fought her like a crazy man, slamming a foot into her shin and getting a good punch to her ribs before she managed to get him to the ground, with a dagger at his throat and a fist in his hair for good measure. "Check the cottage!" she shouted to her companions. "Stop fighting!" she yelled at him.

He let his muscles go limp, but then, wild-eyed, turned his head and sank his teeth into her forearm. Zanja cut him then, and though it apparently took a moment for his pain to register, the man released his teeth from her flesh to shout in outrage, "You've killed me!"

"Dead men don't argue," said one of Zanja's companions dryly, having come over, somewhat puzzled, to help restrain him.

Emil came down from the man's cottage. "That little house is built like a fortress and is crammed with guns. With the clear shot he's got of the bridge he could have held us off all day."

They trussed the bridgekeeper to a tree, where he screamed curses until they plugged his mouth with a kerchief. Besides the cut in his neck, he had broken his hand punching it into the pistol that came between his fist and Zanja's ribs. Anger seemed to be keeping him from feeling it, but he certainly would regret losing his temper soon enough. Zanja went up to the cottage to have the bite in her arm washed with soap. She and her companion returned to the bridge, lugging baskets of food ransacked from the cottage: preserved meats, bottled pickles, dried fruit, tins of crackers. Emil and the others had finished inspecting the bridge by then, and, standing in a group, they fished pickles from the jars with their fingers, chomped the dried fruit, and smeared preserved meat on crackers and ate them in a single mouthful. The luxury was wasted: they would have eaten raw horsemeat with just as much enjoyment.

"A good team of dray horses is what we need," said one. "But that little horse on the hill won't be worth the effort it will take to catch him."

"What we need is Annis and a couple of bags of explosives."

There was a murmur of agreement.

"What we have, however, is a couple of axes and our bare hands," said Emil.

They glumly studied the sturdy bridge, jaws working, passing the pickle jars. "I guess we'd better get busy," someone finally said.

They chopped through the massive timbers one by one, and pulled apart the rubble pilings, stone by stone. By sunset, the bridge had begun to groan. The river joined the game, pushing and pulling at the teetering structure, until the bridge collapsed into the water, and the river broke it up as though it were no more substantial than a sugar cake. Not one member of the company was unbloodied by then, but no one had been carried away in the collapse of the bridge, so they found the energy to utter a ragged cheer that was more relief than jubilation. Then Perry looked around at the battered company and said wryly, "Well, we're in slightly better shape than the bridge, though not by much. Good thing there's been no sign of the Sainnites. Rather than fight or escape, I'd beg them to put me out of my misery."

The sun was setting. They dragged themselves a little way into the woods and lay down on the ground like wounded animals.

Zanja awoke with rocks embedded in her cheek and big black ants crawling through her hair. The members of her company were strewn like corpses across the hillside. Others moved among them in the mist, shaking them awake, offering to fill their porringers with porridge spooned from the kettle that two people carried between them. She turned and saw Willis squat down beside Emil to shake him vigorously by the shoulder.

"What were you thinking? You left the bridgekeeper tied to the tree, and he told us exactly where you had gone. If the Sainnites hadn't turned around in their tracks—"

"What?" said Emil in a voice blurry with exhaustion. "When did they turn around?"

"We met them on the road before dark."

"That was before the bridge fell." Emil sat up, rubbing his face. "Shaftal's Name! Were they just a decoy? What are the Sainnites up to in the flatlands, while all of South Hill Company is out of the way?"

Zanja felt a peculiar, urgent impulse to be alone. She got to her feet with difficulty, and limped into the woods, where night had not yet given way to dawn. With the awakening voices of her company sounding far away behind her, she sat upon a fallen tree cushioned with damp moss. She felt only half awake: some part of her still dreamed of the ringing ax and the scraping away of her skin on the heavy stones. Her wandering thoughts vaguely considered a young man, a Sainnite, cleverer and further-seeing than she, who knew before she did what she was going to do next, and danced her on strings like a puppet at a fair. She noticed that in her bloody hand she clasped one of the bridgekeeper's crackers, and she gazed at it in some bewilderment.

"What am I doing here?" she asked. Then, the storm-battered doors of her mind creaked slowly open, and she broke the cracker to pieces and lay them on the log beside her. Like a shadow untouched by daylight, Karis's raven appeared from the shadows and landed softly beside her.

These seven months of her reclaimed life had largely been filled with hectic and dangerous effort. In the peace of the wood, Zanja felt how illusory was all this activity, how empty her life truly was.

In a voice as racked as any smoke addict's, she said, "Good raven, I brought you this bit of bread."

The raven ate. Zanja said, "Your help has been vital these last few days. Even though the Sainnites may have tricked us, I am sure that if we had not destroyed the bridge, the Sainnites would have crossed it."

The raven, his cracker eaten, turned on Zanja an intelligent gaze. "Zanja, at dawn for just a little while, my soul inhabits the raven."

"Karis!" Zanja saw her hand reach out under its own power, as though to grasp the muscled arm of her friend and not the raven's rasping feathers. "Karis!" she cried, but said no more, for the words that crowded forward were dangerous and filled with longing.

Karis said through the raven, in a voice as hoarse and frayed as her own would be at this hour, "I also am surprised. The raven is not supposed to be in South Hill."

"I understand that. But I think he is watching over you. He intervened to help prevent the Sainnites from crossing into Darton."

The raven—Karis—was silent. Whether her silence meant confusion or displeasure was impossible to know.

Zanja said cautiously, "Surely you did not think it would be too difficult for me to realize you live in Meartown."

"Well, you aren't supposed to know."

"Like everyone in South Hill Company, I have good reason to protect the forges and furnace that provide our weapons. My reason is just more personal than most." Zanja added, "And thank you for my dagger. It is such a fine blade that I sometimes think it could fight on its own. I often wonder why you have not made more of them."

"Every time you bloody the blade, I know it, and I feel my responsibility. Therefore, I make carpenter's tools, mainly. They are rarely used for killing."

Zanja said, "Dear gods—and Norina allowed you to forge me a blade?"

"I never told her. I have the same problem with her blade, but she rarely has to use it. Listen, we haven't got much time to talk."

Zanja said hastily, "There's a danger here that you should know about. The Sainnites have a seer, who is now in South Hill, using his vision to direct the actions of the soldiers. Do you know what happened in Rees?"

"Yes, I have heard about it."

"That was the work of this seer. And now the same disaster is happening in South Hill. Emil and I together are clever, but I believe the seer has just proven to us that he is more clever still."

The raven stared, then said in a low voice, "Now I am unnerved."

"No more than I." And Zanja, was, indeed, deeply afraid, with the kind of fear no soldier dares admit to, upon realizing that defeat was all but predestined.

Karis said abruptly, "I must go."

"But won't you tell me what you can do to help us?" Zanja cried. But the raven spread its wings and was gone, and she sat alone in the bird-loud wood, as the rising sun dropped down through the darkness a thousand streamers of gold.

Chapter Thirteen

In the disordered camp of South Hill Company, Emil took the first few steps of the day, his face white with pain. Five years ago, when a pistol ball had shattered his knee, for a while he had both hoped and feared that his career as a Paladin commander at last would be over. But Jerrell had put his knee back together again, and, disappointed, he had continued on.

In South Hill's river valley, the farmers stood in their fields, puzzled by the pall of smoke that sunrise had revealed. What had burned? Why had the fire bells not been rung? Someone spoke of hearing far-away screams during the night, and thinking it was a dream. Slowly, they began to fear that something terrible had happened.

In the Sainnite encampment by the east-west road, a young man sat up in his blankets, fumbled for his spectacles, and cried in the language of his mother, "Oh, what have I seen?" A camp cook turned from his busy stirring to glance over at him curiously. But, even with his spectacles on, the young man saw only his vision—and it was like nothing he had ever seen before.

The raven flew east and north across the Midlands for three days, until he came to Norina's cottage in the woods. There she had returned for a rest from her wanderings up and down the length of the region, where she ceaselessly rewove and repaired the fabric of the law, which the Sainnites tore apart again, before and behind her.

The raven tapped on the window to wake her up, and she went into the kitchen to let him in. She bore the weight of the child lightly enough, but she did not awaken as easily or gracefully as she used to. She fumbled at the window latch and then sat heavily by the cold hearth, rubbing her face. "You've been gone over twelve days."

Embodied in the raven, Karis said, "This raven went to South Hill again. And I've spoken to Zanja."

Looking through the raven's eyes was strange, for he had two fields of vision and could see Norina in only one of them. As she leapt to her feet and cried out, "What!" then strode in agitation across the length of the kitchen, she moved from one eye to the other. "I ought to wring your neck!"

"You're right; you ought to. Why don't you do it, then?" Karis flew the raven over so Norina could reach his black neck easily.

Norina's hands unclenched. She lifted them up as though to directly entreat the goddess Shaftal for assistance, though she could hardly be described as devout.

"Zanja told me that it was a Sainnite seer that caused such havoc in Rees last year. And this year he's in South Hill."

Norina walked back to the hearth and sat down. Her face had lost its color and the scar across her cheek stood out like a brand. "Tell me everything that she said. Every word."

Karis told her. Norina stirred the coals and then sat without moving until the few flames that she had coaxed out of the ashes died down from neglect. She covered her face with her hands. When she looked up, she had slipped from dismay back again to anger. If her infant could survive a tumultuous nine months in Norina's womb, Karis thought irrelevantly, the rest of the child's life surely would seem easy and restful by comparison.

Norina said, "What you don't see, and she can't see, is how she endangers you with her concern. If it is in fact true that the only seer in all of Shaftal is a Sainnite—and that the only person in Shaftal besides myself who is devoted to you has made herself his enemy—it will not be long before the seer begins to dream of you. If it has not happened already."

Karis, muddled by air logic, rather plaintively said, "I am not sure I understand you."

"He will know of you through thinking of her. Perhaps he will know more of you than she does—and certainly, she knows too much already."

"For all these months, Zanja has kept her counsel—"

"She will not *tell* the seer. She will not have to. It will come to him, that's all." Norina leapt to her feet and started pacing again. "We have to get her out of South Hill."

Karis said flatly, "She will not go. Not without an explanation."

"She will do whatever you ask her to do, Karis. Her obligation to you—"

"Her obligation to me is counterbalanced now by her obligation to her company, to her commander. They are in desperate straits. She will refuse to abandon them without a reason—a compelling reason."

Norina stopped in the middle of the room. "No," she said. "I will not tell her more, when with every breath I wish that she knew less."

"Well then, it seems there's nothing we can do but hope."

"Hope!" Norina spat it out, like a curse.

Karis, more present in that kitchen than she was in her own body, which, unattended, fought its daily battle to overcome the paralysis of smoke, could feel the closeness of sunrise. This conversation would soon end.

"You have to leave Meartown," Norina said.

"You know I will not."

"It won't take long for this seer to realize that when you're under smoke you'll walk up to him as trustingly as a newborn lamb. Your first obligation is to survive unharmed. Not just for the people of Meartown, but for the people of Shaftal."

Karis said nothing, which Norina would recognize as rebellion. Norina said, finally, "I'm going to write to Mabin. Perhaps she can do something."

Karis tried to remind Norina that Mabin hated her and probably wouldn't care if she were killed by the Sainnites, but the words came out garbled, and she realized that she had come back to her own skin, speaking inarticulate sounds with a mouth still paralyzed by smoke. A speckling of sunlight lay upon the eastward-facing windows, and she heard faintly the sound of Dominy stirring up the coals of the kitchen fire.

He came in with a pot of tea later, and found the garden doors flung open and Karis standing in the doorway, neither outside nor inside, pulling on the twisted locks of her hair as though they were ropes connected to thoughts, and her thoughts were drowning.

It would not be one of her good days.

Before the weary Paladins arrived at Midway Barn, where Emil's messengers anxiously awaited his reappearance, worrying shreds of news had already reached them: tales of farmsteads razed and entire families disappeared. Emil came out from his solitary hearing of the messengers' reports, looking drawn and gray with pain and exhaustion. Four highland farmsteads that had been steady providers of bread and supplies to South Hill Company had been burned to the ground; and of the farm families, even the children, no one remained, though no bodies had been found. Some hundred people in all had gone missing.

He delivered no inspirational speech, but left to closet himself with Linde, whom he had selected to replace Daye, along with Perry and Willis. Zanja sat among the others, a filthy, bloody, half-starved band of ruffians, and waited for her turn behind the healer's curtain. The smell of chicken stew cooking seemed about to drive them all insane, when the one-armed bread runner fortuitously arrived with the donkey, Zanja's old companion, heavily laden with great wheels of flat bread. Without butter or broth to dip it in, the bread was dry as sawdust, but they ate it gratefully. Slowly, Zanja began to hear a murmur of her companions' old stout-heartedness. She sat with them, and ate dry bread, and plotted revenge.

Later, after a chilly bath of water splashed from a stream, with her poorly laundered clothing drying in the hot breeze, and her bitten arm, blistered feet, and raw hands bandaged and salved, Zanja let herself enjoy the illusion of rest and comfort. She was asleep in a patch of sunshine when Emil woke her. His drawn face, dirty clothing, and even the staff on which he now leaned, reminded her how desperate their situation had become.

"That bite in your arm isn't festering, is it?" he asked.

"No, Emil."

"That's fortunate, I suppose. Jerrell tells me that the surviving Paladins are going to fall ill or succumb to one or another infection if they don't get some rest and a few decent meals in them."

"I ate some bread."

He responded with a flash of his old humor. "That's practically a feast. And you've slept, what, an hour or two? That should be more than enough."

"What do you want of me?"

"I want you to find Annis, but it can wait until tomorrow."

"You don't know where she is?" Zanja had thought of Annis in passing, but had been willing enough not to think of her too long. Her name had not been on the list of dead or injured, so she assumed there was no reason for concern.

"No one knows where she is. Her family, though, is one of the three that has disappeared. Her home is burned, they tell me. When she came in from her experiments, she would have heard all this. I am a bit concerned about what she might do."

Zanja got to her feet—stiffly enough, but apparently with enough grace to win her a glance of unabashed envy from Emil. This grueling journey had all but crippled him. "There are others who know her haunts better than I."

"None of them are fire bloods who have been her lover."

She muttered, "Nothing escapes you, does it?"

"By the land, I wish that were true!" He put a hand upon her shoulder. "Listen: you need a place to shelter out the winter. To partner with the daughter of an established farm family can only be to your benefit. But if it turns out you have to bring her to me at the end of a rope, do you think you could?"

"I'd rather not."

"If you had to?"

She said reluctantly, "Yes."

"Good." Emil added, rather bitterly, "But do hold onto what shreds of decency you can."

The next day, Zanja made her way to Annis's family farm. There, the black, burned-out walls of seven buildings gaped like the jaws of corpses. All around them spread lush fields of knee-high grain and white-blossomed potato plants. Zanja stood at the edge of an orchard, where a din of insects made the voices of the man and woman walking through the field seem very far away. Zanja had been watching them for some time. They had walked from building to building, looking in at the tangles of charred wood contained by each stone shell. Once, they ventured inside, but came out again quickly, coughing and wiping away tears. Now they walked meditatively through the fields, pausing sometimes to discuss something vehemently, with sweeping gestures that seemed to include the entire landscape.

As they drew close to the orchard, they spotted Zanja and stopped short in confusion. She stepped briskly out into the field, taking care to avoid trampling the seedlings, but stopped at a distance so they would not be too frightened of her, and bowed. "I am Zanja Paladin of South Hill Company, a friend of Annis's. You are her kinfolk, yes?"

The two of them clutched each other in dismay, but the woman said cautiously, "Everyone in South Hill is her kin."

They looked enough like Annis that it seemed certain all three of them had a parent in common, but then the South Hillers seemed peculiarly indifferent to ties of blood; what united them into families was the land alone. Now that Annis's family was gone, the land they had farmed was an orphan, an event as rare in South Hill as the orphaning of a child. This event presented the entire community with a problem: Who was now obligated or entitled to tend the crops? This must have been the problem this brother and sister had been pondering.

The man said, "South Hill Company should have no interests here. Where were you when the farm was burning?"

"We were chasing the enemy and burying the dead," Zanja said.

"I hear you were off on a hare-chase, tearing down Darton Bridge for no good reason when you should have been here."

The woman jerked his arm roughly, and he fell into sullen silence.

Zanja said, "Please, if you see Annis, would you tell her that I'm looking for her? I'm worried about her."

Both the farmers seemed startled at the suggestion that someone might actually care for their eccentric sister.

"I'd like to look at the buildings. Would you mind?"

The siblings did not respond. Zanja walked over to the remains of the commonhouse. Portions of the walls remained standing, though the roof had collapsed in a crazy tangle of charred timbers that filled the interior. Cradles had hung from those rafters. Now the acrid stink of destruction seared Zanja's lungs, and suddenly she couldn't breathe.

and pain ballooned in her skull as she stumbled through the fierce heat of the flames where people were trapped and screaming and she followed the rhythmic signal of a newborn's cry: the na'Tarwein infant she had last seen in a basket beside her sleeping mother. And the blazing fire swam in her vision, now close and now far, hot enough that it seemed her flesh must cook upon her bones, and she stumbled through smoke, walking on embers, following the sound

"Madam!"

and the infant's voice fell silent and as Zanja stumbled up to the na'Tarwein clanhouse the roof collapsed and the roar and pressure of flames drove her away, wheezing and reeling in a daze of pain and horror

"Madam Paladin!"

The farmer spoke with sharp impatience, but when Zanja turned her face, she stepped hastily backwards. Zanja put a hand to her face and found it wet, not with blood from her head wound or a dead Sainnite, but with tears. "Some of them burned alive," she said.

The woman took another startled step backwards. "But we have not found any bodies."

"In my own family." Zanja rubbed the side of her head, where the rough terrain of a scar crossed her scalp. Until this moment, she had forgotten that, bleeding, dazed, scarcely even conscious, she had walked through the burning village hoping and failing to save just one life from the disaster, a single child.

"Your family?" The farmer said. "Are you from Rees?"

"I'm from the northern borderlands. We have Sainnites there, too." Zanja dried her face with a corner of her headcloth. "What are you and your brother going to do?"

"Well, as for me, I can't endure to see this good crop go to waste. But my brother wants to cry for justice at the gates of the garrison."

"Justice? Does he think this crime was done by a civilized people?"

The brother said angrily, "The Paladins are much too busy to occupy themselves with something so trivial as justice. So there is no law left in South Hill, except the law of the Sainnites."

"Law? You are at war!"

Zanja parted from the farmers with cold civility, and traveled through the woods towards the powder cave. Her anger at the man's stupidity burned itself out, and ashes remained: a fire-gutted village, a corpse-scattered, charred cornfield, the coarse laughter of the Sainnite butchers halfway across the valley. Zanja, weaving through the mists, falling over the bodies of her friends, seeking Ransel among the dead, so that she could lie down beside him, and cut loose her soul from its bindings.

The Ashawala'i also had never realized they were at war.

Chapter Fourteen

At least one keg of gunpowder was missing from the powder cave. Zanja waited there until a summer downpour had lightened to a mist, then she traveled east in dead of night and slipped into the river valley under cover of darkness. She lay in a copse until dawn. Every time she closed her eyes, pain blossomed in her healed skull, her heart began to pound, and she saw flames.

With her weapons and gear tied in a bundle on her shoulder, Zanja joined a group of farmers headed for Wilton Market. They tolerated her presence as a herd of horses tolerates a donkey in their midst.

In Wilton, Sainnite soldiers lounged in the sun like lizards on rocks. Zanja concealed her alien face behind the bundle on her shoulder. The tide carried her into and out of a crush of market stalls, where baskets of beans in a dozen different colors, and round, flat, and finger-shaped potatoes crowded up against caged chickens, squalling babies, vendors of steamed dumplings and roast nuts and honey candy, and the occasional seller of fine goods: silken scarves and ribbons, handmade lace, silver jewelry. A couple of Sainnite officers rode down the crowded street on their jumpy war horses, and Zanja found herself crushed up against one of these rickety stalls, along with a man carrying a basket of mewing kittens and a woman with a sack of potatoes. Unable to move, close enough to the stall's baubles that she could have stolen one in her mouth if she had wanted, she had no choice but to examine them closely, while the stall man shored up the fragile structure by bracing it with his own body. The Sainnites passed and the pressure eased, but before Zanja moved on she bought one of the baubles, a simple pendant like a miniature plumb bob made of deep green stone. What would Emil think of how she was spending the money he'd given her? The thought sank like a rock into still water. She moved on until she saw a sign depicting a flame rising out of stone.

Transformation, of course, is the business of chemists, but the flame-and-stone also was a traditional call to revolution. Nevertheless, no one except her stood in the street outside the chemist's shop, mesmerized by the audacity of the weather-worn sign. Someone bumped into her and snapped at her for blocking the way. She stepped into the dim shop, and bowed briefly to the chemist, the shop's only occupant, who used a pestle to grind a mess of odd ingredients into a fine powder. A thin, vigorous woman with her gray hair braided and tied with a red ribbon, the chemist nodded but didn't leave off her work until the grinding was completed. Then she came over to the counter, wiping her hands upon her apron.

"Yes," she said, "do you have a receipt for me to fill?"

"There's nothing wrong with me."

"Good, then. I hate to see healthy people dose themselves. So you need a potion for someone else?"

"For a friend. She needs something to calm her heart. She's wild with grief, and it's making her ill."

The chemist tutted absently. "Lost a child?"

"Her whole family is gone. The Sainnites burned her farm. Haven't you heard about it? Her name is Annis."

The chemist seemed to hesitate just a moment, then she shrugged. "That's country news," she said dismissively. "So, she's maddened by grief and you want to . . . what? Make her sane again? Make her family come back? What?"

"I want to give her some peace so she can think," Zanja said. "I'm afraid she'll do something foolish. Is there some drug that will make her talk to me?"

The chemist wrote a few glyphs in chalk on a piece of slate. "I'll have it done tonight. Where should I send it?"

Zanja named an inn she had noticed just a few streets over. The chemist jotted down the inn's glyphs on her slate. Perhaps she had studied in a Lilterwess school, and might even have been a healer once. A lot of the old healers were chemists now, according to J'han, and practiced their art on the sly.

"And your name?" said the chemist.

Zanja took the slate from her and drew upon it the Snake glyph, for betrayal, and crossed it out, then wrote out her name, and gave the slate back to the chemist, who accepted it without a word.

She used what remained of her funds to bespeak a private room at the inn. The room overlooked the street, which became only more crowded after sunset. Perhaps it was a holiday, or perhaps the giddy laughter and music on the street below was a symptom of something else: a relentless tide, a surge of rage threatening to break through. Zanja sat in the window and felt her own tide surging. She drank water; the people below drank ale.

There was a tap on the door. "Chemist's delivery."

Zanja opened the door and let Annis in. "It's good to see you. Have you eaten? I can have supper sent up for you."

"I ate." Annis seemed perplexed and even peeved that Zanja had not been more surprised to see her. She paced the room agitatedly. "How did you find me? You can just tell Emil to leave me alone."

Zanja sat in the window again, leaving Annis an unimpeded route to the door, if she decided to take flight. She had no intention of bringing her back to Emil against her will. When she had decided this she could not remember. "I found you by luck and good sense, and Emil has no idea where you are. Tell me what you're up to," she said.

"It's none of your business."

"Then why did you come here to see me? You didn't have to."

Annis glared at her. "Why did *you* come here?"

"I thought you might want some help."

Annis stopped dead in the middle of the room.

Zanja said, "You searched for your family's bodies, didn't you? Like I did."

"They're alive, as far as I know. I suppose the Sainnites figured I'd come begging for their lives, offer myself in their place, tell everything I know about South Hill Company." Annis spat in the general direction of the garrison. "Bunch of idiots."

"On the other hand, you can hardly hope to rescue them."

"I don't even know where they are." For a moment, she looked exhausted. "But even if I could rescue them, my home would still be gone. I have nowhere to go, nowhere to rest."

She began pacing the room. "The Sainnites build with wood, did you know that? Even though everyone knows how dangerous it is to build with wood in a city. Stone is too cold and damp for them."

"My people built with wood also," Zanja said. "And the Sainnites burned the entire village to the ground." They looked at each other. "Tomorrow is the dark moon," Zanja added. "And it's about time the Sainnites lost a village of their own."

Annis suddenly calmed, and sat on the bed. "Emil won't have his people acting on their own. He might put us out of the company."

Zanja looked bleakly down upon the crowded street of a community that would never be hers. "He and I are fighting different wars."

Annis rubbed her hands together gleefully. "You won't believe what I've got to show you. It's made of paper, like a kite, but it flies like an arrow. It's got a fuse up the middle and in the very tip a cargo that explodes."

Zanja said, "That sounds rather startling."

"Startling? It'll scare the Sainnites half to death. Come on, we've got some work to do, and then we'll have some fun."

Zanja stood up. The room moved around her. Her head filled with an appalling pain. Ransel came out of the mist, and put his arms around her. "I knew you would survive," he said. "Now we shall have vengeance."

Any wall can be breached, but Zanja had never imagined that it would be so easy to break into the Sainnite garrison. They did it with a spindly ladder that they had cobbled together in the basement of the chemist's shop. It was a dark night; even starlight was veiled by thin clouds. No one noticed them carrying their ladder through the streets of Wilton. No one cried a warning as they climbed the ladder to the top of the wall, dragged it up, and dropped it to the other side so they could climb down. The wall was nice and wide; it made it easier to maneuver their awkward burdens.

Even as Zanja worked with Annis in the secret factory in the chemist's basement, she had not really expected that they'd get this far. Surely the Sainnite seer would anticipate that they would arrive, reeking of gunpowder and other less common concoctions, bearing their bags full of brightly colored lethal gifts: packages of fused gunpowder, odd constructions of sticks and paper that Annis swore would fly. But it seemed the Sainnites were not expecting them. Perhaps even a seer could not predict something so unpredictable as this night.

She and Annis tucked their ladder into a shadow. The only light came from the smoldering cords they carried at their waists, which Annis called slow lucifers. The lucifers glowed very faintly, like coals in ashes. A pair of Sainnites scuffed past along the wall, talking amiably in a low murmur. One of them carried a lantern, but its light didn't travel far. Zanja and Annis hid the faint light of the lucifers behind their cupped hands.

They had entered an ornamental garden that was rank with the perfume of night-blooming vines. White moon flowers glowed in the shadows, and delicately formed trees drooped across the walkways like lace curtains. They crossed the garden cautiously. Its wooden fence was merely ornamental. They climbed it easily and followed a cobbled walkway between buildings, out into the main yard. Here sprawled the stables and the carriage houses on one side and the barracks on the other, with the headquarters between, facing the gate. The architecture was strange. The rooflines were curved, parts of the buildings jumped forward like arms or wings, and beads of wood dripped from the eaves.

Most of the barracks windows were propped open to let in the night breeze. Annis showed her teeth again, and gestured silently toward the stable. Briefly, her hand was warm in Zanja's, and then they separated. Zanja set out to find a way to the stables. Since all the passageways radiated out from this courtyard, it took some time for her to negotiate the maze. Finally, huddled against the stable wall, she noticed for the first time that there was a guard at the stable door. However, many of the stall windows were propped open. They were too small to climb through, but when Zanja looked in she could see that the stall walls were only shoulder high, which suited her purposes.

She went as close to the edge of the courtyard as she dared, and signaled with the smoldering tip of her lucifer. She could not see Annis at all in the shadows, but in a moment her lucifer appeared as well, drawing the shape of a flame in the darkness. The flame: transformation, revolution. The collapsing poles of the clanhouses, the burned out shell of the farmhouses. Fire for fire.

Zanja started unpacking her bag of flying explosives, and balanced one on the ledge of each open stall window. She held the tip of the lucifer to each fuse and blew on it to make the smoldering red tip flame and catch the fuse. It was rhythmic, meditative work, easy to do even in the darkness. The horses grew restive as she worked her way around the stable. She used some rockets with medium length fuses, and had switched to short fuses when she heard the harsh hiss of the first rocket. Then she saw it fly in a hissing spray of sparks across the inside of the stable, the horses braying with terror at its fiery passage, and then the rocket exploded with a bang and a blinding flash of light. The horses screamed. Shod heels crashed against the wooden walls. Zanja lit the last fuse and started running, though the crazy woman in her head wanted to stay and watch the rockets soar, trailing fire and a glowing white smoke, carrying their explosive cargo to the many things that are all too ready to burn in a stable: hay, for instance. There would be plenty of hay.

She could hear explosions now from the barracks as well, and shrill shouts. Overhead, a balcony door banged open, and a woman rushed out, cursing as she pulled on her shirt. Zanja paused directly beneath her to light one of her packages and toss it through a street-level window into the upholstered cushion of a chair. The package was a lightweight thing, made of little more than paper and gunpowder, with a little bottle of liquid fire at its center, but the sharp report of its explosion echoed down the narrow passageway, and it was followed by a blinding white flame. The night stank of gunpowder, and was filled with shouts and the banging of doors.

Zanja hid in the shadows of a side door until it looked as if all the building's occupants had rushed out to fight the fire, then she went in, pistols in hand. The building was dark and quiet, the stairs easy to find. But as she started up them, a man suddenly came rushing down, and fell into her when she shot him. She managed to catch herself on the handrail and the soldier fell all the way down the stairs.

Zanja stopped in his bedroom, where the bedding was thrown to the floor. She pried a board from the bed, tucked it under her arm, and went out onto the balcony. The drooping roofline was an easy climb from the balcony rail, but after she had put all her burdens onto the roof she went back to set off an explosion in the middle of the straw mattress. The floors were covered with straw mats, as well. No wonder almost every room had a fire bucket filled with water by the door.

The rooflines, which protected the passageways between buildings against weather, seemed almost designed to allow a fugitive to escape across the rooftops. Only occasionally did Zanja have to use her board to cross the gap; usually it was a mere step. She paused at nearly every building to climb in through a window and set off fire bombs in the beds, now that every soul in the garrison seemed to be out on the streets.

From the rooftops she could see the barracks on one side and the stable on the other, fully engulfed in flame. No bucket brigade or even a water engine could have put out those fires; the Sainnites would be devoting their energies to keeping the fire from spreading. As Zanja stood watching, she saw the glowing passage of a rocket shoot across the rooftops. She set one off herself, in reply. It skittered up the slope of the roof and shot into the air, where it exploded in a shower of fire. Almost immediately, Annis replied with another, like a star with wings. "Beautiful!" Zanja cried out loud.

The next time she paused in her aerial journey, she noticed that her backtrail was marked by flames. Some scattered buildings far from her trail also were burning, perhaps set on fire by the burning gobbets that dripped from the rocket. Zanja set off a couple more rockets, but then stopped, fearful that they'd give away her location. Annis set one off as well; she was only a couple of buildings away now.

Zanja climbed off the roof to another balcony, which overlooked the garden. The garden below lay serenely empty; no one patrolled the walls. She could hardly believe her fortune, but clearly the first concern of the Sainnites was to fight the fires. Grinning, she stepped through the balcony door, into the room beyond.

"Stop right there," a man's voice said quietly. "I've got a pistol pointing right at you."

Zanja stopped. Her thoughts were strangely quiet; her heart scarcely even jumped in her throat.

The man was a pale form on the other side of the room. He was breathless with fear or exertion—exertion, she decided, for his voice seemed calm. "I really don't want to shoot you," he said. Strangely, he spoke fluent, unaccented Shaftalese.

"Then don't," Zanja said.

"Just promise not to set my house on fire," he said.

Zanja was poised to duck his bullet and leap out the window. This, though, she had not anticipated.

"I have books," he said. "An ancient, priceless collection. Shaftali books. Irreplaceable books. No civilized person would choose to see them burn."

Zanja said stupidly, "But the house next door is already burning."

"I just need time to get the rest of the books out into the garden, where they'll be safe."

"My war is not against books."

"Well then, I am not your enemy." She heard the sound of him setting down his pistol onto a tabletop. "There's a lamp just to your right," the man said. As she groped in the darkness and lit the lamp with her lucifer, he said, "I've been watching your progress for a while. You are having quite a frolic. I hoped I might get a chance to meet you."

The flame revealed a man remarkably young, dressed in a nightgown. Spectacles glinted in the light. Without the uniform, he looked no more like a Sainnite than she did. "I'm Medric," he said. "I don't know your name, but I know that you are trapped in the past. Would you like to sit down?" He sat in a chair. The lamp illuminated walls lined with nearly empty bookshelves, and a small chest stood half full on the floor. Even with the fire coming at him, Medric had not packed his books sloppily, but had methodically fit them into the chest as though he were solving a puzzle.

Zanja said, "You wanted to meet me?"

"In my dream you were an owl with feathers of fire. You flew back and forth over the rooftops, dripping flames onto the houses. They caught like tinder behind you. Are you truly a seeker after wisdom?"

The garrison was burning in the glass of his spectacles. He had known it would burn, and had not warned his people. The Sainnite seer now sat with his elbows on his knees and his hands clasped. He did not move as Zanja drew a pistol. "The past makes us what we are," he said, "but the present makes us what we will be. If you shoot me, I will have a kind of peace that part of me wishes to embrace, and you will spend what remains of your life—and it will not be long, I'm afraid—refusing to read the glyphs of possibility. If you do not shoot me, however, anything can happen."

Zanja sat down in a chair. She did not holster her pistol; neither did she point it at him. "You let me burn down the garrison."

"It was the only way I could get you here. I need to ask your advice."

"Advice?" Zanja lay back in the chair and laughed like a madwoman, and could hardly make herself stop. When she had gotten herself under control, she wiped her face with her hands, and found them wet with tears. "Well, why shouldn't a lunatic give advice to a seer?"

"My vision has been too small," he said. "And now I think I have begun to see at last, I see most clearly my own corruption. How can I redeem myself?"

"Redeem yourself? In whose eyes?"

He gazed at her, his face flickering with flame. "In the eyes of my mother's people. In the eyes of Shaftal."

"Your mother is Shaftali?"

"My mother was Shaftali, and my father was Sainnite. Somehow I must come to peace with myself, and how can I do that so long as this land is at war?"

A breeze came through the open windows and the air was thick with smoke. Still, Zanja sat contemplating a glyph she could not read. Was this danger? Or was it opportunity?

It was danger for certain if she delayed much longer, and this young man's books would be nothing but ashes if he didn't get back to work. "I can't answer your questions," she said.

"Not right now, perhaps." He stood up. His long, fair hair was caught back with a blue ribbon. He pushed his spectacles up to the bridge of his nose. "There's a grove of trees just north of the city. I'll be waiting for you there in, oh, five days, at high noon. If you decide to send an assassin instead, I'll know. Still, I'll be there, and I won't hold it against you. You must make your decisions just as I must make mine."

"You know perfectly well that I won't send an assassin."

"In five days you might come to your senses."

Zanja had gotten dazedly to her feet and picked up the satchel of explosives. Annis was waiting in the garden, and surely would not wait much longer. When the seer held out his hand she clasped it and then wondered why she hadn't even hesitated. "Won't you tell me your name?" he said.

"Zanja."

He smiled again, less tentatively this time. "Zanja, I dreamed that we were friends."

"That would be some other world you dreamed of."

"Yes. But you are the one who travels between the worlds, are you not?"

He was not much taller than she, and when she found herself caught within his gaze, it meant neither capture nor dominance, but a stare between befuddled equals. At last Zanja spoke, and not exactly to him: "The gods have quite a sense of humor." So she left him, and went down the stairs and out into the garden, where the air was choked with ashes and the brays of terrified horses and the raw shouts of voices scoured by smoke. But now she could not remember exactly what she was doing here, or even who she was or why she had wanted to burn down the garrison. She had crossed a border. And now she was lost.

She found Annis pacing the garden. She was exalted with fire, and once she began talking could not stop until Zanja shook her sharply by the shoulder. They climbed the wall, and this time left the ladder rather than carry it home, but they had to make their way without being noticed through a roused city. The balconies were crowded with onlookers fascinated with watching the fires or fretful with the possibility that the fires might spread beyond the garrison. They passed below, unmarked, and avoided all contact with anyone, lest the smell of smoke and gunpowder that suffused their clothing betray them. By dawn, they were far outside the city, having buried the remains of their explosives, and having bathed with soap and washed their clothing as well. At sunrise they stood on a hilltop on the north end of the river valley. A pall of smoke lay over Wilton, and Sainnite soldiers moved like locusts across the lush farmland of the river valley.

"Emil will kill us for this night's work," Annis said placidly. "But not until he hears how we did it, so he can get the word to other companies. And actually, since I'm the only one who knows how to make those rockets, I guess he'll have to let me live. You're the one who's going to be in trouble."

"Yes, I am in trouble."

They had neither food nor drink, except for water dipped out of a stream and a couple of handfuls of watercress. Annis was still eating her watercress one leaf at a time, and wrinkling her nose at the peppery taste. Zanja could not remember tasting hers.

"I have an idea," Annis said suddenly. "We'll lie."

Zanja put her head in her hands. "Of course." Annis never even noticed that she was laughing bitterly to herself. "Why not?" she said. "What have I got to lose?"

It took more than a day for them to find South Hill Company, encamped at the Fens Overlook, a rise of land on the northern tip of the river plain, that was protected from armed incursion by a marsh on one side and a particularly tangled woodland on the other. The company was too far from Wilton to have seen the rockets explode, but not too far to see the smoke that still lay in a haze across the river valley. Emil, having already received a report from his spies in Wilton of the garrison fire and the wonderful explosions that preceded it, was in a quiet fury. His spies had told him it was wizardry, but Emil had not doubted that it was Annis. He did not question Zanja's explanation that she had been seeking Annis in Wilton when the explosions at the garrison brought her to the garrison wall, when she had intercepted Annis during her escape.

Normally, Emil was not one to vent his anger in public, but he berated Annis before the entire company, a disgrace she endured with rare dignity, perhaps because she could not help but recognize that it was not contempt that made the rest of the company stare at her so, but awe. When Emil had finished chastising her for taking matters into her own hands, the company members welcomed her with suppressed glee. Emil turned his back on the lot of them and stalked away.

Zanja could not sleep, though she was so tired her thoughts kept blanking out, like candles snuffed in a gale. She wandered restlessly until she found herself at the very edge of the fen, which bubbled and stank in the afternoon heat, while a flock of geese uttered shouts of outrage at an outsider that had intruded on their peaceful foraging.

Zanja spread her glyph cards out and stared at them. The Woman in the Doorway: unmade decisions or ambivalence or even lack of courage left her standing there upon the doorsill. Paired with the Raven, it was Karis. Paired with the Owl, it was Zanja. The Man on the Mountain: solitude, contemplation, far-seeing. By itself, it was Emil, Zanja's commander and friend. Joined with the Box and the Flame, it was Medric: dreamer, destroyer, bespectacled book-hauling boy with a blue ribbon in his hair. Zanja realized vaguely that she had a headache. The cards swam before her vision as if they were swirling in a whirlpool. She could not see the pattern; pieces of it were missing. She shuffled frantically through the deck, tossing down cards at random: Sorrow, the Book, the Sword, the Guardian, the Cave, the Lover, and at last the Madwoman.

She turned to find Ransel sitting on his heels beside her. His goat's wool tunic was ragged and bloodstained; the woven pattern that marked him as a na'Tarwein was obscured by dirt. Upon his back he carried three different bows, and a half dozen quivers of arrows. Just as he had been when he died, he was thin from hard travel, hollow-eyed with hunger, anger, and sorrow.

He gestured a hand toward the mess of cards. "What does it mean?"

"A Sainnite has asked me to be his friend. Now nothing makes sense."

Astonished, Ransel leaned towards her. "Why are you listening to the words of a Sainnite?"

"Because he reminds me of you, my brother."

"Am I to be glad of this? Shall I say, 'Oh praise the gods—my sister will betray our people for memory of me'?"

"How can I betray a people who are all dead?"

"We watch you," he said. "In the Land of the Dead, we wait for vengeance. When we saw you take the hand of the enemy, we cried out in dismay."

"You are dead," she said softly. "To you it must seem simple."

"Do you remember how our people were betrayed? It was a Sainnite, who came into our territory. Tarin na'Tarwein called the enemy his friend, and revealed to him all our secrets. Will you not learn from our clan brother's mistakes?"

Zanja could think of no reply. She looked away from him, and when she turned back, Ransel had disappeared. In his place sat Salos'a, with a mouse clasped in her claw. "The madwoman in the middle," said Salos'a, "does she think she can hold all these powers in a circle around her? Does she not know that each one pulling her in a separate direction will tear her apart?"

"The madwoman in the middle is too bewildered to think," said Zanja. "No matter what she chooses, something is betrayed."

"Then choose to cross the boundary. That way, you will not betray yourself."

Salos'a spread her gray wings and the cards lifted up and swirled in the air, and Zanja realized that she had not understood the pattern before because it had been static. She had not realized that it was only through movement, through an endless alignment and realignment, a pattern that was never stable but always changing, that the glyph pattern had meaning. Only by seeing it in motion could it be understood.

When Zanja truly woke up, the sun was just setting, the cards lay in the dirt, and whatever she had understood about their pattern in the course of her vision had been lost as she crossed the border from vision to wakefulness. Once again, she understood nothing.

Chapter Fifteen

That same afternoon, while Zanja was sleeping beside her scattered cards, the volunteers began to arrive. They came because the burning of the garrison had excited their imaginations: young, vigorous men and women whose labor would be sorely missed on their home farms. Some had been sent by their families, but most had simply come of their own desire, convinced that this was the beginning of the end, and the Sainnites would soon be entirely evicted from South Hill.

Emil, preoccupied with the hasty decisions that had to be made, noticed Zanja only in the way he noticed all the members of his company, as a presence or an absence, as one preoccupied with accomplishing a worthy task, or as one currently available for such a task. Zanja looked haggard, and he remembered to ask Jerrell to check on her. Linde had suggested that Zanja be given the task of teaching bladework to the hot-headed young farmers, few of whom actually owned any fighting weapons. The farmers under her tutelage were much cowed, he reported later, and some complained bitterly after two days of drills, that farming was easier work than what they were being subjected to. A few of them went back to their farms, and the rest of them were learning how to fight: nothing fancy, Linde added, but the kind of things that might enable them to survive a fight long enough to get out of it.

Two more days passed, and Emil began to feel like a shipping merchant. Wagonloads of arms and other supplies had mysteriously begun to arrive, more than the company could use or store. He made plans to again divide the company into units, each with a separate supply line. He slept little, and had to devise charts in order to keep track of things.

Meanwhile, couriers reported that the Sainnites seemed gripped by an odd aimlessness, and that the people of Wilton had gotten together a committee to protest some of the punishments that had been visited on them in retaliation for Fire Night. Buried in a welter of detail, Emil began to feel harried. At the same time, he found he had become too tired and preoccupied to think much about strategy.

When he saw Zanja again, she was walking through the camp with three or four of the new company members trailing behind her admiringly. Annis, who seemed to be thriving on the attention showered on her since Fire Night, was talking excitedly as she walked beside her, making broad, sweeping gestures as if she were about to fly like a bird. By contrast, Zanja seemed still as a cat, remote, almost uninterested. She still looked haggard.

Emil jammed his papers heedlessly into his lap desk and set out after her. Her trail of followers dropped away when they saw him coming, and then Annis abruptly ended the conversation and ducked away. He could hardly blame her for deciding to avoid him. Zanja turned to him, and for a moment there was something disturbing in her face, something too vague and fleeting to name. Her foreign manners took over and she bowed stiffly. "Commander."

"Don't do that. Soon the whole camp will be bowing and sir-ing me and I won't be able to endure it. Come and have some tea with me."

She followed him silently to the fire, and silently watched as he fussed over the teapot, and silently sipped from the delicate cup balanced between her fingers, and silently accepted more tea. The camp turned around them like a wheel rolling down a road, but here at the camp's center all was still. Emil waited for her to tell him what was wrong; she had retreated beyond his reading.

She spoke at last, when he had served her a third cup of tea. "Soon it will be midsummer."

He nodded. "We have accomplished little this season, and lost much." He considered again what she had said. "And soon a year will have passed since your tribe was destroyed."

Emil followed the direction of her gaze. She was staring into the few flames that flickered red in the hot ashes of the cookfire.

He was tempted suddenly to douse them. Much had burned lately in South Hill: farmsteads, the garrison, and too many funeral pyres. When Emil thought about it too long he too would despair, as though he saw the whole of South Hill and even all of Shaftal in ashes.

When he looked up, Zanja was holding out the teacup. He took it from her and absently packed it away.

"Emil, with your permission I'd like to spend the day by myself tomorrow."

He felt an overwhelming envy. "Of course. For what, may I ask?"

"I'm trapped in the past and must cross over into the future. The gods demand it of me."

Emil rubbed his face, feeling harassed again. So quickly did his peace fray away lately. "When you know how to get there, take me across with you," he said.

She looked bleakly amused, as though he had asked, like a naive child, for something no one in their right mind would want. She took her leave without replying.

Zanja arrived early at the grove, and hid herself in the bushes to wait. Medric also arrived early, carrying a basket in one hand and a book under his arm. He looked like a Sainnite today, in leather riding breeches and a shirt of bleached linen, though he wore no cuirass and carried no weapons that Zanja could see. His hair lay loose upon his shoulders and kept falling into his eyes as he studied the book in his lap. Before he started to read, he exchanged his spectacles for a second pair that he kept in a pouch around his neck. When Zanja at last decided to come out of hiding and approach him, he peered at her over the top of his lenses. "Zanja, is that you?" Considering that he was a seer, he could not see very well.

She squatted beside him, and he gave a start when she felt the front of his shirt, but he did not pull away from her. His boots concealed no blade; even the basket contained only food. Zanja said, "How were you going to cut the cheese without a knife?"

Medric shrugged, in the middle of exchanging spectacles again, with one pair in each hand. "You have one, don't you? The Way of the Seer forbids me to eat cheese—I brought it for you."

He put on the other spectacles and smiled suddenly, as though she had only just arrived. "But you're no longer a fey creature bristling with marvelous rockets. So daylight pares away the night's illusions, eh? You decided not to kill me, I hope, during all that time you were studying me from those bushes over there."

Zanja drew one of her pistols and showed him that it was not loaded.

"Then what were you watching me for?"

"To make certain you were alone. And when it became apparent that you were, I began to wonder why your people might allow you to go forth unescorted. Surely you are valuable to them."

"They wouldn't allow me to do it, I'm sure, had I asked anyone for permission. You're older than I thought you were."

"My years feel very heavy lately. You look like a little boy to me."

"I'm almost twenty," he said, sounding as young as he looked. "My years feel heavy also."

To bear a seer's burden alone could rapidly turn a boy into an old man. Certainly, though Medric's face was young, his eyes were old. "In *this* world," he said, "this world in which it is possible for us to be friends, perhaps you might share a meal with me. When we go out of this place, what we do here need not matter any more."

"You *are* young if you still can believe that. Whether I eat with you or not, it will change nothing. So I say we might as well eat."

Besides bread and fruit, the basket also contained cheese and butter and sweetmeats. Medric tasted all of these things, as if to show Zanja that they were not poisoned, but then he ate only bread and fruit: the brown bread, not the white. Where he had gotten fresh fruit so early in the season Zanja could not imagine, and she had never seen anything quite like this fruit. He called them grapes, and said that they had just arrived by wagon from the south, where summer came early. They grew on vines, and, unlike most tree fruits, could travel long distances without bruising.

"We use it to make wine, and everybody complains that it's not half as good as the wine from the old country. I used to drink a great deal of it." Medric offered Zanja the bottle in his hand, which contained not wine, but spring water flavored with mint.

"But spirits are anathema to seers," she said.

"So I learned." Medric looked, for a moment, rather haunted. "I seem destined to learn to survive by nearly killing myself first." Indeed, Zanja thought, he must have come desperately close to being claimed by the madness which always is the dark shadow of insight, and that madness still seemed terribly near to him, as though he could reach out at any time and put it on like a hat.

"A seer should have a mentor," she said, as though he were a young man of her clan who had come to her for advice.

"The Sainnite community treats elemental blood like a contamination, not a thing to be nurtured. When it became clear that I might be useful to my people after all, they found me a Shaftali tutor, and then had to kill him within the year for spying. I rather think he encouraged me to become a drunk, and who could blame him? But if he had helped me instead, and if I hadn't spent all last summer in a drunken stupor, perhaps I would have come to my senses before all those people in Rees had been killed. No, I had no mentor," he added bitterly. "Even now, all I have is this, and I haven't had it long." He tapped the book, which lay beside him upon its cloth wrapping. Zanja was curious enough to spell out the title, *The Way of the Seer*. The book looked as though it had been read to pieces.

Zanja ate more of the sweet grapes. For sanity's sake Medric had embraced asceticism, but for her it was only deprivation, which was to be endured like grief and solitude and tedious hard work. Right now, there was food to be enjoyed, and she enjoyed it. For all she knew, she might have only bread and water tomorrow.

Medric smelled strongly of smoke, and she wondered how the Sainnites were enjoying living in ashes. "Did your people blame you for failing to predict Fire Night?"

"Of course they did. What good am I to them if I can't avert disaster?" His young face looked as old and tired as Emil's did lately. "I fear they will never see that they brought disaster upon themselves." With his chin resting in his hands, he gazed across the lush farmlands of the valley. "Only recently, I realized it myself. Everything I have done that my people admire me for—or at least that they don't vilify me for—has been wrong. I am a boy, misusing my talent to prove my worth to the people who will never accept me. To be a seer, the way I have to follow is a difficult one: difficult and terrible."

He hesitated, with his head bowed over his hands. "I have dreamed of you, Zanja, and of the Man on the Hill, your commander, many times. You have a kinship with him, a kinship I first recognized as a danger, for together you constitute a formidable enemy. Together, you do much with little. Alone, I do little with much. So my admiration, I confess, is fraught with envy. I am asking you to give me an entrance to his trust. He is the way by which I might leave my father's people and serve my mother's instead. You are the way by which I might reach him."

Zanja said, a long time later, "First you must find an entrance to my trust."

"Yes," he said. The single word seemed heavy, an acknowledgment, an acceptance, the marking of an irrevocable step already taken. But then, strangely, he began to tell her a story.

"When my father's people, whom you call Sainnites, first arrived on the shores of Shaftal over thirty years ago, they were the vanguard of an influx of refugees. My father was my age then, and from childhood I have heard him talk of the lands left behind, and the battles he fought there, like his father before him. In Sainna and the surrounding countries, people were born into castes, and my father's people were the Carolins, a caste of soldiers. They were mercenaries, really, living in bands or armies rather like your tribes, except that they might be hired by one warlord or another, and they would fight against another band of Carolins like themselves. This was how they had lived, for time beyond memory. Though the old people remember those times fondly, it seems as though they were a poor and even desperate people, especially during times of peace when they had little choice except to turn brigand.

"Well, I don't really understand the entire story, because the Carolins themselves never wholly understood it—it was their business to do as ordered, not to understand. Apparently, Sainna and all its neighboring countries went to war with each other, a war that lasted many long years, in which thousands of Carolins died on both side. It seems as though it was the nature of this kind of war that it was ultimately a war of resources: How long could the warlords afford to field their armies before the resources ran out? As it happens, Sainna began to lose, and it became apparent that all the Carolins of Sainna would be executed without mercy. So the Carolins began casting about for a place to flee, and their only choice really was to set to sea. They bought, borrowed, or stole ships and over a period of some five years many thousands made their way here to Shaftal, though thousands of others died and continued to die in the last years of the war.

"My father was among the earliest to arrive, and the people of his band found ways to make themselves welcome in a small seaside community. Others, though, were met with hostility and fell into their old habits of thievery and brigandry, which brought the Paladins upon them. The Carolins did not know about Shaftali winters, and a good many of them died because they entered the season unprepared. Tradition and ignorance made it impossible for them to farm; they got no help from the people of the coast who rapidly grew intolerant of them, and I'm sure there were good reasons for it.

"In some places they turned to old methods of slavery, which is why the drug the Shaftali call 'smoke' first arrived here. Enslaving the farmers was a failure, for farming is far more complex and difficult to learn than we ever imagined it to be, and once the smoke killed the knowledgeable and experienced farmers, we were worse off than we had been. Perhaps some ten years had passed by then, and at last the Carolins realized that they were not going to survive except by making war upon Shaftal, and so it happened that we became what we are today: we ourselves are warlords now, and I have to say that the whole history of the Carolin relations with Shaftal has been characterized by a kind of ignorant incompetence brought about by our inability to break with the past. We can only do what we have always done, even though it is destroying Shaftal and ourselves along with it."

He stopped to sip some spring water. Because he seemed to expect that Zanja would make some comment she said, with genuine astonishment, "Although I have fallen in with learned friends, not one of them knows this history. And you talk about ignorance on the part of the Sainnites!"

"Well, here is an example of it. The Carolins teach their children that the Shaftali are better off because of us—that we've released them from servitude to the Lilterwess magicians, and that most of the Shaftali secretly love us for it. At the very least, it is argued, the Shaftali have exchanged one bondage for another, which surely is no more onerous. They have no idea that the Shaftali were never subject to the Lilterwess, but that all of them were subject to the law. They can't imagine that Shaftal had no lords. It doesn't help that the Shaftali and the Carolins speak different languages," Medric continued. "Even my parents could barely communicate with each other."

Zanja rummaged in the basket, but she had eaten all the grapes and she didn't like the sweetmeats. She cut herself another piece of cheese, thinking about how much more likely it seemed that Emil might accept Medric, not because of everything he had told Zanja but because he clearly was, or should be, a scholar.

The silence had lasted quite some time. She glanced at Medric, and found him staring blankly over the top of his spectacles. She did not disturb him from whatever vision he was having, but in a moment he shook himself out of his reverie and murmured in his father's language, "Almost I can see it—an ordinary winter day, writing my book by the fire—except that it's in a Shaftali cottage and the windows open into vast spaces." He sighed.

"What are you saying?" Zanja asked, so he would not know that she understood Sainnese.

"I'm sorry, I was talking to myself."

"Your mother must have had fire blood, didn't she? Did she fall in love as fire bloods do, for no good reason, and pay a high price for it?"

Medric said quietly, "Well, she always said there was a reason, a good reason that she herself could not explain, but I always had the feeling it had something to do with me. Certainly, if ever a fire blood felt herself driven by a sense of destiny and obligation to a future she could not wholly envision, that person was my mother. You're a bit like her, I think, else why would you be here?" He smiled his tentative smile, like a man too accustomed to receiving a hostile reception. "You know the old saying, fire bloods are the hinges of history."

Zanja did not know the old saying, but she replied with odd bitterness. "You will not lay your mother's project upon me, Medric. You must open and close your own doors."

"I know."

After a moment, Zanja picked up his battered book and leafed through it. The book surely had been through the war before it ever made its way to the hands of a man who could actually read and use it. Much of it seemed to be philosophy, but it also contained whole chapters of practical advice on how to live. One phrase struck Zanja: "Live for the future or not at all." She shut the book and gave it back to Medric, who had been anxious during the whole time she held it.

"All my books have come from the bottoms of soldiers' footlockers," Medric said. "They keep odd things sometimes. The soldier who sold this book to me had it from a Lilterwess school that she helped burn down."

Zanja said, "Do you happen to know why the Carolins attacked the Ashawala'i? They were a peaceful mountain people, famous for their woolens . . ."

"Oh, I know all about it. That whole incident is infamous, you know. But it was particularly important to me. There was another Shaftali-born Carolin seer, a year or two older than I. She had a dream that she interpreted to mean that the Ashawala'i were going to defeat and destroy the Carolins. Not one of the Ashawala'i could be left alive, she said, or her prediction would come true.

Medric opened his book and said, as if reading from it, "Such dreams should cause self-examination, reassessment of purpose and intention. But to simply react to dreams like puppets on strings leads to panicked, superstitious insanity. The best seer in the land sees only a very small part of the truth." He shut the book. "The Carolins don't understand that, and neither did the other seer until perhaps she realized, after the Ashawala'i had been destroyed, that the insane enterprise itself might be the cause of the Carolin downfall. We lost an enormous number of soldiers on that one campaign, and you cannot imagine what an impact such a loss had on a practically childless people. Anyway, she killed herself."

There was a silence. "I don't know why I didn't learn from her mistakes," he added. "Why do you want to know about the Ashawala'i?"

"They were my people," Zanja said.

She felt the presence of the ghosts: the infants burned in their baskets, the children massacred in the arms of their parents, the old people shielding the young, the *katrim* with their light weaponry broken in their hands. Medric studied her through lenses glazed with light, and said quite softly, "So now you are the arrow in the bow we ourselves have strung."

"Tell me how I am going to destroy the Sainnites. I am very curious."

He gazed at her steadily, long enough that she began to feel uncomfortable, and finally said, "I don't know what you are going to do. If I did know, I would not tell you. But I will tell you this, for what it's worth: The elemental flame either transforms or destroys, and we fire bloods have the power to choose which of those it will be. I have made my choice. When you have made yours, I will meet you here again."

He took a folded piece of paper from where it was tucked between the pages of his book, and gave it to her. It was a map, roughly sketched, though it was easy enough to identify Wilton, and the river, and the fens, and the location of South Hill Company's encampment, which was clearly marked, along with the locations of the pickets. It wouldn't have been too difficult for the Sainnites to locate such a large encampment, but still it was a shock to see it all neatly laid out like this. "We're going to attack tonight," Medric said. "We'll come up the river, here, and through the woods." He traced a path with his fingertips. "And we'll surround you, trapping you between us and the swamp. We won't attack until near dawn, so we'll have enough light to shoot by."

He took the map and put it back in the book. "Zanja, now I ask your mercy. It's hard enough to live with the betrayals I've already committed, the deaths I've already caused. Please don't use this knowledge to ambush the Carolins."

Zanja could think of nothing to say, no promises she felt able to make.

Medric wrapped his precious book in linen and packed up the basket. He looked very tired. "I have been acting as my own enemy, finding ways to undermine my own plans. Our gaol is full of South Hillers who I insist must not be harmed. I have allowed you to burn down the garrison. Now, tonight's attack will surely go awry. As you might well imagine, my position among the Sainnites will soon become impossible. But I will no longer dream for them, no matter what disasters result. I must find my way with a larger vision."

He stood up. "I wish the same for you."

Chapter Sixteen

During the half day of furtive travel along back ways and across planted fields, and finally across a portion of the fens which entailed much wading but at least was passable, Zanja had plenty of time to consider and reconsider her situation. Now, as sunset approached and she stopped on firm ground to strap her boots on before starting the last climb up the slope to the overlook, she marveled at how visible the campfires were. As she approached the camp her wonder only increased. No picket challenged her, and she walked into the heart of the encampment practically unnoticed.

There was much distracted hustle and bustle, with goose being roasted on spits, the mess of occupation being tidied up, and many excited people clustered in arm-waving conversations, for there never was a South Hiller who could talk without gesturing. At the smoky heart of the encampment, though, there was a stillness where Emil bowed and poured tea from his porcelain teapot. His three lieutenants flanked him, their faces pink with washing, dressed in their cleanest longshirts, their heavy boots tucked up close to their stocky farmer's bodies. Annis sat among them, charmingly flushed by something being said to her by the erect, gray-haired woman who sat beside her upon Emil's stool. This woman was boldly dressed, like the three other strangers who sat somewhat behind her, in Paladin's black. Even from a distance Zanja could see the flash of three golden earrings in her left earlobe. The three earrings of Right, Rank, and Regard had once been worn only by a high commander, a general. Only one such person remained alive now, in all of Shaftal.

Zanja felt a great weariness, a heaviness so overwhelming she could not continue forward, and scarcely could continue to stand. Transfixed by this exhaustion, she did nothing when Councilor Mabin turned her attention to Zanja, as though, of all the gazes that were turned on her, it was Zanja's that mattered. For a long, strange moment they looked into each other's faces across the distance that separated them. Then she spoke to Emil, who hastily set down his teapot and walked over to Zanja.

"What's the matter?" he asked her.

"The Sainnites are going to attack us tonight, here at Fen Overlook."

It seemed a measure of their friendship, or perhaps of Emil himself, that he did not even make her explain further, thus making it possible for her to avoid directly lying to him.

He said, "Well, our watchers would have noticed if a company had left the city gates yet—it's still light enough to see. So we have some hours at least in which to decide what to do."

"I think so."

"You look weary to death." Emil gripped her by the shoulder and somehow she became able to walk with him up to the smoky fire.

The general had never taken her gaze from them. Now she rose to her feet. "Zanja na'Tarwein?" All the other conversations around the fire fell abruptly silent.

"Madam Councilor," Zanja said, "you may not remember, but we have met before."

Mabin said, "I remember you. You are much changed in fifteen years."

Zanja scarcely could fumble a reply as Mabin, the legendary author of *Warfare* and the head of Shaftal's shadow government, expressed her sorrow over the massacre of the Ashawala'i and welcomed her formally into the Paladins. It was, or should have been, a triumph for Zanja to be greeted like this by the councilor herself, with all the company watching. But her status in South Hill no longer seemed relevant.

"Norina Truthken has written to me about you several times," Mabin said.

Zanja felt quite witless. Emil said quietly, "Sit down—maybe some tea will help."

Zanja sat beside Annis and held up her porringer for Emil to fill with tea, for he had distributed all six of his teacups already. She drank too quickly, scalding her mouth, while Emil said to everyone at the fire, "Zanja thinks the Sainnites are going to attack Fen Overlook." He added, for those who did not know, "She is a presciant."

Silence greeted Emil's announcement, and then a fierce argument and discussion which Zanja could not heed. In the midst of it Annis put her mouth against Zanja's ear and whispered, "Mabin's taking me away with her, to make rockets for the Paladins!"

"That's good," Zanja said, then realized, when Annis pulled away sharply, that she should have said something else. "I'll miss you," she added belatedly.

Annis showed her teeth. "Sure you will."

Zanja tried to pay attention to the discussion that swirled around her. Willis argued that South Hill Company should set a trap for the Sainnites, if Emil was so certain that Zanja's prescience was dependable.

"We must not attack them!" Zanja cried. They all looked at her, but Zanja couldn't think of an explanation for her reluctance to ambush the Sainnites. She put her head in her hands and wished desperately that her skull would simply explode. "If we attack them," she said, "it will be a disaster."

Emil said, "Annis, please find Jerrell and tell her to bring a remedy for a headache."

"Are we to spend the entire season running and hiding from a figment of the imagination?" Willis's big fist had clenched. In the twilight, with the light of the flames moving across it, his fist seemed monstrous. It pounded upon his knee in a fever of frustration and Willis's voice rose to a shout. "It is a coward's way!" His fist opened up, and he pointed across the fire, at Zanja. "Before this—foreigner—came to South Hill, we were not cowards! Here we have a perfect opportunity—*she* says—to do the Sainnites some damage. But no, we dare not—because *she* says no. Prescience is nothing but an impulse—an instinct—and maybe it's the instinct of a warrior who has lost her nerve!"

Emil's hand pressed down heavily upon Zanja's shoulder. She had not even noticed him coming around to her side, but the hand on her shoulder shored up her disintegrating discipline. Emil said,

"Willis, since you hold fire talent in such contempt, perhaps you might be happier in a company that does not have a presciant as its commander."

Willis sat back, his face flushed. "I'm just sick and tired of missing our opportunities. Now that you have new counsel you pay no heed to the old."

Emil could seem astonishingly harmless, but he did not look harmless at that moment. "You question my judgment, the councilor's judgment, and gravely insult a fellow Paladin who has repeatedly risked her life this season, and this is all you have to say?"

There was another silence, then Willis, his face bright red, said, "I beg your pardon—sir. I meant no insult. I was over-zealous."

Emil said nothing. His hand still lay heavy upon Zanja's shoulder.

Willis looked directly at Zanja and said, "I hope you will pardon me as well." There was no mistaking the hatred with which he said these words.

Zanja wanted desperately to challenge him to a duel and win a more sincere apology on her own terms. But this was not the Asha Valley, and Willis was no *katrim*. She said, as stiffly as he had, "Of course I will pardon you."

Everyone began to talk then, as though nothing had happened. But no one else suggested ambushing the Sainnites. The discussion focused on the logistics of retreat, for their fifty fighters had swelled to a hundred, and they had precious equipment to protect.

Jerrell's infusion did little for Zanja's headache. When Emil's circle dispersed to spread the word that they were breaking camp, Zanja got to her feet and nearly fell over.

Emil caught her and said, "What is it? Are you ill?"

She said, "Willis thinks you are ripe for replacement and is just biding his time, waiting for you to prove yourself incompetent. But my precipitous rise in your esteem has made him think that I am a pretender to a position that he considers rightfully his."

"Yes, yes," Emil said patiently, and felt her forehead.

"You trust me because I'm so much like you. Even a fool like Willis can see it."

"No, I trust you because I know you're trustworthy. What is the matter with you?"

"Last summer, a Sainnite war horse kicked me in the head. I was like this for months afterward."

"Sit down. I'll have someone get your gear. I want you to stay with me tonight."

By full dark, South Hill Company had dispersed, with a third of the Paladins under the command of each lieutenant, hauling gear and supplies to new encampments on the various overlooks. Zanja traveled in the smallest group, which consisted of Emil, the distinguished guests, and a few fleet-footed couriers. They traveled in a wide circle, north through woods so thick that the dignitaries had to lead their horses, west through farmlands, then south upon the dark road, back to the end of the lowlands, just to the southwest of Fen Overlook.

Mabin had insisted on accompanying Emil, though Emil was concerned that the Sainnite seer might detect her presence and send the soldiers out hunting her. The two of them sat awake while the rest of their small company slept, though Zanja was only pretending. Without witnesses surrounding them, the two commanders acted less formally, and it seemed apparent that they had a long acquaintance, though they did not act like friends. After a while they walked away, and Zanja was able to doze upon the hard ground. When she woke up later it was still dark, and her head seemed ready to finally split open and spill its contents.

No doubt Emil was keeping watch upon the stone overlook, waiting to know for certain whether Zanja's prescience had been accurate. She could go to him and tell him the whole truth: that she had lied to him, that she had twice failed to kill the Sainnite seer, that she feared she was being tempted into treachery by a man who understood her better than she understood herself.

She got up and made her way through a haze of darkness and pain, until she could actually see him, a thin, still silhouette against the stars, the Man on the Hill. Her affection for him washed over her and brought her to a standstill. Wasn't he already making his precarious way between the fragile and competing loyalties that held South Hill Company together? Already, he had to know the minds of his people, the minds of the enemy, and his own mind. Surely it would do him no good if she imposed her burdens upon him, in the selfish hope that somehow they would become easier for her to bear.

"Zanja," said a low voice. "Are you having trouble sleeping? Sit with me a while."

It was Mabin. Like Emil, she sat alone in the darkness, waiting for the dawn. Zanja went over to her reluctantly. "Councilor."

"It's not a good night for sleeping. I've been watching the torch bugs swarm. Sit down, sit down."

Zanja squatted nearby, wishing that she'd had the sense to stay in her blankets until sunrise. Even with Mabin just a dark shadow, still she felt too closely watched, as though Mabin were a fox, and she a mouse.

"I hear that fire bloods are often tormented by nightmares," Mabin said.

"Yes, madam, so I hear." Was Mabin lonely, or troubled, to be inviting a total stranger into intimacy like this? She added, lest she seem too rude, "But I am just tormented by my headache." A swarm of torch bugs swirled in a nearby bush, like sparks in a wind, except that the air was warm and still.

"Emil seems to think highly of your abilities."

"I think highly of his."

"So do I," Mabin said after a moment, as though she'd had to think about it. "Yet I confess, I am concerned. Like that man to-night—Willis was his name?—I wonder that he is willing to let an opportunity go by like this, just on your say-so. How can we even be certain of the existence of this Sainnite seer?"

"How can we not be certain of it?" Zanja said reasonably.

"Because it seems so unlikely! And it's always possible that the Sainnites are just better strategists, or luckier than we. And perhaps the whole point is to make South Hill Company cautious, so that at the very moment when you *must* act, you will hesitate. And we must not lose control of South Hill."

For a dizzying moment, Zanja realized how likely it was that Medric was using her for this very purpose Mabin had described—that he had discovered in a vision her closeness to Emil, and so had realized that he could subvert the entire company by subverting her. This was the nightmare that caused Zanja such dismay, but she could not endure to consider it directly for longer than a moment. She said, though she was sick of explaining herself, "I can never depend upon my prescience to serve me when I need it to. But when it does serve me, it has never been completely wrong. And Emil's and my talents seem to complement each other, for when he forms the questions I can form the answers, and he has the knowledge to interpret those answers, and I in turn can sense whether or not his interpretation is the right one. So we are more certain together than we would be separately: certain of each other and certain of what we know."

"'A steeliness disguised in ritual humility,' Norina wrote of you."

Irritated by this reminder of the Truthken's heavy hand, Zanja said, "My people believed that courtesy comes from strength, not from weakness, and that it was no shame to be constantly reminding each other that without this fabric of ritual courtesy our tribe would have fallen apart."

After a moment, Mabin said, "Norina also wrote that you are wasted in South Hill. I want to bring you with me, to help me plan strategy for all of Shaftal."

"Thank you, madam, but Norina is wrong. I belong where I am."

Mabin's head lifted as though now she was surprised. If she had ever been turned down before, which seemed unlikely, certainly it had never been so promptly and directly.

"Well then," she said, with ill-disguised irritation, "It is your choice, of course. Let me ask you directly what concerns me. What makes you think the Sainnites have a seer?"

"The glyph cards told us."

"It was a *divination*?" Mabin sounded appalled.

Zanja rose abruptly to her feet. "Madam, Emil surely is better qualified to explain our method. I know you will excuse me, for I feel quite dizzy and must go lie down."

But as she returned to her blankets, Zanja heard Emil utter a grunt of surprise from atop the pile of boulders where he kept watch. She reached him in a few strides, in time to see the fading aftermath of a rocket's faraway explosion.

"Oh," Emil said, "it was beautiful. Did you see it? That Annis is a genius."

Mabin had come up behind Zanja, too late to see the fireworks. "What happened?"

Emil said, "One of the scouts set off a rocket. Not over trees, but over the river. That explains why we've seen no sign of the Sainnites on the road. They came up the river."

"By boat?"

"No, not against the current, surely. More likely they simply walked up the riverbank." Emil's teeth showed in the darkness; he was grinning with relief. "The Sainnites are nervous now, I'd wager, after seeing that rocket. What do you think they'll do, Zanja?"

"I don't know," Zanja said. She was sick of her talent, sick of being asked questions and then being challenged for knowing the answers.

"Well, let's pretend they continue onward and find the camp empty. They'll take the road home, won't they, rather than walk home on rocks?"

"Then they'd follow the edge of the fen and come out just below where we are," she said.

"So we'll get a good look at them, anyway, and be able to see how they're judging our strength."

Perhaps just to be certain that the message had been received, or perhaps out of sheer delight, the scout set off another rocket over the river. "Oh," Mabin said when it exploded, "that is a sight. We could set those off just for show. A waste of good gunpowder, though."

The sun had fully risen when the soldiers finally appeared. They had not fled the woods in panic at the prospect of an ambush, and instead they seemed to have spent the time since dawn scouring the woods.

Mabin, peering at them through a spyglass, muttered as they marched away, perhaps repeating to herself the advice in *Warfare* to never make a direct attack on a large company in broad daylight. She turned on Zanja a glance that was almost a glare. "Well, your prescience seems reliable enough. So perhaps this business of a Sainnite seer is also to be believed."

Emil rescued Zanja, taking her to the fire where camp porridge cooked in several porringers tucked into the hot ashes. Emil used his own porringer to mix up a horrid, bitter concoction that he made Zanja drink.

"I dared not give this to you last night," he said, "for if it's your old injury doing this to you, I feared you would sleep so deeply you would never wake up. I've seen it happen."

They were sitting by themselves, so Zanja said in a low voice, "Did you hear my conversation with Mabin?"

"Most of it. Apparently, she's got some kind of hornet in her hat."

"Is it so bizarre to practice divination?"

"Not at all. Mabin probably played at it herself when she was a girl."

Zanja was beginning to feel very odd, as though her head were separating itself from her shoulders. The nearby Paladins seemed very distant, and the birdsong seemed to come from another world entirely. "Emil," she said, carefully shaping the words lest they come out strangely, "I think she wants me dead. Since I will not come with her."

"I think that you're delirious," Emil said gently.

"She wants me out of South Hill. I don't know why." The pain abruptly drained out of her and she stared at Emil, stunned by the suddenness of it.

"Finally!" he said.

"This is a very strong potion." Her words came out like polished jewels. "Sometimes your knee hurts a great deal, doesn't it?"

Emil pretended he hadn't heard, or else Zanja was so confused she hadn't actually said anything out loud, but only in her head. Emil said. "I have to tell you, I see nothing sinister in Mabin wanting to snatch you away from me. I wish I had a hundred more like you, myself."

"A frightening prospect," Zanja said seriously, but Emil laughed out loud.

They traveled through the forested heart of South Hill. As she walked, Zanja imagined the ambush they could have planned. In her mind, they killed some twenty soldiers. Those twenty could never be replaced. And now that she thought of it, Zanja realized she had never seen a Sainnite child, and precious few soldiers who were younger than Medric. Were the Sainnites, like *katrim*, forbidden to bear or beget? If so, then they depended upon outsiders to bear and raise their children for them. Of course, the whores of Lalali were one example of how to make this happen, though a brothel village was hardly the place to raise soldiers. The babies would be taken away somewhere, perhaps to a garrison operated by disabled and retired Carolins whose job it was to raise and train the next generation of soldiers.

If the Paladins could find and kill those children then that, surely, would destroy the fighting spirit of the Sainnites.

"Dear gods," Zanja whispered.

"Careful." Emil, who had not been out of arm's reach all morning, caught her, for she had nearly fallen.

"Do the Paladins make war on children?"

"Of course not."

"The thoughts I'm having."

"Here." He moved her aside so that others in their party could pass. "The potion I gave you to drink sets the thoughts askew, like a fever."

The black-garbed dignitaries, with their audacious earrings and upright attitudes pushed past them, one by one. How simple life must be for them, Zanja thought. To never have to distinguish right from wrong, and simply follow the law.

She and Emil walked behind them, side by side. Theirs was a far more complicated path.

Chapter Seventeen

Mabin and her entourage left with Annis in tow, and Zanja, despite her presentiments, remained unmurdered. Neither pain nor disordered delirium returned to trouble her.

It soon became apparent that Mabin had mobilized all of Shaftal to the defense of South Hill, and the steady tribute of food, supplies, and hardened veterans from all across the country rapidly transformed their rebel band into an army that Emil was hard put to organize or command. These were not soldiers, but guerrilla fighters, and Emil, though he could convince anyone to do anything, was no general. Nor, he complained rather wearily to Zanja, had he ever aspired to be one.

Zanja traveled ceaselessly among the five units of thirty that Emil, who needed no longer be so fearful of the Sainnites' greater numbers, positioned on the high ground that rimmed the river valley. Whenever the Sainnites left their garrison, South Hill Company knew of it almost immediately, because Emil's spies set off signal rockets that could be seen for miles around. Always conscious that each time she bloodied her blade Karis knew about it, Zanja fought in the three clashes that proved the Paladins' new strategic dominance. What followed might have been called a siege, except that between the Paladin encampments and the Sainnite garrison lay some of the richest farmland in South Hill. The Sainnites began to do what they seemed best at: methodical, thorough, mindless destruction. While the ancient orchards were toppled and the farmsteads and fields were burned, the valley farmers, bitterly angry at Paladin and Sainnite alike, hauled their children and animals and what belongings could be salvaged out of danger. Wagons crowded the roads of South Hill. The farmsteads outside of danger were overwhelmed with refugees and their belongings. At a time when only steady, careful attention to the crops could prevent the coming year from being a hungry one, all of South Hill lay in chaos.

Though South Hill Company could not prevent the Sainnites from razing the valley's rich farmlands, they also could not endure to stand by and do nothing. Despite their disadvantage at direct, hand-to-hand combat, scarcely a day passed without at least one skirmish in which the Paladins crept up on Sainnites under cover of waist-high corn or drainage ditches choked with rushes, exchanged gunfire, and then fled in much the same way. The Paladins who spent their days crawling through the weeds took to calling these engagements hide-and-seek raids. It was no game, though, but a deadly, dangerous business that put Jerrell's bone saw in high demand.

With every casualty Emil seemed another year older. Willis's unit alone aged him by ten years, and Willis's gloating reports of thirty or more Sainnites injured and killed did not make Emil less grim. He sent Zanja with a brusque message that she delivered, word for word: "We are not engaged in a contest to determine who can kill the greatest number of Sainnites. And the people of South Hill will not thank us for burdening them with an overwhelming number of crippled fighters. You are to have no more casualties, even if that means that you conduct no more raids."

Willis heard this message with amazing equanimity. "No more casualties," he said. "Well, I suppose he thinks I have his prescience, eh? Oh, but you do have it, don't you?" He turned to his cronies, for, unlike Emil, he took his strength from numbers, not solitude. "It seems a worthy experiment, doesn't it, to see if prescience can protect us from casualties?"

"Oh, yes," they murmured, and Zanja did not need prescience to know that this conversation had been long planned.

"You want me to go out on a hide-and-seek raid?" she asked.

"We're going out on one today."

Zanja looked around that circle of hostile, grinning faces, and felt very tired. What was the price she would have to pay to be a full member of this company? They cared only about Sainnite corpses, it seemed. Well then, she would give them some, though she doubted it would be possible to give them enough.

So she found herself, in the company of some ten others, creeping through the corn plants towards one of the few valley farmsteads left standing. An earlier check with the spyglass had told them that the Sainnites were out in force, but once the Paladins had slipped into the valley they could no longer see how the enemy was deployed, and could not even be certain where they themselves were, in relation to the farmstead. The corn rows were as straight as a planting plow could make them, but still Zanja could not see more than a few feet ahead, and at times could scarcely see her own companions. Surely the Sainnites are expecting us to come down the corn rows, she thought, and turned to suggest to the Paladin closest to her that it might make more sense to approach from the drainage ditch. But her companions had all disappeared.

She turned as a breeze parted the corn leaves to reveal the soldier keeping watch at the end of the row. She dove crossways into the corn. Something like a hot poker punched her in the thigh. She turned and jumped the other direction, like a rabbit evading a wolf. Perhaps the fickle wind would not betray her again. Another gunshot. Someone shouted in Sainnese that she had gone towards the corncrib, whichever direction that might be. She headed away from the voice, cross-row. She fell, and was puzzled that she could no longer walk. She crawled instead, until she tumbled out of corn plants into mossy water. She lay among the rushes, her pistols under water, thinking how nice and cool it was there in the ditch. It seemed impossible that she would be found. She rested her head in the crook of her arm and thought she might sleep for a while, she was feeling so tired.

The pain inserted itself slowly into her unwarranted peacefulness, irritating as a voice telling her to get up and do some more work. She ignored it—she had felt worse pain and lived. But it grew worse, much worse, and finally she sat up, and noticed with surprise that the water she lay in had turned a bright scarlet. She found a neat hole scorched into the canvas of her breeches, and pulled them down to reveal another neat, blood-weeping hole in her thigh. *Such a small wound,* she thought, pretending that she did not know that a pistol ball's worst damage was usually below the skin. She could not make a bandage—her clothing was muddy and soaking wet—and so she buttoned up her breeches and lay down again in the water, and forced herself to listen to what the world would tell her.

She heard a rapid volley of gunfire. After a long silence, she heard a second volley. The Paladins had circled around, she thought sleepily, after using her as an uninformed, unwilling decoy. She heard the sound of flames, and for a while she lay wounded in a different valley, listening to the sound of Sainnites burning a different village. I must get up, she thought, and woke to find that she already was crawling down the drainage ditch, though not until she saw the smoke and saw the soldiers did she realize she had gone the wrong direction. She watched them curiously, these angry soldiers stranded far from home in a hostile land, and understood too well what it was that made them want to burn everything to the ground.

She turned away from the burning farm, and began dragging herself down the drainage ditch again.

From the bottom of the ditch, she watched the shadows move and the sun set. Despite the summer warmth, the water's cold set into her bones. She hauled herself out of the ditch and into the road, where she lay shivering. She heard the far-away bells of Wilton ringing the hours. Until it was too dark to see, she watched her blood seep into the dirt. At last, the search party that she knew Willis would have to send for her, if only for the sake of appearance, found her and carried her back to camp.

"I'm not going to die," she told Jerrell, "and you're not going to cut off my leg."

Jerrell argued, but Zanja was adamant. Jerrell removed the pistol ball instead, which was bad enough, since it took some cutting to even find the ball, which was embedded in the thick muscles above the knee. When Zanja awoke in the afternoon, Emil was sitting beside her, with his legs stretched out before him and his back against a tree, gazing with a strained expression toward the smoking ruin that had once been one of the richest farmlands in Shaftal.

"What's wrong with that seer?" he asked.

She began to sit up, and he turned to her. "I'll get whatever you need. Jerrell says you are to lie still."

"What I need can't be gotten."

He smiled wryly, and set himself to fetching and carrying the small comforts that he could provide: a cup of water, a bag of beans for a pillow. He checked on her clothing that hung in the sunshine, declared it not dry yet, and settled once more against the tree. "So," he said, "in famine the Sainnites also go hungry, and famine is exactly what will happen in South Hill this winter. What seer would be so short-sighted? These Sainnites don't behave like people with insight at all. In fact, they act like mindless brutes, as they always have. Could the seer be dead, or gone?"

"Maybe he's lost his mind," she said.

"Maybe he's stopped dreaming. It happens."

"Maybe he had a bad love affair."

"Maybe he's fallen ill."

"Maybe," Zanja said, "he's had a change of heart."

Emil looked out at the smoke-hazed valley, then back at Zanja. "Surely not. We fire bloods are cursed with loyalty. To turn traitor against the people we call our own—it's not in us."

"Sometimes insight overrides loyalty," Zanja said, too bitterly.

They sat in silence for a while. So long as Zanja didn't move, the pain in her leg was not unendurable.

Emil said softly, "Every time I close my eyes, I dream the same dream. A man sits before me, with a wooden box in his lap. He holds it up to me, as if proffering a gift, and opens the lid. I can't see what's in the box, but I know that I want it desperately."

"What does he look like?"

"The man? Oh, I don't know. It's all in shadow: a big, dark room with a single lamp flame. Why does it matter?"

"It matters," Zanja said, but felt that she could not explain. *Later I will explain,* she thought wearily, *but now I cannot endure any more consequences.*

"Well then," Emil said, "next time I dream of him, I'll try to get a look at his face." He took her hand in his. "My dear, with only one leg, you'd still be invaluable to South Hill."

"Of course Jerrell sent for you."

"When a member of my company chooses certain death—"

Zanja said, "Do you remember when the bridgekeeper bit me?"

"It wasn't so long ago."

"Which arm was it?" She held out both her arms, and after some hunting, Emil found the scar, nearly faded to invisibility.

"So you heal clean," he said. "But a pistol ball—"

"Sir, Jerrell has already lectured me."

"Sir!" He sat back a bit.

"My brother," she amended. "I am not choosing death out of despair. I know my leg will heal."

He looked at her for a long time, as if studying a particularly complex pattern of glyphs. "Someday," he said finally, "you will tell me your secrets." He took her hand again. "I'll instruct Jerrell to trust your judgment, if you tell me the truth about what happened yesterday. Willis says that your companions lost you in the cornfield. They realized the Sainnites were watching for them and retreated, and only then noticed you weren't with them."

"I'm sure they abandoned me deliberately," she said. "But unless one of those who was with me in the cornfield admits to it, I don't see how it can be proven."

"One of them will admit it soon enough," Emil said quietly, "and I'll finally have a good reason to rid myself of Willis, though I suppose his kinfolk will hold it against me forever, no matter how good my reasons are." He sighed. "Do you know, in the old days, the G'deon might drive a spike into the heart of a particularly irritating enemy, and from that day every beat of the heart would lie in the G'deon's control. That's the way to solve my problem with Willis—keep him alive, let him continue as a lieutenant, but let him know that at any moment I might choose to let him drop down dead."

He drew up his knees, looking for all the world as if he meant to continue talking to her all day. "Unfortunately, my powers are limited, and whatever I do will have unwanted consequences. Tell me something," he added abruptly, "Do you feel up to reading the cards?"

"I don't even know where they are."

"They're drying in the sun, like everything else you own." He fetched them, and counted to see that all of them had survived, warped and mud-smirched though they were. As Zanja shuffled the cards aimlessly, he asked, "What characterizes the state of conflict between South Hill and the Sainnites?"

Zanja picked a card she'd not studied yet. It depicted a balance, or shopkeeper's scale. Emil glanced at it and nodded without much surprise. "What would tilt the balance in our favor?" he asked.

Zanja could not choose a card. "Are you thinking too much?" Emil asked after a while.

"It's as though every card is the answer."

"So in order to tilt the balance we'd have to alter the entire

Universe? Well, try this question instead: What is the most important factor in tilting the balance in our favor?"

Zanja chose a card and tossed it down before looking at it. It was the Owl. "Hmm." Emil grinned without much humor. "Well now, this is getting interesting."

Zanja shifted uncomfortably. Her injured thigh ached.

"So tell me, what is the Owl to do?"

Zanja laid down another card without looking at it, then saw that it was the Door. She sighed.

"What will immediately result from this decision that the Owl must make?"

She lay down another card, and Emil gave a small start, but said nothing. The glyph was one Zanja did not know; the picture showed an opening into a hillside.

Emil shook his head, and asked, "What will be the long term result of this decision?"

The last card seemed the most ambiguous of them all: it showed the silhouettes of a ridged horizon, with the sun above, either rising or setting. Emil moved the cards into an organized row and scowled unhappily at them. At last, he said, "Well, either this is a piece of arrant nonsense or a message of great portent. Based on what I see here, I want to say that it appears that you, Zanja, are a crucial factor in events with implications that reach far beyond South Hill. You are in a position where you must make a difficult decision even though you feel you cannot decide. Your decision will result in some kind of grave danger: a danger of spirit of body or both. It may very well lead to death." He touched the card with the opening in the hillside. "This is the door to the labyrinth, the underworld. It is always dangerous but not necessarily fatal. Now, it is not clear who or what is endangered, but it may be you, or South Hill Company, or something much more important than any of us here. In the end—" he touched the Sun card "—there will be hope or loss of hope. An end of everything or a new beginning. It could go either way."

Then there was silence.

Emil contemplated the cards. "Surely if this were nonsense I would recognize it. So what am I to make of this?" Then he grinned with a wry amusement. "Or, more specifically, how can I help you to make the right decision?"

"Anyone else would insist—demand—that I explain," Zanja said.

"But if this is a true reading—and you would have told me by now if it wasn't—then I have to assume that you don't feel able to explain. If you don't feel able to do it, then for me to insist that you do would only complicate your situation when it seems I ought to be making it simpler." He looked up at her. "I must somehow help you without actually understanding what I'm doing or why I'm doing it. Tell me what to do."

"In truth, I—am at a loss. These portents—they do not explain anything."

"They tell me that you are caught up in something that's much more important than you realize." He turned the Door card so that it was right-side-up for Zanja and tapped it with his fingertip. "What can you tell me about this?"

Zanja said, "If I decide wrongly, then you are the one that will be endangered."

"Me personally?"

"Emil—you have made yourself my friend. How could it not be personal? But it's difficult to imagine that what happens to you won't affect South Hill Company, our entire enterprise here, or the whole history of Shaftal which brought us to this point."

"So. You've been avoiding me ever since the night we evacuated Fen Overlook—maybe even longer, since Fire Night. Something happened that I don't know about." He clasped his hands across his knee, as though restraining himself from doing something else: hitting her, embracing her; it was impossible to tell. "How can I help you?" he asked again. "Or is it absolution you need?"

"Tell me, in your dream—"

He raised an eyebrow. "You think my dream is relevant to this?"

"What is in the box?"

He tapped a finger on the Sun card. "Hope," he said. "Or at least the hope of hope."

"Would you die for it?"

"Yes, I would. So—am I going to die for desire's sake after all, like every other fire blood since the dawn of time? Should I get my affairs in order? You understand," he added gently, "I think it's about time I had something worth dying for, something better than this idiot's war."

He held her hand for a while, then offered her a handkerchief from his breast pocket, and picked up the cards that she had let fall. Then he fetched Jerrell, who checked Zanja's bandage and agreed to arrange for her family to give Zanja a safe place to recuperate, as soon as she could be moved. She gave her another potion to drink. The memory of Emil sitting quietly beside her, cleaning and oiling her pistols for her, accompanied Zanja in her sleep, in her dreams, into the day that followed, and into the night that followed that. It was such a small thing, and yet at the time she most needed it, it gave her a great peace.

Chapter Eighteen

In the silent night, the warm air lay heavy and still, and starlight blurred behind a lingering haze of smoke. Leaning on a staff, Zanja shuffled through the silence where accuser bugs should have shouted from the tree branches. But the trees all had been cut down, and without the intervention of their uplifted hands, the sky pressed down upon the earth like a smothering blanket. Here on the dark plain, the farmers slept by smoldering barns and clenched their fists in their dreams. It seemed the whole world had been put to the torch.

Zanja's staff scraped gravel. Her foot dragged behind her; her patience wore thin. She had left the Paladin camp as early as she dared, but by the time she reached the grove outside of Wilton she had heard the city bell ring midnight. The grove, of course, had been cut down. She saw no sign of Medric, and sat upon a stump to wait.

She waited, listening to the clock toll out the passing hours. At last, she accepted that he was not coming. All her distress, it seemed, had been for nothing.

She thought she had allowed enough time to reach the camp again before summer's early dawn overtook her, but her leg had stiffened as she waited, and then the wound reopened as Jerrell had warned it would if she didn't keep it still. Her leg was bathed in warm, slow-flowing blood, and a lassitude came over her. So the horizon had begun to lighten when she climbed the steep path through the trees, past the inattentive pickets and back across the boundaries of the Paladin camp.

As she headed for her abandoned blankets, she heard a camp cook bang a pot as the flames of a cookfire began to crackle. It still was dark among the trees. She walked in shadow, careful, worried, wondering what had become of Medric and what she should do now. When Willis rose up from beside her empty bed, she stared at him, stupid as a rabbit in torchlight, unable to imagine what he was doing there, or what it meant.

She heard the others rise up out of darkness where they had been hidden. She let her staff fall, lest they mistake it for a weapon, and held out her empty hands. Contrary to what Ransel used to say, she did in fact know when to give up.

"So you deign to return to us," Willis said. "Where have you been all night?"

I should have put up a fight and gotten myself killed, she thought, now that it was too late.

Willis struck her. She fell, and the earth did not catch her. She fell into the darkness, into the vortex of that catastrophic year.

A grinning Sainnite forced her to watch what he did to her, even though she could not feel it.

The Paladins lifted her up, and he struck her again.

He cut off her toes, one by one. His companions held her head by the hair, so she could not look away.

"Tell me where you have been!" he cried. He raised his fist.

A war horse's hoof struck her in the head. She fell.

Ransel jerked her up by the hair. His familiar, battered war blade shone in a light too vivid to be sunlight.

"You are a traitor!" he cried, triumphant. The Paladins, startled and bewildered, or angry and jeering, gathered around.

"You are no longer one of the people!" Ransel cried. The Ashawala'i people stood silent, accepting his judgment.

He struck her, and she fell. She did not know anymore who was her brother, or her companion at arms, or her enemy. She fell, and she fell.

She opened her eyes, but could scarcely see. Upon bare ground, she lay bleeding, unwatched. It was a contemptuous inattention, for they certainly knew that she could not flee: she had no toes; her back was broken. Ransel had cut off her hair, thus rejecting her from the tribe. Why had they not brought her the suicide drink? The Ashawala'i had given all other outcasts that mercy: why not her?

She felt blindly for her weapons. The dagger was gone, and the pistols. But her small knife was still tucked into her blood-smeared boot.

She held the blade to her own throat, but could not cut deeply enough. She began to weep. "Lord Death, now I choose you." Her fingers were painted with bright red ink. She wrote a message to him upon the shining metal of the blade. Then someone noticed, and with an exclamation snatched the knife out of her hand.

At the height of a stroke, Karis dropped her hammer. The red hot piece of iron fell from the tongs, and those also clattered onto the stone floor. A boy rushed over with the water bucket, but she dropped to her knees upon the stone floor, and swept her hand across it to clear the debris. With a scrap of iron she scratched a line upon the stone, then another crossing it, then a third.

"That's the Raven," said the boy helpfully, water sloshing out over his feet.

"What?"

"That's the Raven glyph. Isn't it?" The boy peered down at the marks she had made. "Your mastersign!" he said, apparently trying his best to make sense of her crazy behavior. "The messenger of good and bad fortune. It just came to you, right? And you wanted to write it down before you forgot, right? And now you can be a forgemaster, and you'll take me to work for you?"

"The Raven." Karis looked again at the marks she had drawn on the floor. "Something has gone terribly wrong."

Zanja lay paralyzed in a blood-stained hay cart. At a distant mountain peak, the moon lifted her pale face to the starry sky. Except for the occasional calls of the soldiers on watch duty, the Sainnite camp lay silent. Zanja watched the sky, able only to wait, now that all choices had been taken away from her.

A slight sound made her turn her head, and a slim shadow separated from the darkness: lithe and silent, grinning teeth shining with moonlight. "Oh my brother," she breathed. "Why do you risk your life for me? I am already dead, but you can still live."

He came to her, though, silently laughing his raven's laugh. "You trickster," she said. "You have come to take my life in mercy at last."

Yes. His blade was in his hand. She smiled at him, her courageous friend. "Come, then," she said. And then a Sainnite uttered a warning shout, and they rose up and killed him.

It had happened again. It would happen again, again, and again, while she lay hopelessly screaming, and Ransel's sturdy heart pumped his lifeblood onto the ground. Over and over, he came to deliver the mercy blow, and over and over they killed him.

A heavy door grated open. There was a terrible blaze of light and a flapping shadow, like a big bird's wings. "Come out of there," Willis said.

"She's been unusually quiet the last few hours," another voice said doubtfully.

Emil's voice, low and quiet, said, "She has been shouting and you left her unattended? She has a serious injury!"

For Emil, quiet meant angry, angry almost beyond speech. "I'm going in after her," he said. But Zanja had managed to get to her feet by then, and shakily walked into the light. Emil was just a shadow she could see even with her eyes closed, and surely she was no more than a shadow to him, a being of the Underworld, a house habitated by memory.

"Give me your hand," he said.

He should not be merciful to her, or he would die. But she took the hand he reached down to her, and let him haul her out of the darkness, into the dusty, milling chaos of a hot and sunny farmyard.

Through a blaze of tears brought on by sunlight, she saw farmers in their summertime work clothes, come to see who had been locked in their cellar and why. She saw each of Emil's lieutenants, who had never, even at a funeral, seemed so grim. She saw many other Paladins, some who had jeered at her, some who might eventually have become her friends. All of them stared at her, and at the dignified man she'd had the temerity to call her brother, not so long ago.

His rage was masked, but she felt it like knife on bone. "You have made friends with a Sainnite," he said.

She knew what she had to do. "Yes, sir."

"And you went out the other night to meet this person?"

"Yes, I did."

"What for?"

This time, he would not die. He would not help her as his enemies lay in wait. Better for him to hate her than to die because of her. She said, "I went to lead an attack on Willis's unit, but they said they were not ready."

His hand rested on his pistol. This close to her, he would get a good shot, and even in anger would shoot well, kindly, remembering his affection even as he knew it was betrayed. But then he sighed, and all was lost. "I know that is a lie," he said.

A voice spoke behind Zanja. "She intends her lie as a gift."

Zanja did not have to turn to know who had spoken. A black shadow flapped upon the ground in front of her. Her frail courage faltered.

Emil said, his voice still soft with anger, "A misguided gift."

Zanja said, "Sir, it is my calling to transgress, but it is my duty to cause no harm by that transgression. Let me do my duty."

Emil gazed into her eyes, expressionless, unblinking. And then he turned away, to speak to his lieutenants. "This matter will not turn out the way any of us might expect. It seems ill-advised to do this so publicly, when so much damage already has been done to our community."

Willis said, "No," as though he already was the commander. This was, certainly, his spectacle.

Emil smiled oddly, without amusement. "Well then, at least let's get into the shade, for courtesy to our guest." He gestured toward an arbor of flowering vines, where there were some inviting benches in the shade.

Zanja turned then, and looked into the scarred, sun-browned face of Norina Truthken. "What are you doing here? It is not your business."

Norina said, "Who did you think would come?"

Though Zanja had lived with her until four months ago, she'd had no idea that Norina was pregnant. Even the heavy clothing of winter could not have concealed it now. Though her dust-stained clothing and red-rimmed eyes suggested a heroic journey had brought her here so quickly, her jutting belly hinted that at any moment she might deliver a child. Just the thought of her as a mother made Zanja's head hurt.

Karis's raven rode upon her shoulder. It was a most uncanny sight.

Zanja could barely walk the short distance to the arbor. The bullet wound in her leg had not healed at all as she lay helpless in the Underworld. At least she could escape the sun and sit upon a bench, though everyone else except Norina remained standing. A man-at-arms stood beside Norina, bristling with weapons like a brigand.

Willis began, "I found Zanja's bed empty shortly after dark, and—"

Emil said, "I know what happened, Willis."

"But the Truthken—"

"If Madam Truthken wishes to know something, she may ask."

The watchfulness of Norina's gaze, and the black bird on her shoulder, hardly seemed calculated to set anyone at ease. She said, "Lieutenant—Willis is your name?"

Willis jumped, and Zanja felt something, the faintest prickle of anticipation. "Madam Truthken," he said belligerently.

"You have not told the truth."

"I am not lying! Anyone who was there will confirm—"

"You wanted Zanja dead, and were desperate for an excuse. That is what you have not said."

His face went white, but his chin came up. "I admit I had my men abandon her in a firefight. But I did that because I knew she was a traitor, and Emil would not see it, just as he will not see it now. I did it to save the company."

Norina gazed at him, expressionless. "So you named yourself commander."

Dazzled and bewildered by the vivid shine of truth in the midst of this nightmare, Zanja said, "He acted under Mabin's command."

She heard the faintest sound from Emil: a grunt of pain or surprise.

Norina's gaze on Willis's face never wavered. "She says the truth?"

"Yes," Willis said, with more apparent pride than fear.

Norina blinked, once, and turned to Emil.

Emil said in a strangled voice, "What did she offer you?"

But Willis, seeming to think he had the upper hand, said loftily, "That's between me and the councilor."

The bloody fool would get command of South Hill Company. Zanja could feel no more horror; the betrayals had accumulated until she hardly noticed them. But the look on Emil's face was worse than her own pain.

Norina stood up. "Commander, I need to speak to you alone."

They stepped aside. The five lieutenants, two of whom Zanja scarcely knew, shuffled their feet and muttered to each other. The man-at-arms stood stolid as a plowhorse, but his gaze never ceased to flick from one person to the next. Zanja ached in every part of her body. She felt her face with her fingers, to find her eyelids swollen, her lip split, her cheekbone raw and bruised. Her leg hurt with a dull and insinuating pain. She kept forgetting where she was, and the faces of the lieutenants and the observers kept changing, from Paladin to Sainnite to Ashawala'i.

Norina and Emil returned. Emil said somberly, "I will communicate with Mabin on what to do with you, Willis, but meanwhile you are relieved of duty."

Willis's face turned red with anger. "And the traitor? You'll let her go unpunished, of course!"

"We have not yet addressed the problem of Zanja," said Emil evenly. "But I have relevant information that I doubt any of you have yet heard. The Shaftali prisoners were set free from Wilton garrison last night. Some of those from Annis's family came direct to me and told me about how they'd been freed by a Sainnite man, who unlocked the doors and escorted them safely out of the garrison and out of the city itself, all under cover of darkness."

"A Sainnite?" repeated Willis in disbelief.

"Yes. In fact, the freed prisoners carried a letter to me from him." Emil turned to Zanja. "What did you tell this Medric, the night Willis found your bed empty?"

Zanja said, though it took a great effort, "I never saw him that night."

Emil glanced at Norina. "Madam Truthken?"

"Truth," Norina said.

"What were you intending to tell him?"

"I was going to bring him to you, to have you meet him."

"Truth," Norina said.

"Why?"

"He wanted to join the Paladins."

Norina said, "I can't judge the truth of hearsay."

"Ah, yes. But Zanja believes what he told her to be true?"

"I can't be certain, Commander. She wants it to be true, but for this very reason she does not trust her judgment—and for other reasons as well," Norina added, as though she were reading words being written as she spoke. "I think she is unbalanced. How long has it been since she ate, or drank?"

"Just two days," Willis said defensively. "Maybe three."

"Wounded and bleeding. And your man says he heard her screaming."

"What matter? She's a traitor!"

"You believe that she's a traitor," Norina corrected him. "The truth, however, has yet to be determined, and cannot be determined when she is scarcely even in her right mind. Commander, I am here for my own reasons, but since you have asked me to arbitrate I must insist that you at least get her some water."

Emil sent someone for water, and while that was being brought, Norina took a cloth bag out of the pocket of her doublet and tossed it to Zanja. It contained some kind of old dried fruit, gone hard as rawhide and practically as tasteless. Zanja held a piece in her mouth, and as it softened and dissolved a sudden clarity came to her: enough at least for her to realize how weak she was, how worn out with despair and horror. With the second piece the pain in her leg was eased, and with the third she sat erect and pushed some loose strands of hair from her face, and thanked the girl who had brought a dipper of water for her.

She said, "I met Medric on Fire Night. And though I was and am still half afraid that he might be engaged in some kind of elaborate trick, I took the risk of talking to him, because I thought the benefits could be great. It's he who told me that the Sainnites were going to attack us at Fen Overlook."

There certainly were some huge gaps in this story she'd told, but Emil at least seemed able to fill them in. He glanced at Norina, who said, "Clearly the truth."

"What have you told him in return?" Emil asked.

"He asked only to meet you, Emil, and I told him nothing."

"Truth," Norina said.

Willis exploded. "What does it matter! She spoke to a Sainnite! She did it in secret!"

There was still something Zanja might do. She said, "Medric is a better man than you, Willis."

Norina said, "Zanja, be quiet."

"He said he would prove his trustworthiness to me, and he has proven it. Meanwhile, you have proven that nothing matters to you but your own ambition."

Norina said, "Silence her!"

But Zanja cried, "There is just one traitor here, Madam Truthken!"

With all her strength, she flung herself at Emil's weak knee, and he toppled like a rotten tree at exactly the moment of the pistol blast.

Zanja lay across him, gasping, terrified that she might have flung him into the line of fire rather than away from it. Then, Emil raised a hand and gently laid it on the back of her head. "Quite a display of prescience. What in Shaftal's name do you think you're doing?"

She said, for his ears only, "That man just guaranteed that he would never command South Hill Company."

His chest heaved: was he laughing? She could not tell, he was otherwise so solemn. "Careful!" Linde had rushed over and seemed ready to disentangle them by flinging Zanja wildly out of the way. "Calm down, Linde, I'm not hurt. But she already was injured and it's only worse now."

Linde lifted Zanja and set her on the bench, then helped his commander to his feet. Linde's face was white with shock, but not so white as Willis's, who half stood and half hung within the grips of the other lieutenant and Norina's man-at-arms. "I did not aim at Emil," he said desperately to Norina, who had not moved from where she sat, and if anything seemed uninterested in the chaos before her. "I would never shoot my commander! It was her, the traitor—I lost my temper, is all!"

Emil walked over to him and hit him, a contemptuous blow that scarcely left a mark on Willis's face, but silenced him effectively enough. Across the yard, that contemptuous blow registered in the faces of a dozen or more people, who although they had not heard what was said, surely could read the language of the scene, like any other staged drama.

"And you think that a man who cannot command himself can command a whole company?" He added, "Madam Truthken, is there a traitor here?"

Zanja felt so strange, so empty, so tired, that she wondered how she could still be present in this strange place. Norina said, "Zanja has merely exercised a fire blood's usual foolhardiness. As for Willis, it is most ambiguous. Willis meant to shoot Zanja, but he meant it as a blow to you. So in the eyes of the law, perhaps it might be argued that you were his true target. In any case, I would refuse to hear him as Zanja's accuser, for he only loves the justice that serves his interests, and only sees the Law as a tool to achieve his desires. He is untrustworthy, but technically he is not a traitor."

"Let Willis go," Emil said. Willis was released. "Get out of my sight," Emil added. "And get out of my company. If you want to complain to Councilor Mabin, you are free to do so. The rest of you, please step away. I wish to talk to the Truthken alone."

Reluctantly, they left. Emil sat heavily on the bench beside Zanja. "This is a fine mess!"

Across the green, Willis had already reached his people, and no doubt he quickly began to explain his version of what they had seen. But they stood back, apparently uncertain whether they wanted to be known to be his supporters any longer.

Norina said quietly, "Shall I leave?"

"If you don't mind, Truthken, I think it best that I avoid the appearance of conspiring with Zanja and so it would be most useful to me if you remain." Emil folded his hand and rested his forehead upon them in an attitude of utter weariness. "Zanja—You and I are at cross-purposes, of course. I am much more interested in saving your life than I am in saving my position. At the same time, you are trying to save my position and seem little interested in saving your life."

Zanja said, "My brother, you have died for me a hundred times. I could not endure it anymore."

Ransel looked at her blankly.

"Don't be a fool," Zanja implored him. "Every time you try to help me, you die. Do not burden me with the terrible memory, I beg you! If you do not die, you cannot blame me for failing to avenge you."

Ransel took both her hands in his. "My sister," he said gently, "the past is done and cannot be changed. Come forth out of the Underworld."

Emil was holding her hands. He said quietly, "Madam Truthken, this must be the anniversary of the massacre of the Ashawala'i."

Norina's eyes narrowed, as though she had been handed a package that might or might not be a gift.

"I think she's half out of her mind," he added, "and she certainly cannot recover here. I ask you to take her under your protection, and bring her to a healer."

Norina stood up. "I will, of course. But first, I think I'd better guarantee that the rogue lieutenant of yours can't get his forces organized, or we may find it difficult to get safely out of South Hill.

I'll leave my man here, to give you the appearance of propriety. I don't think any of your people have noticed that he's deaf." She picked up the bag from beside Zanja and gave her a handful of the dried fruit. "What became of your blades? You don't know? All right, I'll find them for you. Is there anything else you own that's too precious to leave behind? All right, eat that. Come, raven."

The raven flew to her shoulder, and, gesturing to her man to remain, Norina walked over to the knot of people that had formed around Willis. The knot loosened as Willis's people stood back to let him face the Truthken on his own. No doubt she would use her substantial powers and authority to make his present and future life as unpleasant as he deserved.

Emil commented, "A formidable woman, even for a Truthken." He took some folded papers from his doublet's inside pocket. "My first letter from a seer. He devoted most of it to successfully con-vincing me to spare your life at any cost. As for the rest, he says he had a dream that the land would recognize him as her son, and so he's going forth into Shaftal on his own. He wrote that he has left me all his books—had them shipped downriver to a storehouse in Haprin for me to pick up. I feel like I've been bequeathed a child by a total stranger."

Zanja said, "I wish you could have met him. You would have liked him."

"I admit I find his letter both intelligent and convincing. It's a very strange sensation to be saying such things about a man who has helped to kill so many of my friends."

"But he was trapped. When the walls of the House of Lilterwess fell, the Sainnites themselves were buried in the rubble. And we all are buried there with them, crushed and suffocating under the stones."

"Hmm. Now you *are* talking treason. Good thing there's no one but me to hear." Emil unfolded his letter from Medric again, and Zanja saw how creased and smudged the paper was. This letter had forced Emil to subject it to uneasy and intense scrutiny, and perhaps its contents still were being delivered to him as he glanced at it once again, still seeming uncertain how to read it. "He wrote some glyphs here at the bottom, do you see? It seems like a message to you. At least, here is your Owl, your Raven, your Door."

In fact, Medric had written at the bottom of the page each of the glyphs from Zanja's frantic card reading the day after Fire Night. But now, no madwoman lay at the center of the circle, holding together or being torn apart by contrary forces. Instead, there was a glyph Zanja did not know how to read. She touched it with her fingertip, and Emil said, "That's Fellowship, the union of friends to serve a grand design. What do you think he means by it?"

"I think he's nineteen years old and hasn't yet lost his hope."

"Zanja na'Tarwein," Emil said, "may that hope one day be yours and mine as well."

When Norina returned, Willis walked behind her, carrying some of Zanja's gear, including her missing blades. One of his people also followed, leading the horses like a servant. Truthkens must be obeyed, in small things and in large. Zanja hastily chewed and swallowed the dried fruit. It lay within her, warm as earth in summer. The wound in her leg stopped seeping blood, and when she stood up, her vision remained clear.

Emil buckled her weapons belt onto her and put the knife into her boot sheath, and helped her mount one of Norina's horses. She must have looked a ruin as she rode out of that place, tired unto death, with her breeches blood-encrusted and her face marked and swollen from Willis's fist. When she looked back, she saw Emil, standing serenely alone in the middle of the roadway. He lifted a hand in farewell. So long as he stood there, Zanja knew, no one would dare chase after them. He was still standing there when the road took a turn, and he was gone from sight.

Part 3

The Hinge of History

All love is made of insane hope.
　　　　　　　　　　　—MACKAPEE'S *Principles for Community*

*The past is always with us. For the blood that soaks the earth cries
out for justice. And without justice we never will have peace.*
　　　　　　　　　　　　　　　　　　　　—MABIN'S *Warfare*

*Between victory and defeat, between offense and revenge, lies
a third possibility: neither a compromise nor an abandonment, but a
marriage.*
　　　　　　　　　　　　—MEDRIC'S *History of My Father's People*

Chapter Nineteen

Like a great wheel the year turned; and now the sower dropped to the horizon, and up rose the gatherer with her arm outstretched to capture the ripe stars and put them in her basket. All day, in kitchens across Shaftal, the ripe fruits had been cut up to be dried in the sun, or cooked with sugar to make preserves, or covered with hot syrup to be baked into pies during the dark half of the year.

Now it was night, and in the most northwestern borderland, the general of the Paladins sat awake in her lamplit study with a bowl of golden apricots untouched upon her desk. The aging general of the Sainnites also sat awake, drinking wine and pacing restlessly as he made the messenger from South Hill explain again and again how the South Hill garrison had managed to lose track of the Sainnites' only seer.

Somewhere between these two generals, in a silent glade well away from the road, Zanja lay staring into the darkness, and did not flinch or even seem to notice when Norina began to peel the bandage from her wounded leg. And on the river which runs east past Wilton, Emil stood at the bow of a boat that lazily rode the current towards Hanishport and the sea. After fifteen years as the commander of South Hill Company, he had left South Hill, and never would return.

How could he continue to command, when his general had proven herself such a fool? Norina Truthken had told him quite forcefully that Mabin had valid reasons for her actions that would never be explained. But whatever Mabin's reasons, no matter how valid they might be, that did not make it any less impossible for Emil to continue as commander. He wrote Mabin a letter, he delivered South Hill Company to Perry's capable command, he bid his friends farewell, and he left South Hill.

His lifetime of service had left him impoverished by Shaftali standards, for he had no family to go home to, and the friends who had served as family in the old Paladins were dead or fighting in the war. Still, he could not seem to bring himself to be concerned about his own future. He felt only his freedom.

The boat reached Haprin at mid-afternoon. He made his way to a storehouse near the docks, where he showed a woman his letter from Medric and she waved him into the building without even looking at it. "It's four big trunks, halfway back on the right side," she said. "You'll be needing a wagon."

Once beyond the light of the doorway, he walked through a darkness that rustled with mice and bats. He hoped that the trunks were good ones and he would not find the books chewed to pieces. Halfway down the long, dark building, a sudden light flared as though someone had lit a match. The flare became a lamp wick's steady glow, and the flame disappeared, though Emil could track it by the light it cast. In his recurring dream, he had followed that glow of light through shadows just like these. He remembered these half-seen crates, the dusty, dim shadows, the rustling of the mice. His heart's desire waited for him here.

The crowded shapes would form an open space here, which would be filled with light. And so he found a glowing nest of blankets tucked among the massive trunks. The man from Emil's dream sat quietly beside a small brass lamp, which did not illuminate his face. Upon his knees lay a plain, flat wooden box with a broken latch that once had locked with a key. The man said nothing, but held the box up to Emil.

Emil knelt and took the box. He opened the hinged lid, and laid the box down upon the floor so that the lamplight shone inside. The papers carefully preserved within were padded with small pillows of down and silk. On the top page was written, "Principles for Community," and underneath, scarcely readable in faded ink, the name "Mackapee."

Emil did not touch the fragile paper, but he bent his face close to it, and breathed deeply. He could smell, so faint it scarcely was there at all, the scent of peat smoke. The Mackapee manuscript had not been burned after all.

He saw that his life had been a spiral, first veering away from loss, but now turning back to a new beginning. He had done his duty. Now, at last, he could follow his heart.

"You can only be Medric," he said.

"Sir, can you return this manuscript to its rightful place?"

"It belongs at the library at Kisha, which has been destroyed." Emil carefully closed the lid of the manuscript box. "I'll have to build a new library, and a new university. And first, I'll have to make Shaftal a place in which libraries and universities can be built."

The young man said, "That's not a bad idea."

"It's an undertaking so large I doubt anyone alive now will live to see the end of it."

"Oh, no, I think you're wrong. But in any case, 'What's worth doing is worth merely beginning.'"

"So wrote Mackapee, the first G'deon of Shaftal. Have you read the manuscript?"

"The manuscript? No, sir, it has not been removed from its box. I've studied a printed copy."

Emil took up the little traveling lamp by the handle, and lifted it so it illuminated Medric's face. The seer's lenses glowed with flame. "You *are* young," Emil said.

"I suppose. You're exactly as I dreamed."

"You dreamed of me? What did you dream?"

Medric's gesture took in the dark warehouse, the glowing lamp, the fortress of books. Emil set down the lamp rather sharply, and sat back on his heels. When two fire bloods share a dream, it is said, their fates are linked forever.

Medric peered at him. "Are you all right, sir?"

"You'll help me build that library."

"You'll accept my help?"

"Why wouldn't I? Oh." Emil began to laugh. "That's right; you're the enemy."

It seemed to also strike Medric as terribly funny, and his hilarity didn't run dry until his spectacles fell off and he had to retrieve them by feel.

Emil said, "A few days after Fire Night, when Zanja was on her way to meet you—though I didn't know it then—she said she was trapped in the past and needed to cross over into the future. I foolishly asked her to take me with her. So here I am, bewildered mainly by my lack of regret."

Medric smiled. "I crossed over also, knowingly and willingly. But what became of her?"

"I managed to get her safely out of South Hill. That's all I know. But let me thank you now, while I'm thinking of it, for your letter. It helped me to do what was right, and I needed that help desperately."

"Well, I'm glad I've done some good for once."

"Have you eaten? May I buy your supper?"

Medric gathered himself up and rose to his feet. "I confess, I haven't eaten in a day or two, and not because I'm fasting for a vision."

"You're penniless, of course, which is why you're sleeping with your books."

"*Your* books."

"My books, if you insist. Yet it seems that you accompany them."

"Sir, the books are not a bribe. Ever since I began to collect them, I knew that I would have to deliver them to a proper caretaker. I simply could not bear to leave them unguarded." Medric offered his hand to help Emil rise.

Emil took Medric's hand and let himself be helped. Medric was slightly built and had a soft hand, but he was not without muscle. Only a fool would underestimate him: no accident had brought them to this place, but the active, determined intervention of a gifted seer. His air of uncertainty was merely an affectation.

Emil said, still holding his hand, "My name is Emil. If you call me 'sir' again, I'll start calling you 'Master Seer'."

Medric looked appalled. "Please don't, Emil."

"Let's get some food in you."

Emil could not bear to leave the manuscript unattended, so they took it with them. At the inn, Medric asked for bread and vegetables, causing the cook to look at him askance, but Emil accepted roast capon and a pie of fresh peaches. Over food, their conversation turned from somber to hilarious, and Emil laughed until his ribs hurt, wondering if that lightness in his chest could possibly be his heart. If it was his heart, it was on holiday.

After supper, he purchased a wagon and a sturdy dray horse, using almost all the money he had taken with him. Haprin had a ferry that would take him across the river; from there he would go to the western border where he could store the books with his friend the shepherd. After that; well, he supposed some plan would come to him.

It was nearly dark when they returned to the storehouse. Medric showed Emil the other rare books in his collection. He had found them one by one through dreams, he said, stored at the bottom of one or another soldier's footlocker. He had collected a couple of hundred books by the time he finally got the one he was looking for, *The Way of the Seer*, and each book had its own adventure story of unlikely survival in a hostile world. They talked about the books until the lamp oil ran out and left them sitting shoulder to shoulder in a sudden darkness.

Medric said, "Sometimes this summer I have envisioned myself in another place: a stone cottage in a lonely land, with sleet tapping on the shutters and a warm fire burning. And I'm not alone there. I ask a question, and you come and sit down next to me. You tell me how the past became the present. You get a book down from the shelf and read it to me."

Emil said, "It's still a long time before sleet taps on the shutters, but tomorrow is close by. I hope you'll be traveling with me."

"I will," Medric said. "Don't go."

Emil could feel Medric's warm breath stirring the air between them. He found Medric's face by feel and carefully took off his spectacles and put them safely atop the trunk. Then, in a bed that was made of as much book as blanket, he made love to a son of the enemy. It occurred to him later that even his oldest and most loyal friends would not forgive him this transgression, or even worse, they'd misunderstand and pity him. He lay in the rustling darkness of the warehouse with Medric asleep in his arms, and could not bring himself to care what anyone thought of him. He had broken with the past, and the future was a book he could hardly wait to read.

Chapter Twenty

After a day or two of travel, Zanja stopped expecting the upbraiding she deserved. In fact, Norina accorded Zanja a certain kindness, though from outside it might have looked more like indifference. She had looked after Zanja's injuries, patiently soaking loose the bandage from the wound, and rebandaging it every day after that with an expertise that she must have acquired from J'han. She insisted that Zanja rest even though she could not sleep, and hounded her into eating. She and the man took turns riding, while Zanja rode all the time, and she would not permit Zanja to do any of the work at all, except small things she could do while sitting down. It was easier to acquiesce to her iron will than it was to resist, and so, in spite of the circumstances, Zanja's injuries began to heal.

Other than insisting brusquely that Zanja obey her, Norina left her alone. Zanja rode blindly behind her companions, carried forward only by the momentum of the journey. She did not know where she was, or in what direction she traveled. She did not care that she lived, and took no interest in what might happen to her next. Days passed, and she did not even speak. She wept without noticing her own tears.

One morning, she raised her head and noted that they were traveling northward. They followed a rutted, unmarked track through rugged, mountainous country. Some time passed, and she looked down and noticed Norina walking at her stirrup, breathless, putting a hand occasionally to the horse's side for balance. "You'll miscarry," Zanja said.

"I'm as likely to miscarry as you are to die from sepsis," Norina said.

Some time later, Zanja said, "I feel I could die from sorrow first."

But Norina said, quite sensibly and with surprising kindness, "You'll start feeling better soon. The first year is over."

A long time later, Zanja asked, "Will Willis get control of South Hill Company?"

Norina laughed. "That man? Not even in his dreams."

That night, Zanja plunged into a deep and restful sleep, from which she woke as if rousing from a summer fever. She bathed in a cold stream, washed and mended her shirt, and took out her blades to check and clean them. The small knife in her boot was blood-encrusted. She fingered the scab on her neck, remembering what she had done, amazed that her crazed logic had brought aid after all.

"The raven is gone?" she asked Norina, as they ate camp porridge by the fire. The man-at-arms was already saddling the horses.

"Naturally, I sent him with a message to Karis that you are all right."

"I want to send Karis an apology. I must have startled her when I wrote that message on the knife blade."

Norina ate a few mouthfuls of her porridge before commenting, rather wryly, "I have to say, your methods are ingenious."

One night they were kindly welcomed and generously fed in a woodcutter's camp, where the people were desperate for news and stories of any kind at all. Zanja lay gazing at the stars, which had not been so close since she left the mountains of her people.

Soon, they climbed down out of the mountains and followed a river to the northwest, and slept one night at a farmstead, in the hay. The farmers fed them even though they were respectively too injured, tired, and pregnant to work; they would not hear of a pregnant woman going hungry; and they nearly convinced her to sleep in a bed instead of the barn. Norina was not tireless, and when Zanja turned to look at her that night she caught her off guard, and just for a moment could see how worried she was. Then Norina turned her head, and her face was stone again.

At midday, they entered a village at a crossroads, which Norina said was called Strongbridge. The bridge was indeed impressive, and was frequently crossed by heavy wagons. The inn-yard they entered served as a kind of depot where huge dray horses stood harnessed while the drivers paced the cobbles, stretching their stiff legs, eating the meat and bread hauled out to them in baskets, and swigging tankards of ale against the oppressive heat. The inn itself was of startling size, recently painted red and green, with flowers cascading over its roof from an enterprising vine. Among the flowers a raven stalked. In the rectangular gap of a second floor window a very tall woman was intricately folded, nearly invisible in shadow. She looked as though she might be trapped there.

"Zanja," Norina said sharply, to call her attention to the girl who waited for Zanja to hand her the reins.

Zanja dismounted, and left horse and companions standing in the yard. She could not run yet on her injured leg, and the front door jerked open before she had reached it.

She had half forgotten how big Karis was. She filled the doorway, her shoulders almost wide enough to touch both doorframes, head bowed to fit below the lintel, big hands clasping the timber frame as though she might simply collapse it, and make the inside out, and the outside in. And then it was as though the earth itself had clasped Zanja in a bruising embrace and lifted her half off her feet, and made as though to completely encompass and engulf her.

Her ear was against Karis's heart. She gripped her with all her strength. She would not let Karis go again. All the forces of the Universe might range themselves against her, but she would not let Karis go.

"Just leave us alone, Nori," Karis said after a while.

A long time later, Zanja lifted her head a little, and realized that Karis had practically folded herself around her, and seemed not at all inclined to release her, though she did raise her cheek somewhat from the top of Zanja's head when she felt her move. Zanja said, "I'm making a mess of your shirt."

"How would anyone know the difference?" But Karis produced a sweaty handkerchief from somewhere, and Zanja used it to wipe the remaining tears and dirt from her face. "We're making spectacles of ourselves," Karis said.

Around the bulge of Karis's bicep Zanja could see into the public room, where a couple of hardened drinkers stared at them. "Surely there's a path by the river," Zanja said.

Zanja's limp gave them as good a reason as any to walk arm in arm despite the sweltering heat. She felt dazed, in a strange land, with no familiar landmarks. *Dear gods*, she thought, *what boundary did I just cross?* As they walked through the town, Karis stopped to buy some steamed buns from a stall, which did a desultory business. The streets were largely deserted, dogs lay panting in what shade they could find, and every window was propped open. On a day like this, the entire population of Asha Valley could have been found in or near the river, and so it was here. The shady shoreline was crowded with lounging or dozing adults, and still more swam along the banks, keeping an eye on the shrieking children. They found a solitary place at last, where the current was probably too swift for swimming, and they sat side by side upon the damp earth. Damsel flies covered a branch over the water like jewels on a rich man's jerkin. Karis gave Zanja a dumpling. Its meat filling was so spicy it made Zanja's eyes tear up again.

"Now stop that," Karis said

"It's really spicy. Gods know I'll cry at anything lately, but this time it's not sadness."

Karis took a bite, and closed her eyes in concentration, chewing. "I guess maybe I can taste something," she said finally.

"It's like eating coals from a fire," Zanja said.

"Is that good? It certainly sounds interesting."

"In a painful kind of way."

Zanja had not quite remembered the utter chaos of Karis's hair, which grew in every direction and was twisted into vinelike tendrils that looked impossible to comb or tame. She had not quite remembered the intense blue color of her eyes, or the fine lines that radiated out from them like the splines of a fan. She had remembered that Karis's physical presence was a kind of a shock, like a stone tossed into water or a live voice penetrating a dream, but when they last met Zanja had been unable to truly feel the impact of it. Now, with every breath that lifted Karis's shoulders, every pulse in her throat, Zanja felt her own heart turn over. When Karis turned to her, she did not know what to do. Should she confess? Should she look away?

Karis said, "I've thought about you constantly."

Zanja opened her mouth, but didn't trust whatever might have come out of it. "How is it possible that you can act like this without desiring me?" she might have said.

Karis said, "Take off your pants."

Zanja felt a disorientation, then got a grip on herself and said with difficulty, "My leg is healing."

"Please, Zanja, I beg you. The trajectory of the pistol ball has torn up the muscles of your thigh. Even if it heals you'll have scarring inside your leg, and the muscle won't work right because of it, and I'll never be at peace if I don't fix it."

Zanja unbuttoned and pulled down her breeches and lay upon her side while Karis cut the bandage from her thigh. She would turn this experience into a test of discipline, for she seemed to be sorely in need of such an exercise. "Can you leave the scar?"

"For bragging rights?" Karis sounded amused.

"I was abandoned by my fellows in the middle of a firefight because they wanted me dead. That hardly seems a thing to brag about. But I'd rather not have to explain why I don't have a scar to show for it."

"All right. I'll try to restrain myself."

The violence of metalsmithing had not spoiled Karis for more gentle crafts. She almost made the healing seem as if it were not work at all, except that occasionally a drop of her sweat fell and landed on Zanja's skin. Zanja worked to keep her breathing steady and her muscles relaxed; her old trainers would have been proud of her. When Karis's warm hands lifted from her thigh, it was a relief but also a loss.

"That's better," Karis said.

Zanja pulled up the bloodstained remains of her pants. "How do you do it," she asked shakily, "without being able to feel?"

"I feel a little. It's not much, but it's all I have."

"When I think of what you could do . . ."

"Don't think about it."

"The man that got you addicted to smoke—"

"He's dead already, not that it does me any good."

"I'd like to kill him again."

"You'd have to wait your turn."

Behind the clear eyes, the powerful, passive muscles, the soot ground into her skin, and the quiet, waiting expression of her face, lay a deep anger. Zanja said, "Karis, you are not tame, merely caged."

Karis made a sound as if she had accidentally sliced a finger. "You know, talking to you is a bit like chewing on hot coals."

Zanja broke into a startled laugh.

"My raven said you were in a black despair."

Zanja said grudgingly, "Norina has been as kind as I would tolerate, and I guess it's done me some good. You must have done something dramatic, to force her to treat me so gently."

Karis showed her teeth. "Oh, I did."

"Did you threaten to come get me yourself?"

"Threaten? No, she is immune to threats. I started to South Hill moments after I'd gotten your message, and I challenged Nori to give me a reason to turn back and let her go in my place."

Karis lay upon her back and gazed up into a sky as blue as her eyes. Her shirt collar was unbuttoned and sweat collected in the hollow of her throat. Zanja shut her eyes and begged the hot afternoon to anesthetize her. After a long time she said, "But Norina seems desperately worried, and much as I don't like her I must respect her. I wish I understood what she understands."

"Mmm. This is what you sound like when you're being diplomatic. It's not chewing coals anymore, it's more like—oh, I'm no good at metaphors. You tell me one."

Zanja tried to think of texture, for although Karis could not taste, she surely could feel enough to be able to tell soft from hard. "Those crisp cakes with chewy pieces of fruit in them," she suggested.

"They feed those to me when I've forgotten too many times to eat. They must be mostly butter. What are you laughing at?"

"You don't like those little cakes?"

"I hate being treated like I'm an invalid."

"I apologize. It's my own ignorance that makes me resort to indirection. I don't know what I'm supposed to say or know. I don't know what might hurt or offend you."

Unlike the sun-parched sky at which she gazed, Karis's eyes were a bright, unfaded blue. She squinted them shut suddenly, as though sweat stung them. "When Norina takes you away, you won't know any more than you do now."

"That's not going to happen," Zanja said.

Karis turned her head. "Norina is my protector because she's dangerous."

"Yes, but she has more to lose than I have."

"Are you going to make me demand that you obey her?"

"Are you going to treat me like a servant?"

"Are you going to make me choose between you?"

"Why not? Norina makes you choose."

"She has a good reason."

"What good reason could she possibly have?"

Karis said unsteadily, "I can't tell you."

"Why not?"

"Because I'm bound by obligations I can't explain to you. Why are you so cantankerous? Is it the heat?"

Zanja said, "From beginning to end, this year has been a disaster. But I've learned something that you and Norina both don't know: how impossible it is to really make a choice, when the best choice of all is an option you couldn't even imagine."

Karis blinked up at the glaring sky. "Say that again, but fill it up with human experience and leave out the abstract words, and maybe I'll understand it."

"The Sainnites defined my choices for me. And before that, the Ashawala'i did the same. Because I am a *katrim*, and because the Sainnites are fools, I am living a life that I hate. I'm thinking I should do something else."

"I see," Karis said.

"In much the same way, Norina makes it possible for you to live within your cage. And so long as she helps you tolerate captivity you never will break free. You'll have no reason to try."

"Shaftal's Name!" Karis sat up abruptly.

Now ends our friendship, Zanja thought.

"Oh, you are dangerous," Karis said.

She settled back onto her elbows, and in the heated silence the accuser bugs suddenly began to shrill. After a long time, she said, "Norina has insisted that you be left in ignorance, lest you do something disastrous. But now it seems that you have done something disastrous because of your ignorance."

"Names of the gods! What have I done?"

"I can't tell you—that's Norina's business. But I think I will point out to her that to continue to leave you in ignorance seems, at best, ill-advised," Karis said. "And to treat you like a servant seems ridiculous, since you will not—cannot—act like one—except as a kind of play-acting. And to send you away has proven impossible since no matter how far you go I continue to hold onto you in spite of all advice and common sense. Norina insists that I must not—cannot—simply call you my friend. I am a smoke addict, and she is a Truthken. Only an idiot would trust my judgment over hers. So tell me what I am to do, Zanja, for I am at a loss."

Zanja said, "Why don't you seek the advice of a seer? It just happens that I know one, and—"

She had to stop, because Karis had begun to howl with laughter. Nonplused, she waited for Karis to recover from her mirth, which had a certain bitter edge to it, for she seemed almost to be sobbing by the end, and had to wipe her tears on the tail of her shirt. "You have no idea—" she gasped.

"No idea at all," Zanja agreed.

"I'm sorry," Karis said. "Tell me about your seer. Tell me how you met."

"I met Medric on Fire Night," Zanja began. "Emil had sent me to find Annis, who had gone rogue after the Sainnites torched her family's farmstead, and my search brought me to Wilton, where I found her. But along the way, something began to happen to me, and I began to do things that made no sense . . ."

But at least one thing she had done did make sense. She opened the pouch that held her glyph cards, and shook out from the bottom, where she had nearly forgotten it, the pendant of green stone and silver wire. "That day I bought this for you, though I had no reason to even imagine that I would see you again. I thought I had lost my mind. I was starting to remember things in a way that seemed insane. But perhaps it was, after all, a kind of prescience. When the veil between present and past tore apart, so also did the veil between present and future. I hadn't lost my mind; I merely knew something I had no business knowing."

She put the pendant into Karis's hand. "You see, now I have given you the pendant. I look forward to someday understanding how everything I did that day makes as much sense as buying this pendant did."

Karis seemed dumbfounded, and said not a word as Zanja resumed her tale, but lay back in the grass with the pendant in her fist, resting against her breast, until Zanja had described her last sight of Emil standing in the middle of the road, and then fell silent.

Then Karis said, "Name of Shaftal, it does make sense. Norina has been wrong—wrong from the first moment I sensed your presence in Shaftal. Zanja—" She swallowed. She was breathing as though she had run a race. "Yes, I do want to speak to Medric, very badly."

"I can bring him to you. Unless I've sorely misjudged him, he would make himself easy for me to find. He wants nothing more than to do some good in Shaftal. It doesn't bother you that he's half Sainnite?"

As Zanja talked, Karis had gotten to her feet. Now, she gazed down at Zanja, and her face seemed very far away, and shadowed suddenly as her height blocked out the sun. "What is it exactly that you think I am?" she asked.

Zanja stared up at her. The people of the Juras tribe were yellow-haired, blue-eyed, extremely strong giants. But Karis's Juras mother had been a Lalali whore. "Your father would have been a very big man," she said.

"And a Sainnite."

"No doubt. I suppose that would matter to some people."

"To some people, it is the most important thing about me."

"Well, Karis, you know some tremendous idiots."

Karis leaned over, and took hold of Zanja with both her hands, and set her on her feet. "So long as you're not one of them," she said, and Zanja saw that she was smiling.

Beyond the inn-yard and the inn, behind the kitchen, grew an undisciplined garden where climbing roses and fragrant herbs tangled into a blooming thicket, over which bees operated in a hum of industry. The beehives stood at the garden's edge, nearly half a dozen of them. Bees bumped into Zanja and Karis as they walked across the flight path, their feet crunching in the dried bee corpses that littered the ground. Zanja followed Karis into the tangle of roses, and Karis in turn followed a path to a lathe house overgrown with rich, green vines. The door had fallen off its hinges. Within, Norina lay upon a bench in a mossy shade garden planted beside a spring. The bubbling pond was filled with sodden wooden crates that contained bottles of milk and wine, kept cool by the cold water. The shade garden seemed damp and almost chilly compared to the sun-sodden outdoors. Norina lay on her side with her head pillowed on one arm.

Zanja hesitated at the doorway as Karis knelt beside Norina and lay a hand upon her gravid torso. She smiled so sweetly that Zanja wondered how anyone could remain angry with her. Even Norina could be cajoled, for after a moment her scarred face creased with a rare smile. Bits of sunlight that came in through the lathwork speckled them with sparks of brilliance.

Leaning upon the rotting door post, Zanja saw how it must always have been between them: bound by an affection sturdy enough to survive all the disagreements and power struggles that were inevitable between two such willful women.

They talked in low voices, then Zanja heard Karis say, "Are you certain you want to know?"

Norina opened her shirt and Karis put a hand inside to feel her belly like the midwife or healer she would no doubt have been, had the elements in her blood been less radically out of balance, and had the story of her life been less out of true. "It's a daughter," Karis said. "Ready and restless to come out of there. And a vigorous child she'll be—how could she not be?"

"How indeed?" Norina grumbled. "Conceived by an earth witch's meddling—" Norina buttoned up her shirt. "It's been a bittersweet year," she said heavily.

They both were silent then, until Norina said quietly, "Karis, it's a terrible position you've put me in. Ten years ago, when I offered to help you, I never offered to be your jailer."

"You've given me ten years I wouldn't have had otherwise. Nori, I want you to tell Zanja what you're afraid she's done."

Norina sat up. "No, Karis, I told you . . ."

Karis looked over at Zanja, who would be just a shadow against the blaze of sunlight. "Zanja, come here."

The grotto smelled of mold and rotten wood, but it certainly offered relief from the heat. Zanja used her porringer to dip some water from the spring; it was so cold it made her teeth ache. She brought some more for Karis, who drank it with the air of one accustomed to doing as her caretakers told her. Karis said, when Zanja had squatted on the ground beside her, "Since Norina refuses to talk, perhaps you would talk to her instead. Tell her about Fire Night, and about Medric."

Zanja told her tale again. When she had finished, there was a silence. Norina gazed into Zanja's face as though she were reading and re-reading an unexpected letter and could not decide if the news it contained was good or bad. Then she put her head into her hands.

"Truth?" Karis said.

"A fire blood's truth," Norina said grumpily. "As full of mystery and metaphor as a blasted book of poetry. I don't know what to make of it."

"Well, I think it only sensible to accept this seer. In fact, if what you fear is as inevitable as you say, I don't see what else we can do."

"You want to trust him?" Norina seemed appalled.

"Put him through your Truthken's meat grinder first if you want."

"A seer? His truths will change from one moment to the next. There is no point."

"There must be a way."

"No, Karis." She sat forward on the bench, implacable. "No."

Karis said, "Nori, I can't continue like this."

Norina stood up abruptly. "Near fifteen years you've trusted me—"

"Sit down," Karis said.

There was a silence. To Zanja's surprise, Norina sat down. The spring made soft, lapping sounds, like a cat drinking milk. "You are not infallible," Karis said. "I intend no insult by pointing this out, no more than you intend to insult me when you remind me of my many weaknesses. This time, I want you to trust me. Tell Zanja the truth. Let her find this seer and bring him to me."

"No." Zanja had never heard a voice so cold.

"If you don't do it, I will."

"Then you have no further need for my advice. And I have no desire to either struggle with you further or to participate in your folly. You'll go to your doom without my help."

In the dim light, Karis's face seemed very pale, but this time she made no move to stop Norina from standing up and leaving. It was Zanja who leapt up and blocked the door.

"Are you insane?" Norina said softly.

"You're making a mistake."

They looked at each other, eye to eye, more than long enough for Norina to figure out that Zanja was no threat to her, and her entrapment in the lathe house was an illusion. But Norina didn't move to push past Zanja. She turned and said to Karis, "No matter what I do, I am forsworn. Only you could put me in such a position."

Karis said, exasperated, "You're too angry to think. Even I know a way out of your dilemma."

It was unusual, and gratifying, to see Norina so taken aback. To see her cold face quirk with wry humor was even more surprising. "You're getting very subtle for an earth witch," she told Karis. And then her unnerving gaze shifted to Zanja's face. "I assume you're wondering why Mabin arranged your murder. It was to prevent you from delivering to the enemy one of Shaftal's most guarded secrets. But you had already done what she most feared, when you crawled through Medric's window on Fire Night."

"I had? What had I done?"

But Norina apparently had said all she would say. She shifted her heavy, off-balance torso, pressed her hands to the small of her back, and waited. Beyond her, Karis sat with her elbows on her knees and her chin in her hands. Whatever they were waiting for, they seemed prepared for it to take a while.

Perhaps they expected Zanja to determine for herself whatever it was that Norina's vows prevented her from telling her. Zanja took her glyph cards from their pouch. "You say I know an important secret, but what secret do I know?" She looked down: in her hand she held the Woman of the Doorway. "Karis is Shaftal's most guarded secret? Why?" She sorted through the cards, wishing for Emil's insight. Her fingers stopped: she held the card called Death-and-Life. The G'deon's glyph.

She could not take a breath. Norina held her arm in a painful grip. She must have seemed on the verge of falling over. "But Harald G'deon didn't—" she protested, and stopped. Who really knew the truth of what had happened the last day of Harald's life? Not many people would have been in his sickroom, and almost everyone had been killed by the Sainnites soon afterwards. She looked up from the card to Karis, who was making a serious study of the dirt beneath her feet. "He laid his hands on you before he died. He vested you with the power of Shaftal."

Karis raised her gaze and said to Norina, "Now may I speak? I think she is under a misapprehension."

They waited rather long for Norina to calculate a grudging answer. "Yes."

"When Harald died, I was the only earth witch in Shaftal. They found me and brought me to him at the last moment of his life. As he died, he dumped his load of power into me. I did not know what was happening, and it was done without my consent. After it was done, and could not be undone, my unworthiness was discovered. It became apparent to everyone that Harald could not have intended to make me his successor, but only to use me as a receptacle."

"By the nine gods!" Zanja turned to Norina. "For fifteen years Shaftal has been in turmoil—"

Norina said quietly, "Despite having been so foully treated, Karis serves Shaftal with more honor and consistency than anyone thought possible."

It was a statement amazing in its sincerity, for Zanja had come to think that Norina admired and respected nobody. Even Karis looked rather surprised.

Zanja said, "I mean no disrespect, but I don't see how."

"She accepts obscurity, she chooses not to exercise her significant powers, she resists the lure of smoke as much as she can, she lives when sometimes her life is unendurable, and someday she will pass on the power she carries, and give Shaftal a G'deon."

Shaken, chastened, Zanja could scarcely think of a response. So this was how a woman so dishonored might reclaim her honor and even be a hero. Yet the tragedy of Karis's life made her own tragedies seem almost ordinary. She said, "How can I help her?"

Norina said, "I guess I should have trusted you from the beginning."

It was like a river reversing its course by an act of will, with a new current just as inevitable and irresistible as the old. Zanja must have been staring at Norina in blank amazement, for Norina's grim expression finally gave way to one of sardonic humor. "Now, Zanja, get yourself in hand. The ritual must be completed."

"You acted as your duty required," Zanja said.

"Formidable enemies can make formidable friends."

"I'm hardly in a position to refuse—"

"Well, that's a bit half-hearted," Norina said.

"There's no point in lying to you."

"That's true, but this little drama is for Karis, not for me." Norina glanced at Karis. "She's satisfied enough." She took Zanja's arm, and propelled her back to the bench and to Karis, who got up and fiercely embraced them both.

Norina said, "You were going to let me leave."

"And you were going to go."

They examined each other rather cautiously. For the length of their friendship, Zanja thought, Norina had been reading Karis back to herself like a book read to a blind woman. Surely she must have been unnerved to look up from her reading and find the other chair empty and the door standing ajar.

Zanja said, "You're afraid that Medric knows of Karis, even though I told him nothing?"

"She created you," Norina said, "just like she created these blades we carry, just like she created the ravens. So she is in you, and when Medric met you, he met her as well. It may take some time for the small bit of truth he's seen to become a whole, but if he's the seer you say he is, then it will happen."

"So I must find him, just as Karis says."

"Well, I must consult with Mabin before we do anything."

"You know that won't work," Karis said. "Giving birth will lay you up for a while, and you won't even be around to consult with anyone. And if Mabin forbids us to contact him, as I'm sure she will, what then? You know that Zanja won't stand quietly by while Mabin's assassins hunt Medric down."

"Good luck to them," said Zanja. "That man has already out-smarted the smartest commanders in Shaftal. But no, I don't owe Mabin any loyalty. Medric, however, deserves all the help I can give him."

Norina said, "Unlike both of you, I still answer to the councilor, and will until I die. So what am I to do?"

"Go ahead and write her a letter," Karis said. "Tell her what we're doing, but don't ask permission."

"She won't be happy. She'll say you're over-reaching yourself, and she'll blame me."

Karis said, "Oh, I'm sure she will. But you can endure it."

Chapter Twenty-one

"Don't send that letter!"

Awakened by Medric's cry, Emil put an arm around him. Sometimes, when Medric became restless in his dreams, Emil could soothe him without awakening him. But Medric turned away, mumbling urgently.

The sky had clouded over. A summer shower would give relief from the dust, thought Emil. He got up to check the oilcloth that covered the trunks of books in the back of the wagon. When he returned, he found Medric sitting up in the tangle of blankets, fumbling frantically for his spectacles.

"We're running out of time!" Medric looked around himself rather wildly.

"Are you awake? Or still asleep?"

"I'm not sure. I can't see."

Emil found his spectacles for him. Medric peered up at him and said, "I'm awake."

Five days they had been traveling lazily, following the wagon down the dusty road, holding hands. It was summer, and all across Shaftal, Sainnites and Paladins were desperately killing each other. Emil knew this holiday of his could not last long, but still he asked, "What are we running out of time for?"

"Zanja is looking for me," Medric said. "She needs us both, more urgently than she knows. But we can't leave the books. How much further do you think we have to go?"

"Four days travel, or thereabouts. Where is she?"

"Oh, I don't know." Medric disengaged himself from the blankets. "I'll tell you if I can see a map."

Emil fetched the map and lit the lantern. When he sat down, Medric leaned against him. Emil tucked him close and kissed his head.

"Maybe we can just ignore everything," Medric suggested.

"I don't believe that's an option you'll find in *Way of the Seer*." Emil kissed him again, and unfolded the map. Medric pointed. Emil asked, "Strongbridge? What is she doing there?"

"Being a hinge of history." Medric sighed. "Oh, well. The letter's going to be sent, and nothing I can do will stop it. If I could, maybe it wouldn't make any difference anyway." He studied the map. "I suppose that to find me, Zanja will go to where she knows I was last, and wait for me to come to her. She'll wait a few days, and eventually work her way to Haprin, for she knows I shipped my books there, doesn't she? And then she'll be able to find out that you and I left together, and perhaps even which way we headed. So she'll guess where we're going, because she's been to your shepherd's cottage before, and come after us."

"She will," Emil agreed, stunned by the simplicity of it. So this was how Rees Company had been systematically slaughtered, one person at a time. It was best not to think about it.

Medric rolled up the map, and blew out the lamp. "After we've secured the books, we'll turn back and go to her, and meet her on the road somewhere. Now we can sleep."

But when Emil awoke at dawn, Medric was still awake, and had spent the night pacing back and forth, watching the clouds gather and then disperse without issuing a single drop of rain.

Karis came home again to Meartown, to the furnaces and the forges and the teams of gigantic horses hauling wagonloads of ore from the nearby mines. Because Meartown was less than a day's foot journey from Strongbridge, Norina had reluctantly let her go as she had come, alone. Norina had her own journey home to make: to her first home, the seaside village far on the southern coast, to the rambling house in which she had been born, and where her older sister now ruled, a benign matriarch by all accounts.

The region of Mear was a place of hostile, stony hillsides and occasional, straggling trees, home to many kinds of mice and the foxes and hawks that ate them, but unfarmable and, except for a few places, too barren even for sheep. In spring a few tiny flowers bloomed among the stones; in winter the snow blanketed the land and blew into drifts taller than Karis could reach. Yet, for hundreds of years Meartown had thrived in the middle of this wasteland, its fires stoked by coal mined from the same hills that the iron came from; all its other needs came in by wagon. The road to Meartown was like a heart's artery, and there was no road better laid or maintained in all of Shaftal. All summer long the road crew wandered that road, filling potholes and replacing stones; all winter long that same crew worked the snowplows.

The barren land inspired a barren kind of love, an intellectual and passionless appreciation for its empty spaces and harsh, stony ridges. By day, the sky was brown with coal smoke, and she spent most of those days within the gray city of the forges. Hemmed in by stone and metal, she longed for green and living things. She sighed as she walked into Meartown that afternoon and waved a hand at Mardeth, who collected the gate toll from outsiders. "So you're back," Mardeth called. "Have you eaten today?"

Karis sat down by the town well and ate the lunch that the inn had packed for her that morning—more of those dumplings that had made Zanja cry, there by the river.

Present yet absent, Zanja moved across the countryside like a spark of light through darkness. If Karis had shut her eyes and started to walk, she would have walked directly to her side. With her whole being, she yearned to do that very thing.

In Strongbridge, Karis had bought Zanja an ugly, hammer-headed, evil tempered horse. With one touch, Karis had won the willful horse's abject devotion. The horse, who she named Homely, proved himself a sturdy mount, with an easy, light gait and an eagerness to run that Zanja did not always rein in. She had left with most of Norina's equipment: her saddle, her spare shirt, her cooking gear, and her maps. Zanja had never seen such beautifully drawn and detailed maps, though many of the details made no sense to her. They were judicial maps, Norina said, copied from an original that still survived in a secret archive. But Norina had overwritten the maps with her own notations, which had been incorporated when the map was re-drawn by an artist who could not resist ornamenting what blank space remained with drawings of boats, trees, castles, and the like. The maps had been re-drawn perhaps a dozen times since Norina first began carrying them, and now she admitted that even she sometimes had difficulty distinguishing the roads from the welter of detail.

Following obscure but direct routes, along byways and cowpaths that are usually known only to locals, Zanja traveled east and then south, and in six days hardly saw a single soul. Not until she drew close to Haprin and camped for a few days just over the hill from the main road did she even have a conversation—with an enterprising farm girl who visited every day to sell her eggs, bread, and milk. With nothing to do but wait and think, Zanja found herself sorting through the events of her life as though they were glyph cards, picking and choosing which ones had significance, and deciding what that significance would be. She had not spent such a peaceful time since she could remember.

At last, she roused herself to go into Haprin and make inquiries. A watchwoman at one of the warehouses was much taken with her, and for the price of a dinner told of a bespectacled young man who had slept beside his shipment for some days before he was joined by an older man, and they left with the trunks, by wagon, headed for the ferry. Yes, a man with hair going gray, his face creased by wind and sun, but definitely not a farmer. "A Paladin," said the watchwoman, who by the end of the meal was speculatively stroking Zanja's knife-scarred hand.

"I don't suppose he had a limp."

"Yes, he did. But a night with that young fellow did him a world of good."

"You amaze me," Zanja murmured, more amazed, in fact, than she let on. Though the friendly watchwoman was appealing enough, Zanja disappointed her hopes, and went back to her solitary camp, to gaze up at the brilliant stars and think of Karis.

In Strongbridge, after Karis had gone to her room to smoke and then sleep under the watchful guard of Norina's tireless assistant, Norina and Zanja had shared a fine supper. As was inevitable, Norina commented on how well Zanja was comporting herself, and particularly complimented her efforts to keep secret the fact that she was in love with Karis. The Truthken was not as unsympathetic as Zanja had feared she would be, but neither had she held back the facts, both about how Karis had been brutalized in Lalali, and about how smoke irrecoverably destroys sensation. The unpleasant conversation certainly had helped to cool Zanja's ardor.

But she lay now, thinking of Karis's big, gentle hands stroking her injured thigh. That touch had ruined her, she thought wryly, for now she wanted nothing else. She could only hope, as she had promised Norina, that she would recover quickly.

The next day, as she rode down the main road to the ferry, Karis's raven dropped out of the sky onto her shoulder. "Something is wrong!"

A startled farm family that shared the road with her drew back, staring fearfully.

"What do you mean?" she asked the raven. "Did Karis send you to me? Did you see something from the air that I should know about?"

The raven uttered a strangled caw, as though he had half-forgotten how to talk. "It is Karis," he managed to say. "Something is wrong with Karis."

Zanja never got on the ferry.

Seven days later, in an evening that had turned suddenly cool after sunset, Zanja rode up to the Meartown gates. The stars had come out, and the gate was closed: a gate of iron forged in the form of ivy climbing a trellis, with spear-shaped leaves tipping the gate's top, edged, no doubt, with sharpened steel. Though Zanja had allowed Homely regular rest, she had scarcely slept, and now she saw the beautiful, deadly gate with a terrible clarity of exhaustion and panic. Not since the night of the frogs had she been forced to function in spite of such horror. "Something is wrong!" she shouted at the cranky old woman who came too slowly out of the metal-hinged door of her stone house. The town stank of dust and coal.

"Stop ringing the cursed bell," the woman said, holding her ears. "The town's children are asleep."

Zanja made her hand stop pulling the bell rope. Her exhausted horse had not even jumped at the noise of the ringing.

"And come back in the morning," the woman said. "You can sleep by the road there. There's a pump so you can water your horse."

"I'll climb the gate if I have to, and come pounding at your cottage door."

The woman said dryly, "This is Meartown. We know how to make a gate here."

She started to turn away, and Zanja shouted at her back, "Do you know Karis? Do you know her best work? Look here!" She thrust her dagger through the gate's bars. "She doesn't give these blades to many people, does she? For pity's sake, look at me, look at the raven on my shoulder. I am her friend!"

The woman took the dagger from Zanja's hand, scrutinized it, and gave it back. "You do have a fine blade," she said doubtfully. She peered through the gate at the bird on Zanja's shoulder. "And a strange pet."

"Mardeth," the raven said, the first word he'd spoken in many days. "Help her."

"Shaftal's Name!" The woman snatched up the key at her waist and unlocked the gate. Zanja all but fell through as it swung open. "You're not the one I expected," Mardeth said.

"I'm Zanja. Norina's pregnant."

"Well, blessings upon her," Mardeth said automatically. She examined Zanja, then stepped forward to take Homely's reins. "You've had a bad time of it. Come in and take a bite to eat, before I show you the way to Lynton and Dominy's house. You'll be needing your strength, won't you."

Zanja followed her, too dazed with hunger and weariness to protest or demand an explanation. It wasn't until she sat in the woman's kitchen with the teakettle starting to hiss and some bread and cold meat before her that she thought to wonder why the gatekeeper might have been expecting Norina to come frantically ringing the gate bell in the middle of the night. She nearly leapt up and ran out to the yard, where the woman was watering the horse and giving him some hay, but she made herself eat instead. She'd be needing her strength, Mardeth had said.

Mardeth came in, and cut her a piece of pie. "Your horse isn't in too bad shape. Leave him with me tonight, and I'll have him shod in the morning. Looks like you've been keeping him in oats but not feeding yourself. Are you out of money?"

"I've got enough for the shoeing."

"As if the blacksmith would accept a single coin from you. I'll send around to the other mastersmiths and take a collection to help you on your way. We were getting ready to send out some people ourselves. It's taken us this long to figure out that she's not somewhere nearby, off her head or injured somewhere. Six days we've been scouring the countryside. What's the matter with you?"

Zanja had knocked the pie into her lap and sent the plate spinning to the hearth, where it clanged on the stones like the gate bell, and set the woman's dog to barking. "She's disappeared?"

"Yes, of course she's disappeared. What else are you here for?"

"The raven couldn't tell me what was wrong. I thought she might be ill."

"Well now, that's odd," the woman said, looking askance at the raven, who paced restlessly along the back of a chair. "Very odd indeed. Not that I know a thing about elemental ways, but they say a witch's familiar knows everything she knows, and if the raven doesn't know anything, what does that mean, I wonder?"

Mardeth rousted up a neighbor to let them out the gate and keep an eye on it while she was gone. "Lynton and Dominy live up there a ways." She pointed into the nearby hills. "Karis has lived with them, oh, for some years. There's some trees up there, and a bit of a spring, and it seems to make her happy."

As they hurried up the steep, scrupulously maintained road, Mardeth told Zanja how it had happened that Karis disappeared in the middle of the night, but no one realized anything was amiss until the next evening, when the forge master finally came looking for her at her house. They had wasted all the time since then trying to find her in the environs of Meartown, having assumed that she had come to harm somehow on one of her wanderings. That her harm might have come in the form of a human being seemed not to have occurred to any of them until finally one of the two men noticed a broken door latch in Karis' room. "In all the years they've known her," Mardeth said, "she's never broken anything. She can be clumsy as an ox, but she's never even cracked a teacup. And it was a good, strong, Mearish latch. No, someone must have broken it to get into her room from outside. But why would anyone wish to do her harm? Especially someone from around here?"

She glanced at Zanja and realized she was weeping. "Now then," she said awkwardly. "I'm sure we'll find her."

Something about the image of Karis blundering around a kitchen with a fragile teacup in her hand had left Zanja devastated, and she could scarcely stem her tears even when they arrived at the cottage, where two aged men welcomed them in. They seemed eager when they realized Mardeth was at their door, perhaps even hopeful that she brought good news. But when they saw Zanja's face, they fell to weeping themselves. "She's dead, is she?" said one.

"Now calm down, you," Mardeth snapped. "We know nothing

at all, and the stones themselves would defend her from harm. Put on the kettle there, Dominy. This one's just in tears because she didn't know until now what had happened. She'll be all right in a minute, when it's done sinking in. Now all of you sit down and I'll make the tea."

"No, I want to see her room," Zanja said. Lynton took her down the dark hall through a wide door at the end, and Zanja stood there in the doorway to Karis' bedroom as the man hurried to light a couple of lamps. The flames illuminated a high, raftered ceiling, high enough that even Karis would not have to worry about banging her head on it, and several pieces of oversized furniture: a chair, a work table piled with books and debris, a settle by the fireplace, a huge, high bed with the linens in disarray, and a double door constructed almost entirely of glass that looked out upon a garden. The old man swung the doors open and showed Zanja the broken latch.

"Was her room in such a mess when you found it? The bed and such?"

The old man shrugged. "No different from usual. We'd come in every few days and clean for her, not that she noticed. She never had time for tidying up, and never lost anything, anyway."

Zanja sat on the settle. She was learning more about Karis now that she was missing than she'd ever learned in her presence. "Would you leave me alone, please?"

"Of course. Madam." He touched his forehead, an old-fashioned gesture of respect rarely seen these days. Not only had they all assumed she was a member of the Lilterwess like Norina, but he, at least, apparently assumed she was a ranking member. He left the room without another word.

The room was still imbued with Karis's presence. The raven, who had come in with her, flew to a claw-scarred chair back near one of the windows and fluffed up his feathers sleepily. Faintly, Zanja could hear voices in the kitchen, and the sound of water being poured for tea. She picked up a book from the floor, and spelled out its title: *Principles of Clarity*. Some of its pages were bent, as though Karis had tossed it impatiently aside. A small pot on the hearth contained a hardened, resinous substance—hide glue, Zanja thought, which would soften when warmed, and harden again when taken off the fire.

Zanja stood up abruptly, and began methodically searching the room. In the trunk were more books and a few articles of clothing, some clean and roughly mended, some dirty and stinking of the forge and Karis' sweat. The sheepskin jerkin that Karis had been wearing when they first met lay in there, and several pairs of socks, badly darned. The men who looked after Karis were not much good with a needle, apparently.

Small models of machinery, constructed of slips of wood and amber dabs of glue, cluttered the tabletop. A book lay open to a page of diagrams of waterwheels, but this was no grain mill Karis had been designing. Zanja turned one of the miniature wheels, and watched it operate a thing like a hammer. Another one operated a bellows, of the kind used in the forge. Karis's model was so precise that it even blew little, rhythmic puffs of air.

Zanja hunted through the room, but though she found Karis's belt on the floor, with sheathed knife, tin cup and various small tools still dangling from it, she did not find pipe or smoke purse. Zanja checked for loose boards in the floor, felt the stones of the wall, and finally found Karis' hiding place in the chimney, where a small stone had cracked loose from its mortar. A wooden box was crammed into the hollow behind it and could only be worked loose with great effort. At last Zanja slid open the lid and folded back the oilcloth covering; it was filled to the top with small cubes of smoke, at least half a year's supply. Since Karis's kidnappers had not hunted for this supply, they must have brought some with them. Surely a woman who could unlock doors with a touch would easily escape, unless her captors kept her continuously under smoke. She was being poisoned three or even four times a day.

Now Karis would be—had already become—like all the other smoke users. Something was wrong, the raven said, and then he began, inexorably, to become ordinary. The evidence had lain before Zanja all along. Karis was not dead yet, but she might as well be dead.

Zanja began to think again: cold, hard thoughts. She took out her glyph cards and picked out the four glyphs that, among other things, symbolize the four directions. Ten times in a row she plucked the same card from the four in her hand, the one with the glyph that meant "north."

She fell asleep on Karis's bed. One of the men came in later, to take the boots off her feet and tuck a blanket around her against the chill. She tried to say something to him about the morning, but he hushed her, saying, "We'll take care of everything." One by one, he blew out the lamps.

Chapter Twenty-two

They brought Homely to her at dawn. He had bitten the man who tried to ride him, and so they led him to her, ignominiously tethered behind a stolid cart horse. His hooves were newly shod, his tack and all Zanja's gear refurbished, and his saddlebags were filled with food. "Is the blacksmith all right?" Zanja asked Mardeth.

"Oh, he's used to temperamental horses."

Homely bared his teeth at Zanja, and she had to grab the raven by the feet to keep it from taking flight at the sight of all the people who had come to see her off, but horse and raven both calmed down once she was mounted. Mardeth handed her a money pouch, and Dominy gave her sweet rolls and boiled eggs to eat as she rode. Two or three dozen other people had made the trek to the hollow for no other purpose, it seemed, than to stand around and look at her. Mardeth murmured that some of them stood ready to accompany Zanja, if she wanted them.

"It's not numbers I need," Zanja said, though she would have given almost anything to have Ransel, or Emil, or even Norina, at her side. As she rode away, a chorus of good wishes shouted after her. When she looked back, the townsfolk all stood in a forlorn huddle around the two old men, who were still waving their red kerchiefs. Ten years they had looked after Karis, as much as she would let anyone look after her. "Idiots," Zanja muttered. She needed someone to rage at.

At noon, the raven spoke. "Pendant," he said.

Zanja had been riding cross-country, following whatever animal trails and streambeds she could find that went more or less northward. She had recently stumbled onto a deeply rutted dirt road. While the horse rested, Zanja searched up and down the stretch of road, sometimes kneeling in the muck that remained from a recent rain storm. Finally, she found it, buried in the mud: the pendant of green stone that she had given Karis beside the river in Strongbridge. A torn piece of green ribbon trailed from it as she pulled it out of the mud. Karis must have torn the ribbon that first dawn, when she started to come out from under smoke, and realized something was wrong, before her kidnappers forced her to smoke again. That was the dawn that the raven had flown to Zanja with his dreadful message.

"You're watching, aren't you Karis?" Zanja said, after she had started on her way again, with the raven on her shoulder. "I can't feel you any more, but at least sometimes you still see me through the raven. I must seem very far away to you, just as you seem to me. Can you hear me now?"

"Yes," the raven said.

"Can you tell me where you are?"

"Mabin," the raven said.

"Mabin? Has she been captured also?"

The raven looked at her blankly, and said nothing more.

The countryside remained treeless and desolate, and the road she followed northward seemed to go nowhere, though wagons traveled it often enough to keep the grass from growing in the ruts. Norina's maps showed empty, un-annotated countryside.

One morning, as Zanja saddled her horse behind the knoll where she had spent the night, a single rider loped past. The only remarkable thing about him was his horse, a luxury Zanja could not have afforded if she hadn't been given money so generously by friends and by strangers. She continued more cautiously, traveling far to one side of the road rather than upon it. Here and there were sudden fingers of rock pointing at the sky. She noticed, atop one of these, a watchkeep huddled in the shade of a lean-to that looked almost like a pile of brush, if one didn't look too closely. Zanja slipped past in the countryside behind him, where the lean-to blocked his view, and from there she could see the little bell tower upon which he could ring his alarm.

She soon came upon the thing he guarded: a lush green valley much like the valley of her birth, with a small, but busy village at one end—a village with walls, and a sentry at the gate. The valley had been carved out of the earth by a river that cut a deep swath across the countryside as far as Zanja could see in either direction. This river, at least, appeared on Norina's map, though the valley and the village did not. As she watched the village from the rim of the valley, Zanja realized it was not a village at all, but a military settlement—not of Sainnites, but of Paladins. She had found the hidden heart of the Shaftali resistance; Shaftal's government in exile.

Both the glyphs and her own judgment pointed inexorably into the valley. Zanja wanted to violently brush away the possibilities that tickled at her skin. Had Karis been kidnapped and cruelly drugged, not by Sainnites, but by the Paladins?

To break into a Paladin stronghold without assistance or even the vaguest idea of where to hunt for Karis seemed insanely fool-hardy. She would do it tonight, she decided, and shut her eyes to think.

It was a warm summer afternoon, and the accuser bugs droned their shrill curses down in the valley. Nearby, Homely chomped away at the grass, and the raven, perched overhead atop a pointed rock, cleaned his feathers busily. It was a commonplace kind of sound, like the rustling of paper. In the midst of her dismay, Zanja felt a sudden, unlikely sensation of peace.

When she opened her eyes, the summer sun hung low and red, glaring into her face like coals of a fire. She could still hear the rustling paper sound, but she could not see the raven. She rolled over, groaning, for she had fallen asleep with her back against the pile of rocks. The man sitting nearby turned a page of the book in his lap, nodding and chuckling to himself. His spectacles were glazed red with sunset. "Dear gods," Zanja said.

Medric looked up from his book. He seemed rather the worse for wear: a rag tied back his stringy hair, and dust covered his drab clothing. "I guess you were tired. Some warrior you are."

Two additional horses grazed companionably with Homely on the other side of the clearing. She got stiffly to her feet, and found a smokeless fire burning at the other side of the rock pile, where a soot-black pot stood empty, and a porcelain teapot steeped upon a stone. Emil sat there on his folding stool, just looking up from the book upon his knees. "You're awake at last. Now we shall have some answers."

"You've left South Hill?"

He closed the book carefully, and wrapped it in a jacket of leather. "It was time I remembered what my life was about."

"I hope you're here to help me."

"Sit down. Despite that nap, you still look ready to collapse." Emil opened his padded box and took out two teacups. "Why else would we rush up here into the wilderness like madmen chased by rabid hounds, except to help you? Help you do what, by the way?"

Medric sat on Zanja's other side. "Zanja, I see history rippling away from you."

Emil smiled affectionately at the Sainnite seer. "Medric is full of wild stories he's made up from reading too many books."

Medric said, "It's not possible to read too many books. To read too few, now that's possible."

"Medric says there's a third road for Shaftal. We—the three of us—are at the crossroads, he says." Emil offered Zanja a cup of tea. The cup might have been made of flower petals that released a delicious fragrance. Somewhere, Emil had invested in some very expensive tea. She took a sip. Her hands were shaking like any smoke addict's.

Medric said, "Zanja, where is the lost G'deon? Somehow, she must be saved!"

Emil murmured, "Set that cup down before you drop it. It's irreplaceable, you know."

Zanja put the cup on the ground.

Medric said, "I saw her in a dream, a woman like a mountain, but shackled hand and foot, blinded, with her tongue cut out. . . ."

Emil put his arm around her. Zanja lay her head back upon his shoulder and stared up at the sun-red sky, which swirled and swam in her vision. "But she is not the G'deon."

"She is. I know what I dreamed. The land cries out to her to give it healing."

Emil said, "Zanja, have mercy. Who is she?"

"Karis. The Woman of the Doorway. How can she be G'deon . . . a half-Sainnite smoke addict?"

"She's a smoke addict?" Emil cried.

"She's Sainnite?" said Medric.

"But if Harald G'deon meant to choose her, and not just to use her as a kind of storage, then every moment, from the day of her birth—and even before—the people of this land have failed her." And then it came to Zanja, the truth she had not wanted to know, and she started wildly to her feet, crying, "Mabin did this to her, and it's my fault! Dear gods—" Something was impeding her, and she struggled with it blindly until a mild voice entered her awareness, saying her name. Medric stood before her, his hair having come loose, somewhat out of breath. Emil had her by the arms, from behind.

"Sit down," he said. "You're off your head and that's never good when someone carries weapons as sharp as yours. Sit down and explain."

She sat back down, her knees gone weak, and let Emil talk her into some semblance of calm, until he trusted her with a teacup again.

Medric said, "The G'deon's choice of a successor had to be confirmed, isn't that right?"

Zanja said, "Norina told me that Harald waited until the last possible moment to send for Karis, and then he did it in secret. But perhaps he did it on purpose, so he could get around the council, for everyone knows that he was at odds with them, and with Mabin in particular."

"Well, it's true that Harald's last years were fraught with controversy," said Emil. "For he insisted that we accept the Sainnites, which was a very unpopular idea. Are you saying that for fifteen years we have had a G'deon vested but not confirmed? And that she has been willing to live in obscurity all this time, while the land is torn to ruins around her?" Emil paused, and shook his head, and added more gently, "By Shaftal, what else could she honorably have done? To exercise such power outside the constraints of the Lilterwess—"

Zanja said, "She was constrained, not just by smoke but by Mabin, who indirectly controlled her through Norina, who exercised all her formidable powers to keep Karis tractable."

"Norina?" Medric said.

"The Truthken, Karis's oldest friend."

Emil said dryly, "Ah, I see. Air logic. Inflexible and absolutist. No doubt Norina believes she is doing her duty. But what do you mean when you say Mabin did this to her? What has been done, and why do you blame yourself?"

"Someone sent a letter," Medric said.

"Norina sent a letter. To Mabin."

"And Mabin did what?"

"She kidnapped Karis. And holds her prisoner down there, in that garrison."

Medric said, "So whatever was in that letter convinced Mabin she needed to act, and quickly."

"The letter told her that Karis had sent me to find you, and bring you to her."

Medric looked baffled, but Emil said, "Oh, I see."

"What?"

"Well, what would you have told Karis, when you met her?"

Medric said, "That she is the hope of Shaftal."

"And that," said Emil, "Would be the one thing Mabin never wants Karis to hear. Not from a seer, anyway. Not if she intends to keep Karis from knowing the truth."

"Mabin doesn't command the border people," Zanja said, "so she doesn't command me."

"Me neither, obviously," Medric said cheerfully. "How soon do you want to leave, Zanja? Shall I load my pistols?"

Emil put his head in his hands. "She still commands me. Which of my vows and beliefs shall I betray today?"

Zanja said, "Well, the truth is—" She had to take a breath to steady herself. "Truth is, I have no hope of rescuing Karis. All I can do is to rescue her living remains. She has been under smoke day and night for over ten days now. To save what little can be saved is hardly worth becoming forsworn for."

Emil raised his head. "But fire logic can encompass the grandest of contradictions, and I have done my share of encompassing these last few days. Why should I not continue?"

On Zanja's other side, Medric uttered a snort of laughter.

Emil continued gravely. "So of course I will go with you to rescue what survives of our G'deon. And perhaps once we have done that we will find something else to save from this disaster. Surely three fire bloods together can redeem even the most hopeless situation."

Medric went away to load his pistols, which was a task complex enough by daylight, but which seemed to give him no difficulty even in the darkness. He had been raised to be a soldier, after all. Zanja said to Emil, "I thought you were a celibate."

"Hmm. Of course my position required a great deal of restraint, but surely you didn't think it was by choice. Fire blood and celibacy? You know better than that."

"Yes," she admitted.

"So. I always suspected that with Annis you were settling for a poor substitute."

"You know more than I did," Zanja said. "You're usually very good at minding your own business, Emil."

He chuckled. "And you're usually better at protecting yourself from a prying old man." He took her hand. "A smoke addict. You might as well be celibate. Why do you say this disaster is your fault?"

"When I first met Karis, Norina said I would endanger her, by making her restless. If Karis had simply stayed as she was, passive and invisible as she has been, Mabin would have had no reason to do anything to her."

"That certainly sounds like air logic," said Emil dryly. "But you and I, we know better."

Though the village walls were well guarded, it was not particularly difficult to breach them. Two presciants and a seer could hardly help but recognize the moment it was safe to climb the wall. They scrambled over and huddled in the shadows on the other side as a watchman passed, and then Zanja whispered, "This place has never been attacked, I gather, or they would not be so relaxed."

"It's never even been discovered," Emil said. "The closest Sainnite garrison is a long way from here, you know, and the Mearish folk are notoriously secretive. But the few survivors of the fall are housed here, and so I doubt anyone ever becomes complacent."

They set forth, walking in a group, like soldiers done with the day's work, and what with the dark night and the unlit streets they were able to cross from one end of the small village to the other without attracting notice. They saw no taverns or shops, just a series of residential buildings that looked a good deal like military barracks, and a great exercise yard at the village center, with a huge horse stable. The settlement was even about the same size as the Wilton garrison, and Zanja noticed Medric shaking his head as though bemused.

"I have no idea where your Karis is," Medric said, when they had crossed the village. "She's here, though."

"We've got the whole night to wander the streets," Emil said. "And tomorrow night, and the night after that."

Zanja pulled the four glyph cards from inside her shirt, and shuffled at them while looking at the stars to establish a sense of direction. The card she chose told her to go south, back the way they had come.

They paced back down the wide boulevard, pausing at every cross-street to shuffle the cards. "Now this is very conspicuous behavior," Emil commented.

Prescience had a way of fraying away into ambiguity and uncertainty if it was relied upon too deliberately. When, while standing upon one street corner without moving, the glyphs told Zanja to go south, then west, then south again, she was not much surprised. "I guess we're finished," she muttered, and stuck the cards into her shirt.

Emil nudged her and pointed at Medric. He had wandered up against the wall of the tall corner building, which had no windows at all on the first floor, and he was gazing upward at a lit window. He gestured at them sharply, and they dove into the shadows against the wall as a big, slump-shouldered, shambling figure moved restlessly to the window, only to be eased impatiently away by another, smaller person.

Emil put his hand on Zanja's shoulder. She was, she realized, scratching at the mortared stone with her fingernails, as though to dig through into the building with her bare hands.

Medric came up to them. "Just for a second there, I felt the mountains turn over in their sleep."

Emil grabbed them both by their sleeves and marched them a distance away. "There's a good reason why nobody quite trusts us fire bloods. One minute we're inspired visionaries, the next we're drooling idiots. Don't you two turn idiotic on me."

A black shape hurtled at them from out of the darkness overhead. Zanja snatched the raven out of the air before he plummeted into Emil's stomach. The raven uttered a squawk, then settled down and let Zanja perch him upon her shoulder. "The good raven doesn't see well in the dark," she explained. Then, a thought came to her. "Karis, do you hear me?"

"Yes," the raven said, and Medric and Emil both jumped with surprise.

"Lie down and pretend to sleep, and be patient. Can you do that?"

"Yes," the raven said.

"Then do it now. We are coming for you, but you must wait for us."

They walked through the village and came back at the building from another direction. The building's only door opened into a walled courtyard rather than directly to the street. The courtyard's arched gate stood closed and locked. The wall was smooth, impossible to climb. Nor was there enough space to slip over the top of the gate even if it could be surmounted. In any case, the courtyard had an alert watchman, who paced determinedly from one end to the other, and paused every couple of rounds to peer through the gate and examine the roadway. The other three walls of the house presented blank faces, and offered no access to the roof, either, even if it were possible to get from the roof into Karis' room.

Zanja drew her companions away from the building again, to the shadows of another street corner. Emil was vigorously shaking his head, though she had not said a word. "We are not assassins," he hissed.

Zanja turned on him in a fury. "Well then, if we can't attack the guard, what are we supposed to do? Rattle the gate and ask politely to be let in?"

"Zanja, these are our people, not our enemies."

"It doesn't matter!"

"Right now it doesn't. Later, when you can't forget that once you were a warrior, but then you became a murderer, it will matter very much. You have a good reason for killing that young man. All murderers have a good reason for doing what they do."

Medric hushed them urgently. "This is not the place to argue moral philosophy."

"I should never have accepted your help," Zanja muttered.

"But you did, and now you're stuck with me. Zanja, listen to me: If they were going to kill her outright, they would have done it by now. So let's study the problem and come up with a solution we all can live with. We have time."

They found a sheltered place within sight of the walled courtyard, and settled down in the shadows. Medric promptly fell asleep, with his head upon Emil's shoulder. Emil seemed to doze as well, but Zanja kept watch as the night settled into a stillness broken only by the ring of the guard's iron-studded heels upon stone.

The stars gradually disappeared, and there was a faint rumble of thunder. As lightning flickered suddenly over the village walls and the first scattered drops of rain began to fall, she heard hurried footsteps and a man in a rain cape came around the corner and rushed up to the gate, cursing. The guard in the courtyard came over, and they argued bitterly as the gate lock rasped open. The gate swung open and now both men stood outside of it, still arguing. A blinding flash of lightning illuminated their faces, distorted with rage and streaked with rain. The two men flinched from the light. Then they wordlessly traded places, one stepping into the courtyard, one starting angrily down the street.

Zanja had braced her pistols, one upon each knee. As the angry guard disappeared from sight, she slid the guns back into their holsters. Emil, whom she had thought was asleep, said, "There will be a way in."

"Guns make killing too easy. It becomes a habit, like it has with Willis and with Mabin. It keeps us from thinking of other ways." But she could not take her gaze away from the gate, which had been open, and now was closed. The new guard began pacing across the courtyard, in the pouring rain. She could hear his boots ringing on the stone.

"Rockets!" Medric exclaimed suddenly, his voice blurred with sleep. "Who made the rockets? On Fire Night?"

"You mean Annis?" Zanja said blankly. Then she said it again. "Annis." She got hastily to her feet. "Of course. Mabin brought her here."

The raven leapt from Zanja's shoulder and dove into the rain. They followed, but lost sight of him. They circled around into the alley, and finally spotted the raven, sitting miserably in the downpour upon a second floor windowsill, tapping patiently on the glass. The men ducked into the shadows, but Zanja stood in plain sight, with the rain running down her face. The raven tapped steadily, as though he meant to keep tapping until he drowned. Zanja stared up into the downpour, her eyes blurred and stinging. When the window jerked open suddenly, the wet raven fell off the windowsill with a squawk.

Annis stared down at her.

"Have you got a moment for an old friend?" Zanja said.

"Zanja!"

"Myself."

"What are you doing here?"

"Emil's in trouble. I think you can help."

Annis disappeared, then reappeared to toss a rope out the window. Of course, Annis would never tolerate being shut up in a building, unable to come and go as she pleased.

Knots tied regularly in the rope gave Zanja better purchase than she might have expected on such a wet night, but climbing the rope to the window was no easy task, and hauling herself over the windowsill was even more difficult. Annis dragged her into the room, and then helped her up from an ungainly sprawl. "How's the rocket business?" Zanja asked.

"I'm making big, nasty ones now." Annis started to pull the rope up, but let it go when Zanja clasped her hand. "You've got quite a chill on you. You better get those wet clothes off."

"Would you make a fire for me?"

"Oh, sure." Annis knelt on the cold hearth to lay a fire. She had some big sulfur matches to light it with, but everything seemed to be a bit damp, and it took her some time to get a fire going. Zanja talked as she got undressed, so that Annis would heed her voice more than the sounds outside. She told Annis a tale of selfishness and betrayal in South Hill, a tale that ended with Emil imprisoned by his own company for treachery, with his life endangered by Willis's assassins, who could not afford to wait for a Truthken to arrive and sort the whole mess out. The situation required Mabin's intervention, Zanja said, and she had burned through three horses getting here ahead of Willis's men.

Annis blew the tinder into flame, then sat back on her heels. "You're right; I've got to help him somehow. He's been like a father to me. I suppose I have some influence with Mabin . . ." As she looked up, Zanja contrived to be taking off her last item of clothing, her shirt, which she innocently hung on the chair back. Then, feeling Annis's gaze, she looked directly into her eyes. "I really have missed you."

It was easy, almost natural, to embrace her and kiss her. Annis wore only a hastily-buttoned shirt, and was more than willing for it to be unbuttoned again. Zanja took Annis to the bed and laid her down upon it, with a knee between her thighs and her tongue in her mouth. She dragged the shirt from Annis's shoulders so it entangled her arms. Annis was entirely distracted when Zanja heard Emil grunt as he hauled himself over the edge of the window. She jammed a fistful of the bedsheet into Annis's mouth, tossed her onto her belly, and twisted the tangled shirt into a fetter. Annis struggled, but Zanja held her face into the pillow until she fell still, no doubt half smothered.

"Well," Emil said, as he came over to the bed, breathing heavily, "an unconventional solution." He helped Zanja to contrive to bind Annis more securely to the bedframe. Then he covered Annis modestly with the blanket and sat on the edge of the bed, admonishing her to behave herself, while Zanja hauled Medric through the window. Annis stopped fighting the tethers after a while.

The raven flapped heavily on sodden wings to the windowsill. Zanja patted his feathers with a towel to sop up the worst of the wet. Medric had knelt on the hearth to take apart and clean his pistols and re-load them with dry gunpowder. He did it as if he had an impatient commander screaming at him to do it faster. As Zanja came over to put on her wet shirt, he asked, "Now what?"

"I don't know. Any ideas, raven?"

The raven shook his wet feathers and brooded.

Karis lay rigid in the too-small bed, with the rain sound rushing past her. From far away, she watched three bedraggled rescuers crawl through an open window. One was like a knife blade white hot from the forge—one was like a knife blade tempered and honed and one was like the forge itself. Fire and earth makes the forge; fire and earth makes the blade.

She must not sleep. *Oh Shaftal*, she prayed. *Oh Shaftal I must not sleep.* She could not remember why. *Oh Shaftal I must not move lest the watcher awaken. Oh Shaftal.*

The raven turned his head and now she saw Zanja: wet and thin and grim as death. Zanja—implacably loyal—*Oh Shaftal protect her heart, she is so true, the truest blade I ever forged. Zanja save me I am gone to smoke, I am gone.*

Karis. I know you can hear me. Karis, I am at your door.

The rain whispered now. The voice whispered in her raven's ear. *Karis do you feel me I am here.* Silence. Presence. *Do you re-*

member when I was imprisoned doubly imprisoned and you freed me. In bed, Karis remembered what a good night that had been, how tired she had been, and then the hunger that drove her was sated and she could rest for a while. She remembered Zanja, limp as an exhausted child, sleeping in her arms as the snow fell. For a few hours, for a night, the world had been as it should be, and her heart had been at peace.

Now I am here for you but you must unlock the door.

A whisper: *Unlock the door. Dear gods Karis unlock the door.*

Karis touched stone through plaster, the stone of the wall which was rooted in earth, and breathed in. Presence. She sat up in the bed.

Dear gods Karis unlock the door.

She stood up. Her body was stone. She could not move except when pushed. The white hot blade, the forge, the pumping bellows. Fire and earth makes the forge. The room swirled around her, dark and blurred with smoke. She stepped. The floor shall not creak. She stepped. The watcher shall sleep. She stepped. I am the key. Open. *Oh Shaftal.* And now she is looking at herself and the room is full of smoke and she opens her eyes and she sees the raven looking at her. Presence. Zanja has touched her. *Dear heart.*

"Dear heart," Zanja breathed.

Karis opened her mouth. The raven croaked, "Zanja."

Emil whispered, "There is someone in the room."

With Karis's limp, cold hand clasped in both of hers, Zanja listened. She heard even, deep breaths. She looked around the door-jamb. A candleflame flickered on a tabletop; a woman's head rested on the table, her arms dangling, as if she had been hit from behind with a hammer. Zanja grinned into Karis' vacant stare, and in a moment saw the faintest twitch of a smile. Slow-witted was not the same as no-witted.

"Hurry!" Medric hissed. Then Zanja felt nearby, a faintest stirring, the restlessness of a time-tempered intelligence and a bitter, ruthless heart. Someone was awakening; someone had heard something. Mabin.

Karis could not be hurried. One step at a time they took her down the stairs. When they came up they had climbed at a distance from each other to keep the treads from creaking, but now they could not be so artful. Karis had no shoes. Her steps were silent but her weight was not. The building sighed under the burden of her.

On the floor above them, a door opened and there were footsteps. A moment later the four of them slipped into Annis's room and Emil eased the door shut. "It has no lock," he breathed, and began moving furniture to block the door.

A shout echoed down the stairwell. Medric had already gone out the window and was halfway to the ground. Footsteps thundered up the stairs. How long would it take for the building's occupants to figure out what had happened? The confused guard out in the courtyard would insist no one had come in or out. How long would it take for them to realize that rescuers must have come in through a window? Emil was pulling up the rope. They would have to lower Karis, who scarcely seemed able to place one foot in front of the other and certainly could not be expected to climb down a rope.

Zanja abruptly took out her knife and hacked Annis's bindings to tatter. Annis jerked the gag out of her mouth.

"I need your help," Zanja said.

"After you made a fool out of me? I think I'll just do the same to you. It seems fair!" Annis leapt off the bed and started for the door, clearly expecting Zanja to jump her.

"Annis, this is no game. Karis is the G'deon of Shaftal. Settle with me later, if you must, but help her now."

Annis stopped short. "What? Is this another one of your tales?"

"It's the truth. Come and help us lower her to the ground—she's too heavy just for the two of us. Come! There is no time!"

Annis hesitated, but she had always been impulsive. "Oh, all right!" she said, but her face glowed with excitement.

Emil was ready. Despite, or perhaps because of the smoke, Karis looked panicked as they dropped her over the edge. The three of them popped their shoulder joints and burned the skin off their hands lowering her safely to ground, but then Medric had her, and Zanja could breathe easier. Annis went out the window, followed by Emil. Throughout the building, doors were being slammed open, but no one had yet been sent out to check the surrounding streets. Mabin's people still thought that Karis was still somewhere in the building.

Emil had reached the ground. The sky opened up in a fresh downpour. Zanja swung out the window and only then remembered the raven. His feathers were fluffed comfortably in the warmth of the fire, and he seemed disinclined to leave, but finally flew to the windowsill the third time Zanja called him. She slid down the rope as Annis's door crashed open.

There was a pistol blast, and the raven exploded like a feather pillow ripped open. In the street below, Karis uttered a terrible, wordless cry, and fell to her knees.

Chapter Twenty-three

Annis said, "This way."

They ran, propelling Karis forward with one person pulling at each arm, and another pushing at her back. Annis darted ahead, light-footed, grinning like a child set loose to play. They ducked into a narrow back way. Behind them, Mabin's people jammed the house's single doorway, struggled into the courtyard, and shouted at the guard to unlock the gate. With no idea which way the fugitives had gone, Mabin would have to divide her forces at every turn. Soon, Zanja and her companions would outnumber the pursuers. Pistols would not fire in the rain; she and Emil might well be testing their long unused daggers before the night was done.

"This way," Annis called. They fled down an alley where garbage piles awaited the trash wagon. They trampled through a vegetable garden, where squash vines tripped them and soft mud clung to their ankles. They crashed through a gate into another garden, and then between buildings to more gardens, and at last to the wall.

"There's a door in the wall right around here," Annis said. "So people can escape to the river should they need to." She hopped on one foot, belatedly putting her shoes on muddy feet. She had put on a shirt, but her breeches were still tucked under her arm.

Zanja could hear Mabin's people shouting the village awake behind them. Karis leaned in her embrace, cold and soaking wet, gasping for breath. She heard a bolt shoot open, and Emil said, "Annis, don't take the path. That way, through the woods." Annis leapt forward, happy in the chase. The three of them followed, compelling Karis through the thicket, where a tracker might be able to follow their route, but not until daylight and not until the rainfall had ceased. They made their way to their horses and put Karis on Homely. The rest of them went on foot, heading westward, into the wilderness.

It rained all night and well into the morning, and then the sun split the clouds open like a bright hammer upon gray stone. Zanja, trudging across the rocky landscape with her hand on Homely's stirrup, sensed a quickening in the giant riding beside her, and looked up to see that Karis had lifted her hanging head and was squinting up into the sun. "Karis, are you awake?"

Karis glanced bleakly down at her.

Zanja put her hand upon Karis's sodden knee, wondering if she would even feel the touch. A steady tremor ran through the muscles under her hand, like the vibration of a heavy wagon upon cobblestones. "Should I explain what has happened?"

Karis shook her head.

If reason and will broke free of smoke's paralysis before bone and muscle did, then Karis had been considering her situation for some time already. Perhaps she felt the vacancy of amputation where her raven had been; perhaps she had sorted through the dreamlike memories. She seemed, now, to become aware of the hand upon her knee, and she covered it with her own. Her hands already were trembling.

Zanja said, "I took the box of smoke from your room. You still have your smoke purse."

Karis dried with her sleeve the wretched tears that had streaked her face. "Can we stop?" she slurred.

Zanja shouted ahead at her companions, who had outpaced Homely and his heavy burden, then led the horse to a bit of a rise, which she hoped might be less muddy, and helped Karis to dismount. Karis lay down with her back against the earth, like an uprooted plant digging herself back into the soil.

Zanja took hold of her hand again.

"Help me."

Zanja had cobbled together courage before, using whatever poor bits and pieces of strength she had at hand. But to do it for another person, when she herself felt hopeless, was not an easy feat. She stated the bitter facts, as Norina would have. "If you continue to use the drug as you have been doing, you'll die. But if you stop, that also will kill you."

A tremor rippled through Karis's form, like a small wave running ahead of a devastating flood. "Another choice," she gasped.

Wouldn't there have to be a tenuous route, halfway between one death and the other? If there wasn't one, what harm was there in pretending like there was one? "A dance," Zanja said. "A balance. Use enough smoke to keep you alive, but not enough to kill you. Every time you smoke, wait a little longer. In time, you will be using the drug just once a day again."

Karis said hoarsely, "And in the interim, this agony. Death sounds easier."

"No doubt it is easier. No doubt it would have been easier had I chosen death a year ago, when your raven gave me the choice. There's been a number of times I wondered why I didn't."

"Why didn't you?" she gasped. Her eyes were blank with pain.

"I knew I was caught up in something, and could not endure to die with my curiosity unsatisfied."

Karis smiled faintly. She placed Zanja's hand upon her breast, where the hard outline of her smoke purse lay under the shirtcloth. "Take it."

"I don't want to decide for you—"

"Don't be so scrupulous." Another tremor, stronger than the last, shook through her, and Karis took a shaky breath. "It won't be pretty. I've seen smoke addicts die—because they could not—light a match. And no one thought to light it for them."

Zanja unbuttoned Karis's shirt and lifted the purse from around her neck. Then, she put the green pendant in its place, knotting the torn and mudstained ends of the ribbon.

Karis seemed to find it difficult to breath. But she asked, "Are you—all right?"

"Is this earth logic, to worry about me when it's your life that's at risk?" Zanja added, "When I saw the Sainnite army crossing the Asha River in dead of night with my people helpless before them, that tried my courage. This is not any worse."

"This is my worst fear."

"Don't face it alone."

"So that's the secret."

Karis sat up so Zanja could hold her: against her shoulder, within her arms, between her legs, an embrace that could have scarcely been more intimate if they'd taken off their clothing. When the first convulsion came, it had Karis's shocking strength behind it, and Zanja could no more hold her still than she could have reined in a maddened plowhorse. She learned to ride it through, evading Karis's flailing limbs, holding on by gripping her own wrist across Karis's ribs, so that she still would be there when the seizure was over. Each time a seizure passed, Karis lay limp against her shoulder, sobbing for breath, clammy with sweat, and later weeping, bleeding from a bitten tongue and lips. Finally, she scarcely seemed conscious anymore and Zanja lit the pipe for her and helped her smoke. The convulsions stopped, and then the tremors, and Karis's head grew heavy and her hands slid down to rest upon the grass that she had torn up earlier by the roots. Her eyes glazed and closed, and Zanja could not rouse her.

She must have uttered a cry, for when she looked up Emil was kneeling beside her. He felt the pulse in Karis's neck and said, "Zanja, surely you don't think either one of you can repeatedly endure such a torment." He must have watched from a distance and been hard put not to intervene.

Zanja's exhaustion washed over her then, as though Emil's acknowledgment had raised a water gate. "I am the only one who can help her to walk this hard way, though watching her do it breaks my heart."

"For the gods require you to show the way across the borders. I understand that. But if you lose her, you will lose yourself. It's a poor friend who would stand by and let you do such a thing needlessly."

"Needless?" She considered for a while. "Heedless, certainly. Haven't you heard that hopeless passion brings out the worst in the na'Tarweins?"

"I'm afraid this is the first I've heard of it." Emil uttered an unkind snort. "I take that to mean you'll try to listen to me, but you're making no promises. Well, even when I was your commander I couldn't depend on you to follow orders." He felt Karis's pulse again, and said, "She's got a strong heart, doesn't she? Earth witches are notoriously hard to kill. I say you need not be so impatient for a cure. Let her move more slowly out of her darkness."

Zanja let the reassurance calm her own more volatile heart, and as if in response Karis stirred, and Zanja looked down to find her eyes open, though blank and senseless.

"We can try to get her back on a horse," Emil said. "My horse looks the best of the three now, though that's not saying much. I doubt we can travel much further, but Medric says we've entered into an elemental's domain, unlikely though it seems in this wilderness, and he says this man or woman will investigate our presence and either offer us hostility or sanctuary. Let's hope for the latter, shall we?"

They continued to travel in the direction they had been going, with the river canyon to their right. Some trees had begun to appear in the pathless waste. Just after passing a grove of these at mid-afternoon, a ululating cry echoed behind them. Zanja turned to find a rag-tag group of people emerging from among the trees—children she thought them at first, until she saw that at least two of them had hair gone to gray. Over Emil's objections she walked back to them alone. Even alone, with her hands held out in friendship, she seemed to frighten them, for they drew back, wide-eyed, as she neared them. Some wore only necklaces and girdles of white shells, and others wore strange woven garments of rough linen. Some carried spears of wood, split into three sharpened points. An old man emerged from their midst and came out to her. He spoke in a language she had never heard, a language like water on stone.

Surely they had traveled beyond the borders of Shaftal, into the wild lands of the west, which, like the northern mountains and the southern plains, was tenanted by tribal people. This tribe into whose territory they had wandered clearly were too anxious to be warlike, and probably it was usual for them to avoid strangers, rather than seeking them out like this.

Zanja said, in Shaftalese and then again in the language of her own lost people, "We must have shelter. Will you help us?"

The man replied. She was too tired to listen, too tired to even try to distinguish one sound from the next. He took a step forward, and held out his hand. A large leaf in his palm unfolded to reveal a bit of fish, brown with the smoke that had preserved it. Enemies do not eat each other's food, so Zanja took the warm piece of smoked fish and put it in her mouth. The wild people immediately stepped forward, peering at her curiously.

Emil had the wit to bring out some of their own meat and bread, and the wild people all ate a mouthful of their food, while those of Zanja's company ate some of the wild people's fish. During this necessary waste of time, the old man walked up to Karis, cautious of the horse, and stood for a while beside her, looking up at her. Then he put a hand upon her bare foot, and Karis, who throughout the day had scarcely seemed conscious, heavily lifted her head. He seemed startled—perhaps by her size or blue eyes—but did not step back. Karis opened her mouth as if to speak, though she could not, and the old man bowed to her. He turned to his people and spoke to them, and they all bowed to Karis, with their hands upon their hearts.

The old man was a water witch, Medric enthusiastically told Zanja, delighted and amazed by such a rarity, despite his own exhaustion. Zanja felt no amazement, only relief that she needed not cross the boundary of language in order to explain herself to the man, at least not today.

They followed the tribal people down a steep and crooked path into a deep cleft in the earth. Here, captured between cliffs as steep and barren as stone walls, lay an island-scattered azure lake carved out by the river long ago, with a cattail marsh along one edge and a stony beach along another. Here a half dozen tiny boats of lath and hide lay upon the shore, and dozens of others sprinted across the water's surface like paddle bugs. The sound of laughter echoed across the waters, and some curious children came swimming up the shoreline, slick and bright-eyed as otters. Somewhere, Zanja supposed, there was a village, but weariness and sunlight reflecting off the water blinded her so she could scarcely see to keep her feet from wandering off the path.

They walked along the stony beach to a place where the floods of ages had undermined the cliff face, making a wide and shallow cave, which a crowd of industrious people had nearly finished walling off with gathered stones. Upon a simple hearth, a row of fish pierced on a green wand were being roasted, and a pile of flatbreads warmed. When Zanja came out from helping Karis into the cave and laying her down upon the rush mat within, Emil already had started water heating for tea, and the people seemed intrigued by his iron cooking pot. Medric and Annis had gone away with the horses, and all their gear lay in a pile upon the beach.

After Zanja had spread the damp blankets out to dry in the sun, she joined Emil, who was drinking a cup of the bitter bark infusion that eased the pain in his knee. The water witch and a few others sat with him, sipping with some astonishment from porcelain cups of green tea. Zanja bowed to the water witch with her hand on her heart, as his people had done to Karis earlier, and he gravely bowed to her in return. Emil said, "What will you have, green tea or willowbark or both?"

She took both, and when Annis and Medric returned they shared the hot fish, flaking the meat from the bones and wrapping it in the warm flatbread. Medric said, "These people live on one of the islands out there, and hardly ever set foot on ground at all. I wish I knew the language; there's so much I want to ask!"

Zanja already thought of them as Otter People: a lithe and small and playful folk. She taught Medric the words she had already learned involuntarily while listening to the Otter People talk. She knew "water," "fish," "boat," "bread," and the word by which the Otter People referred to the five of them, which she supposed meant "guest" or "stranger." The verb patterns would take longer for her to grasp, but she expected she would be speaking simple sentences in a day or two. All of them, Otter People and stranger alike, engaged in the game of word exchange, and soon the Otter People roared with infectious laughter. The water element had something to do with time and weather; very little else was known about it. Apparently, it made a people of great merriment.

Zanja found that humor difficult to endure, and finally she excused herself to check on Karis. Tucked within her womb of stone, Karis lay curled upon her side, with a hand resting palm down upon the rock. Sweat plastered the hair upon her face. She opened her eyes at Zanja's touch, but her gaze remained dull and blank.

Medric had come in behind her. "She has a fever," Zanja said, and added in frustration, "Despite all the elemental talent gathered there on the beach, she is our only healer, and if she could heal herself we would not be in this predicament."

Medric said quietly, "And the smoke will not easily let her go. There's a reason why my father's people use it to enslave."

"What does the future hold for her? Have you no idea?"

"I feel that we'll be safe here, at least for now. I cannot see beyond that, because Karis's life is in the balance."

"There must be a way to tilt the scale."

"Zanja, I don't know. I don't know what to do."

Though Zanja sat beside Karis that night, waiting for just a word or two with her before she slipped away again, Karis went directly into convulsions without ever leaving her stupor. It was all Zanja could do to get some smoke in her, and afterwards she paced up and down the length of the stony beach in a bitter rage, unable to endure the fact that she was losing a battle she did not even know how to fight. She did not sleep at all.

All night and all day Karis burned with fever, and not even water remained long in her stomach. She had already gone thirteen days without food, and could not survive much longer. Zanja could not endure watching her starve to death like every other smoke addict, and, in desperation, withheld the drug from her one night. After a long while, the violence of Karis's seizures began to alternate with a death-like stillness. Zanja finally lit and smoked a pipe herself, breathing the foul-tasting stuff into Karis's mouth and lungs for her, one mouthful at a time, until Karis opened her eyes and stared at her in bleak horror. At least, Zanja thought, she seemed to be conscious for once.

Then her wits deserted her entirely, and the gift of smoke was thrust upon her willy-nilly, if a complete cessation of rational thought and physical sensation could be called a gift. Later, she would remember that she had become like a worn-out child, who curled where she was upon bare stone and shut her eyes to sleep.

She awoke puzzled, heavy-bodied, tortoise-slow. A big hand smacked her cheek, and the dull shock of pain and surprise brought her upright. It was morning, well past dawn. She dimly smelled the cookfires' smoke, and heard the laughter of the Otter People as they gathered up their nets. A fist caught her braids and she was jerked back down onto the pallet beside Karis, and a muscled arm embraced her throat.

Karis's voice rasped in her ear. "You will not smoke again. Swear."

Clawing at the blacksmith's muscles, Zanja choked, "No."

"Swear!"

Black spots swam before Zanja's eyes. "Only—to save—your life," she gasped.

"My life is not worth such a price!"

And then she was shoved irresistibly away onto the bare stone, where she lay until her vision stopped swirling and she dared sit up, rubbing her neck and testing the hair at the back of her head to make certain it was still attached. "It's good to see you feeling so well," she said, speaking with some difficulty.

Karis lay upon her back, breathing convulsively, tense with rage, as though she was about to leap up and wreck the cave and all its contents, like a berserker. Zanja got up and went to the door. Emil and Medric lay in each other's arms on the stony beach, groggy with love and sunshine. She shouted imperiously at them to bring some porridge, and they both stared at her.

She went back in, and knelt at Karis's side, and begged her pardon for taking a risk she'd had no choice about and had every intention of taking again should the need arise. Her patent insincerity was enough to make Karis smile weakly. "I guess I didn't make much of an impression."

Zanja rubbed a bruised elbow. "You made an impression all right."

As Emil came in with the porridge, followed by Medric, they each in turn blocked the sunlight and cast the cave into shadow. Emil still limped badly. He bowed ironically as he handed Zanja some porridge. "I had checked on you just minutes ago."

"I was rudely awakened and it made me ill-mannered. I am sorry."

"Well, you've been under a strain," Emil said more kindly. "How is she?"

He looked directly into Karis's face and recoiled with surprise.

Zanja remembered then what it had been like to meet Karis for the first time, to feel the shocking, palpable presence of her intelligence, like a handshake that leaves the hand aching. Emil, whose talent made people's hearts transparent to him, dropped heedlessly to his knees. Karis gazed at him in some puzzlement, then at Medric, who had crouched, wide-eyed, beside him, and then she turned to Zanja and said, "I should know these people."

"They helped in your escape and have been with us ever since. These are my friends, Emil Paladin and the seer Medric."

"How could this be?" Karis said blankly.

Much to Zanja's relief, Emil's look of astonishment gave way to a genuine smile. "Well, Karis, Medric had a dream that Zanja needed us, and so as soon as we could we traded our dray horse and wagon for a couple of riding horses, and nearly killed them coming here cross-country, rather to Zanja's surprise. But for us it was very simple, really."

Karis looked from him to Medric.

Medric said, "Karis, you are the hope of Shaftal."

There was a silence. Karis said, "So I see that, like all seers, you are mad."

Zanja convinced Karis to eat while she explained where they were and how they had gotten there. Before she finished the tale, Karis's tremors began again, and Medric and Emil delicately took their leave. Karis set the mostly empty bowl aside and lay back upon the plain pallet, wan and hollow-eyed. She said, "I didn't want and never would have chosen the ancient office of G'deon. But your fire blood friends seem enchanted by the glamour of it."

Zanja said, "Oh, yes, it is quite glamorous. I myself am struck dumb by the glory of it."

Karis shut her eyes, and said heavily, "I know I should laugh. But the truth is too bitter. For fifteen years I have carried this weight within the flawed receptacle of my flesh and bones, and as if that weren't enough, have also borne the burden of Mabin's unremitting censure and Norina's overbearing solicitude. Mercy could only be had from the secrecy that allowed me to be a mere earth witch and metalsmith of modest ambitions. Now that mercy is gone."

Zanja said, "So now you must become accustomed to being treated with affection and respect by three fire bloods. Why is it terrible to be so richly perceived now?"

Karis flinched as a particularly strong tremor shook her frame. "If I live—then I will fail your hopes. Shaftal—I am so tired."

"Our hopes for what?"

Karis shuddered again. Sweat beaded her forehead as if she endured an intense pain. "Whatever you want. Deliverance. The healing of the world. All things I cannot do."

Zanja said softly, "Even the gods could not save my people from destruction. So if Shaftal is to be saved, it seems it must happen in a more ordinary way. Karis, how can I give you peace? Shall I tell you that I'm simply fulfilling my long overdue obligation in a trade agreement? You broke into a Sainnite prison and saved my life and rescued me; now I have broken into a Paladin prison and saved your life and rescued you. It's a simple exchange. Or would it make you feel better if I tell you that once I've made you indebted to me I have every intention of abusing your sense of obligation? That *would* make you feel better."

Karis began to laugh, but it was painful to watch.

Zanja said, "But the truth is that I dare not let you die, nor dare I release your secret to the world, for Norina will hunt me down and skewer me."

"That's true," Karis said. "But it's not the whole truth."

"Well, of course, I am devoted to you. So why can you accept devotion from Norina and not from me?"

Karis's hand clenched convulsively in Zanja's, her palm sticky with sweat. "I accept Norina's duty," she said. "But you have no excuse."

The convulsions began.

Even the worst of battles has an end, but for Karis the siege never seemed to lift. Three times between each sunrise, Zanja sat beside her as she fought her tedious, horrifying struggle, only to give in, over and over again. With slowness that seemed unendurable, Karis won back her life from smoke, gaining ground so slowly that many a time it seemed as though she won nothing at all. It was a wearying, desperate, grinding labor of will that yielded too little reward. Days of sudden fevers and devastating fits of nausea gave way to days of dispirited exhaustion and irritable boredom. Then, Karis made a water clock by piercing a hole in an empty pot and hanging it to drip water into a container. This clock became her enemy, and the changing containers Zanja put down to catch the water defined the progress of the combat. For seven days the time Karis called her own could not fill one of Emil's tiny porcelain teacups. But then the teacup overflowed and Zanja's battered tin porringer replaced it.

Ten more drops of water today than yesterday, and tomorrow it would be ten more. Medric timed the water drops with Emil's watch, then worked a cipher on the stone floor with a piece of charcoal. At this rate, a year would pass before Karis was smoking only once a day again. Zanja made him erase it before Karis could see the grim numbers.

One afternoon, when Zanja came out of the shadowed cave into the rich warmth of the late summer sunshine, Medric was waiting for her. Karis had just smoked, and had fallen into an exhausted sleep. This was not the first time either Medric or Emil lay in wait for Zanja, but only now did she realize that it was no accident. "The two of you are taking turns," she said.

Medric grinned. "It's a measure of how preoccupied you are that it took so long for you to realize it. Here, sit down. I want to talk to you."

She sat on one of the large stones that served them as furniture. The entire population of the Otter People's village seemed to be out on the lake this warm afternoon. One of the young people engaged in a raucous boat race was a stocky, brown-haired South Hill farmer who seemed on the verge of tipping her boat into the water. It hardly mattered, since Annis wore no clothing. The sun had cooked her brown as a loaf of overcooked bread. Someone dumped Annis into the water and she came up laughing.

"There is a shadow over Karis," Medric said. "And it lies over you as well, since you have bound yourself to share her fate."

"What shadow?" Zanja asked. "Death, is that it? Madness? Neither one seems worse than this torture."

Medric said, "A moment of decision is coming upon you, a time when you must see clearly and speak with courage. But you have lost your vision. Karis's whole attention is on the water dripping from her clock, and there's a kind of madness in that—one that you have come to share with her. Here, eat this."

He had given her a piece of the Otter People's flatbread, with some of the ubiquitous smoked fish rolled up inside. Zanja ate it rather as Karis would have done, obediently, without hunger or pleasure. Medric pushed his spectacles up onto the bridge of his nose and gazed rather blearily out across the water, blinking in the glare. "These water folk make me see how much we fire bloods are bound by our seriousness. Everything we do seems fraught with importance. It's easy to lose perspective." He took off his spectacles and put on the other pair. "Aha!"

Zanja said, "What can't I see?"

"I have seen Karis lift a hammer and strike, and the sparks fall around her in a shower of gold. I see her shaping the world on her forge."

There was a silence. Zanja said, "Will you stay here for a while and keep an eye on Karis? I want a bath."

She took the cake of soap and bathed in the downriver end of the lake, washing even her stinking clothing and dirty hair, and when she came back with her dripping laundry in her arms, Medric loaned her a clean shirt to wear and combed her hair for her. Then, as Zanja braided her hair, he read out loud from one of the half dozen books that he and Emil continued to haul around with them, though most of the library was safely stored. He read a history of a time so ancient the story seemed more myth than fact, yet the tale had an eerie familiarity: a tale of people arriving by sea to a land inhabited by tribal folk, and how at first they had been conquerors until at last the land tamed them and taught them how to live upon it. That land had been Shaftal.

Zanja lay back, with her hair only half braided, dazed by cleanliness and sunshine and the easy rhythms of Medric's reading voice, and the ancient cycles of history. Medric broke off and said, "Here's Emil, looking grumpy, and the water witch."

Zanja sat up and rubbed her eyes. Two boats had landed on the beach. The water witch, carrying a heavy jug, went into Karis's cave. Zanja started to get up, but Emil's hand restrained her. Medric went back to his reading, and then he and Emil sat talking about history for hours. When at last the water witch reappeared, he crouched down beside Zanja and said, "Give her the water to drink until she has drunk dry the jug."

"Esteemed sir, as you will," she said, and bowed.

He got into his boat and rowed away.

"You absorb language like paper absorbs ink," said Medric admiringly.

"Land have mercy," Emil said, "isn't the man tired yet? He took me on a half-day journey upstream until my arms were about to fall off from rowing, and then we had to climb the cliff to a little spring that bubbled out from a crack in the stone. I'm certain he explained it to me, but unlike Zanja, I don't understand a word he says."

Zanja said, "You obviously are the elder of our tribe. Therefore, you stand witness on our behalf."

"Witness to what, though?" Emil said, rubbing a stiff shoulder.

Medric lifted his head and smiled suddenly. Zanja turned to look at what he was seeing, and leapt to her feet and ran to the doorway of the little cave, where Karis stood, braced between stones. Karis said thickly, "If I'm to receive guests now I should be more presentable." She dropped her shirt, which she had been unbuttoning, and walked across the beach and into the water.

Zanja picked up the shirt, which was even more rank than hers had been, and stood there feeling like a parent must feel when her firstborn suddenly ceases to be a child.

When Karis came out of the water, Emil wrapped her in a blanket, and gave her the last cup of tea. She sat by the coals of the fire, watching Zanja stew her shirt and spice it heavily with shavings from their solitary bar of soap. "You never told me what a peculiar feeling it is to have someone work magic on you," she said to Zanja.

"Well, I didn't want to seem as if I were complaining."

"What did he do?" Medric asked.

"Water magic makes no sense to me. He did something very ordinary."

"Surely not!"

"It was ordinary, I tell you."

Perhaps Karis was incapable of appetite, but she ate an astonishing quantity of bread and fish, and then pursued a lengthy argument with Medric. It was well past sunset by the time the tremors began, and when Zanja went into the cave with her, the porringer under the water clock had filled to overflowing, and was surrounded by a small pond of spilled water, with the water clock nearly empty.

"I guess we need a bigger bowl," Zanja said.

Karis sat upon her pallet of woven reeds.

"Here, you're supposed to drink dry the jug, he said." Zanja picked up the water jug from the floor, but it already was empty. "What did he do to you?"

Karis said, "You know how people wish for more time."

Zanja looked at the overflowing porringer. Another drop plunked into it. "Time is water?"

"For him it is. I told you it made no sense."

"How is it ordinary that he gave you more time?"

"People give each other time fairly commonly, don't they? You're giving me some of yours right now. I tend to be miserly with mine, however. I always feel like I don't have enough of it." She lay down. "Am I tired?"

"You should be."

The spasms, when they came, were not nearly as violent as they had been. Afterwards, in the few moments between smoking the pipe and going under smoke, Karis said, "I think I might live."

"You've faced your ordeal with great courage."

"What choice had I?" And she was gone.

Chapter Twenty-four

The night had been edged with a bit of autumn's chill, and when Zanja awoke, she remembered that she had crawled into Karis's bed in the middle of the night and covered them both with her blanket. She lay alone now upon the reed pallet, and a bowl with waves painted along its edge sat beneath the water clock, collecting time. She went out and found Karis beside the fire with Emil. He had unbuttoned and rolled up the leg of his breeches to reveal the knee that plagued him so. It was a wonder that he could walk at all, Zanja realized as she got a closer look at the scarred, distorted, swollen joint, much less run and fight the way he did. Karis laid her hand upon his knee and he began arguing with her.

"Just concede," Zanja advised him. "She's bigger and stronger than you are."

Her clothing had dried enough to wear. She took Medric's borrowed shirt to put it with his gear, and found him asleep on the reed bed he and Emil shared. He often slept late, for he often sat awake for half the night. When Zanja returned to the fire, Emil's knee had been transformed. "I don't know," he said bemusedly. "Somehow, this seems like cheating." He worked the new knee as he might work the trigger of a new pistol.

Karis said, "Five years of walking on a shattered knee seems long enough to me."

"It's just as well I haven't known you all these

267

years. How could I have kept from entreating you to heal my friends, who all are dead now? What a horror I would have made of your life, laying upon you a burden of moral quandaries, matters of life and death, that no one person should have to resolve by herself. It used to take an entire government and strength of tradition to relieve the G'deon from having to decide how to dole out his favor. You have no such protections."

"Not even the protection of being able to pretend that I'm superior to everyone else. Good morning," she added to Zanja. "Is it too early for such serious talk?"

"We're out of tea," Emil said sadly.

Karis had already eaten, but sat down with Zanja to eat again, and told her that Annis, who seemed to be living with the Otter People, had rowed over at dawn with the new bowl for the water clock, the day's delivery of food, and a pair of sandals for Karis. "Have I met Annis before?" Karis asked.

"I doubt you remember. She's a genius at blowing things up, and comes from a good family."

"That's better than I can say about myself."

Emil took a few steps, testing his new knee. "Oh blessed day," he said, "You're a genius, anyway. You can always get a good family."

Karis was still smiling as, after breakfast, she took Zanja's arm and walked her down the beach. "You must have been cold last night."

"I'm afraid it made me presumptuous."

Karis had turned her face away to look over the busy waters of the lake. Now she looked back, and Zanja did not think she had ever seen such unhappiness. "Presumptuous?"

"I—"

"Let's pretend I don't understand why it might be presumptuous for you to share my bed on a cold night," Karis said.

"All right." The pretense was certainly preferable to any other alternative.

"But if I'm to be your torturer . . ."

"What torture? I have no false hopes." Zanja kicked at the stones. "I thought we were pretending we didn't know what we're talking about."

"I guess that's not going to work."

"Well, then let me say my speech about how I hope you won't let this come between us, and how in time I'll come to my senses—"

"Come to your senses! Oh, have pity!" Karis dropped to her knees and drove her fists onto the stones with enough force to send them flying and clattering across the beach. Zanja grabbed her wrists, fearful that she would break the small bones of her hands without knowing it. Karis cried, "Let it me be who comes to her senses! Let me taste, let me feel hunger and pain and weariness and even pleasure! Let me know the name of the desire that drives me! If there be gods—"

Karis was taken by a spasm of grief as sudden and violent as the smoke convulsions that made her life all but unendurable. She struggled in Zanja's embrace, but finally let her head rest in the cradle of her shoulder while she wept. At last she was still, and said hoarsely, calmly, with her head heavy against Zanja's breastbone, "Zanja na'Tarwein, you're in love with a madwoman."

Zanja kissed the tangled mess of Karis's hair. "I'm not entirely sane myself."

Karis convulsed again; Zanja could only hope it was with laughter this time. And then they both lay still, while the sweet laughter of the Otter children echoed across the water, and the warm sun rose above the canyon rim. In that silence that came in the wake of sorrow, Zanja felt the heavy weight of the moment resting upon her like a door upon its hinge. She said, "Councilor Mabin has proven herself so ruthless, it seems that something about you must terrify her. I wish you would explain it."

Karis groaned against Zanja's chest. "Shall I explain why water runs downhill? Shall I name the forces that bind together and tear apart? That I can do. But why Councilor Mabin hates me and has always hated me, that I can't explain. It's not for anything I've done—I've done so little—so it must be for what I am."

"Once you lived with her, you and Norina."

"No, Norina lived with her, but I was her prisoner, for Mabin doled smoke out to me, one piece at a time, like a reward given a trained dog. Mabin is the one who taught me that no matter what else I did with my life, I had better learn a trade so I didn't have to depend on anyone except myself for my smoke supply."

Zanja stroked a hand down Karis's unruly head, but had to stop because it was too much for her to endure.

"Agreeing to help me escape her cost Norina too much," Karis said. "She became as bound to me as I am bound to smoke."

"She was what, Medric's age?"

"She was never young," Karis said. "When she was crowning between her mother's legs, her mother shouted, 'There's been a mistake! My baby is an old woman!' "

"That explains a lot," Zanja said gravely. "But I've never understood exactly why Norina agreed to help you. If you were not to be the G'deon . . ."

Karis said wearily, "No, Zanja, she told you the truth when we were at Strongbridge. It is her duty to make it possible for me to survive to vest the next G'deon."

"That's all you live for? To lay upon some child a burden you could not yourself endure?"

Karis lifted her head then, and Zanja let go of her. Having felt the force of her anger before, Zanja thought it prudent to put some distance between them.

"I am not completely without hope," Karis said, with great restraint. "I can yet believe that the future can be different from and better than the present. I even have the audacity to imagine that I might yet win some small honor for delivering Shaftal's inheritance to its rightful heir."

Zanja said, "But why are you not Shaftal's rightful heir?"

"You have to ask? Just look at me."

"Do you believe that Harald G'deon picked you as thoughtlessly as he would pick a whore, and raped you with his power merely because you were convenient? Or rather, is that the story Mabin wants you to believe? This same Mabin who hates you and controlled you first through smoke and later through your beloved friend, and finally, rather than have you escape her control, all but murdered you? You still trust that woman's judgment?"

A long time the silence lasted. Karis rubbed her eyes as though to clear away a blur of tears.

"Tell me what happened when they brought you to Harald," Zanja said.

"It was afternoon. The night before, I had managed to use smoke without Dinal realizing it, for we were sleeping under stars. But once we came to the House of Lilterwess, I began to worry, for it was such a crowded place. Dinal had been so kind to me, I feared to lose her regard by telling her the truth, but I thought that I would have to. That was the only thing on my mind as she brought me into Harald's room. The room was full of silent, dignified people, who all turned in surprise to stare at me. Dinal's hand was on my shoulder. She pushed me forward, and the dying man on the bed opened his eyes and held out his hand to me. I felt a surprise, a kinship—he was an earth witch like myself. I knew so little that I didn't even realize this must be Harald G'deon. I thought that he might teach me what to do with myself, if he lives. But his life fire burned so faintly, I knew he would only live a few more hours at most. So I took hold of his hand, to bid him a safe journey. That is what I remember clearly. Norina says he died immediately after empowering me, without saying a word."

"Who decided it was not Harald's intention to name you his successor?"

"It was the Lilterwess Council. Once Dinal explained who I was, and it became evident I was a smoke addict, the council decided not to affirm me as G'deon."

"But Norina was not party to that meeting, was she? And Mabin is the only councilor who survived the night."

"Norina has her faults, but she has never lied to me."

"No, but it's possible she doesn't know the entire truth. I'm asking because I don't understand why Mabin fears you enough to kill you."

Karis said quietly, "I have been vested with a stunning power, and nothing can stop me from exercising it as I choose. Don't you find that frightening? I'm certain Mabin fears that I will challenge her, and claim the G'deon's right. That I have no desire to do so must be unbelievable to her."

"But what if Harald G'deon knew what you were when he sent Dinal for you? Even if he was out of his mind, as some say he was, he was not a fool. So let the G'deon's chair remain empty if that's what seems right to you, and wander the land in rags and die unknown like Mackapee did. Scholars like Emil and Medric will study the obscure history of your life a hundred years from now and never quite make sense of it. So what, so long as it makes sense to you?"

Karis uttered a short laugh.

"What I see is that your life has been decided by people who seem determined to keep you within boundaries and to keep you from realizing that they are controlling you. And I see that as a result you never have made a choice for yourself except one time, the time you saved my life. And it put all of your keepers into a panic, which surely reveals how illusory are the boundaries they've put around you, and how easy it would be for you to simply step outside of them. So why not set yourself free of them? If you were free to live as well and joyfully as you could, exercising with honor what powers have been given to you, what would you do? Can you even imagine?"

Karis muttered to herself, as her raven would have, "Oh, I am in dire danger."

She laid her hands flat against the stony beach. "I know exactly what I would do," she said. She got abruptly to her feet. "Excuse me." And she was gone, striding quickly back the way she had come, to where Medric sat awake in his bed. Perhaps it was a trick of the light reflecting from his spectacles that made it seem as if he were staring at them across the length of the beach. Karis sat beside him and they had a long, sometimes agitated conversation, which ended only when Karis got up to go back into her cave.

Zanja looked in on her after a while, and Karis raised her head from where she sat in a huddle upon the floor, with her filled smoke pipe in reach, and the water clock plunking the occasional drop into the bowl. Zanja said, "Since you were kidnapped twenty-one days ago, one keeper or another has been hovering over you. It's not a role I relish much myself, so I hope you'll just tell me when you think you're strong enough to need no looking after. Are you strong enough today?"

Karis shook her head. She looked frightened and worn out, and Zanja remembered that Karis had no way to judge what her limits were. "Shall I come in?" she asked.

"You're very formal."

"Well, I'm making up this dance as I go along. I can't get it right all the time."

Karis smiled. "That's better. You know, you aren't always the most restful of companions."

"Are you admonishing me?" Zanja sat down beside her. "I'll be boring if you will."

"No," Karis said, "and no again. But let's not talk about the future anymore."

So Zanja diverted Karis with tales of her lifelong friendship with Ransel, until the water level in the bowl had risen high enough, and Karis reached for the pipe. She suffered no life-threatening convulsions, and because of her rapidly increasing strength, she remained awake after she had smoked. Zanja supposed she could take her for a walk, like a pet, but the very idea was so unsettling that she got up and left the cave instead. It was more than disconcerting to see Karis go from the morning's robust passions and willful vigor to this helpless passivity. The contradiction between the two Karises was not at all easy to encompass, and Zanja began to understand a little of why Mabin and Norina and even Karis herself had been unable to imagine her as anything other than a flawed vessel, to be patched together until it could be replaced. But if fire talent could not encompass a grand contradiction, what good was it?

It seemed strange that the nights had turned chilly, until Zanja examined the night sky and realized that any day now, the stars of summer would set. Karis took Zanja exploring up the river canyon, which required more stamina than Zanja would have thought Karis possessed. Karis's energy seemed inspired by the grand scale of the landscape: the broken rocks as big as houses, the foaming river, the looming stone cliffs, the narrow strip of sky. Her fascination with the place worked as a camouflage, and it took some time for Zanja to realize that the quality of their conversation had changed, and not for the better. They skated across the surface of a conversation mysteriously opaque and impenetrable, like water turned to ice.

By the time they returned to Otter Lake, Zanja was utterly confounded. Karis had used herself up by then, and they stopped to rest on a rock at the edge of the beach. The sun had dropped below the canyon rim, but the rock retained its warmth, and Zanja lay back upon it and shut her eyes, only to be assailed by a chaos of emotion that her disciplines could hardly keep in check. So this was love, she thought ironically, and hoped she'd soon discover the remedy for it. Then, she felt a mouth touch hers, tentatively, curiously, and she opened her eyes to find Karis's somber face, carved into hollows by her hard fight with smoke, so close that Zanja scarcely would have had to move to kiss her again. Zanja said desperately, "Now you are torturing me."

"I'm torturing myself," Karis said. She sat back, but Zanja still could scarcely breathe. "If my hands had been cut off I'd still be interested in picking things up, and I might even try it once in a while."

Zanja said, in a voice that did not seem hers, "Please don't try it again."

"Then how am I to live as well and joyfully as I can? You pose me quite a paradox."

Karis had given Zanja's scarcely functioning mind a glyph of words to figure out. While Zanja floundered in her divination, Karis sat with her chin upon her fist. Sometimes, a trembling passed over her. At last, Karis spoke again. "Maybe you've been merciless for good reasons, but you've been merciless nonetheless."

"It's a wonder you can stand my company," Zanja said stiffly. "Surely it's not pleasant to be reminded constantly of what you cannot have."

"Zanja, I could have whatever I wanted, if only I *could* want it. But I'm not like you, for even when you lay paralyzed, with your back broken, you still could want something. So you could imagine a life worth living, though there was much you might want and be unable to have. It's not the having that matters to you, am I right? So you can imagine living your whole life beside me, in a state of unfulfilled desire, and that's acceptable to you because it is desire itself that gives you joy. But I am an earth witch and no matter how rich my life of heart and mind become—and I am rich now, richer than I ever have been—it never can amount to joy. I need the earth, the flesh, the life of the skin. Without that, this whole thing—" she gestured at the shadowed canyon, the vivid sky, "—is just an intellectual exercise."

Zanja sat up, more bewildered by herself than she was by Karis. "I can't explain it, but I know that what you've said is only half the truth. You're standing in a doorway looking in one direction and thinking that what you see is all there is. But if you turned around you'd see something else entirely."

If Karis had received a classical education, then surely she would know that the Woman of the Doorway faces danger any way she looks. But Karis did not state this obvious objection, and she sighed and seemed relieved, as though this very peculiar conversation had served a purpose only she could comprehend. "All right," she said. "I'll try to turn around. I apologize for my behavior," she added. "It seemed like you wanted to give me some comfort yesterday with all your talk of Ransel—a model friendship, untainted by desire. But it only made me realize how much I detest the compromise you're offering. So I thought of how I've learned to feel the metal beneath my hammer, not by touch, but by knowing it from within. I thought I might know you that way."

"How is that different from what you had to do in Lalali?" Zanja put her head in her hands. "You can know me without touching me."

"If I were a fire blood, yes."

"I see," Zanja said, in the grip of a deep dismay.

After a while, Karis's big hand stroked softly down the back of

Zanja's shirt, and Karis said, "There's no point agonizing. I just want you to understand."

"I can't understand without agonizing," Zanja said. But she lifted her head and added shakily, "You'll be wanting to get back."

Karis stood up and they started down the beach, and after a while Karis closed her hand around Zanja's. "Norina already has left her child and is traveling north. I had promised to send the raven before her labor began, so if I know Norina, she's in a panic now."

Zanja said, "Well, we can't have her tearing apart the countryside looking for us, with no idea of what the dangers are. I'll have to go find her, somehow, before Mabin does."

Karis nodded. Zanja's hand felt like it was pinched in a trembling vice.

"How soon do you think I'd have to leave?"

"She's traveling very fast, and we'll want to catch her well before Strongbridge. The's what, six day's travel from here?"

"At least."

"At least? Then you should leave tomorrow."

"Tomorrow!"

Karis said softly, "I agree. It's much too soon."

"She'll come rampaging in—"

"She will," Karis agreed.

They had walked in silence almost to the cave before either one of them spoke again. Zanja said, "The last time I left you, you disappeared."

"Well you could be the one who disappears this time. I'm sure Mabin is looking for you. You should take Emil with you."

"No. Emil stays with you. Emil and Medric both."

"With Medric and the water witch looking out for me—"

"They don't have Emil's knowledge and experience."

Karis sighed. "You want Emil to stay with me for the same reason I want him to go with you. Well, let's not get into an argument about whose life is most worth protecting. I always lose that one."

They were standing at the entrance to the cave, and Zanja realized that this time Karis did not want her to go in. Karis said, "I'll be awake long before the sun tomorrow."

"Wake me up once you're awake."

Karis nodded. Her sorrow might have been a load of iron, yet she smiled wryly, as though she recognized that she was accepting the very compromise she detested: an arm's length intimacy that must inevitably be corrupted by bitterness. After she had gone in-side, Zanja sat alone upon the beach, wishing futilely for one easy choice, one option that did not leave her bleeding and bereft. The sky grew dark, and Emil and Medric came walking down the cliff path, hand in hand, talking earnestly, carrying a brace of rabbits and a basket of mushrooms for supper. Between the two of them, they were more kind to her than she could endure, and she went to bed early to get away from them.

After sunrise, Emil walked with Zanja to the top of the canyon path where their horses were picketed. Emil decided not to tell her about Medric's restless night; she did not need to worry more. He promised to look after Karis. From Homely's back, Zanja looked down at him and said with something of her old irony, "So now you're nursemaid to two rogue elementals. Your elevation has been meteoric."

"I can stand it a little longer," he said. "Just look out after yourself."

She did not remind him that her survival up until now had bordered on the miraculous. "A warrior shouldn't have so much to lose," she said. "Especially knowing as I do just what it's like to lose it."

"Nothing will be lost." He took her hand and lightly kissed her knuckle. "I'll look for you in twelve days. Medric and I will hunt some fowl, and we'll have a feast. And then all of us will decide what we're going to do with ourselves. Now go."

Her ugly horse pranced across the pathless ground as though he thought he was on parade. Watching her go so lightly and yet so heavily, Emil had the odd thought that she did not yet know what she had to fear. Yet, knowing her way was fraught with unknown danger, she had set forth. *And so we all are Paladins,* Emil thought, *every last one of us who sets forth so lightly upon a dangerous road.*

He had this same thought again, later, when Karis came out from under smoke and spent the afternoon with him and Medric in a hilarious attempt to circumnavigate the lake. Karis feared deep or flowing water and, like all earth witches, could not endure setting foot in a boat. While scrambling up and down the rocks, Karis made herself entertaining, with a humor that was deep and subtle and utterly entrancing. But the charming afternoon left Emil with an aching heart, and he and Medric spent a strangely silent evening afterwards. That something of great import was at work in both of them seemed clear. But what they struggled with Emil could not fathom, and both of them kept their own counsel.

Six days Zanja traveled across a familiar landscape. She skirted Meartown to the west and forded the river north of Strongbridge, then worked her way south, cross-country. A day's journey south of Strongbridge, she took lodging at a farm near the road she and Norina had traveled, and settled down to watch the road. In the afternoon of her second day of watching, Norina appeared. She traveled in the company of her gentle husband, riding horses so tired they dragged their hooves in the dirt.

Zanja greeted J'han first, who said in some bewilderment, "Zanja? I hardly can believe my eyes!" She clasped his hand, thinking how incredible it was that he had endured Norina's company long enough to claim a husband's right, and yet his wife did not trust him enough to explain where they were traveling, or why.

To Norina, Zanja said, "Some terrible things have happened, but Karis has survived."

Norina subjected her to a remote examination. "You are not confident of her well-being, though."

"At that farmstead over there, you can have your horses looked after, and perhaps even eat some supper and get a night's rest. It will take some time for me to explain."

"We'll go to the farmstead, of course," J'han said, and started his reluctant horse forward. In a moment, Norina followed. J'han laid his hand on Zanja's shoulder as she walked at his stirrup. "So this is all about Karis? I should have known."

Norina said, "And it's not your business, as I've been telling you all along."

"Your health and safety are not my business," J'han said, as though agreeing. Norina glared, and fell back out of hearing rather than be further subjected to the criticisms she could not help but hear, no matter what words her husband chose to use.

J'han said to Zanja, "We have a hearty daughter, with a healthy set of lungs on her. She's down there on the seacoast, no doubt screaming fit to raise the dead." And I should be with her, his tone of voice said, so clearly that even a non-Truthken easily could hear it.

Zanja said, "Perhaps you'll be able to return to your daughter."

J'han smiled sadly. "I have every intention of doing that."

"Without Norina?"

"Norina chooses differently from how I choose. And as you know, she is uncompromising. So this is how it ends."

Later, having situated the horses and made suitable arrangements with the farmers for lodging, Zanja sat with Norina in the guest room and told her how Mabin had tried and failed to kill Karis. Norina listened in unnerving silence. She asked no questions, neither did she argue. For a while she lay upon the rope bed, then she got up to pace the room, then she sat down and picked the dried mud from her boots. When Zanja had finished, Norina went to the window and leaned out to shout for J'han to come inside.

"Have you ever heard of someone using less smoke?" she asked him when he came in, wiping his hands on a towel.

"Less than what?" he asked blankly.

"Karis was forced to smoke more frequently than her usual amount, much more. Enough to nearly kill her. And now she's decreasing that frequency, trying to reduce herself back down to once a day. Have you ever heard of such a thing?"

"No," he said in some astonishment. "Is she being successful?"

"Yes, apparently, though it hasn't been easy."

"I always have heard the smoke users inevitably increase the amount they smoke, until they die of the poison or else from their inability to buy as much drug as they need. If it's possible for them to use less . . ." He paused, shaken and distressed. "Then we have abandoned them to a fate that we always assumed to be inevitable, when in fact we should have been trying to help them."

"Karis is different," Norina said.

"She is an extraordinary person of great wit and will. But she is human, and her body is no different from mine or yours."

"You don't know what you're talking about," Norina snapped.

J'han set his lips and visibly restrained himself from a sharp reply.

"What is wrong with you?" Zanja said to Norina later, after she had sent J'han away again. "I can hardly endure your company, and I don't see how bringing you to Karis will do her a service."

"Watch your words, Zanja na'Tarwein. I'm not in a tolerant mood."

"I would never expect you to be tolerant."

Norina sat again on the bed and dug her fingers into her short hair, which was stiff with dirt and stood upright like wheat stalks. "Go away."

After a long silence she looked at Zanja, who had remained sitting where she was, at the table by the window. Norina said, "You tell me that Karis's true enemy is my commander and a hero of the people, and that somehow I, a Truthken, never noticed. You tell me that when my dearest friend needed me the most desperately, she nearly died in my absence. And now you imply that you have the ability and the right to keep me from her unless I behave myself according to your high standards. Your very presence chides me. Go away and chide someone else."

Zanja left her, and found J'han out in the kitchen, examining a collection of dirty and impatient children, who clearly wanted to make the best of the remaining daylight and saw no reason to be subjected to a healer's scrutiny. J'han sent them away, reassured the gathered parents about their health, and took Zanja by the arm out into the privacy of the yard. They sat upon the edge of the well, and for some time neither of them said a word.

"The people of air are not easy to love," Zanja said at last.

"Nor even to like sometimes," J'han said.

"Would you at least come and have a look at Karis, before you start your own journey? I'm weary with caring for her."

"Yes, of course. My child's in good hands, and I am afraid Norina will kill herself with this hard traveling. It was not an easy birth."

Zanja sighed. "I was beginning to see how being friends with a Truthken might be invigorating enough that I could put up with the exasperation. But now I can't see it anymore."

J'han laughed heartily, without anger for once.

"And I fear for Karis, should she be trapped between air and fire. In truth, I wouldn't blame her if she decided to get rid of us both, just so she could have some peace."

They talked until after dark, when one of the farmers called them in to supper. Norina did not appear at the supper table, and J'han slept out in the barn with Zanja. In the morning, their journey north began, an angry journey made even more grim by the weather, which turned wet and stormy only after they had traveled beyond the reaches of civilization and there was no shelter to be found. By the time they reached the canyon path they all had been wet to the skin for two days and nights, and the nights had been cold as well as wet. They had been sleeping huddled together for warmth, but relations between them had not thawed much.

In all, thirteen days had passed since Zanja had last traversed this rocky pathway down to the lake. Then the lake had glowed like a jewel; now it was gray, with the muted colors of tree and canyon bleeding across it like ink on a wet page. Halfway down the path, Zanja spotted Emil riding up to meet them. He also rode on horseback, with his horse muddied to the belly and rain dripping from its mane, and he looked as wearied and worried as Zanja ever had seen him. Before he even spoke she knew that something terrible had happened.

"Karis has disappeared again," he said. "Five days we've been hunting for her, and haven't seen a trace, not even a footprint. Zanja, listen—before you ride off in a panic and kill yourself on the slippery stones—I swear to you that she was not taken away. She has written a glyph upon the space of her cave, and the message, I think, is intended for you."

In the cave shelter, the water clock was not merely shattered, but pulverized to powder. In the middle of the cave floor lay Karis's box of smoke, with the lid broken to splinters, and the interior burnt to charcoal. Of the contents, the half year's supply of smoke, nothing remained but ashes.

Yes, Zanja could easily read this glyph. She dropped to her knees beside the incinerated box. Of course Karis could not imagine herself free from Mabin's control and Norina's expectations if she could not also imagine herself free of smoke. Nearly a month of battling back the smoke must have given her an insane hope that she might be able to defeat it for good. That was the doorway she had decided to enter, the doorway where certain death lurked.

And then Norina was shouting at her: "What have you done! What did you do to her!" And it did not even occur to Zanja until too late that she had to defend herself, and Norina's heavy boot slammed into her side—once, twice, a third time—before Zanja had managed to catch Norina's foot and take her down. And then they were rolling, their blades of folded steel ringing like bells, a sweet, terrible sound. But no matter where Karis was, at the very moment that Zanja's blade cut into Norina's flesh, Karis would know.

Zanja flung her dagger away and blocked with her forearm a stroke that could have killed her, and felt the dagger slice through cloth and flesh and all the way to bone. She brought her knee up reflexively into Norina's crotch and heard her shout, and then she was rolling away and rising to her feet, but Norina's heavy boot cracked into her knee and Zanja heard, rather than felt, the bone shatter like pottery. Then Emil took Norina from behind and the fight seemed to be over. And then the pain came.

"Hold still," J'han said, his voice deadly calm.

"Gods burn her to ashes—"

"Zanja, hold still. Your ribs might be broken and you could be killed yet."

Zanja had seen the kind of death that came when a rib pierced a lung, and she held herself still, or as still as she could. A very bad time followed. There was much frantic activity around her, and sometimes J'han's voice penetrated the haze of pain, always calm, measured, talking steadily to her or to someone else: "I know it's bad, Zanja, but there's no time to brew a potion. Just keep breathing—you know how to keep the pain from taking control of you—Now, sir, give me the bandages, and that grayish bottle—yes, that one. Put more pressure on her arm; it's starting to leak again . . ." He faded out, and when he came back he was working with needle and thread like a seamster—nice of him to mend Zanja's shirt—except that it was her arm he was mending—and she couldn't take a deep breath for some reason. "You're awake again?" he said. "Almost done now. Amazing how easy it is to do this kind of damage and how much work it takes to fix. You can't breathe very well because I've got your ribs bound, but they're just cracked."

"What happened to my leg?" she croaked. Her entire leg seemed to be immobilized with a splint of some kind, but the pain was dazzling and nauseating.

"It's not good at all—sir, can you cut that?—Your kneecap's shattered so badly I don't know if it can mend. At the very least it'll be a long time before you can move about at all, even on crutches. I've got it in a splint, but—"

Zanja shut her eyes to understand him better, but the information seemed beyond comprehension. All she could think of was Karis, incinerating her entire smoke supply and walking away. How long would it take for her to die? Would Zanja feel it, when Karis died?

"What happened to Norina?" she asked.

"She went away," J'han said distractedly.

Zanja glanced sideways and saw Emil, holding Zanja's arm still so that J'han could work on it, watching J'han's work with professional interest. There was blood everywhere. Feeling Zanja's attention, Emil raised an eyebrow and said mildly, "Now that was the dirtiest fight I've seen outside of a tavern. Too bad you were at the receiving end."

Zanja gasped, "I'd hurt Karis if I hurt Norina."

"Unfortunately, Norina had no such compunctions. But this is an amazingly clean wound."

J'han said, "With the right blow, a blade like that could kill you before you knew you were hurt. I wish my surgeon's knives were that sharp."

"Where's Medric?" Zanja said.

"Now you're starting to think," Emil said. "Karis seems to have convinced Medric to keep his mouth shut. He's refused to help look for Karis, as have the Lake People refused. It's been just me and Annis, chasing around the countryside like a couple of wastrels. I even tried your trick with the directional glyphs, but it doesn't work for me."

"Hold still!" J'han said.

"Gods' curses on that madwoman," Zanja gasped as a fresh wave of pain washed through her. "I'm the only one who can find her!"

"You'll have to accept that you're not going anywhere," J'han said.

Annis brought over a steaming bowl of dark, stinking fluid and held it out for J'han's inspection. He dipped in a fingertip and tasted it, and made a face. "Practically undrinkable. That's about right."

"No one's been able to find Medric either," Annis said. "He's around, but no matter where you are, he's just left moments before."

Medric said at the doorway of the cave, "I'm here now. Good gods." He looked around the blood-smeared cave.

"You didn't dream this part?" Emil said bitterly.

Pale, red-eyed with sleeplessness or sorrow, Medric dropped to one knee beside Zanja. "Karis promised to make it possible to find her. She said she'd go west along the canyon rim as far as she could go in five days travel, and then she'd hole up in some hollow place where she could see the sky. She asked me to beg your pardon, Zanja, for deceiving you, but she had to fight this battle alone."

"She brought enough smoke to last until today?"

"Yes."

"All three of you must go find her, then. If she can be saved—"

J'han said, with that terrible honesty that was sometimes the only gift a healer could give, "Zanja, there is no hope of that. Even if we can find her before she dies, the only thing that could save her is smoke, and we have none."

Emil said in a low voice, "Mabin has some."

There was silence. Zanja said, "Karis would rather die." She made the mistake of moving, and for some time she could do nothing but breathe and struggle to stay conscious. When J'han put the bowl to her mouth she drank just a swallow of the bitter pain killer. "J'han, Karis is vested with the power of Shaftal," she said.

He sat back sharply, nearly spilling the bowl of potion. "What!"

"Go with them to find her. If she is dying, at least she should die with dignity."

"Annis can take care of Zanja," Emil said.

Annis grumbled because her long recess with the Otter People had come to an end, but she did not refuse her old commander's will. They settled Zanja onto the pallet with the potion beside her, and within the time it would have taken ten drops of water to fall from the water clock, they were gone.

Zanja took one more swallow of the bitter potion, and told Annis to leave her alone. After that came a merciful darkness and stillness.

As she slept, Zanja dreamed that she was an owl, flying across the face of the earth, with the river flowing to her right, black as blood, and rocks below, like scattered bones. At last, she found Karis, a broken and twisted body in a grassy hollow where sharp stones broke through the earth like teeth. Her body was cold; no breath passed her lips. Emil, Medric, J'han, and Norina knelt in a circle around her, digging with their bare hands to cover her with earth. Norina was weeping, racked with a grief made all the more terrible by the bitter strength her sorrow had overcome.

Zanja must have cried something in her sleep, for she opened her eyes to find Annis beside her, with a cool hand upon her burning forehead. Zanja's throat felt scoured raw, and her voice came out a whisper. "They will find her too late. Is there any word?"

"Zanja, it's much too soon."

"But someone is here."

"What do you mean?"

"I feel it."

"Maybe the potion is giving you hallucinations." But Annis went to the doorway, where Zanja could see a bit of star-scattered

sky above, and a bit of star-scattered lake below. "I don't see anything," Annis said. Then her body gave a jerk and she uttered a
surprised grunt and lifted a hand as if to investigate what had struck
her, but before she could understand what had happened, she fell.

It happened so suddenly that the sound of the pistol's report
didn't register until after Annis's knees buckled. There was nowhere
for Zanja to go, even if she'd had the ability and will to flee. Her
blade lay within reach, but thanks to Norina her blade hand was
useless. Her pistols were still in Homely's saddlebags, and the three
men had taken Homely with them. Five people came into the cave
and made certain that Zanja was indeed helpless, and then Mabin
came in. "Where is Karis?"

"Karis has returned to earth."

Mabin struck her across the face. "The truth!"

Zanja tasted blood. She said thickly, "Karis has delivered herself
to the smoke."

Mabin sat back on her heels, rigid with frustration. "She makes
no sense."

"There's no one else here," one of her companions said. "We've
searched all along the beach. No horses, no equipment, no nothing.
Just the two of them, and Annis is dead."

Mabin hissed in her breath, and then released it. "If I'd known
it was Annis—well, there's no help for it now. So long as we've got
this one, we've as good as got the one I want. We'll have to settle
for that."

"This one seems to be newly injured. Broken ribs, it looks like,
and—" Zanja felt her injured arm lifted and examined. "She was
cut defending herself, with healer's stitches closing up the wound.
A nice, clean job of it."

"A healer, and someone with a nasty temper—that would be
Norina and her consort. No doubt there's been a disagreement and
Norina has taken off with Karis." Mabin fell silent a moment, and
then she muttered, "Shaftal, what have I done to deserve this?"

Zanja was tired to the bone, and tired to the heart. She shut
her eyes and did not open them again until her captors lifted her
onto the litter they had made for her, and the pain began again.
The Paladins had to step over Annis's body as they carried Zanja
out into the cold night. And Karis—Karis also would soon be dead.

Chapter Twenty-five

Emil, Medric, and J'han traveled through the afternoon and across the dark span of the night as though demons were after them. "I think we're close now," Medric said, sometime after dawn. Soon afterwards, they spotted the white flag lying limp in the half light: Karis's shirt, they realized when they had drawn near, tied to a tree branch by the sleeves. They untied it and soon had found their way into a hollow of earth that was cupped like the palm of a giant hand. There in the center Karis lay in the wet grass. Norina, whose long intimacy with Karis must have helped her to find her first, lay beside her, embracing her naked body with her own.

"She's too cold," she said.

Emil lay down on Karis's other side and they sandwiched her between them. After J'han had listened to Karis's heart, he covered her with blankets, and sat upon a stone with his head in his hands, as though he could not bring himself to speak. The Truthken, though, began to weep. Having emptied herself of anger, Emil thought, now only grief remained. She had indeed loved Karis, however badly she might have done it.

Emil held Karis tightly, as though to keep her from falling. Her powerful muscles lay limp and cold; her heartbeat was intangible, the motion of her breath so weak it seemed illusory. She'd bitten her mouth, battered her hands, scraped her skin raw upon the stones, in a terrible, solitary agony that had mercifully ended now. She would die without ever opening her eyes again. The healer did not have to say it out loud.

Norina sat up. Her hair was plastered down with water and mud, her face pale with exhaustion beneath the grime of hard travel. "J'han, what can we do?"

"Only smoke could save her," J'han said.

The Truthken shuddered, as though she'd been cut with a blade. "I have some smoke," she said. "Ten years I've carried it with me, as a surety."

J'han leapt to his feet. "We must improvise a pipe."

"But this one time I will not fail her." Norina took a pouch out of her shirt and emptied its contents into the palm of her hand. One by one she untwisted the spills of paper and crushed the contents to powder between her fingers, and rubbed the powder into the wet grass where it could not be reclaimed. None of them made any move to stop her.

J'han said, "Medric, perhaps you will start a fire and we'll warm some water to bathe her. And then we'll put her clothes on her."

Throughout the night, Medric had traveled silently, except for an occasional hoarse word to direct their path, a directive which they had accepted in silence. From time to time, his face had seemed to come at Emil out of the darkness: drawn with sorrow, wet with tears, hollow with a terrible weariness, as though he had borne the whole weight of history upon the frail hinges of his vision, and could not carry that weight much longer. But now Medric stood back, gazing at this desperate, hopeless scene as distantly as a general gazes on a battle. "There's a reason why she took off her clothes," he said.

Norina wiped a sleeve across her eyes as though to clear a fog, and looked at him in that way which makes even the bravest warrior flinch back from a Truthken's stare. "By the land, what are you?" she said softly.

Medric did not flinch under her gaze.

She said, as quietly as before, "Better people than I have given you their trust. Tell me what you see."

"Madam Truthken, when you destroyed that smoke, I saw you close a door. And I saw another door open. There is no one in this land who knows Karis like you know her. So tell me, why did she take off her clothes?"

"Even though Karis cannot feel the wisdom of her flesh, there's times she knows exactly what she needs to do. I suppose it is earth logic."

"So wouldn't it be even more logical if she lay on soil rather than grass?"

Norina began pulling up great handfuls of grass by the roots. J'han and Medric helped her, and by the time the sun had risen, they had cleared a patch big enough to lay Karis upon with her skin pressed against the damp black earth.

"It looks like a grave," Norina said.

"But it is a garden." Medric's eyes had seemed glazed with sleeplessness and sorrow, but he was, Emil realized suddenly, in the midst of a waking vision.

Emil said, "Medric, what should we do now?"

"Plant her," Medric said. "Plant her so she will grow."

Emil went creeping through the nearby brush until he managed to kill a couple of heavy ground birds with some lucky shots. Plucking and cleaning the birds took nearly as long as hunting them had, and then he dug up some roots that would make a poor substitute for potatoes, and picked greens. He returned with his heavy gathering bag to find that nothing much had changed. J'han had dosed Medric with a sleeping draught to stop his hallucinations, and Medric slept, pale and exhausted even in sleep, his face still creasing sometimes with worry or fear. J'han, a botanist like all healers, had collected a pile of strengthening herbs. Norina knelt at Karis's side like a mud-covered statue, watching her breathe. Karis, except for her face, was covered with a blanket of soil that steamed now in the warm afternoon sun. She had not died yet, and that was surprising.

Emil filled his pot with the fowl and the roots and set it on the fire to stew, then went off again to gather wood and fill their canteens. Normally, all the walking and riding and worrying would have crippled him by now, but when Karis laid her hands upon his knee she had repaired much more than that one badly healed old injury. He had returned to their camp, and was stirring the pot that had started to simmer, when he heard Norina say in a voice destroyed by weeping, "Karis."

Emil feared what he would see, but what he saw was that the soil had cracked over Karis's chest, and those cracks widened and narrowed in rhythm with her deep breaths. Karis lay quiet, eyes open, gazing at Norina with an expression Emil would not have liked to have directed at him. She turned her face away and Norina sat back, as if she had been hit.

J'han scraped away the earth so he could listen to Karis's heart. He said, "Well, Karis, it seems your heart wants to keep beating."

He put his head near hers, for she seemed to have spoken. "Emil, she's asking for you."

Emil went to kneel beside her. Her voice was just a whisper, like a sheet of paper being torn. "Zanja," she said.

"We left her in the cave by Otter Lake. She and Norina had a fight and she was unable to travel."

On Karis's other side, Norina covered her face with her hands. Zanja's blood still spattered her shirt.

Karis opened her mouth again, and the tearing paper sound resolved itself into a word: "No," or perhaps, "I know." Then she said, "Where is she?"

Emil gazed at her, baffled. Norina dropped her hands and said, "Karis, I swear I didn't kill her."

Karis did not look at her or seem to have heard her.

"She is alive," Emil said. "She was bitterly angry at Norina and desperately worried about you, last I saw her."

Karis said very carefully, as though to a stupid child, "Where. Is. She."

Silence, then Norina spoke, looking at Emil and not at Karis. "Something has befallen Zanja. Karis cannot perceive her presence."

"What!" Emil leapt to his feet.

"I will accompany you. I won't anger her any longer with my presence."

J'han began to protest, but stopped himself and said in exasperation, "There's no point in even talking to you. Emil, if I give you some powders, will you find a way to make her take them? Slip them into her drinking water if you have to. She has not even rested since giving birth, and seems determined to kill herself."

"I'll take your powders," Norina said. She stood up and began to gather her gear, making the jerky, mechanical movements of a body strained beyond endurance.

Karis continued to gaze at Emil. Only the earth had brought her back from the threshold; she had no business being alive at all. Anger burned in the depth of her sunken eyes, and suddenly, Emil could imagine her as G'deon of Shaftal.

Emil said to her, "We'll wait a little while for Medric to wake up, in case he can tell us what's befallen her. We will find her. You have plenty of evidence that fire bloods do not lose what they love."

Some time after Karis had eaten and been taken hostage by a healing sleep, Medric awoke, not with a start, as he usually did, but slowly; so that Emil, who had been doing what he could for the exhausted horses, could contrive to be beside him when he finally awoke, and place the correct pair of spectacles upon his nose. Medric said thickly, "I recognize you even as a blur."

"I certainly should hope so," Emil said.

Medric smiled, and so it seemed that they would survive the anger and disappointment of the last few days. Still, Emil said, as was right, "I feel as if I failed you by being angry at the choices you felt you had to make. Surely it was a terrible time for you, and my anger only made it worse."

Medric said in some astonishment, "Are you trying to tell me that—"

"Karis is going to live, as far as J'han can tell. And, apparently, she's going to live without smoke."

"Oh, Shaftal," Medric said, sitting up in a daze. "Oh, earth and sky, do you feel it? The door is swinging open, and the breeze is blowing through . . ."

Emil said, though he hated to dampen the young seer's enthusiasm, "I'm so worried about Zanja and Annis that there's not much else I can think about. Something has befallen them, Karis says, and that something can only be Mabin."

"Karis doesn't know what happened?"

"She can hardly talk, but Norina says that Zanja is beyond Karis's ken."

"Well, that puts her over water then, doesn't it? It seems obvious enough." He took off his spectacles and rubbed his eyes.

It had not been at all obvious to Emil, but, remembering Karis's discomfort around water, it began to make a kind of sense. It was said that Shaftal is the G'deon's flesh and bone, and nothing happens between ocean and mountain that the G'deon does not feel. If Karis could not feel Zanja, alive or dead, then it could only mean Zanja was no longer in physical contact with the earth. He said, "So she's somewhere on the river."

"I'll come with you."

"Medric, my dear, if Karis ever needed a seer beside her, now is the time. I'll find Zanja without your help. You know I can. And I have Norina, who is the equivalent of an entire battalion."

"But it's an awfully big river."

"You forget about our friends the Otter People. Surely the water witch will know what's happened on his river." Emil kissed Medric, not too hastily, and then he kissed him again. Before he could stand up, he had to disentangle himself from the fist gripped in his hair. For the first time in days, it was not just weariness that made him so dizzy.

And so the next day Emil and Norina found the empty cave and fresh blood splashed across the stones, and then the Otter People came and took them to the island, where they showed them Annis's body. They had laid her in a little boat with her knees drawn up to her chest like an infant curled in the womb, and they had filled her boat with journey gifts: a net and fishing spear, tiny people of twisted reed to accompany her, a bottle of good spring water, a supply of dried fish, and many small items of great value: knives and beads and pieces of worked fish skin, the kind of gifts that are given to a beloved friend when bidding her good-bye. At sunset they all escorted Annis across the lake to the river outlet, and they let her boat go and watched until she'd slipped out of sight. They uttered encouraging shouts to send her on her journey, but many of the people seemed devastated with grief. They'd loved her more, and better, than her family ever had.

Emil had seen many a Paladin killed or maimed, but always had been able to explain the death as having served a cause. This death could only be explained as a betrayal. When he wept for Annis, he wept also for himself, for an entire adulthood spent serving under the command of a leader who would kill an innocent like Annis simply for being in the way.

Emil understood perhaps three dozen words of the Otter People's language, which was not enough to ask the question he needed to ask. But the old water witch was dismayed by the terrible, sudden violence that had occurred on the shores of his lake, and told what had happened using story dolls, like the little reed poppets that had accompanied Annis on her last journey. The doll that had Zanja's long hair was in a boat two day's journey to the east of Otter Lake.

Emil and Norina left at dawn to journey to the Paladin garrison where all that remained of the old traditions of Shaftal were preserved, all except the traditions of honor and open-handed generosity. These traditions were not even mentioned in the letter of the law, but without them the law was just a mindless formula. Emil had dared to read a little of the Mackapee manuscript before he carefully put it away in a mouse-proof chest, in a dry attic, in a stone building unlikely to burn down. And what he'd read there was the spirit of a man who valued change. "The peaceful speech of strangers transforms the world," Mackapee had written in his crabbed handwriting. If Emil had laid eyes on the manuscript fifteen years before, he'd have hurried past those words, looking for more subtle revelations, words to argue about in the university.

Zanja na'Tarwein had lived by and nearly died for that transformation. Mabin Paladin, the hero of the people, had chosen another way, the shortsighted way of the bitterly conquered, the vengeance by which the wronged becomes the wrongdoer and the whole world gives way to war. When Emil lay down in love with a son of the enemy, he had abandoned that vengeance, and he was only now beginning to realize what that meant for him. And Norina Truthken, whose devotion to the law had not been able to keep her from betraying her dearest friend, what was she going to do now?

Norina had scarcely spoken a word on this entire journey. She was far from recovered from childbirth, and her bandaged, milk-swollen breasts must have hurt her greatly. She took the powders her husband had given her: reliably, publicly, as though she was doing a kind of penance. In fact she was doing the only thing a person of honor could do in her position: accepting disgrace, humbling her pride, making reparations. She would put her life at risk to do these things, and her life wouldn't be worth much if she could not accomplish them.

When they stopped to rest the horses and eat their dinner of cold fish and flatbread, Emil said, "I'm curious how the law would resolve this paradox we're in."

Norina snorted in bitter amusement and passed him the jug of water. "Everyone who breaks the law does it for the same reason: because her own desire, she believes, should take precedence. The question is, which of us is in fact the lawbreaker, when our governor under the law falls into the error of thinking she rules the law rather than being ruled by it? Are we right, for serving Karis's personal interests and thus opposing Mabin? Or are Mabin's followers right for serving Mabin's personal interests and thus injuring Karis? This situation is a judge's worst nightmare."

"But if Karis is G'deon . . ."

Norina lifted her head, as though genuinely surprised at the idea. "That has never even been a possibility. But now that she is no longer addicted to smoke, perhaps everything has changed. If Karis is G'deon, that certainly resolves the moral difficulty. The G'deon's role is and always has been to protect the land, to remember the people, even if that means going beyond the law. And we are required by law to serve the G'deon first. However—"

"She's not the G'deon."

"It's not as if we had the power to decide such a thing."

"So we have a paradox, a puzzle that defies resolution. But not a dilemma, for we both know exactly what we must do, and we intend to do it. That is what intrigues me, you see. It's a purely philosophical problem."

Norina groaned, as people often do when they hear the word "philosophy," for the Truthkens are always wanting their truths to be unarguable. So she seemed to be curing herself with self-mockery, the only cure for the obsessiveness that is the bane of all Truthkens, and no doubt she was practicing it as deliberately as she was taking her husband's powders. A woman of her age and experience could hardly expect to be re-schooled by anyone except herself. But if she had a true community such schooling would be the service her people provided. And if Karis were to lack such a community as well, who would then school her in the right use of her power?

Oh, but if there was one thing Karis did not lack, surely it was wise and strong-willed friends. And they all would be well advised to not get into the habit of servicing her whims, even now, when she was so desperately ill. To do her will without question was no service at all, but an abdication.

"What are you thinking that makes you so happy?" Norina asked.

"Just when I was thinking with despair of a dishonorable and unappealing retirement, I realize that I may yet have an interesting few years ahead of me. Madam Truthken—"

"Oh for pity's sake, call me Norina."

"Why don't you lie down and rest for a while, and I'll make a good report to your husband."

She was not so humorless as she had seemed. She was still

chuckling when she lay down on the blanket he brought her, and shut her eyes.

Before dawn the next day, the two of them stood on the canyon's edge overlooking the Paladins' Valley, and waited for sunrise. They actually had slept for most of the night, and awakened before first light to travel the last mile on foot, leaving their horses and gear hidden in a glade. If there was an additional watch being kept on the valley, somehow they'd managed to avoid the trap, and they sat peaceably upon stones overlooking the magnificent landscape of the canyon. As the sun lifted, pink and gentle light set the stones to glowing like coal. Norina took a spyglass out of her shirt—she was astonishingly well equipped—and scanned the valley below. Without a word she handed the spyglass to Emil.

The boat was anchored in a deep eddy near the walled village, which had been built on high ground to avoid being destroyed in the periodic flood times. The river still lay in shadow, and even at this distance Emil could see a spark of lantern light upon the deck. As he watched, the sunlight hit the river, turning it to glowing amethyst, and he saw the figure pacing on the boat deck, back and forth, like a lion in a cage.

He thought of Zanja, being hauled from a rowboat onto the deck of the riverboat. Considering her recently broken bones, it was an unpleasant thought. He gave Norina back her spyglass. "She's on that boat," he said, as certain as he'd ever been of anything.

Norina peered down at the river, muttering, "I all but gave Mabin the bait for this trap. What am I going to do about it now?"

"We," Emil corrected. "It's a boat because Karis can't endure boats?"

"Over water she's an ordinary mortal, and a seasick one at that. No doubt Mabin will demand that she come aboard, however. And she will comply, if that will save Zanja's life. We'll have a sorry time trying to stop her, for now that I've lost her regard she won't listen to my advice."

"I think Karis will listen to me. Certainly, Zanja would want us to prevent her from putting herself in Mabin's power."

"That's one argument that might dissuade Karis," Norina said wryly. "Let's think up a few more on the way back, shall we? We're going to be needing them."

✠ ✠ ✠

When they returned to Otter Lake, they were greeted with an astonishing sight: black smoke billowing from a crude chimney made of gathered stones, boatloads of ore and coal drawn up to the shore, a line of Otter children taking turns at pumping a monstrous bellows, and Karis in the middle of it, swinging a huge stone hammer to shatter the ore and keeping an eye on Emil's cookpot, which had now become a smelting pot.

"She always was incorrigible," Norina said.

J'han came across the beach to greet them, a harried and frustrated man. "Are all elementals so willful?"

"Some of us are worse than others." Norina stopped at the edge of the beach and would proceed no further, but her gaze yearned to the hammer-swinging, half-naked giant standing spread-legged on the stones. It was a magnificent sight. Then, Karis turned and looked at her, and Norina turned quickly away. "I'm not welcome here. I'll stay at the top of the trail with the horses."

"No, you stay right here until I've talked to her." Emil walked across the stony beach to the amazing cobbled-together forge and the rock-shattering woman. From the midst of the smutty, laughing children, Medric grinned at Emil, his face black with soot, his eyes afire with joy. Emil wanted nothing more than to embrace him, soot and all, but he went to Karis instead, and said, "By our land, you're a beautiful sight."

There probably was nothing he could have said that was more likely to stop her in her tracks. She all but dropped the gigantic stone hammer.

"Such beauty lifts the heart," Emil declared, and knelt. "Dear Karis—"

"Emil—"

"Dear Karis," Emil persisted, "your lifelong friend and I have found Zanja, but rescuing her will not be easy. However, we have some ideas that you might like, when you care to hear them. But for now let me ask you on Norina's behalf what else she can do to make amends—"

Karis stepped over, took him by the shirt, and lifted him bodily until he stood once again on his feet. She was not particularly gentle. "Kneel to me again and I'll make it so you'll have no choice but to stand." And then she stopped, breathing heavily from her exertions, and added after a moment, "I suppose you want me to realize that if I don't want to be treated like a sovereign I'll have to avoid acting like one."

"I'm so glad I succeeded in getting your attention," Emil said. "You were looking rather dangerously single-minded."

Karis gazed at him, suddenly just a tired, wasted woman whose great strength seemed about to fail her, fueled as it was by a rage that surely could not sustain her much longer. "I want to hold my love in my arms," she said. "She doesn't even know—"

Emil said, "This is Zanja na'Tarwein we're talking about, not some fool."

"But when she gives up hope—"

"I have seen her under the most desperate of circumstances, and she does not surrender."

"That's what I'm afraid of."

"She would want you to listen to your friends," Emil said.

There was a silence. Karis said bitterly, "I'm listening to you. Just don't ask me to insult Norina with a false forgiveness. If you want to tell her something, tell her I have no respect for someone who can't cherish what I was willing to die for."

"I'll tell her," Emil said. "But she can't make peace with her husband when she feels like she has to sleep with the horses to avoid irritating you with her presence."

"She doesn't have to sleep with the horses," Karis said. "Just tell her not to talk to me. I'm going to kill someone, and I'd rather it wasn't her."

Emil stepped back involuntarily.

"Medric already has talked me out of tearing Mabin's precious village to pieces, which I could do."

"I do not doubt it," Emil said. "I'm glad you heeded him; I don't think I could endure it if the House of Lilterwess were to fall a second time. Can I ask what you're working on?"

"A hammer," Karis said. "A hammer for working steel."

He waited, but she explained no further. She did add after a moment, "Let me finish with this, and then I'll stop and rest, which will make J'han happy, and we can talk about what to do."

She turned back to her rocks, and the sound of them shattering under her hammer followed Emil back to the edge of the beach.

"What is she making?" Norina asked. She had sat upon the ground and was reorganizing her clothing, having perhaps submitted to an examination of some kind.

"She's making a hammer. What she'll make with it I can't imagine, but she'll tell me. What I want to know is where she got coal. That's not the sort of thing that can be picked up off the ground."

J'han shook his head. "The water witch and she are like hand and glove. Who knows how they're doing it."

Norina, seated among the stones, said, "By tradition, the people of the borders are protected by the G'deon. If the water witch recognizes her, no doubt he thinks he owes her a certain fealty."

"That bodes well," Emil said.

"Doesn't it, though." Norina stood up. "Well, am I an exile?"

"No, but you should not talk to her."

"I guess that's an improvement. Why did you kneel to her?"

"I thought she needed to be taught a lesson. She is very teachable."

Norina smiled, though not with a lot of vigor. "I know this all too well. But some lessons, I fear, she will never learn."

"Norina—" Emil hesitated to say this in front of J'han, but it would have been too awkward to ask him to step away. "Karis says to tell you that she has no respect for someone who can't cherish what she was willing to die for."

Norina accepted this fresh censure with surprising equanimity. "I thought as much," she said. "J'han, is there any hope she'll recover her physical sensations, or is that damage permanent?"

J'han said irritably, "My impulse is to say that it's permanent, but what do I know? She's still having convulsions at sunset every day—one of the strangest things I've ever seen. Maybe this is as well as she will ever get."

Norina looked at Karis as her heavy hammer once again smashed into the ore. "She deserves better," she said.

There was a silence. Emil took the reins of the horses, to unload their gear and take them up to graze. Norina said to J'han, "How do I keep my milk from drying up?"

J'han looked at her in some astonishment.

Of course there was a way, but lacking a spare child to give suck to, this seemed like a husband's problem. Emil left them to work it out.

That night, he seduced his beloved Sainnite seer and did not care when their groans became cries that anyone trying to sleep upon the beach could hear. If Karis was awake, she'd know that at least two of her companions knew how to cherish what they had.

Chapter Twenty-six

When Zanja opened her eyes, she lay in a shallow, strangely shaped wooden room, which was lit by a gently swinging lamp that hung from a hook. "She's awake," said the man who sat near her upon the steeply sloping floor. He held a pistol.

Mabin came in. The ceiling was so low she had to walk crouched over. The entire room seemed to move. The lamp swung as if in a breeze. Zanja had never in her life been in a boat, and had not guessed that they might have enclosed rooms like this, not a place for people—it was not shaped right—but apparently for storage. Now, except for the pallet upon which Zanja lay, it was empty as a coffin.

"Give me the pistol," Mabin said to the man. He handed it to her and went out, closing the door behind himself. Mabin squatted upon the floor, grunting with tiredness.

Knife fights often are won and lost in the first moments of battle, when in the first movements and first contacts of blade on blade, the fighters discover whether or not they've met their match. A good strategist learns to use those moments to deliberately mislead the opponent into misjudgments that there is no time to recognize.

Zanja hastily considered her situation. Annis was dead. Mabin had assumed that Karis was still alive, in the company of Norina and J'han. Although Mabin could not know that Karis had won back many hours from smoke, she would not be confident of Karis's subjugation to the drug, because even under smoke Karis had been able to use her power to aid her own escape. Mabin could not know about Emil, and she had expressed no interest in Medric, so perhaps she assumed that Zanja had rescued Karis unassisted.

She expected that Karis would come for Zanja, at any cost to herself, as Karis had already demonstrated she would do. She did not know that there were other credible witnesses to the enormity of her betrayal, and she would not know about them unless she stumbled across them while searching for Karis. She did not know that Zanja had a tribe, half-formed and tiny though it was, and that she would protect her people. She did not know what it meant to be a *katrim*. Above all, she did not know that Karis was dying, or perhaps already dead.

Zanja said, "After the Sainnites captured me, they took symbolic vengeance upon me for the humiliations I and my fellow *katrim* had subjected them to. They tortured me, just as you are doing. For some reason, I always expected the Paladins to be different from the Sainnites."

"Who do you think you are, to—" Mabin began, but it was too late to raise her defenses; the blade of accusation had cut deep into the flesh of her complacency.

"I know exactly who I am," Zanja said.

"A traitor to the people—a traitor under the law!"

"The Ashawala'i are not subject to the law of Shaftal."

"What!"

"You wrong my people in wronging me. Does not the law require that you respect and protect the people of the borders?"

"You have no people—"

"Where one survives, the tribe survives."

"You fight our war, you are subject to our laws."

"I refuse to be subject to a law that allows people like you to commit murder."

"Murder?"

"Annis is dead," Zanja reminded her.

"Another traitor."

"Is that the way the law works? You kill whomever you like, then declare them traitors?"

"We are at war—"

"At war to save the very law you are destroying. It is you who are the traitor."

"Don't be absurd."

"It is not treachery to deliver the vested G'deon into a certain death by poisoning? What is it, then?"

"Who made you judge, Zanja na'Tarwein? You are nothing but rogues, you and Karis both—a couple of fools with too much power and not enough wisdom. You must be restrained, for the future of Shaftal. If you will not accept restraint, then you must be killed. I regret it, yes. But it is you who have made the choice, not I."

"I have too much power?" Suddenly the entire conversation did indeed seem absurd, and Zanja uttered a laugh, quickly choked off by the pain of her ribs.

"You are all the more dangerous for not knowing what you are doing. Fifteen years ago Harald G'deon made the last and greatest error in his life of errors, when his courage failed him and he cursed Shaftal by filling a weak and inappropriate vessel with his power. For fifteen years I have managed to keep Karis in control. Yet the moment you came to Shaftal, before Karis ever met you, before she ever even knew your name, she began to break her restraints. That is your power, Zanja na'Tarwein: the power to attract, the power to influence, the power to awaken that which should be left asleep. If I allowed you to exercise that power, this very land would be destroyed."

Zanja said, "You lived with her for years, and yet you do not know her. She would destroy nothing."

"Your people were destroyed by the very Sainnites that Harald allowed to get a foothold in this land!"

"My people were destroyed," Zanja said, "by the dream of a misguided seer. If the people of Shaftal had given that seer proper guidance, rather than calling her their enemy because her father was a Sainnite—"

Mabin leapt to her feet and struck her.

Zanja said, "You see, you are not defeating the Sainnites. You are becoming them."

Mabin struck her again. Then, without a word, she left Zanja alone in the darkness, taking even the lamp with her.

Zanja lay still, hoping for the pain to ease, waiting for her breath to slow. Four witnesses there were to the true nature of Mabin's betrayal of Shaftal, one from each of the four ancient orders of the Lilterwess. They would have a credibility that Mabin herself could not contravene. And Norina, for all her faults, would not rest until she'd seen justice done. Zanja lay silent in the dark hold of the boat, willing Medric to see her, to understand what she was doing, to convince Emil and J'han and Norina to flee to safety while Mabin, rather than pursuing them, waited for a visit from a woman who was dead.

"Accept the willing sacrifice of a *katrim*," Zanja entreated them. "Don't waste your lives trying to save mine. Go, and make my death and Karis's death be of some significance. That's all I ask."

Several times a day, they came in to lift her up over the bucket that served as her toilet. Often, they also left her a meal and fresh water. Usually, Zanja scarcely even noticed the food, except as a means for measuring the time. She felt no hunger, and even to drink water required more effort than it was worth. Though the worst of her pain began to ease after a few days, she hardly got up from her pallet, for her splinted leg and bandaged ribs made movement nearly impossible in that cramped space. She heard Mabin pacing up and down the length of the boat's deck, for hours at a time, like a wild animal in a cage. Zanja lay starving in the darkness below where she walked.

Twenty-one meals had been served when Zanja's door opened and Mabin stepped into the cargo hold once again. "We will force you to eat if we have to," she said.

Zanja had been expecting and preparing for this visit all morning, for her prescience seemed enhanced by hunger, just as a seer's ability to envision the future might sometimes be enhanced by fasting. "I cannot stop you from doing what you like," she said.

"Such despair is unbecoming in a warrior."

"Despair is what makes my confinement endurable. I would give you some as a gift if I could, then perhaps you would be less restless. The sound of your pacing interrupts my thoughts."

"Your thoughts will be even more interrupted if my Paladins have to pour cold gruel down your throat and force you to swallow it or drown in it." Mabin hung the lamp from the lamp hook. She held a pistol, and despite Zanja's apparent weakness took care not to turn her back on her. "I expected Karis would come for you by now."

"No doubt," Zanja said.

"Tell me what you think she is doing."

Zanja closed her eyes, and there she saw Karis, as she had never seen her in life, lifting and swinging a great hammer, with the molten metal flying at each blow. Sweat polished the great muscles of her back and shoulders, and sunlight caught on her skin, and in her hair, as if she were made of gold. "She is working at the forge," Zanja said. "All these years you knew her, and you never knew how strong she is."

"Nonsense," Mabin said. "If she had returned to Meartown, I would know."

But Zanja felt a little peace. Karis seemed so intent on her work, surely that meant she had found contentment at last.

Now the time Zanja had bought for her friends' escape was indeed running out, and she could only hope that Medric's dreams had brought them all to a place of safety. She began to eat a little— enough to placate Mabin, she hoped, but not so much that it would dull her heightened senses. Mabin came into the cargo hold and talked to her for hours at a time, and Zanja devoted all her energies toward making the experience more unpleasant for Mabin than it was for her.

She was aided in this endeavor by an astonishing run of bad luck that began to plague her captors and to harry Mabin in particular, as only small annoyances can. Zanja learned firsthand about the mice and maggots fouling the food supply, but she also heard hints of other irritants as well: an infestation of fleas, broken ropes and fouled lines, unseasonably cold and wet weather which forced her captors into close quarters, and an unpredictable tendency for the boat to slip its anchor. Already tormented by these unremitting vexations, Mabin could not endure with any grace Zanja's deliberate attempts to infuriate her.

By the end of another two days of questioning, Zanja knew she had put herself in grave danger. This battle of wills between the two of them operated with its own logic, and had long since become far more than a mere delaying tactic. Though she lay awake that night, she fell into a restless sleep at last. Night upon the river was a silent time, and Zanja slept with her ear against the wood that separated her from the water. Sometimes, in her dreams, it seemed she could hear the water sliding past, but tonight she heard something else: a faint, rhythmic tapping, sometimes close and sometimes far away, almost as though someone were swimming up and down the length of the boat, drumming lightly upon its hull.

Near dawn, Zanja awakened abruptly. She was cold—and wet.

Her pallet and blankets were soaked with cold water. The water was collecting in the lowest point of the hold, where it stood in a puddle a hand's width deep, but she could not figure out its source. Every part of the hull seemed wet, as though the wood was weeping. She dragged herself up the slope of the hull and waited to see what would happen next.

By the time the door was opened for her morning meal, the water was knee deep, and the man who had opened the door uttered a surprised yelp at the little river that flowed over his feet when he forced open the door. Soon the boat echoed with pounding footsteps, and Mabin came with three guards behind her to search the cargo hold for the puncture that they assumed Zanja had somehow put through the hull. "After we repair the leak you'll sleep in water," Mabin said. "You'll have only hurt yourself." But they had scarcely begun their search when someone came to the door with the news that the aft hold was half full of water as well.

"Mabin," Zanja said, as the councilor turned away to investigate this new disaster.

"What?" she snapped.

"Karis is dead."

Mabin stood very still in the doorway, with the lamp beyond her, silhouetting her. A hard, pitiless woman, it seemed the only thing that could stop her in her tracks was the thing she most wanted to hear.

Zanja said, "The smoke did kill Karis. She endured so much, but in the end she decided to die rather than use smoke any longer."

"Why have you kept this from me?" Mabin asked. Her voice was nearly a whisper.

"You have murdered the G'deon of Shaftal. While I've been playing games with you here, witnesses to that murder have gotten safely away. Now, there will be an accounting."

Mabin turned away without a word, and closed and locked the door behind her. Alone in the darkness, sitting upon the weeping boards, with the collected water slopping gently in the silence, the vast wilderness of loss opened up within Zanja, and for a long time she wept, as the water level rose higher and people rushed back and forth across the length of the boat, their voices edged with disbelief and dismay. Soon they would abandon the boat and leave Zanja here to drown in the rising water. It seemed a lonely and cold death, but it was as good as any, she supposed.

But Mabin came back with two others, and fought open the

door, and had her men haul Zanja out of the hold and up into a misty, cold early morning where the sun was nothing more than a haze of light. There they bound her hands and put her into a rowboat, along with so many other people that the little boat also seemed in danger of sinking. It was so crowded the rowers could scarcely move to row it to shore. Mabin sat beside Zanja, glowering at her.

Zanja could not imagine why Mabin had come back for her. Perhaps she was haunted by Zanja's declaration that she was no better than the Sainnites. Perhaps she wanted the satisfaction of killing Zanja with her own hands, rather than letting her drown. The hazy light was almost too bright to endure after Zanja's days of darkness. As the rowboat lurched toward shore, the riverboat settled deeply into the water behind them, like a hen settling onto her nest. Soon it would be sitting on the river bottom.

The muffling silence of the fog crept across the rowboat. The grumblers fell quiet and Mabin stared bleakly across the water, where the shore now came hazily into view, as stony as any other bank of this harsh river, with boulders that huddled in the mist like bodies upon a battlefield. Beyond the shore, the fog loomed like a wall. Something lay within the mist: a universe of possibilities, thousands of routes through the wilderness, thousands of days yet to dawn.

It seemed very strange that a perfectly sound boat had suddenly begun to leak, and not just from one place, but from everywhere at once. Fingertips had drummed on the boat's hull in the dark of night, as if slender swimmers, playing like otters, had swum up and down, sometimes coming up for air, laughing gleefully, with their faces in the water to muffle the sound. What a fine game it would have been. And to repeatedly slip loose the boat's anchor, to make deliveries of fleas . . . this was guerrilla warfare indeed.

The rowboat ground into the stony shore, and the rowers shipped their oars. Grumbling again, some of the people in the boat got out and hauled the boat into the shallows. The boat tilted and its occupants got out. Two men dragged Zanja from the boat, and hauled her through the knee-deep water onto dry land, holding her by the elbows. They lay her down upon the shore and she immediately began, quietly, to drag herself away.

"I don't like this fog," Mabin said. "I don't like anything about this day. Let's get to town, and quickly." She looked at Zanja. "Where do you think you're going?"

Zanja uttered a cry of longing and anger, and struggled under the knee that dropped onto her back. It took two men to get her under control. When she hung like baggage from their iron grips, she noticed Mabin, standing several body lengths away, with her pistol drawn. "That was stupid of you," Mabin said. "I don't know why I didn't simply shoot you. You have little value for me anymore."

"Why don't you let me go?" Zanja said. "What harm can I do now?"

Weather magic is water magic. The wall of fog was dissolving now, and the wretched, flood-distorted trees that grew along the shore seemed to step forward, one tree at a time. And then one of the trees lifted its head like a horse catching a familiar scent, and the tree beside it was a person holding its reins. The fog rolled back like a curtain folding away from a bright window. More people. More horses. A gaunt scarecrow leaned upon one of the gnarled trees as though upon a cane. And then the sun washed across her and she drew herself erect.

Karis.

"Councilor Mabin," she said, in a voice heavy with irony, "this time you have brought your fate upon yourself."

The pistol hammer clicked as Mabin pulled its trigger. The powder pan did not ignite, for gunpowder is earth, nothing more than earth.

Karis stepped towards her. Those among the trees remained at a distance: a Healer, a Truthken, a Paladin, a Seer; witnesses from each of the four ancient orders of the Lilterwood. There was laughter in the river. Mabin seemed unable to look away from the giant woman who confronted her. "Councilor Mabin," Karis said again, softly. "One way or another, you will let her go."

Mabin cried, "Kill the captive!"

Zanja threw herself forward, breaking the grip of her captors and collapsing again onto stones. Then they had her again, but they paid her little attention. A rag-dressed collection of muscle and bone, Karis took another step forward, and Mabin toppled backward at her touch, as though she had been pummeled. She sprawled upon her back, and Karis took her by the shirt and tore open the heavy fabric as though it was gauze. She lifted a fist as though striking a hammer upon the forge. But she held a glittering needle of steel in her fist, bright and terrible in the sudden sunshine, and she drove it without hesitation into Mabin's heart.

Mabin uttered an awful cry. Blood gushed, vivid scarlet in the bright sunshine. Karis pressed her palm to Mabin's breast. Mabin clawed empty air as though to pluck the cold steel from her heart. The Paladins stood transfixed.

"Before Shaftal," breathed the man who knelt upon Zanja's back, "she's spiked her heart. Shaftal, what have we done?" He got up hastily and made as if to offer Zanja a hand, but she did not even look at him.

Mabin lay still. Karis stood up, breathing heavily, her hand painted scarlet. Mabin lifted a trembling hand to touch the blunt end of the steel spike embedded in her flesh. Karis said, "Mabin Paladin, Councilor of the Lilterwess, you live now at my tolerance. My advisors have convinced me to let you live, for the sake of the people who honor their old oaths. It is for them, and them alone, that I give you your life. See that you give me reason to continue to tolerate you."

Mabin gasped bitterly, "I know the law. You need not instruct me."

The old man who had tried to help Zanja to her feet cried out, "Lady, we didn't know! We thought it was our duty to serve the councilor! How were we to know who you were? Mabin, you can yet ask for pardon—"

"Pardon?" Mabin said, and sat up, though she clutched an agonized hand across the spike. "Shaftal will not come into the hands of a Sainnite pretender, the smoke-addicted daughter of a whore! I will tell the people what you are."

Karis's bloodied hand clenched into a fist. A horrified silence fell, so profound that Zanja, with her ear to the stones, could hear rocks grinding in the bottom of the nearby river. Then Karis said, "I always thought that you hated me for what I am. But if I am Shaftal, then Shaftal is what you hate. Isn't that true, Mabin Councilor? Don't you hate Shaftal, the land and the people both, because we are half Sainnite? Don't you hate Shaftal because this land is, now, the child of violence and rape? Don't you hate the land because of its subjection and paralysis? And isn't it true that your hatred is killing the land, just as it nearly killed me?"

But Mabin cried, "For the land's sake, kill her! Can't you see what she'll do to Shaftal?" No one moved or even seemed to have heard.

A hand touched Zanja's shoulder. Norina and Emil had walked fearlessly into the midst of Mabin's people. The old man seemed to know them both, and said, nearly in tears, "Take her, take her! How were we to know? Tell her—tell the lady—tell her we are not all such fools."

He helped to haul Zanja to her feet. She could not stand on her own, but Emil braced her from behind, from foot to shoulder holding her erect, with his arms wrapped tightly around her. Norina knelt upon the stones and buckled Zanja's belt around her waist. With her head bowed she said, "I have wronged you and don't expect your forgiveness. But I will make amends." She looked up then, and Zanja saw how even humility can be an act of unbending pride. Norina read her thoughts as though they were words written upon Zanja's face, and she smiled, showing all her teeth. "You really should savor my abasement while you can, for I assure you, you will never have an opportunity like this again."

Zanja said, "One opportunity is enough. I'll savor this moment my whole life, and remind you of it incessantly."

"That seems fair." Norina rose and put her arm around Zanja's waist, and took half her weight onto her shoulder. So she and Emil walked Zanja across the river-washed stones, while the frightened, speechless Paladins let them go, and Mabin did not disgrace herself again by shouting commands that no one would have obeyed. Karis stood waiting, a woman of iron and stone and soil and everything that grows. At the last moment, Emil stepped away, and it was Norina alone who delivered Zanja into Karis's arms.

Chapter Twenty-seven

Medric would not be appeased. "I am a historian," he insisted. "Now that you need not keep these secrets any longer, it would be criminal to refuse to tell me."

Norina said, "Young man, you have appalling nerve to call a judge, a servant of the law, a criminal."

Medric grinned. "You wouldn't waste your time admonishing me if you didn't like me." He sat down beside her, and folded his ink-stained hands expectantly. "I'll trade you. You tell me the past, and I'll tell you the future."

The six of them had camped fearlessly upon the open plain, where grass and stone stretched to the horizon, flat as water and rippling in the wind. They drew knobby, weathered rocks up to the fire for chairs, and Emil brewed tea, using J'han's supply, as he'd long since run out of his own. They had told Zanja what had happened, and what they had done. Like Karis, who scarcely had said a word even when she unwound the bandages and healed Zanja's broken bones, Zanja inhabited a place of stunned silence and could not seem to find the pathway out. But Emil sat beside her, and sometimes he lay a hand upon her shoulder, or clasped her hand in his, and slowly Zanja felt herself re-enter the world. She thought, the future: these people will be my companions as long as we are alive. And she felt the years spread before her, like a wonderful new country.

"I don't know why I didn't recognize your strategies until the end," she said to Emil. "I should have known when I heard about the fleas that it was your kind of war."

Emil grinned. " 'Drive the enemy insane and she will defeat herself.' "

Zanja recognized the quotation from Mabin's *Warfare*, and laughed until Emil had to pound her on her back.

Emil said, "It was easy to do, with four elementals under my command. Ah, to think of the misery this little company could inflict . . . but no, those days are past." He sighed with false regret.

Karis had walked away on her own and had not yet returned. At sunset she needed to be alone, J'han explained. It was a clear night, and the sky was filling with stars. There was a stillness, a vastness, pressing down upon the little tribe camped here upon the heath. They'd stepped through the door and now found themselves in this open, lonely place, a handful of people in a universe of stars. From now on, each step they took would be on a path of their own forging.

Norina said to Medric, "No, I don't want to know the future. It's the not knowing that gives us heart, it seems to me. But I think I will tell you a bit of history, for Dinal's sake. And for yours, Zanja, since I must still earn your forgiveness. I witnessed very little myself: I was a child, a student, who happened to live in the House of Lilterwess, like many other students. But the night Harald G'deon died, Dinal and I sat beside Karis's bed, where she lay unconscious from the blow of power that Harald had struck her with—brutally, out of necessity, for he was breathing his last breath. By then we had discovered the bitter truth of Karis's smoke purse inside her shirt, and all the council knew, and had been arguing for hours what to do. Dinal took me to Karis's bed, and asked me to bind myself to her with an oath. After I had done this, she told me this history, and I, of course, know that it was the truth. So listen, Medric."

Medric managed to look even more expectant and alert. Norina began her tale.

Harald had been G'deon of Shaftal for thirty-two years. He had always refused to identify a successor, and, since the G'deon owes no one an explanation, no one understood why. As word of his illness spread across the land of Shaftal, even the most ardent and loyal of his followers—already distressed due to the harrying of the

Sainnites—were thrown into confusion and dismay. Some asked if the G'deon had lost his mind, to have grown old without giving any thought to those who would outlive him. Others, more cynical, declared that he had failed to choose a successor out of spite, to irritate his lifelong critic and opponent, Councilor Mabin.

During those last, terrible days of the G'deon's life, Dinal kept vigil by his bedside. She neither wept nor slept, and would allow no one else to be his honor guard. When Dinal broke her vigil, as she occasionally did to bathe or seek out a mouthful of food, she saw that gloom and panic now reigned unchallenged in the House of Lilterwess. Meals went uncooked, children ran wild, scholars stood about in the unswept hallways, councilors hurried with an odd aimlessness from one room to the next.

On the seventh day, as Dinal returned to the G'deon's room to resume her watch, Councilor Mabin herself, who kept vigil in her own fashion, snatched at Dinal's sleeve as she passed. "Ask him what will become of Shaftal, when we have no G'deon. Ask him how we can keep the godless Sainnites at bay."

Dinal eased her sleeve from Mabin's grasp. "Excuse me, Councilor."

"Ask him if he has forgotten his calling, and his people!"

"Councilor, Harald G'deon cannot answer your questions. Though his heart continues to beat, his spirit has departed. We both know that he would never have chosen to die with so much left incomplete. But death comes when it comes."

"Then will he be the last G'deon of Shaftal? This is a bitter destiny."

"His life has been bitter," Dinal said. "Why not his death?" She turned her back, and Mabin wisely let her go.

That night, Harald G'deon uttered a sigh, and Dinal sat up sharply in the chair in which she had been dozing. The healer, who read a book at the table in the corner, came softly across the room. The G'deon sighed again, and it almost seemed as if he had said Dinal's name. She took his hand in hers. "Harald, why do you suffer so? You need not remain in this world any longer. Your time is done, and we will find a way to live without you."

Shadows filled the hollows of his wasted face, but within his eyes the light of the guttering candle flickered. "Go," he said.

"Where am I to go? My place is by your side."

"Lalali."

"Lalali! What can there be of value in Lalali?"

Once again, he lay silent, with only the faint tremor of a heart-beat to let Dinal know he had not yet departed.

She kissed his hand and laid it down upon the coverlet. She stood up, bones aching with weariness, and went out into the corridor, where some of the councilors slept upon benches. In her own rooms, she made no noise as she rolled up some blankets and tossed a few things into a bag. Yet, despite her quiet, her foster daughter awakened and came to stand, sleepy and disapproving, at the bedroom door in her night shift. Norina said, "Did you intend to leave without bidding me good-bye? Where are you going?"

"Lalali."

"Lalali! Surely not alone! Let me come with you."

"The only thing that could make this journey more burdensome would be having to worry about your well-being as well as my own. You will remain in the House of Lilterwess."

There was a silence, then Norina said quietly, "I'm afraid I won't see you again."

Dinal slung her sword belt over one shoulder, her bag over the other, and kissed Norina farewell. "Know I love you." She left her standing in the darkness.

She took a loaf of bread from one of the kitchens, and, out in the yard, saddled the first horse to come at her whistle. A weary, bent, aging woman wrapped in a black cloak, she rode out of the House of Lilterwess. Hoping to avoid the plague of violence that made the main roads unsafe to travel any longer, Dinal took the mountain road from Shimasal to the coast. This isolated and wind-blown track took her through the tablelands, along ridges which overlooked the rich Aerin River Valley. She traveled from before dawn to long after nightfall. She made her bed on hard ground, under cold stars, and she lay awake, counting the years of sorrow and naming the dead. She spoke the name of Harald G'deon himself in that grieving litany. Perhaps even now he breathed his last breath, as the mother of his sons dutifully followed his last whim on this lonely road to the sea.

Long before sunrise, she rose from her cold bed. She tied her hair back to boldly reveal the three earrings of Right, Regard, and Rank, and called her horse to the saddle. She rode in darkness down the steep track from the highlands to the coast. As the sky lightened, dawn winds carried to her the scent of the sea.

The sun had just risen when she rode into Lalali. The city gates stood open, guarded only by a pretty-faced boy dressed in purple silk. He ran up, boldly clasped the heel of her boot, and gazed winsomely up into her face as he invited her to have her way with him. When he suggested what they might do, she jerked her foot away in disgust. Undiscouraged, he latched onto the empty stirrup. "Speak your secret desire, and it shall be yours. Is it a girl you'd prefer? Is it not power you seek, but rather to be overpowered?"

"Stand away, boy! I travel on the G'deon's business!"

She threatened him with her lifted foot. He stepped away from the horse, crowing with amusement. "The G'deon's business? Tell the G'deon there is only one business in Lalali!"

Dinal's horse jumped forward at a kick of the heel, and left the young man to enjoy his hilarity in private. His laughter swooped and howled through sunrise's silence. "The boy seems half mad," Dinal muttered.

On horseback, she wandered the streets of Lalali as the sun gradually chased away autumn's chill and cast a shimmer of light across the copper-tipped towers. Sunlight glared on walls of white sandstone. It gilded three nude marble figures in the center of a fountain, engaged in a complicated sexual act.

Dinal passed a crew of blank-eyed, starved and sore-riddled street sweepers, who were so numbed by smoke that they did not even flinch when the foreman laid into them with a switch. Other than these, Dinal did not see another living soul until noon approached. Then, a few early-rising whores came out to sit naked in the sun. Their pierced and bejeweled nipples glittered; last night's golden paint peeled away in patches to reveal bruises, scars, scabs, and bloody wounds. Lounging in chairs dragged out into the middle of the road, they cushioned certain parts of their bodies with pillows, and watched Dinal pass with the same stunned and incurious gaze they turned upon each other. A street doctor made her rounds, dispensing poultices and headache remedies.

They smoked to dull the pain, Dinal supposed. But a whore under smoke was helpless to defend herself against injury. So the trap closed, and there was no escape.

Dinal's horse stopped dead in the middle of a deserted square and looked at her over his shoulder. Dinal could offer him neither explanation nor purpose for their continued wandering. It was her lot and joy to serve at the beck of the G'deon. She would have to remain in this cursed town, and await either the bidding of her heart or the long-expected word that the G'deon had finally breathed his last.

She allowed the horse to drink from one of the pornographic fountains, then she turned him toward the eastern end of town. Here, the nearby ocean scented the air with a sweet reek of seaweed and salt. In the debris of narrow alleys, rag-dressed people huddled against moldy stone. When the sun suddenly came blazing over the edge of the rooftops, they began to awaken, in a mutter of groans and curses.

The narrow street led Dinal to a plaza, where a broken-wheeled carriage stood with the horse still in the traces, and the driver, asleep or dead, slumped to one side with the reins in his hands. A few newly risen drunks had gathered to dunk their heads in the fountain. Two shouted at each other, and seemed on the verge of blows. One vomited onto bare stone, as another looked speculatively at the carriage. Others still lay like soldiers mowed down in a desperate rout and left behind to rot. Dinal's horse picked his way squeamishly among the fallen.

Not much liking the look of this plaza or its occupants, Dinal turned her horse toward the nearest alley. Directly across from her, in a windowless wall scabrous with the remains of a decaying mosaic, a door opened. Out came a barefoot girl, dressed only in a night shift, with a water jug balanced upon her hip. She was extraordinarily tall and thin. The invading sunlight passed across her face as she stepped through the human debris. At Dinal's hail, the girl neither stepped forward nor stepped away.

Dinal held out a hand, with a silver coin in the palm. "I have lost my way. Will you take me back to the main road?"

The girl examined Dinal from toe to head, her gaze lingering longest on the telltale gold earrings: three of them, marking her high rank. "All roads lead to the main road. No one will ever believe you are lost. Who are you?" Her body was all arms and legs; she had been growing with astonishing speed and her breasts had started to form. And she had come into her power, and had only just begun to realize what she was. This Dinal saw, imprinted in the girl's very flesh. She was earth.

"I'm Dinal Paladin. I've come here to find you."

"Now there's a story," the girl said. Yet her body had shivered, as with yearning, before she spoke with such quick cynicism. Perhaps she had half expected someone to come and find her, thinking that surely someone, somehow, would realize that an earth witch had emerged in the back streets of Lalali.

"I was sent by the G'deon," Dinal said. "I am the mother of his children."

After a moment, the girl said, "You must speak to my master and hire my services. Do you have a kerchief or a length of cloth, something to cover your face? And let loose your hair."

Dinal untied the thong that bound her hair, so that it fell forward and covered her earrings. She took a black scarf out of her baggage, and the girl helped her to tie it so it covered her entire face, except for her eyes. "Now, stand so, holding the reins." The girl demonstrated an attitude of impatience and boredom. "You must seem eager, but do not agree to pay more than you have there in your hand."

The girl's master, a thin, hard-faced man with a grimy red ribbon tying back his greasy hair, seemed none too willing to let the girl go with Dinal, even for so little time. They dickered until the girl reappeared in the open door, fully dressed in a plain, serviceable tunic and trousers. Dinal, who had been holding the coin between her fingers where the girl's master could see it, abruptly closed her fist and mounted her horse. "Never mind, then. I was particularly taken with your girl's unusual appearance, but I will find someone else."

"Lady, if you knew what it costs me to keep her!" Defeated, the girl's master reached behind himself to grab the girl and shove her forward, but smacked her cheek when he got a good look at her. "What are you wearing? Will you shame me before the entire city?"

Dinal said, "Her plain clothing pleases me." She held out the coin. "Come here, girl, and take your payment."

Expressionless, the girl took the money and dutifully delivered it into her master's hand. A handprint had appeared on her cheek. "Bring her back by sunset," the man warned, as the girl mounted behind Dinal.

When the girl pressed against Dinal's back, the tension in her muscles belied the calm, even indifferent expression on her face. They rode down the cluttered alley. As they turned the corner, Dinal said, "He assumed I wanted a whore, and I let him believe what he liked. But you must understand that you are free now, and it is your choice whether or not to come with me. I intend to take you to the House of Lilterwess, where you belong. Will you come with me, of your own will?"

The girl said, "Yes."

"What is your name?"

"Karis," she said.

The girl directed Dinal safely to the main boulevard, where masked men and women now sauntered arrogantly down the rows of whorehouses, surveying the exotic beauties beckoning wearily from the steps. At the city gate, a dozen boys and girls now gathered, each more beseeching and desperate than the last. Dinal rode past them, as a bell tower counted the second hour of the afternoon, and a drunken troubadour balanced his way along the top of the wall, incoherently singing.

Then they passed through the gate, and Karis sighed, as though she had been holding her breath. Dinal never felt her turn to look back at the city, not even once.

Several days later, Harald G'deon vested Karis with the power of Shaftal, and died. It was the last night that the walls of the House of Lilterwess would remain standing.

In the twilight, Zanja spotted Karis coming toward them across the ragged plain, stumbling because her head was tilted back so she could watch the sky. Zanja stood up, unsteady from the lingering weakness of starvation. "I want to be alone with her for a while."

"See if you can get her to sleep," J'han suggested, offering a blanket. "She doesn't seem to know how to do it."

Zanja walked across the treeless heath. Karis was a tattered shadow, with fraying hair and raveled shirt. Her hand caught Zanja by the shoulder as if starlight had blinded her, and she said in a voice as rough as a hoe's edge, "Zanja, what am I going to do?"

Zanja said, "Lie down with me and I'll tell you the stories of the stars."

Karis lay down where she was standing, and starlight filled her eyes as water fills a cup. Zanja had to fit herself around the sharp stones and prickly plants that Karis had not heeded. The blanket that she drew over them smelled of smoke and mildew and the detritus of a long, hard journey; a journey far from over, perhaps never over.

Karis said, "Emil fought me for Mabin's life. And even now I wonder if it was wisdom or cowardice that I didn't simply kill her. I could have." She sounded both amazed and horrified. "Accept the burden of responsibility, Emil says, or become what Mabin imagines I am."

Zanja said, "Now you will become something else."

"Something better, or something worse?"

They lay in silence. Zanja said, "It *is* possible to exercise power well."

"You think so? Did I exercise it well when I deceived you?"

"I suppose you thought I wasn't strong enough to let you choose to go to certain death. I admire your courage now, of course, but in the moment of decision, I would have begged you not to take the risk."

Karis said, "I never feared that you would hold me back. I did fear that if I made you part of my decision, you would choose to die with me if I died."

They had been quiet long enough for the crickets around them to start to chirp, when Zanja finally said, "Karis, thank you for this year."

"What? It's been the most lonely, miserable, forsaken year . . ."

"But even the gods must be amazed by it."

"Amazed?" Karis said in a choked voice.

Her shirt smelled like plain lye soap, with a lingering scent of old sweat and coal smoke. That smell was the only ordinary thing about her. Zanja got up on one elbow and stroked the springy tangle of Karis's hair. It pushed back against her palm, and when she raised her hand, it went back to its wild shape. Karis took a shaky breath. Perhaps Zanja had frightened her, or perhaps the tenderness had sunk through senseless flesh to some deep place where Karis could feel it.

Zanja said, "Of course you are uncertain. That's the way it is."

"For everybody?"

"Do you think I know what I am doing? I see a universe of possibilities, and some of them are very unpleasant. Perhaps the people of Shaftal will turn against each other. Or perhaps they will destroy the Sainnites, trading one massacre for another. Perhaps the people will claim you as G'deon and you'll be consumed by them until nothing is left. Perhaps our little tribe will come apart like a herd with too many stallions."

Karis uttered a hoarse, ragged gasp of laughter.

"Perhaps desire will never be fulfilled. But to live is only worth the effort if you live in hope. And living in hope is a discipline, a practice that can be learned."

"Is that why you insist on teaching it to me? I'll never do it as well as you do."

"But I do it so badly. Blundering through the thickets like an ox, tripping and falling into traps of despair, bleeding and raving and starving like the refugee I am . . ."

"How could anyone resist the attraction of such a life?" said Karis.

Side by side, they gazed up into the close-crowded constellations. At last, Karis added, "Weren't you going to tell me the stories of the stars?"

"That's what I have been telling you."

A long time they lay talking, a peculiar, fragmented, spiraling conversation that Zanja filled with pieces of stories which Karis kept interrupting with stories of her own, so that none of the tales were finished. The silences grew longer, and then silence took over the entire conversation. Zanja opened her eyes, and realized she had been dozing. Karis lay prostrate, wholly surrendered to sleep. Zanja rolled her onto her side without awakening her, and cleared away some of the stones from underneath them both, then folded herself against Karis's back. Karis's shirt had slipped down from her shoulder, and Zanja kissed the bare skin that pressed against her cheek.

She dreamed that the kiss had been like flint on steel, and Karis had ignited like tinder.

Zanja awoke at dawn, but Karis slept well into the morning, utterly collapsed in the greensward, with the ripening seedheads bobbing over her and the sun bringing out beads of sweat on her forehead. J'han checked on her and said simply, "Let's leave her alone unless Mabin comes after us." So they improvised a sunshade for her, and spent the morning in aimless repairs to their gear, sorting their baggage and sharpening their knives, like soldiers awaiting orders. After eating three servings of camp porridge, Zanja found she finally could walk steadily. Emil sewed up her breeches, where they had cut open the seam to splint her leg. Norina and J'han seemed engaged in extremely complex negotiations, which no one dared interrupt. Medric was suffused with restlessness until he calmed himself by reading out loud from a book of poetry J'han carried with him. Zanja had never before heard such poetry, in which the words worked like glyphs or like doors, doors upon doors upon doors.

In the middle of a poem, Karis came stumbling groggily over to the smoldering cookfire and half sat and half fell onto the stone chair that Emil vacated for her. Medric finished the poem and looked up from J'han's book.

"I think I had a dream," Karis said uncertainly. Had she never dreamed before? She rubbed her face with her hands. "Dreams are like poetry, aren't they?"

"Yes," Medric said.

"Well, I'm no good at metaphors. I dreamed I was naked and so I started to put on my clothes, but then I looked down and realized that I was putting on my own skin. What does that mean?"

"Oh, my." Medric closed the book and hastily put on his other spectacles.

Emil, squatting by the coals to pour water into a fresh teapot, set the pot of water down suddenly. "Karis, I've been thinking that perhaps the best gift we might give you is a season of solitude."

Karis looked at him, and finally said in a voice gone blank with shock, "What?"

J'han had been examining her from across the cookfire. Now he said, "Certainly, it doesn't look like you need me anymore, and Norina and I have already agreed to return to our daughter, to raise her together through winter, anyway. The spring is still an open question, of course, but the sooner we leave the better."

Karis glanced at Norina, who neither spoke nor looked away. In fact, Zanja realized, Norina had yet to speak a word in Karis's presence, which surely required an inhuman discipline on her part. "Of course you don't know what to do in the spring," Karis said, as though she had not realized before now exactly how much her friends' decisions depended on hers. She accepted a steaming porringer from Zanja, along with the spoon from her belt, and obediently stuck the spoon into it.

Emil said, "Medric and I can go to my winter home, perhaps. It's distant, but not so far that we couldn't visit you if we needed to, or you us. Medric, what do you think? It's a lonely and wild enough place. Will we get sick of each other?"

"We'd better not. You're going to help me write my book—"

"I am?"

"—and there's that library to build."

"Hmm. Not this year, I don't think."

"That's what I mean," Medric said. "You are I are in it for some years at least. Karis—"

She looked at him, sullen as though she were the youth and he the elder telling her what to do. "Go back to Meartown," Medric said.

"Why?"

"Because the most important journeys all begin at home."

Karis opened her mouth, but said nothing.

Zanja said, "Then we all should come to Meartown. The tribe should stay together."

They all looked at her in some surprise. Then Medric said, "Tribe? A community, maybe, after Mackapee."

"No, a company," said Emil.

And J'han said, "Or a family, perhaps."

Norina put her hand over her mouth to stop herself from speaking. Perhaps she would have demanded that they found a new order.

"But not yet," said Emil. "The last thing you need, Karis, is to be surrounded by people who are slavishly waiting for you to tell them what to do with their lives. You must answer your own questions first."

Karis said mutinously, "So you're all going to abandon me out here in the wilderness instead?"

Emil said, "Why, yes, I believe we are."

Medric added irrelevantly, "Slavish? That's a bit of a hyperbole, isn't it?"

They argued amicably and finally settled on "obsequious." Norina seemed to be trying to tear her hair out of her head. Karis glanced at her and said irritably, "What?"

"Eat your porridge," Norina said.

Karis seemed flabbergasted. "The first words you've said to me in ten days—"

"Eat your blasted porridge," Norina amended.

"You'll be a rotten mother," Karis muttered. She put a spoonful of porridge into her mouth.

There is a stillness that comes across the earth sometimes, at dawn, or just before a storm, a stillness as if the entire world lies stunned by possibility. So Karis became still, and so the agitated, half-hilarious talk of her friends fell silent, and so the breeze itself seemed to take its breath. Karis looked at the bowl of porridge as though she had never seen food before.

"Porridge is pretty dull, as food goes," Norina said.

"Dull?" Karis took another taste. "This is dull?"

Comprehension struck Zanja like a stinging slap in the face. "Dear gods," she whispered.

"Oh, my," said J'han.

But Medric grinned complacently and gave J'han his book, and Emil calmly poured out onto the ground the pot of tea he had just made, and packed his tea set away. Zanja caught a glimpse of how irritating fire bloods could be when they have realized a truth before anyone else. J'han got up and began fussing in his saddlebags, taking things out and putting them in again. Norina laced her fingers across her knees and in silence watched Karis eat another astounded spoonful of porridge. Of course, to a Truthken there is no such thing as privacy, but Zanja felt it proper to look away, if only to hide her own expression. She would have found something to do, like Medric and Emil, who were fretting now over how to distribute the weight of books and food between their two horses, but it just would have made her feel as foolish as they looked.

Karis scraped the porringer clean. Zanja took it from her and filled it up again with oats and dry fruit, and set it in the coals. Norina stood up without a word, and went to help with the packing. Karis wiped her face with the ragged tail of her shirt. "I think I'm hungry," she said, as though there were nothing extraordinary about her hunger. Then she looked at the cloth of her shirt, and touched it to her face again. "What—"

Zanja felt the shirtcloth. "It's soft, the way old shirts get."

Karis alternately felt her face and the cloth. Then she looked at her callused, soot-black hands. "I am alive," she said. "It feels very odd."

The flat heath spread out before Zanja, oddly out of kilter. When Zanja looked at Karis, she hardly could endure the sight, and had to look away again. The silence became awkward, and at last Karis said in a strained voice, "Well, I must ask you, since you haven't volunteered. Where are you going to go?"

Zanja turned, startled, pained that Karis would even think of sending her away.

"Because I'm going with you," Karis continued.

"I think I'll go to Meartown."

"Well."

"Karis—"

"Be careful," she said hoarsely. Her attention seemed intensely concentrated, as if she had been rescued from deep water and needed to breathe.

"With your permission," Zanja said, very carefully, "I'd like to court you."

Karis uttered a sharp laugh, but even her laughter had no peace in it. "And up until now, what have you been doing?"

"Well, if this whole year has been a courtship . . ." Zanja paused, and said, "Perhaps it has."

"I don't think the earth sent me out to rescue you on a whim."

"It seemed whimsical enough at the time."

Karis was smiling, her panic passed for now. But Zanja knew, quite clearly, how uncertain was the path on which she trod.

Zanja said, "I would like to make a suggestion. Take Norina into your good graces again."

"Have you forgiven her?"

"I will, before I bid her good-bye. She makes amends the same way she goes into battle. Gods help the fool who gets in her way. If you forgive her, we all will be the safer for it."

Karis uttered a snort of laughter and unfolded herself a bit. "Well, since you've gotten in her way before, you know what you're talking about. Nori!"

Norina came over with J'han's book of poetry and gave it to Zanja without a word. Without a word, Zanja stood up and gave Norina her seat, and pointed out to her the porridge cooking in the ashes.

Karis said to Norina, "You must be bored with penitence by now."

"My boredom is only just beginning," said Norina morosely. "But J'han is never bored. Why couldn't he be the one with the breasts? That's what I want to know."

Zanja went for a desperately needed walk across the flat, rocky countryside. The yellowing grasses were weighed down by seedheads, which in places had been cropped neatly off by their wandering horses. She reached the clear rivulet that had served as their camp's water source. When she looked back, Norina sat at Karis's side, talking earnestly. Karis listened somberly, speaking little. It seemed like old times.

Zanja walked in a wide circle around the camp. The next time she looked at the cookfire, Norina had been replaced by J'han, who seemed to be systematically giving Karis most of the contents of his healer's pack: a brown bottle of something to soothe her throat, herbs to build her strength, and a great deal of advice. But in the end he seemed to offer some kind of reassurance, and Karis must have said something amusing, because he burst out laughing.

The next time she looked, Emil and Medric sat on either side of Karis, and all three of them were roaring with laughter. The sound of it carried far across the plain. J'han and Norina were saddling their horses. Zanja started back toward the camp. By the time she reached the fire Karis was sitting alone, with packets and bottles piled at her feet like homage. Zanja took the small fortune that the people of Meartown had collected to fund her rescue of Karis, and divided it up among them. At least none of them would go hungry or cold this winter.

Zanja first said good-bye to Norina. "Karis should never have to choose between us," she said.

"You'll wish a thousand times that you had never said those words."

"I already wish I hadn't."

"That's once."

Zanja said seriously, "If you have any advice, I would hear it."

The sardonic side of Norina's mouth lifted at the corner. "You're the one who threw yourself into the middle of this avalanche. Are you trying to tell me now that you're worried about where it's taking you?"

"Not at all," Zanja said. "And I'll never forgive you for trying to murder me."

Norina said, "In all my days of seeking the truth, I've never met a worse liar."

When Medric embraced Zanja in farewell, he said, "Do you ever think about that other Sainnite seer's vision? The one that predicted that the Ashawala'i would defeat the Sainnites?"

"I try not to," Zanja said.

"That's good," Medric said. "I never would have told you about it had I known who you were. But if the fate of my people is in your hands—"

"Then that puts it in your hands, doesn't it?"

Medric looked taken aback. "It does? Oh, it does." She left him fumbling for a different pair of spectacles.

Emil's hug was bracing. "You know where to find me," he said.

Her arms were aching and empty as she stood beside Karis and watched the four of them ride away. Homely, laden with their food and bedrolls and a book each from Medric and Emil, nibbled a few sprigs of grass and then snorted impatiently at them.

Karis said, desolate, "How I'll explain all this to the townspeople I have no idea."

Zanja's patience had never been so tried by travel. Karis slept insatiably, ate ravenously, and in what daylight remained dawdled on the path, infinitely distracted by a curiosity as global and undisciplined as any child's. The barren heath was to Karis an extraordinarily complicated living puzzle that she could not resist figuring out. But the more she understood, the more there was to understand, and they would starve to death before Karis was satisfied. The rigors of the last month had melted Karis like a candle. It had taken only a sense of taste to make her devoted to food, and when Zanja pointed out their shrinking food supply, their pace picked up substantially.

Still, Karis touched everything, meditatively, absorbedly; and often smelled and tasted it as well. She wore herself out with sensation, and Zanja wore herself out with trying to explain to her the marketplace of physical experience that she had always taken for granted. Karis could not distinguish between hunger and thirst, between tiredness and sleepiness, between softness and smoothness; and teaching her the difference was not nearly so simple as one might think.

Late one afternoon, after several days of leisurely travel, they climbed steadily up the steep road to the Meartown gate, but long before they reached the gate, people had begun to come rushing out and down the road, one or two at first, and then dozens more as the word spread of Karis's arrival. Faster than seemed possible, the entire town turned out to welcome her home. In the heart of a celebrating crowd, Zanja clung grimly to Homely's reins and to Karis's elbow, tempted sometimes to beat the people back so that Karis at least could breathe. Karis, however, seemed resigned to the attention, and patiently embraced the babies born since her disappearance, and shook the hands of forge-jacks and forge-masters and hundreds of other muscular, smoke-begrimed people who had not even taken the time to remove their scorched leather aprons.

They sat Zanja beside Karis in a place of honor in the town's largest tavern, into which the townspeople packed, elbow-to-elbow, like beans standing in the pickling jar. The tavernkeepers did not have enough tankards to go around, and a dozen toasts had to be drunk, with the tankards being passed from hand to hand until everyone in the tavern had drunk at least a swallow to Karis's health. All this took an inordinate amount of time, and at one point Karis glanced aside at Zanja's face and said dryly, "You endure some trials more gracefully than others."

"We should have crept to your house under cover of darkness."

"Sooner or later they'd have discovered I was home. We might as well get this whole thing over with."

She disappointed the folk of Mear later, though, when they demanded that she tell what had happened. "I was kidnapped by brigands, and Zanja found me and saved my life," she said. "So I've learned the value of having a hero or two among my friends. Now are you going to hold me hostage to your good will much longer? Surely you have work to finish, and the day is nearly over."

The townsfolk dispersed reluctantly, clearly unsatisfied with the two-sentence tale, but sunset was drawing near and they all knew that Karis had to smoke or die. Karis gravely bid her well-wishers farewell, and only Zanja knew what the glitter in her eye was all about. At sunset Karis often was overwhelmed by desire for smoke, and by a lingering fear that somehow her miracle of liberation would prove to be illusory. After sunset came the jubilation at seeing the stars, yet again. She had gone through the cycle enough times now that she seemed to be starting to trust the jubilation and to distrust the fear.

Now they stood alone in a surprisingly empty street rimmed by soot-gray walls. Someone had taken Homely to the common stable; others had carried their gear away. Karis hesitated in the street, as though she had abruptly lost her sense of direction. After a while, Zanja sat down upon a stoop and tightened her bootstraps. When she looked up, Karis was gazing down at her with a curious expression. Zanja looked at her curiously in return.

"You've been very patient," Karis said.

"Actually, the discipline of peaceful waiting is one I never learned to do with grace. Emil is a true master of patience. You should watch him sometime. The contrast will show you how deliberately and awkwardly and unnaturally I wait. We na'Tarweins are notoriously impatient."

Karis seemed bemused. "But I don't want you to wait on me, well or badly. Why don't you just stop doing it?"

Zanja stood up and took hold of Karis by the shirtfront, and dragged her, startled, to the high stone stoop. With Zanja standing on the stoop, she could kiss Karis's mouth without having to climb her like a tree. Though Karis seemed affrighted, she did not pull away. Instead, in a moment Zanja felt a shudder run through that long frame, and Karis's fist clenched in the cloth of Zanja's shirt. She seemed to want to crawl inside Zanja's very skin. The shirt cloth started to tear. It was Zanja who took a step back, unnerved by the sensation that she had not so much chosen this moment as she had been delivered to it. Karis lost her balance and sat down upon the stoop as though her knees had given out on her. The breeze, cool with the coming evening, inserted a curious finger into the hole in Zanja's shirt. She and Karis both were breathing as though they had just sprinted up a hill.

"Blessed day," Karis gasped.

Zanja knelt at her feet and said with mock seriousness, "The Ashawala'i call that feeling 'being struck by lightning.' Shall I explain the sensation to you?"

Karis said shakily, "I understand enough."

Zanja felt the entirety of Karis's attention focus upon her. She thought of Karis exploring the landscape of her body the way she had been exploring the heath, and her heart began to wobble in her chest. "Would you rather I go back to being awkwardly and unnaturally patient?" she said.

"Could you?" Karis asked, then answered her own question. "No. And if you could, I'd be offended."

Zanja grinned. "Well then, it's completely impossible."

Karis looked away. Her hands clenched each other like shy children before a stranger. "Zanja, it's not you I'm afraid of. It's my ghosts."

"I have my ghosts too. So what?"

"So maybe lovemaking will be an embarrassing, disastrous farce."

"We've survived so much worse than that already."

Karis looked back at her, stricken.

Zanja said, "Karis, I can always find a way across. It's my gift." She gave her a hand, and helped her to her feet. They walked all the way to Lynton and Dominy's house without saying another word, and without letting go of each other.

✠ ✠ ✠

The delivery of their gear had prematurely announced their home-coming to Lynton and Dominy, and they arrived to find everything in chaos as the two men frantically tried to make Karis's bed with fresh linens, cook a celebratory dinner, and heat the bathwater, all before sunset. Karis left Zanja to sort things out while she walked off by herself toward the green trees that clustered around a small pond. The sun was nearly down.

Zanja repeatedly explained to the two men that Karis no longer used smoke and there was no rush, but nothing she said seemed likely to overcome their disbelief. Finally, to calm them down she took over some of the work. She had never made a bed in her life; but it proved, as she suspected, to be largely a matter of common sense. She took out Karis's two cleanest shirts and hung one to warm by the fire. The second she took with her to the bathhouse, where the washkettle had come to a boil. Buckets of cold water stood waiting to mix in the tub with the hot. There was a crock of herbs and flowers to sprinkle in the water, a crock of soft lye soap, and a bath brush worn soft with use.

Clean, dressed only in Karis's shirt, which hung to her calves, carrying her knife belt, she walked back to the house and let herself quietly into Karis's room by way of the garden. It was full dark by then, and she could hear Karis's voice in the kitchen. Zanja built up the fire in the fireplace and combed her hair with her fingers as it dried. She supposed she was missing dinner.

She fell asleep in the warmth of the fire, and when she awoke, Karis stood nearby, buttoning her clean shirt. She had set a burning candle into the chimney nook, and gazed down at Zanja with her eyes set into dark hollows by the angle of the light.

Ordinary and commonplace words could have filled the silence, but Zanja did not move or speak.

Karis knelt beside the settle and lifted a hand to awkwardly brush the loose hair out of Zanja's eyes. Her fingers were steady, but her agitated breathing revealed how close her ghosts hovered. She smelled unlike herself: of soap and herbs rather than of smoke and old sweat. She abruptly leaned over and kissed Zanja's mouth. Then she tried to pull away but Zanja couldn't seem to release her. Karis easily could have broken free but she held herself still, trembling like a wild horse trapped into the traces. Carefully, Zanja let go of her. She told herself she could wait as long as she needed to, and she could do it gracefully, without resentment. She was a *katrim*. She could sleep on the hearth in the kitchen and she wouldn't blame Karis, and she wouldn't complain.

She sat up, rubbing her face. Karis sat down beside her on the settle and said miserably, "You deserve—"

Zanja crawled into Karis's lap. Though startled, Karis moved instinctively to embrace her, to accommodate the weight of her. Zanja was so much smaller than she, a tribeless mountain woman lost here in the plains, ready to die of loneliness. Holding her like this, would Karis remember the bitter winter day she rescued her? There had been no coercion when Karis gave her back her life, just generosity: unearned, unsought, utterly unexpected. Zanja felt Karis's hand in her hair, and shut her eyes and thought of Karis stroking the heath's soft grasses. She willed herself to be as passive, and as vital, as the heath had been.

She shuddered alert when she heard Karis's breathing change. Karis's big, gentle hand had found its way to Zanja's face and now she began kissing her, and Zanja made her hands lie still. Time carried them upon a quiet river. The fire died down and the candle guttered in its socket. The moon rose and cast a modest light through the garden door's glass windows. Zanja tasted salt.

She lifted a hand to Karis's face and found her gasping with surprise, awash in astonished tears. Zanja straddled Karis on her knees and the river took them again and the moonlight faded away. Karis stood up and carried Zanja to the bed. Zanja's exquisite restraints snapped, and in a matter of moments she ruined both their shirts.

They'd have nothing to wear in the morning. But between now and then lay an infinity of time.

Though Karis floundered in an agitated ocean of sensation, Zanja's hands anchored her within her skin. Fragmented flesh knitted itself together, shocking her with each new joining: another recognition, another homecoming. Zanja's sculptured face moved across her breast: perspiring, ecstatic, entangling them both in a mess of unbound hair, moaning sometimes like the lion upon her hill. Who'd have thought those knife-scarred hands could be so appallingly gentle, or that a woman of such iron will could suddenly turn so soft?

With one touch Karis could collapse her. She tried it, stroking the soft inside of a lean thigh, and Zanja fell prostrate and inco-

327

herent, as helpless as Karis had ever seen her. For a moment, Karis didn't know what to do. And then she did know.

A strange, irresistible time followed. With Zanja shouting and sobbing and flailing under her touch, Karis felt the shock of her lover's ravishment right through skin and muscle and bone. And then Zanja lay shuddering, gasping for breath in Karis's arms, and beginning to shake with dizzy laughter. "Oh gods of the sky," she said in abject gratitude, and laughed and cried, and Karis held her more closely than she had ever held anything, and could not imagine letting go.

Then Zanja tied her hair up in a knot and said, "Now I will follow the fire."

Zanja lay across her, and Karis saw the callused bottoms of her well-traveled feet. She took one in her hand. It was warm, and rough. The tendons tightened and the ball of Zanja's foot pressed gently against her palm. Karis felt Zanja's hands, and her tongue— unhurried, coaxing. Under that touch, her thighs gave way, and the rest of her gave way as well. Oh, it was fire, but it was also earth: a monolithic presence, waiting, wounded, for healing. Shaftal. She could not refuse.

The earth claimed her.

In the dead of night, Zanja awoke to find herself alone, with the blankets tucked carefully around her and the garden doors standing ajar. She walked out into a chilly breeze, and saw frost sparkle in the starlight. A year ago she had never thought she'd see stars again. Now the cold night felt huge around her, cupped within the folded hollow of the hills, but expanding out into the bright universe. The garden lay breathless and silent, the accuser bugs silenced at last, the frog song long since ended. It would be a sudden winter.

Karis lay naked on her back in a bed of thyme, staring up at the stars. Zanja paused. She knew there had been a mystery at the end of their lovemaking, when with the moment of consummation upon her, it was not to Zanja, but to the land itself that Karis cried out. Perhaps Karis had not slept at all since then, and all their lovemaking had been for her the opening of another door. Perhaps everything they did would ripple outward in the vast future: every breath, every word.

"Now you are afraid," Karis said from the thyme bed. Her voice was hushed.

"I should be afraid."

"Yes," Karis said peacefully. "Anyone should fear to possess such powers as we possess." Then: "Do you remember when I healed you?"

"I'll never forget that day." Zanja knelt down in the thyme. "You restored me to myself."

Karis said, "Now you've done the same to me. So it was the land that sent me forth, to make whole the one who would make me whole. I'll never again question the logic of my life."

Chapter Twenty-eight

At mid-autumn, when the ground began to freeze, South Hill Company disbanded. The malaise that had affected the Sainnites seemed also to have affected the Paladins, like a plague jumping across the battle lines. By then, half the people of the company had no homes to go to, and only food delivered from outside would keep the people of the region, including the Sainnites, alive until spring. Even Willis had succumbed to the bitterness of that year. He was gone from South Hill; no one knew where. One of Emil's friends had gotten a brief and inexplicable letter: *I am released. I wish you the same.* Though she shook her head in pity that so fine a commander had fallen victim to the silliness of middle age, she lay awake that night, thinking of the ways that her own service to the war had imprisoned her over the years.

Emil and Medric, on their second trip for supplies to the nearest town, outran the storm by less than an hour. They had scarcely finished unloading the wagon when the rain began to fall. Medric, who had insisted that they augment their already substantial supply of food and lamp oil, took on the project of cramming their purchases into the already packed storeroom of the little cottage. Emil went up to the attic to check for leaks, and wound up sitting for quite some time on one of the trunks of precious books, listening to the rain pounding on the roof, and peering out the one small win-dow at the gray landscape below. When he climbed down the lad-der, he found Medric curled in an armchair by the kitchen fire, with a book in his lap and a pen in his teeth, and the ink pot precariously balanced on a pile of papers on the arm of his chair. He looked up, took the pen out of his mouth, and said, "Why has no one ever written about Harald G'deon?"

"Chaotic times have brought us a dearth of historians," Emil said. "And so many have blamed Harald for the Fall of the House of Lilterwess, I suppose that there is an impulse to erase him from history."

"But some day people will wish they could know more about him," Medric said. "And another thing: the House of Lilterwess came into being around Lilter, the second G'deon, largely to keep her powers regulated. So once Mabin made it clear she would not confirm Karis as G'deon, at that point, it could be argued, the House of Lilterwess lost its reason for existence."

"Now that's hardly true," Emil began. He chopped some vege-tables for a bean soup while he explained as well as he could how the Orders of Lilterwess had gradually become the unifying heart of Shaftal's government and culture. As he put the pot onto the fire he caught sight of Medric's smile, and leaned over to kiss the top of his head. "Do you hear?" he said. "The rain has turned to sleet, just like in your dream. What are you thinking about?"

"I was thinking that 'The House of Karis' just doesn't sound very impressive."

"That's because it's impossible to imagine her as an institution."

"That's probably what they said about that woman Lilter, and look at what happened."

Medric wrote for a while in his weird mix of languages and alphabets. Emil did not feel like doing anything, and made himself a pot of tea. Although it had been a long day, Medric still would sit up with his books and papers for half the night. Emil would go to bed, and wake up before dawn with Medric curled against him like a friendly cat. In the kitchen, Emil would find both the lamp reservoir and the wood box empty. He would go out on a solitary walk to watch the sunrise, and when he came back he'd start some bread and write a letter to Zanja, though he could not imagine how to arrange for its delivery.

Emil got up to stir the beans. The wind flung sleet at the shut-tered windows. By now it was full dark, and the storm would rattle the shutters all night long. Within the cottage, here in the bright kitchen, it was easy to forget about the storm.

Zanja looked up from the uncertain text she was deciphering as someone came into the tavern, and she saw as the door closed that it was past sunset. The people clustered nearest the door shouted in good-natured protest against the bitter wind that came blowing in. The tavern's convivial cheer grew noisier by the moment, as miners and smelters came in to celebrate another day's survival at their inevitably dangerous jobs. Zanja closed her book. Her tutor had gone home some time ago.

The door opened again, and Karis came in, accompanied by a half dozen other metalsmiths from her forge. The other smiths lined up to get tankards of ale, but Karis took cider instead, and a loaf of bread and a wedge of cheese. She set her burdens onto a nearby table and then mounted Zanja's table to engage her in a startling kiss, while the people in the vicinity burst into laughter, and the tavernkeeper shouted good-naturedly across the room, "Hey, now, that's no way to treat fine furniture!"

Karis grinned wickedly. "Greetings, wife."

"Whatever that means," Zanja said.

Karis sat down decorously on the bench across from Zanja, and retrieved her cup and plate from the other table. "It means whatever I want it to mean."

"Well, that's convenient. What does it mean tonight?"

"Tonight, it means you can share my bread and cheese without asking. I've been daydreaming about supper ever since dinner, haven't you?"

"No, since breakfast. I missed dinner." Zanja took some bread and cheese.

Karis tasted the cheese, and shut her eyes. "Oh, my."

Throughout the short months of autumn, Karis had immersed herself in the ordinary, which to her was not ordinary at all. Meartown was a busy, everyday kind of place, and Karis seemed steadied by the straightforward effort of labor. Zanja gathered that she had never worked so hard or so brilliantly, and some of the more perceptive townsfolk had already come to Zanja to ask plaintively whether Karis needed help in setting up her own forge, as though they hazily recognized that Karis's talent could not be contained much longer in the narrow patterns of her earlier life.

To be the speaker for a single person was a role Zanja did not much savor. She advised these people to talk to Karis, but none of them did. Instead, everyone participated in Karis's pretense that nothing of significance had been changed. They accepted Zanja as Karis's lover and apparent dependent, they were puzzled by Karis's recovery from her addiction, and their labored lives continued unaltered. The mysteries of Karis's late summer disappearance lay in the past, and now the preoccupations of winter distracted everyone's attention. Karis seemed to prefer it that way. Zanja alone knew that Karis's senses had developed far beyond the limits of Zanja's experience or vocabulary, and that sometimes she could only understand Karis in the same way she understood glyphs or poetry, through the faith and vision and intellectual recklessness that Emil would have called fire logic.

It had been a preoccupied autumn. Love had not so bedazzled Zanja that she did not regret its cost. She had finally ceased to be a *katrim*. What she was becoming instead she did not know, but she found Karis's joking use of the undefinable word "wife" to be deeply unnerving.

Something in the tavern distracted her: a strange quality to the sound, perhaps. Someone from the forge had come over to engage Karis in a technical conversation that Zanja ignored. She got up to refill her cider cup, listening closely as she worked her way through the crowd. Ale and good cheer had made everyone a storyteller tonight, and although not all the stories she overheard had to do with the metal crafts, she heard nothing extraordinary. "Are there any strangers here tonight?" she asked the girl who poured the cider.

The girl pointed at a corner table which was surrounded three-deep by soot-smudged listeners with tankards in their hands. As Zanja edged her way over, she caught sometimes the tenor of an unfamiliar voice, and spotted a wool-clad shoulder and arm as the speaker gestured.

"What?" someone said, with an astonishment so deep and sharp that many more heads began to turn. "*What are you saying?*"

"I'm only telling you what I have heard," the voice said, its articulation blurred by drink. "But I heard it from the people who saw it happen."

The tavern was rapidly falling silent, like a noisy audience that realizes that the play is beginning. Zanja began to work her way back to Karis, but the hush passed her and reached Karis before she did. Karis turned around on her bench, curious, relaxed. Zanja made a glyph with her hands: Danger. Karis leaned forward and rested her chin in one hand, disguising her height, making herself momentarily invisible in a room full of muscular, soot-stained people.

"It was a big woman that did it," the man said, his voice reaching all the way across the crowded room now. "She came out of nowhere, and knocked Councilor Mabin down, and drove a spike into her heart. And Mabin still lives, that I can tell you for certain. At summer's end it happened, and her heart is still beating this very day."

"This is a wild and dangerous tale," someone objected, and there was a murmur of agreement.

The rest of the people sat in stunned silence, however, some with their drinks half lifted, others staring at each other in disbelief. "That big woman," someone finally said, "Who is she?"

"Well, Mabin certainly knew who she was," the stranger said. "And perhaps only Mabin knows the whole story, a story she's not telling. But *what* is that big woman? That's what I want to know."

Everyone spoke then, in a cacophony of wild disagreement. Karis sat without moving, her face slightly pale in the shadows. Zanja knelt beside her and murmured, "If we try to slip out now, everyone will look at you, and at least some of them will truly see you, and put all the pieces together."

Karis's ragged hair frayed out into the darkness, but when she straightened up from her crouch, her eyes filled up with light. "Zanja, it's time for the journey to begin."

Kneeling beside her, Zanja's thoughts began to fragment strangely. She thought of how Karis had insisted that they build Homely a paddock up at Lynton and Dominy's house, rather than stable him in town. She thought of the money Karis had earned in these few months, quite a lot more than had been spent. She thought of the random tools that had begun to accumulate mysteriously under Karis's table, taken home one by one from the forge. She was not surprised when Karis stood up, and faced the accumulating stares and the rising silence of the tavern.

Karis said, "I had to make do without Meartown steel, but I don't think you'd be ashamed of the workmanship. It was a fine spike."

She picked up her doublet from the bench, and left the tavern, with Zanja behind her. Outside, the storm clouds had begun once again to extinguish the stars. Breathing clouds of white, fastening up their buttons against the cold, they walked briskly away from the tavern. Karis said, "My accounts are all settled. I've hinted to the forge-master that I'm leaving. Lynton and Dominy tell me my responsibility for them should not hold me back, for they both have lived well beyond their time already. I'm afraid we'll have a miserable night's journey—this storm will drop some snow before it's done. Is Emil's cottage big enough for the four of us?"

Zanja's heart had filled up with fire, like a furnace. "What does one cottage matter, when we have the world?"

Karis tucked her big hand into the crook of Zanja's arm, nearly dislodging the book she carried there. "Meartown bored you to tears, didn't it?"

They walked out the gates, greeting Mardeth as always. Only as the gate closed and locked behind them did Karis seem to hesitate. She turned, and looked behind her. "Mardeth," she said.

The gatekeeper had started to her cottage, but turned back. "What?"

"We're off to see what we can make of the world," Karis said.

The old woman smiled indulgently. "Are you, then? Good luck to you."

"She thinks you're joking, or drunk," Zanja muttered.

Beside her, Karis uttered a laugh. "Maybe that's what they all think."

Arm in arm, they walked up the hill.